Praise for *Flatbellies*

A *Washington Times* Top 10 Golf Book of All Time

"Compelling. . . . A coming-of-age classic—think *Stand by Me*, *The Wonder Years*, *American Graffiti*, and *A Christmas Story* meet on the first tee of a dusty muni in El Viento, Okla., for a fourball in Smalltown, USA. . . . Almost from the start, you'll feel like the sixth member of the gang, because Hollingsworth can turn the most hardened cynic into a sentimental sap."   —Barker Davis, *Washington Times*

"More than just a *Hoosiers* for golf, *Flatbellies* succeeds thanks to A. B. Hollingsworth's engaging characters and what this reviewer recalls as accurate depictions of teen situations and feelings."

—Mike Snider, *USA Today*

"Compelling. . . . A fast-moving account of life and golf in small-town Oklahoma."   —Doug Ferguson, Associated Press

"Equal parts *Stand by Me* and *Missing Links*, *Flatbellies* . . . is a rollicking, lyrical tale of teen angst, rebellions and redemption set in the mid-1960s. . . . Propelled by seamless, sophisticated writing, unpredictable plot twists and well-developed characters, *Flatbellies* blends its robust morality tale with a touching, quirky love story and a healthy dose of beer-fueled humor. . . . A fast-paced, entertaining story that seizes and surprises the reader from its opening paragraph, *Flatbellies* is a rare delight, an emotional, heartwarming testament to the strength of the human spirit and our grand game's magical ability to mold and forge the characters of those who play it."

—James McCarten, GolfWeb at PGAtour.com

"Each generation tends to produce at least one or two good coming-of-age novels. The better ones reflect their particular social history, and also repeat some eternal verities. . . . *Flatbellies* nicely fills that niche. . . . As the story unfolds, Hollingsworth touches upon some fond and deep memories about life in the mid-1960s in Middle America. . . . There's much to enjoy in this engaging new novel."

—Fritz Schranck, (Delaware) *Cape Gazette*

"A remarkable debut. . . . [Sports books] are not always this good, this funny, this moving. It's not a sports book. It's not a guy book. It's about life, and that's pretty universal."   —Ann DeFrange, *Daily Oklahoman*

"The skillfully crafted characters . . . enter their senior years dedicated to achieving the impossible, but love, loss and life keep getting in the way."   —Carol J. Burr, *Sooner Magazine*

"A charming and beautifully written new golf novel joining the elite coming of age stories of a generation. Set in a small Oklahoma town in the mid-1960s, it is a memorable and moving tale of the struggles and accomplishments of a high-school golf team and its quest to win the state championship."   —Golfread.com

UNIVERSITY BOULEVARD

A. B. HOLLINGSWORTH

W. W. Norton & Company
New York   London

Grateful acknowledgement is made for permission to reprint excerpts of lyrics from:

"Hurdy Gurdy Man" by Donovan Leitch. Copyright © 1968 by Peermusic (U.K.) Ltd. Copyright © Renewed. International Rights Secured. Used by permission. All rights reserved.

"Spirit in the Sky" by Norman Greenbaum. Copyright © 1970 by Great Honesty Music (Larkspur, CA). Used by permission. All rights reserved.

Library of Congress Cataloging-in-Publication Data

Hollingsworth, Alan B.
  University Boulevard / by A.B. Hollingsworth.
    p. cm.
  ISBN 1-932202-11-0
    1. Vietnamese Conflict, 1961–1975—Oklahoma—Fiction.
2. College students—fiction. 3. Male friendship—Fiction.
4. College sports—Fiction. 5. Oklahoma—Fiction. 6. Golfers—
Fiction. I. Title.

PS3558.O34975U55 2003
813'.6—dc22

                                        2003018098

ISBN 0-393-32421-4 pbk.

W. W. Norton & Company, Inc.
500 Fifth Avenue, New York, N.Y. 10110
www.wwnorton.com

W. W. Norton & Company Ltd.
Castle House, 75/76 Wells Street, London W1T 3QT

1 2 3 4 5 6 7 8 9 0

Here's to our special season, trivialized by some and immortalized by others. Yet, for a twinkling, the sun did shine on the Age of Aquarius. But it was more than that—for we also saw the moon glow from the Age of Apollo.

—Smoky Ray Divine
(from his toast at a
fraternity reunion)

For

the proud men of Greek letter societies everywhere . . .
and the women who endured them.

Acknowledgments

While writers often deal with "word counts," one word is invariably left out of the tally—the inhospitable "No." This is the "no" delivered to family and friends, to opportunities and events—in short, the very people and things that make life so engaging. Unfortunately, "no" is a prerequisite in order to manufacture time.

However, during the time used to create this book, "no" was countered by "yes" on multiple occasions—from family and friends and readers (even book clubs) who agreed to share their favorite college story with me, allowing a variety of windows to a peculiar era in our country's history. Special thanks, too, are due my unofficial editors—Dee Harris and Cheryl Browne—who tackled the draft phase of the manuscript, as well as to Hyla Glover who helped proof the final version. I am very grateful to Amy Cherry, senior editor at W. W. Norton & Company for her advice and suggestions, and to Lynne Johnson at Clock Tower Press for orchestrating *University Boulevard*. One theme in the book is the paradox of our universal need for encouragement from others, mirrored against the overpowering human compulsion to discourage. I am lucky to have had the help of those above who assisted creativity in the form of encouragement.

I remain very grateful to the original crew at Clock Tower Press (Danny, Brett, and Brian from Sleeping Bear Press days) who found my first novel, *Flatbellies*, in the slush pile and brought it to life. Every step that fosters success is never forgotten.

And I am grateful to my wife, Barbara, for her input on the manuscript and her support. But most of all, I'm appreciative that she understands *why* I manufacture the time to write.

1967–68

I

Chipper DeHart feared for the social survival of his friend, Peachy. After all, the clip-on tie dangling from the neck of his old high school buddy could provide a noose too convenient for the covert hangmen who prowled fraternity halls during Rush Week. This was a new, and perhaps treacherous, world where Chipper reckoned the sculpted shell might be valued over the pearl inside, or the pesky grain of sand, as the case may be.

Twin doors, chiseled from imposing oak, each emblazoned with a cross having thick and fluted arms, greeted the two as they marched forward, lost in the pack of rushees. If one were to pop the mysterious crosses away from the doors with a crowbar, it seemed to Chipper that a hoard of cryptic truths and sacred rites would spill onto the smooth concrete walk, an enchanted, beckoning path.

The two boys' roots remained 50 miles away in the village of El Viento where the crops grew in a wrapping of topsoil no thicker than skin. Crazy as it seemed, Chipper felt as though a dual-action catapult had launched them from the flatbed of their hometown, plopping them into a wonderland of sorority milk and fraternity honey—finally.

From an early age, Chipper thought himself born into a geographical blunder—that Nature had erred when it planted him in the dust bowl, hidden from the world. To be accurate, he had good parents— small town doc with med tech wife—who nagged only when needed, two younger sisters in their own orbits, a wiener dog, and membership last year on the state championship golf team. But he had been held prisoner inside a tiny dot on the map where El Viento was spelled in letters so small it took a magnifying glass to read them. And, for Chipper, the way out was by writing letters.

So, in the fourth grade, during the era of lunch counter sit-ins, he had written a letter to the governor of Oklahoma carefully explaining the equality of Negroes, based on the smarts he appreciated in his mammy, an insightful woman named Lily. It won Chipper an audience with the governor, a spot with the TV cameras, and the firm conviction that a well-written letter can be a passport to emancipation—his own. In the seventh grade, a letter from Chipper brought the *Saturday Evening Post* to El Viento for an inspired story about quadruplets born as two sets of identical twins. And while Chipper had no connection to this event, it proved again that letters touch the outside world, thus harboring an escape clause. Now, it was his letter to the Interfraternity Council that had delivered him and Peachy to the doorstep of College Cooldom on Two-party Day.

Two-party Day meant the fraternities had narrowed their choices, one step away from Bid Day. Pledging a Greek letter society was so fundamental to enrollment on this Oklahoma campus that it was a mystery why anyone would bother to go to college and not pledge. Indeed, for Chipper, "college" was simply a synonym for "fraternity."

But deep inside, under multiple layers of confidence and enthusiasm and future victories claimed, he sometimes felt a pea-sized knot of fear. This gnawing sense directed him to include at least one friend in all exploits. Furthermore, he had learned in high school that nothing tamed these secret willies more than immersing himself in the spirit of teamwork—encouraging *others* to fight the good fight. For him, a Greek letter society seemed a perfect fit.

Chipper fiddled with the half-Windsor knot of his genuine necktie from Danner's clothiers, then made quick confirmation that his uniform was identical to the others in the mob—houndstooth slacks, yellow long-sleeve shirt, club tie. Peachy's patterned, short-sleeved shirt from Woolworth's offered little in the way of rescue for the silly clip-on. *Peachy is loaded with dough*, thought Chipper, *so why the heck can't he get with the styles?* And to make matters worse, his friend's Beatle mop had bushed out over the summer, beyond fraternity cool, until the sandy bangs covered the upper half of his horned rim glasses.

"I'm thinkin' the Peach might wanna stick with a small house. You know I ain't gonna be president or nothin' if I pledge the same place as you. That's why I'm looking pretty hard at the Dekes."

"I never said we had to pledge the same house, Peachy."

The front doors of the Sigma Zeta Chi house swung open to reveal tentacles of groping arms, each designed to encircle a guileless rushee. Within seconds Chipper felt himself lassoed and led to the face of the most famous Sig Zeta who ever lived—movie star Jake Chisum. Chipper almost felt the need to bow to one knee as he stared at the altar. With a spotlight beaming on the countenance of Chisum, the four-foot portrait showed him in western duds, while two stubby candles on black metal stands burned near the bottom of the golden frame, offering auxiliary light to America's Hero.

"Brother Jake Chisum is a Sig Zeta, you know," said a nameless voice at his side.

"Yes, I know," replied Chipper, having been told this umpteen times at open house, then again on Six-party Day.

Although duly impressed with Jake Chisum, Chipper questioned a movie star's role as a "brother" some 40 years after Chisum's college graduation. No one would be a roommate with Brother Jake, they wouldn't party together, they wouldn't sing the Sweetheart's Serenade, they wouldn't even see Chisum shoot the bad guys except on the silver screen. In fact, it seemed peculiar to Chipper for a fraternity to use a famous alum as a rush point. Yet there was a glow around Chisum's flickering face that Chipper couldn't deny. After all, Jake Chisum only took movie roles where he was the man that other men rallied 'round.

Chipper could hear the mutterings about Jake Chisum permeate the living room, a corral now filled with dozens of houndstooth slacks and club ties. The swagger about Chisum was mingling with the sound of another selling point— Sigma Zeta Chi was one of only three fraternities founded on Christian principles. *So what principles were the others founded on?*

When he turned to locate Peachy, he spotted his spectacled friend being dragged down the hall toward the basement door by a goofy-looking, chinless Active. A very bad sign. Ushering rushees away from the crowd, especially at the beginning of the party, meant the ubiquitous "spook patrols" were still in operation on Two-party Day with members maneuvering to segregate the "doughs" from the "studs." Rather than meeting members and other rushees, the doughs destined for the spook patrol would be sequestered for poker or pool in the basement. If this was, indeed, Peachy's fate, Chipper knew the Peach could handle himself quite well. In short order, Peachy would be running the pool table or the poker game, and would empty the pockets of, and thus humiliate, any sanctimonious members who dreamed of joking later about their minions in the spook patrol.

Chipper met one Active member after another, each asking the same questions about hometown and major, some having asked the very same questions of him on Six-party Day, with no recollection of their previous conversation. Other members had memorized Chipper's resume, and they overwhelmed him with unearned praise.

Throughout the living and dining areas, separated only by a long, brick planter, waist-high, filled with green plastic leaves, Chipper heard the bold proclamations of the other rushees, most of them stating majors in pre-med or pre-law. Sugar cookies and oily punch blended with conversations about Sig Zeta and Christendom, then when the well was dry, the rushees were assembled around a cold fireplace to hear formal speeches by the officers.

Chipper took his seat on steps that led to the split-level TV room, craning his neck to locate Peachy, unsuccessfully. The outgoing President spoke about the future of Sig Zeta in its role as one of the top three fraternities on campus. Chipper recalled that at least six different fraternities had made this claim during rush week, apparently realizing the futility of claiming one's house as *the* top fraternity, weighed against the lackluster boast of being one of the "top six."

Several officers spoke after the President, then the Social Chairman described how all the top bands in the country would be playing at the parties during the next year. "We've got the Box Tops for Western Party, Sam and Dave for the Baby Bawl . . . then grab your cocks and drop your socks—" (the Social Chairman turned to tap his cigarette ashes in the fireplace) "—the Young Rascals for Derby Day!"

Chipper was thrilled, for a moment at least, then doubts emerged about this star-studded lineup. *But the Social Chairman wouldn't say it if it weren't true, would he?* It would be tough for any other fraternity to top the Young Rascals. A big-name band, in fact, carried far more weight than a famous alum. He scanned the crowd again for Peachy, but no luck. Chipper suspected the worst.

As the Social Chairman stepped aside, a rather extraordinary figure took the stand in front of the fireplace, beneath an enormous bronze version of the Gold Cross that seemed to rise all the way to the vaulted ceiling. "My name is Ted Boone, and for those of you who pledge Sig Zeta, I'll be your Pledge Trainer next year."

Chipper found it hard to believe that this Ichabod reincarnate was a fraternity man. Skinny to the point that his houndstooth slacks hung from bulging hip bones by one tooth, Ted Boone had an undertaker's face, with thick black eyebrows, a bulbous Adam's apple, straight black hair sprayed to perfection, and dark circles around his eyes. But his voice was liquid gold, elocution à la Paul Harvey or a deejay on Boss Radio.

"I'm from Ponca City, a junior majoring in Letters, and I'm pinned to Dora Taylor who is a Tri-Delt," continued the Pledge Trainer.

What the heck is "Letters?" Chipper wondered if he was catching the first glimpse in his short life of what the world called an "intellectual."

"Those basic facts you'll have to memorize for every Active in the house if you pledge, and you'll eventually claim much more than the basics, especially about your pledge brothers. But as your Pledge Trainer, my impact on your lives will be found elsewhere—between your spine and your soul—quite different than rote memory. It will be my job to nurture individual growth within a framework of conformity. That's right. Every other house on this campus will be teaching you how to look cool, how to dress, even how to think, and of course, how to win the hearts of fair damsels. Conformity. You've heard the word a million times. Little houses on the hilltop, little houses made of ticky-tacky, and they all look just the same. Not here. Not at Sig Zeta. We will define your strengths, your individuality, and bring you to fruition."

Fruition?

"We are the spark to light the inner fire you know to be present within yourself . . ."

Ted Boone rambled on, shepherding words into flocks that Chipper had only encountered on the written page, never in speech—". . . helping you navigate the labyrinthine corridors of college . . ."—and Chipper got lost in their meaning. But one thing for sure . . . this guy was one of a kind, and Chipper felt that it all must be true, that Sigma Zeta Chi had to respect individuality. The mere presence of such an odd duck within the walls of this traditional fraternity meant there was room for a guy to be himself. Not only had the Actives picked Ted Boone to be a Sig, but they also had clear respect for him, electing him to this critical post as Pledge Trainer.

Engrossed in the stirring articulations of Boone, Chipper barely felt the tap on his shoulder. As he turned, he saw the face of Al Marlowe, head Rush Chairman.

"Come with me," he whispered, a dour expression providing overcast for the Rush Chairman's face. Marlowe turned away, lumbering toward the basement door.

No. It can't be. He's taking me to the spook patrol! But how could they? With my record?! Wait a minute . . . they probably figured out I'm friends with Peachy. No, NO . . . I get it . . . that sonuvabitch Peachy knows exactly where he is and why, and now he's told them some cockamamie story about me to drag me down there with him. I'm gooned. I'll be shooting pool in a matter of seconds.

2

With the eight ball sitting comfortably in the side pocket, Peachy turned to the vanquished foe at his side, a fellow spook.

"So, Larry, my man, wha'd you say your last name was? And where're you from again?"

"I didn't say. Not my last name, nor my hometown."

Peachy was taken back at the curt response.

"Twohatchets is the name," the boy continued, holding his eyes in a steady gaze, as if waiting for the shock of his odd surname to register. "And I guess my home is Anadarko."

"Ah . . . the Polack capital of the world. Well, hell, I ain't got nothing against Polacks." Peachy laughed to assure the Indian kid that race was of no consequence to him. The Indian returned a cautious grin, bordering on a scowl, making it difficult for Peachy to use his well-developed radar for identifying suckers.

"Play any sports there?" Peachy asked, still probing.

"Track. And then golf, if you're the type that's likely to call golf a sport."

"Hmm. How's your golf game? I break 80 most days, but then I cheat a lot."

"Did okay at state, placed ninth overall, what with my playin' solo and all. The team didn't qualify for fourball, of course. Not many *Polacks* play golf."

Peachy grinned with the word 'Polack.' He might be able to like a guy who could play along with the jibes. "Yeah, I gotta admit, I did pretty well myself at state golf—"

"Wait just a minute. I remember you," said the Indian kid. "By darn . . . at state . . . you had that fit or somethin' on the first tee. Fell flat on your—. Then, two shanks out-of-bounds, and your team still wins." This time the kid smiled for sure.

"Yeah, that was me," admitted Peachy with swelling pride. "All part of the master plan, my friend." Peachy tapped his index finger against his temple to point out the loft of his genius.

A lone, chinless Active stood across the room, director of the spook patrol. He was showing some enraptured boys the secret handshake of Sigma Zeta Chi, teaching words to fraternity songs, and having a bang-up time, Peachy figured, collecting future stories for the brothers. The spooks sat on the blue Naugahyde cushion of a U-shaped bench that rested smack dab in the middle of the tile floor where they faced the real-live Active. Peachy and Larry stood away from the group, in the corner, chalking their pool cues.

Peachy turned his head from the odd sport of human mockery and sized up Chief Twohatchets once again. He was having to look upward a titch at the Indian, making the kid at least six-foot-two. Half-drooped eyelids left Larry's dark eyes looking like tarnished coins squeezed into the slots of penny loafers. Even for an Indian, his jaw seemed pituitary broad and, of course, no detectable beard.

"Larry, my friend, I guess you realize where we are," said Peachy, always searching for a pupil who would be fascinated with his savoir faire. This Indian kid was no sucker, but maybe he'd qualify as a lackey. "What I can't figure is how we made it to Two-party Day. If we were blackballed, you'd think they would have done it after Six-party Day, not now."

Larry's face didn't change expression as he spoke. "Sure, I know where we are, and I'm pretty peeved off about it. As a matter of fact, it's startin' to get hotter 'n Hades down here in the basement, puttin' up with this—. I made it this far only 'cause of my big sister. Half-sister, that is . . . passes for white, and she's pinned to a Sig Zeta. I don't much like bein' made fun of, and to tell you the truth, I'd like to kick these Sig butts straight to—."

Larry's face turned red on red as he spoke, and Peachy took note that the kid pasteurized his speech, leaving the juiciest words to dangle in the air. For Peachy, there was no excuse for dulling the luster of four-letter gems.

Peachy's father (Peachy Waterman, Senior) had taught his son a poker-ized view of life where odds ruled, and where it was more important to read the players than the cards. Larry's chew muscles were flexing beneath his ears when he spoke, so Peachy could tell already that

Larry was stuffed, stifled, and restricted. The kid needed to under-stand freedom in a desperate way, and he needed someone who could provide expert tutelage in the process. Yet Twohatchet's sad and sleepy eyes had a curious confidence that impressed Peachy that this guy was not going to be anyone's toadie. Still, Peachy placed the odds of his being the captain of this friendship at 90%.

"But do you know *why* we're here?" asked Peachy.

"Sure. These highfalutin' clothes from Danner's don't do crapola to cover up my red skin. That's why. My sister said 'pick out anything . . . if it comes from Danner's, it's cool.' But *cool* is not enough when your hands and face are red. As for you and why they stuck your sweet behind here, I'd say it's that fruity tie you're wearin'."

Stunned at the kid's nerve, Peachy adjusted his clip-on, then fid-dled with his silver tie clasp. He wasn't used to being tossed on the defensive, and certainly not by near-strangers.

"I'll have you know this tie clip has a real diamond, right here in the middle. My dad brought it back from New York, or Las Vegas, or . . . somewhere."

"Oh yeah. How many carats?"

"Uh, I dunno. One. Maybe two."

Larry Twohatchets smiled, a bit too smug. As a matter of fact, it was downright annoying. Peachy knew he shouldn't have bit on the carat question, since he didn't know exactly how big a carat really was.

"Money don't cover up your problem, any more than clothes cover up mine."

Peachy had never heard such insult, at least not recently. "Hey, bud, let me assure you that the Peach doesn't have any problems. And if I did, I could damn sure handle 'em."

"Then why do *you* think we're here? Better yet, Kemosabe, can that mouth of yours get us outta here?"

Peachy could feel the blood rush to his card-palming fingers. There was no greater calling in life than the noble charge to outfox the foxes.

"Larry, my compadre, listen, look, and learn. We are here in this basement because . . . because—" (Peachy felt genius strike, as always)— "because of a clerical error. That's it. A clerical error. And when I'm finished with these bozos, everything will be copacetic."

Larry's response was a muffled laugh, lips held tight, forcing air to whistle through the nose in snorts. "We Indians keep quiet mostly and watch you dadgum whites make fools of yourselves with proud words. Show me why you are not the fool."

Peachy looked across the room at the mesmerized boys gathered at the U-bench. Some of them were perched on the wooden back, clinging to the metal poles that secured the bench, floor to ceiling, perhaps clinging as well to the hope for a bid. The goofy-looking Active was explaining something he called "provisional bids," something about quotas, something about a new gadget called a computer that for the first time would sort and deliver bids almost out of control of the Sig Zetas, and something about the rules of the Interfraternity Council. Quotas, computer, council. Over and over. Peachy figured that most of this mishmash was bogus bullshit, especially the part about provisional bids. But he waited until the Active was through blabbering before he made his move.

3

Granite-faced Rush Chairman Al Marlowe escorted Chipper to the brink of the Bottomless Pit—the salivating mouth of the basement stairway.

"Chipper, I'm sorry . . ."

How? How? With my track record? Chipper was a mere nudge away from plunging to his social death.

". . . that we could only make it to El Viento once this past summer. We've got so many members from Tulsa, we can barely get to the western half of the state. And the small towns are especially tough."

Chipper savored his next breath, giddy with the perfume of cigarette smoke and liquor stirred into the fresh-paint smell of yellow walls, now turning golden by virtue of his deliverance.

Marlowe steered him beyond the basement door, up a flight of blue linoleum stairs, then they zigged and zagged before reaching a short, blind hallway where waist-high wood paneling lined this final stretch. Above the wainscot, on golden walls barely lit by a lone ceiling bulb, were rows and rows of small portraits, each photo framed in simple black. Tacked to the bottom of each frame was a brass plate with a name, a number, and a year.

"Who are these guys?" he asked.

"Past Presidents. This is the officers' hallway. The President has the biggest room in the house, at the end here. After his year-in-the-sun is over, his mug shot goes on the wall. You're looking at every President in the history of our chapter, dating back to 1912."

"What are the numbers here under the year?" asked Chipper as he floated his index finger along the rows back in time. The numbers grew smaller with the year.

"That's their initiation numbers for this chapter. We're well into the thirteen hundreds now. Each pledge is ranked for initiation, then we use that number the entire time you're in the house. So, the outstanding pledge in each class still ends up *behind* the worst pledge in the class before him. Seniority means a lot around here. If you pledge, that number can be more important than your name."

Chipper's eyes zeroed in on 1938, and he felt a shiver when he saw the name of Jody Justice, father of his best friend Jacob. He and Jacob had intended to room together in college, but marital vows to girl-friend Kelly had eclipsed the plan. Jacob and Kelly would be living in the "hunch huts" on south campus, and Peachy had moved in to fill Chipper's best-friend void.

"You act like you know that President," Marlowe said.

Chipper hadn't even realized that his fingertips were touching Doc Jody's nameplate as he stared at the thick-tousled, wrinkle-free version of the man who had shaped his early life.

"Yes. It's hard to believe he was ever my age. He was my best friend's father. Died last year."

Marlowe's squinty eyes widened. "So . . . does that mean . . . Peachy is a *legacy*?"

Chipper was startled from his trance. "Peachy? Oh. I was talking about my friend Jacob Justice who's married now and is going to play golf for the university. Jacob's dad was killed in an airplane crash last year while he was on a medical missionary trip."

"Ah," replied Marlow, with apparent relief. "So it was this Jacob who was the legacy?"

The question faded away. Even in the darkness, Chipper saw his ghosted reflection as a dark silhouette on the glass protecting Doc Jody's photo.

"Come in, Chipper."

He hadn't even realized that ever-subdued Marlowe had opened the door to the President's room. As Chipper eased his way through the entrance, he felt himself turn bug-eyed. Thick, royal blue carpet. Floor-to-ceiling wood paneling. Plaid bedspreads and matching curtains of blue and gold. An air-conditioner! Plush. Ritzy. Fit for a President.

"Have a seat," said a smooth voice coming from behind a colossal desk that seemed not much smaller than army tank. "I'm Perry Crane, outgoing President."

Crane had delivered a speech downstairs only moments before, but Chipper would have recognized his steely eyes and pointed chin from the rush manual where he had memorized the scoop on campus VIPs. Crane had been student body president, a member of the victorious College Bowl team, and most importantly, was engaged to Miss Texas.

As Crane tried to loom over the massive desk to shake hands, Chipper noticed a poster on the wall above the President's head. It was a blown-up photo of Perry Crane at a podium, on stage, shaking hands with *the* Robert Kennedy. Chipper felt his hand lock into the very same mitt that had gripped the former Attorney General's, the man some said would be the next President of the United States.

"Chipper DeHart. My real name's Kyle. Since I usually get down in two from the fringe in golf, they've always called me Chipper."

Marlowe shut the door and stood like a sergeant-at-arms. The rock jaw and Hollywood looks of the blonde Rush Chairman couldn't overcome a face that was austere, almost forbidding.

"It's sure nice and cool in here," continued Chipper, trying to keep conversation alive, though it sounded like mindless patter the moment it gushed.

"Only room in the house with an air-conditioner," said the outgoing President. Chipper wondered if Perry had already hung his picture among the 50-plus Presidents on the wall outside.

He motioned Chipper to sit down in an overstuffed wingback chair that swallowed him with such ease that he felt like lunch for a Venus's-flytrap. President Crane then rounded the corner and hopped his rear onto the corner of the monstrous desk.

"Some very good speeches are going on downstairs," began Crane. "I've always considered myself glib of tongue, but if you pledge here, Ted Boone will cast a spell."

Chipper tried to muster a smile. He knew he was getting special treatment and, by golly, it felt good, especially in view of his near death-by-basement experience.

"There's a reason we pulled you up here to the President's room," Crane continued, "and let me assure you this isn't a hot box. You should judge a house on the basis of the younger men. Hell, I'm on my way out. Off to Harvard Law. Still, when I reviewed the profiles on all the rushees coming through this year, I have to say that I think you and Oliver Kirby from Shawnee are the top two in my book."

Then why did I hear so little from Sig Zeta this summer, he wondered.

"I'll be honest with you, Chipper," Crane continued. "No fraternity is perfect, but I wouldn't trade my four years here for anything. Granted, some of the idolatry can be a bit much, like worshipping the

Two Founders. Quite frankly, I doubt those two had an edge up on me. If I'd lived in the early days of Greek letter societies, I rather fancy myself as a Founder type."

Chipper could hear Marlowe behind the wingback, clearing his throat, but when he glanced up again at the Crane-Kennedy picture at the podium in the poster, he figured the President could pretty well back up his words.

"A new era is unfolding, Chipper. As the song goes, 'the times they are a-changin.' Our chapter of Sig Zeta has embraced a vision and, to be honest, I'm rather sorry I'll miss it." Perry Crane picked up a blue, leather-bound book that had a golden cross on the front. He stroked the stubble of his chin, which seemed to be the only place that grew whiskers. His gaunt cheeks made him look 10 years older, Chipper thought, than the baby-faced freshmen going through rush. "This is The Aegis, our pledge manual. We're going back to basics so we can move forward in time. A group of us old guys have planned a strategy to bring Sig Zeta into a position of dominance on this campus, if not the country. Not dominance in the old sense of the word, which basically means the best parties, but in the *oldest* sense of the word when fraternities were designed to groom men of depth and refinement.

"In the past, we focused on . . . well, jocks and hell-raisers. However, with this year's summer rush, Al targeted student leaders, bookers, athletes in the minor sports, and yes, even musicians. A *new breed*, you might say. Take yourself, for example." President Crane continued without referring to the notes on his desk. "Straight-A average, face man, member of the state championship golf team, All-State Orchestra and, most impressively, I understand you're slated to be the First Term President of the President's Leadership Class."

Chipper nodded in humble acknowledgment of the truth. This was starting to feel good. His skull would just have to learn to accommodate the new size of his brain.

"Why, you may ask, are we changing the face of Sig Zeta? Well, it's my belief that fraternities should be a microcosm of the world. Hell, if we had my way, we'd pledge men of all races and creeds. But let me get to the point. As I said earlier, you and Oliver Kirby are the two rushees I see leading this new breed for our chapter. But since it looks like Oliver is headed for the Sig Alph house to be with his brother, I'll be blunt with you—"

Chipper felt his eyes widen, almost against his will.

"If you pledge Sig Zeta, I'm predicting, with no doubt in my mind, that you'll be President someday. That you'll live in this very room." President Crane eased from the edge of his desk and began to pace.

Chipper swelled inside as he fought hard to remember a conversation once with best friend, Jacob, on the golf course—that extracurricular stuff should have meaning and that one shouldn't waste time chasing accolades just for accolades' sake. Nevertheless, Chipper no longer felt the pea-sized knot of fear, and he could easily imagine his picture in the hall of Presidents.

"And more importantly, I'm not just talking a fancy title for you," said the President. "I'm talking about making a difference. I'm addressing you as a leader who will take the New Breed to new heights. Not simply shooting for Fraternity of the Year, but for the stars . . ."

The mush was getting thick now, but Chipper fought to maintain a somber look to cover the awkward moment.

"I've seen the winds of change on both coasts," continued the President, "and when the winds finally make it to Oklahoma, the entire fraternity system will be threatened. Change or be changed. But because of the New Breed, Chipper, the Sigs will survive."

Chipper knew a snow job in a hot box when he heard one. President Crane had gone a bit overboard. A bit too flowery, a bit too sugary. Chipper could see through it all. Nevertheless, Chipper was swept away by his own significance. His pride was full, and he was ready to sign on the dotted line.

"And that brings me to my final point, Chipper. Traditionally, we don't rush the small towns like El Viento. Not that there aren't good guys there, but it's a matter of efficiency. We can corral an entire group, from Tulsa Edison let's say, in one fell swoop. Why, many of the houses are nothing more than extensions of high school, the guys pledging en masse, year after year. None of us are very good at Small-town, USA.

"No individual rushee has anything on you, Chipper, but what they *do* have in the big towns are *friends*. Friends who are also grade jocks, face men, activity guys. You rush one, win one, and you win the package. But in the small towns, there's not—well, this is a delicate issue—there's simply not a package. It's not efficient."

Chipper was starting to feel nauseous. The doublespeak message was starting to worm its way through his skin. He was up here in the air-conditioned room with the royal blue carpet, building snowmen in the hot box, and his friend Peachy was shooting pool in the basement on his way to social hell.

"I'm told that there are only two rushees from the entire town of El Viento this year. You and a . . . a . . ."

"Peachy Waterman," finished Chipper, a bit more boldly than he intended.

Al Marlowe stepped forward, flipping through a notebook he was holding, as if searching for the one bright spot on Peachy's record. The Rush Chairman handed the notebook to President Crane. When Marlowe turned around, Chipper stared again at the droopy expression of the Rush King, an oddity compared to the merry nature of rush chairmen at other houses.

"Yes, here he is. Is it fair to ask if you two are friends?"

"Yes. We're friends."

"Do you happen to know Peachy's other house today?"

"Sure. It's Deke."

The two Sigs exchanged a concerned glance. Though strong nationally, Deke on this campus was obscure.

"Let's see," said the President, "two-point-five GPA, borderline ACT, clearly not a face man, and no activities at all, it appears. And we musn't forget, there's a minimum grade point to obtain before you can be initiated."

Chipper felt the ropes tighten inside. *Didn't this guy just say that the New Breed was going to be a 'microcosm'?* Yet here sat Chipper, the first rushee ever elected President directly out of Rush Week . . . *as long as I don't rock the boat.*

"Your information's not quite complete," he offered. "Peachy was on the state championship golf team with me. Shot a 77 in the final round at state."

"Oh?" said Crane.

The room was quiet, except for the whirring sound of the air-conditioner.

"And that's not all—" Chipper did not want to cross President Crane or Rush Chairman Marlowe. His voice barely squeaked it out: "Peachy can . . . uh . . . he can dance."

"What?" the two Sigs said in unified disbelief.

"Dance. I mean *really* dance. I'm talkin' people clearing the floor. And what's more, I think you'll find the sorority girls will come to the parties, just to watch him dance. Believe me, it's a sight."

He knew it sounded ridiculous, but he hoped they were hearing a different message: *This is my friend. Maybe he'll go Deke on his own, but if you've taken him all the way to Two-party Day, he really should get a Sig Zeta bid.*

And in a bold stroke in the cool, quiet room, Chipper rose to his feet from the devouring chair. "I better get downstairs to join the others," he said to their quizzical looks.

He held out his hand to President Crane, suddenly unsure if his bold stroke wasn't really a fearful sprint.

"Well, Chipper, I appreciate the opportunity to tell you what a great role you'd play." As the President's hand touched his, he felt the little finger try to snare his into the not-so-secret grip.

Chipper pretended not to recognize the maneuver, refusing its "you're going to be one of us" message, and he shook hands the old-fashioned way.

The message was strong, or so he thought. Be it too strong, he might find himself with the multitude preparing to pledge Sig Alph, his other top choice. Be it too weak, and Peachy would be blackballed. Then what? Chipper wasn't about to pledge Deke. No, the porridge had to be just right.

Chipper thanked and shook hands with Marlowe, then he left the chilly oasis of the President's room and entered the sweltering hallway. In the dim light, he looked at Doc Jody's picture on the wall, and he felt his eyelid twitch. Or was it a wink?

4

Peachy strolled toward the ringmaster standing in front of the U-bench, barely taking notice of the hapless rushees huddled there. *Suckers...every one of them.* Larry Twohatchets was a step behind the Peach.

As Peachy drew close, the Active stopped mid-sentence and slowly twisted his neck, shoulders held still. Peachy could tell from the brown roots and jet-black hair combed straight back in a '50s pompadour that this odd duck dyed his "do." And why? With his pieface, small mouth, beady eyes, the last thing this guy needed was to draw attention to his kisser. Yet he looked strangely familiar. And talk about dressing uncool, this bozo was wearing black slacks and a black shirt. It didn't make sense, so Peachy figured it was just a stunt to mock the spooks.

"Excuse me," Peachy said to the Active. "I've got an idea. Mister Member, sir, what's your name again?"

"Ty . . . Ty Wheeler."

"Ty, my good man, let me introduce my buddy here, Chief Polack, otherwise known as Larry Twohatchets."

Ty seemed to freeze. He didn't acknowledge Peachy's introduction.

Nor did Peachy acknowledge Twohatchets' furrowed, disbelieving brow.

"My friend Larry here is a real live authentic Indian-type guy." Peachy turned to the audience on the U-bench. "And gentlemen, you're in luck. He's gonna show you studs some real live Indian sign language. And he'll begin with this: 'I want to pledge Sigma Zeta Chi.' Take it away, Twohatchets baby, and go slow for 'em on the Sig Zeta part. They don't look none too swift." Peachy gestured his friend to center stage.

Larry Twohatchets' lips parted, apparently dumbstruck, while his low-slung eyelids widened to release a volley of daggers. Peachy figured it was the Indian equivalent of "What the hell are you doing, you stupid, white-assed sumbitch!"

Peachy threw his arm around the rigid shoulders of Ty Wheeler, careful not to touch the oil-slick coiffure. "Step over here with me, Ty. I want to discuss a little item with you."

Ty took a few Frankenstein steps before loosening up and allowing Peachy to drag him to the corner pool table. Looking over his shoulder, Peachy saw still-glaring, still-grimacing Twohatchets popping his knuckles, hopefully a warm-up exercise for pseudo-sign language, and not for a later pummeling.

"Let me ask you, Ty, how long've you been in charge of the spook patrol?"

The Active's jaw tightened, but he looked too silly to be mean. "What are you talking about? Spook patrol?"

"Come, come, Ty, my man. You know—and *I* know—what's going on here. How long you been in charge?"

"I dunno. Maybe five, six years."

At least three demeaning insults popped into Peachy's head all at once, but he held himself in check. Still, *no wonder the guy looks 35 years old*, thought Peachy. *He's a friggin' super-senior, several times over. Ee-gads, he's even got baggy cheeks. Hell, I'm lookin' at the poster boy for rigor mortis.*

"Well, I wanted to draw your attention to a clerical error."

"Clerical error?"

"Yes. A clerical error. You see, my friend Larry over there and me, we're legacies. Both of us. Someone made a clerical error." Peachy delivered his favorite smirk wherein he believed himself to be smiling. "My dad's a Sig Z."

"We don't say 'Sig Z,'" interrupted Ty. "Sometimes, we say Sigma Z or Sig Zeta, but *never* Sig Z."

Peachy was terribly annoyed. In order to reduce people to putty, one *has* to control the conversational flow.

"Did I forget to introduce myself? Waterman's the name. Peachy Waterman . . . Junior. I'm sure you've heard of my old man . . . Senior." Peachy shook Wheeler's hand, pumping it up and down to force a distraction.

"Uh, no. Not that I recall."

"Big alum. *Biiigggg* alum. Rolling in dough. When God Almighty needs a loan, he comes to my old man who still charges two points over prime on the return. Ain't nobody gets no breaks with the old man."

Peachy waited for a return smile, but the Leader of the Spook Patrol didn't bother to wrinkle one inch of the lumpy skin around his mouth.

"Anyway, the old man is a big Sigma Z alum."

"This chapter?"

Peachy felt uneasy, like that gnawing sense that your zipper might be down. Obviously, there was an advantage to being a legacy to this particular chapter of Sig Zeta, but they probably had records and such. Another chapter would take a few days to confirm, but the pledge bids would be submitted tonight.

"Uh, no. He was initiated at Cordell University. Then he *transferred* here."

"Cordell? Never heard of it. I've heard of Cor*nell*."

The hole was getting deeper.

"That's what I meant. And old Larry over there, his brother is an Active right now at . . . uh . . . Slippery Rock. This whole mess is nothing but a clerical error. So here's what I propose. You were talking about provisional bids earlier, so why don't you just write that down on a piece of paper for me and Larry, submit our bids, then check out our legacy status later. If I'm giving you a line of bullshit an acre wide, then Larry and I will de-pledge. I promise."

Wheeler held his ground, not flinching, not smiling. But he wasn't saying no either.

"Ty, what kind of car do you drive?" Peachy asked, moving in from the flank for the kill.

"Fifty-six Lincoln, black sedan, black leather interior. Why?"

"Just wondered. It's about time for me to turn in my red Stingray. It's last year's model and the new ones'll be at the dealers soon. I could let my old one go for . . . oh, let's say, three thousand clams, interest free, payable over five years. Hell, over *ten* years."

"Not interested. I like my cars old and black. It's me."

"Oh, yeah. How so?"

"If you pledge here, you'll find out."

Pledge here? Peachy was pure Cheshire cat. He hadn't thought he was getting anywhere with this weirdo, this five- or six-year flunky.

"But I'll tell you what I *would* like . . ." began Ty.

Bribery at its best, thought Peachy. *I can sniff out the greasy palms of a peckerwood like this a mile away.*

"What's that, Ty, my man."

"A jukebox. No, two jukeboxes. One for the basement here and one for my room. That way the 45s won't get scratched."

Peachy almost shouted for joy. "No problem, Ty. No problem at all. You see, I got this friend, Amy Valente, in fact, she's going through girls' rush right now. A real looker, if you know what I mean. Chipper DeHart's girlfriend. You know Chipper? One of your rushees here now? Six-foot, brown hair, thinks he's God's gift to women? Of course, not. He's upstairs with the others. Anyway, his girlfriend, Amy, believe it or not, she's a Wurlitzer distributor. Gonna work her way through college by getting those friggin' jukeboxes everywhere she can. I'll get you one here in the basement, and I'll throw in the other one for your room at no cost."

"Cost isn't the issue," Ty said. "Control is the issue. I control the records that go in the box. Of course, that'd be expected for the one in my room, but I get thirty slots for the unit in the basement."

Peachy couldn't imagine what this guy's hang-up was, but this was so easy. Too easy.

"It's guaranteed, Ty. Absolutely guaranteed. Hell, you can have *every* damn slot for all I care. Now—we're talking two bids, one for Larry and one for me, right? This, uh, clerical error involved both of us."

"I'm the one who delivers the bids to the IFC tonight. This is the first year they've used the computer system. It'll be a snap. And I'm not doing it just 'cause of the jukeboxes, you understand. I kinda like your style, Waterman. I've got my reasons, and my lips are sealed." Wheeler ran his pinched finger and thumb across the imaginary zipper of his mouth.

Peachy looked over at an anguished Larry Twohatchets whose signaling arms and hands were twitching and seizing in such colorful chaos—falsely spelling out words for the U-bench audience—that Peachy knew he was looking at a rare breed of Indian who didn't know diddly-squat about sign language.

"Deal," Peachy said as they shook on it.

"Now, we've got another 30 minutes to go in this party, and you and your friend should stay down here. The best is yet to come."

Ty Wheeler assumed his rightful place in front of the U-bench, edging the spastic Larry Twohatchets out of the way. Larry and Peachy eased toward the back of the U, just as Ty turned to grab a guitar. He slipped the strap over his head.

Reaching into his pocket, Ty pulled out the most outrageous pair of glasses Peachy had ever seen. With black rims thicker than Buddy Holly's, the lenses were tinted with an auburn hue that was too light for sunglasses, too dark for regular glasses, but just right for Ty the Twit. As he slipped them on, Peachy noticed the U-audience come to attention.

Peachy looked at Larry as their four eyes widened. No one had to guess. They all knew at once that they were looking at a carbon copy, an identical twin, a dead ringer, of the one and only.

But after one strum of the guitar, the Orbison illusion exploded. The chord on the guitar was fine, but the voice—"A candy-colored clown they call the Sandman"—was so sour, so off-key, that Peachy shrank in embarrassment.

5

Rush Chairman Al Marlowe delivered the perforated computer cards, pledge bids, through the crack in the door to Ty Wheeler.

"Remember, Ty, the thick stack with the rubber band is the one for bids. The rest are the rejects."

Ty took the stacks without saying a word, his shifty eyes never fully resigned to his curious role as the house spook. Al watched the Grade-A weirdo walk out of the officers' hallway before the soon-to-be-ex-Rush Chairman pressed the door shut and rested his forehead against the jamb, ending one role and beginning another. His job as Rush Chairman was over tonight. Now, he would be the new President.

Perry Crane had exited today from the fraternity on his way to Harvard Law, shortly after the hot box session on Chipper DeHart (though Perry had been kind enough to leave the Robert Kennedy poster for posterity). Al stared at the Kennedy smile as he dragged himself halfway across the room, collapsing in the blue and gold plaid armchair that had swallowed the DeHart kid hours earlier.

Al hadn't really wanted to be Rush Chairman, but he was born for the role, as generals are born to lead. Gifted with Brando looks, he was just one torn T-shirt away from yelling, "Stella. Stel-la!"

But his looks, his commanding voice, his intramural touchdown skills, his 3.5 GPA, his Mercedes, didn't tell the real story. And the real story was that Al didn't want to be President any more than he'd wanted to be Rush Chairman.

He felt bad that he had ignored Chipper during the summer, but he had grown increasingly distraught with one-on-ones in small towns, and he felt himself enveloped in molasses each time he drove into another hicksville where the conversation burden would be his. Rush in the bigger towns had worked only because he'd delegated schmoozing chores to the Actives who lived there. Al was thankful Perry Crane had agreed to give the hard sell to Chipper.

As he stared at the Kennedy-Crane team on the wall, he felt himself sinking deeper and deeper into the marshmallow cushion of the chair. When he tried to lift his forearms from the blue and gold fabric, they were glued in place. His head weighed so much it flopped to the back of the chair where it strained his neck when he tried to lift it again.

Al was paralyzed. His eyes were fixed on the alarm clock as it ticked away time while lounging on the monster desk, taunting him with spinning hands. 1:00 a.m. 2:00 a.m. 3:00 a.m. How could sleep not come to his body when his mind had already chosen to hibernate? And what was so amusing to Robert Kennedy, smiling through it all?

6

"The door is o-pen," came a singsong voice following Amy's knock.

Amy Valente dragged her pink Samsonite suitcase through the portal to her new dorm room, where she was greeted by the aroma of Shalimar and the upside-down pettipants of her new roommate whose rump was skyward, jiggling in the traditional bicycle exercise.

"Hi, there. I'm Cassie. Cassie St. Clair. We talked on the phone." The pixie-girl didn't miss a rotation as she stretched one hand to greet the new roomie, still balanced, lace-clad legs cycling the imaginary bike. "Sorry to meet you with my *be*-hind in the air, but I gotta keep going. I come from a long line of bubble butts, and if I'm going to be a dancer, I gotta keep trim."

Amy laughed inside as Cassie continued her ride, though nothing more than a gracious smile passed beyond her lips. "Well, I'm Amy, as you might have figured. I could probably use some exercise myself. Golf really doesn't do it, you know." She tossed her luggage on the bed and let her purse drop to the ground.

"You play golf? Why?"

Amy thought it an odd question, but she replied just the same: "Because I'm good."

"Oh. I just never knew a girl who played golf before. I come from a really small town. It's not even a town, really. Two Blinks. Ever heard of it? The first blink you see it, the second blink you don't. Didn't even have a high school. Had to travel 10 miles just to be in a graduating class of seven."

"But didn't you tell me on the phone that you're here on a dance scholarship? How'd they ever find you? Or did you find them?"

Cassie dismounted from her bed, sandy hair in bouncy pigtails. Standing proudly in a baby blue T-shirt and white pettipants, she broke into a series of spins, twirls, and toe-stands before coming to rest in first position, one arm curved to the sky, all in the narrow confines of the matchbox room where scant floor space made a "T" between parallel beds. Amy applauded as she sat on the corner of one of the beds, in the long arm of the "T," near her pink luggage.

Cassie gave a brief and boring account of life at Two Blinks before returning to Amy's question. And in that brief account, Amy found a very good friend. Amy had powerful discernment, she felt, and a friend she could find after an hour or so, but she could spot a very good friend in 10 seconds flat.

"My aunt and uncle run the only business that sits on the highway at Two Blinks. A grocery store with a gas pump. My parents are dead, so I was bounced from an oversexed uncle first, then to Two Blinks with a hermit uncle who lived mostly in a trailer while my aunt was in the main house." Cassie's huge smile was plastered. "I'd sit there in the store working the checkout counter day after day, watching the tumbleweeds play chase with the dust devils outside, and I'd think to myself, 'Someday, *someone* is going to take me away from all of this nothingness.' And I'd practice my ballet five or six hours a day."

"But who taught you, out in the middle of nowhere?"

"A record and a book. They went together. The record explained the pictures in the book, plus had the right music to boot. I got real psycho about getting good."

"No lessons?"

"None. I'd see a little ballet on the neighbor's TV every now and then is all. I worked at my dancing for years by myself. Then, one day, this long black car pulls up to the store while I was working. A tall woman gets out, she's six-footish or so, big ol' sunglasses making her look like The Fly in that horror movie, wearing a fox hat with a leather top, of all things, and a matching coat. I mean it was 90-something degrees out, in October, no less. She's *famished*, and she's *parched*, and she needs a *libation*, and she really *must*. . . ."

Cassie began prissing up and down the "T" as she spoke, mimicking the The Fly, with her claw-cocked, insectoid arms ratcheting into various poses, as she demanded this and that.

"So I start scurrying around getting everything she needs. Mind you, she's got a male servant in uniform, no less, who's aiming some sort of stick at me, telling me to scramble every time she squawks.

Amy, I didn't know what the heck was going on. I was kinda scared 'cause I was at the store alone. I guess to cover up my heebie-jeebies, I went sur les pointes, on my toes you know, while I went around the store to gather her stuff, finally leaping around in grand jetés. All of a sudden, she begins to stiffen up, quits ordering me around, and starts telling me to go through the positions. Ballet positions. You know what I mean?"

"Sort of. I love dancing to rock 'n roll, of course, but ballet? Sorry."

"Anyway, she starts looking back at her valet as she's putting me through the paces. Next thing, she wants to know my name and every-thing about me. To make a long story short, she invited me to try out for a scholarship here at the university. I did, and I won. I made it here on the Yvette Chalot Dance Scholarship. Only one girl in the state gets a free ride to the university, and I'm her."

With that, Cassie bowed low to the ground, letting one arm flow from her body, unfolding until the back of her hand kissed the floor, then she stood tall again, hands on her hips. "Yvette Chalot was The Fly. She's like a professor emeritus of ballet, or something like that. It means she's too old to perform anymore."

"That's a neat story," Amy said.

"I know. I don't even have the classic ballerina shape. Look at me. Too short. My gluteus assimus is too round already at eighteen. And my boobs are so big I have to trot to keep from falling forward."

Amy hadn't noticed Cassie's curves until now, because the girl's Ipana smile and elfin face with slit-like eyes provided her sparkle.

"You, Amy, *you've* got the right shape for a ballerina," Cassie said.

Amy didn't know whether the compliment was a backhand or a forehand. "I never took dance," she said. "Didn't interest me. I don't know why. Always studying, I guess."

Cassie moved to her own bed, across from Amy. "What about you? I know on the phone you said you were pre-med. Isn't that sort of weird for a girl?"

"Maybe so, but I don't understand why. After all, most all the doc-tors in Russia are women." Cassie looked surprised, causing her pig-tails to wobble. "I don't think much about what's right for a boy or a girl, probably 'cause I grew up without a dad. It was just my mom and me. My father took off when I was little. The way I see it, a woman has to be prepared to take care of herself. In fact, I'm putting myself through college working for Wurlitzer. I put jukeboxes every place there isn't one."

Cassie put her palms on her thighs, elbows out, and Amy noticed that faint brown freckles coated her arms where the baby blue ended and more freckles coated her legs where the lacy white ended. Cassie leaned forward and stared into Amy's eyes. "I *know* what you mean, Amy. You've got engine-youity, too, don't you?"

"Ingenuity?"

"Yes, engine-youity. When I was a little girl, I remember my father—I was seven when he and mom were killed in a motel fire—but I remember my father always telling me I had ingenuity. I thought he was saying that I had an engine in me. Engine-in-youity. I shortened it to engine-youity, but to me the word means that I've got an engine inside. And you've got it too, right?"

"Maybe. What do you mean exactly?"

"Power. Cylinders. The drive of an engine. It's always running no matter what's going on around you."

"Well . . . I . . ."

"Home, husband, babies, white picket fence. We're not really sure it's going to happen for us. So we're driven. No, we're *being* driven. By an engine."

"You might say that, but believe me, I'm planning on a husband and babies."

"Me too. I'm just not *assuming* it's going to happen. I'm preparing for anything. So, do you have a boyfriend?" asked Cassie.

"Yes."

"Well, I don't. I'm footloose. What's your boyfriend's name?"

"Chipper DeHart. He's going through rush now, too. In fact, the boys are pledging this morning, you know. I won't be able to talk to him until after our first open house this afternoon. Do you know what you're going to pledge?"

"Are you kidding? I don't even know if I'm going to pledge at all. They say it's a matter of survival at this school, but I'm gonna be pretty busy at the College of Fine Arts. Besides, I didn't have a single letter of recommendation, so I doubt I'll even get a bid."

"Oh, I'm sure you will. I don't have many letters myself. I'm from El Viento, and there weren't many women in sororities there. And no one in my family ever did it. I just thought it might be kind of fun, and my boyfriend is obsessed with the frat scene. He took the rush manual, for gosh sakes, and memorized the names and activities of all the hot shots in all the different fraternities so that he'd know more about the members than vice versa. He gets kind of nutso about stuff like that. I could take it or leave it."

"Are you going to wear that to open house?" asked Cassie.

Amy was dressed in a pink shift with a matching grosgrain ribbon hair bow that separated her bangs from her long, teased hair that ended in a golden flip. "No, I'm going to switch into a pink and white jumper with my mary janes. And I'm wearing enough Aquanet to freeze both Batman and Robin, so I don't think I'll need to curl my hair again."

"Holy hair glue, Batman!" Cassie dropped her smile for a moment and placed her hands on her hips to mock the hit TV show. "That's why I like my hair shortish. Never have to worry about it. Mind if I ask if you frost yours?"

"If I didn't frost it, it would be more mousy than blonde."

"But gosh, you've got the prettiest green eyes," said Cassie. "And I'd kill for your dimples. I need those creases to cut into my fat cheeks."

Cassie kept her smile fixed as an awkward moment of silence passed, then she reached to the ground and picked up Amy's purse.

The bag hung from a large O-ring made of wood, with loops like curtain rings connecting the black leather to the O. As Cassie lifted one side of the O into a handle, the loops rattled with gravity to the bottom of the O and closed the purse. "Why, I've never seen anything like it," said Cassie.

"You're kidding," said Amy. "Every girl I know has one."

From the doorway came a sultry voice: "And if you carry that *monstrosity* into a sorority house, you'll be blackballed quicker than you can say Neiman-Marcus."

The two girls looked up together. Amy thought the girl in the door had a most bewitching face. Huge black eyes—just a little too far apart and pinched into commas at the edges—were almost hidden by silky black hair that hung straight, hugging her face and shoulders. Her skin was pale, begging for a tan base, but Amy had the impression that the girl was wearing no makeup at all. Unless, perhaps, subtle eye shadow might explain the deep-set eyes. Tall and thin, wearing a black suit and heels, she seemed to fill the doorway.

Behind her, a stream of porters were carrying trunks into the room next door, joined by a common bathroom to Cassie and Amy's quarters. When Cassie saw the men in the hallway, she pulled the bedspread over her bare legs, but the porters looked neither left nor right.

"My name is Audora Winchester," the girl said. "I'm your suitemate. My father is paying double for my room, so I won't have a roommate. It shall be the three of us."

As Amy raised her hand to shake Audora's, she found herself mesmerized by the girl's long, unpainted nails and a glittering bracelet studded with diamonds she assumed were real.

Audora hesitated to shake, as if unaccustomed to another woman offering this gesture. When their hands finally clasped, Amy scrutinized Audora's eyes beyond the fluttering lashes, hoping to determine if those spacious eyelids were powdered with shadow.

"My name's Amy Valente," she said, then she turned to Cassie to allow her to speak for herself. Cassie pulled the bedspread around her for a makeshift dress and began to hobble toward the door.

"I love your eye shadow," said Amy, probing. "Who makes it?"

Audora smiled, as if she'd been asked the question a hundred times. "I'm not wearing any. It's all me." She spoke as if she should be waving a feathered fan about her face.

Cassie tripped on the bedspread and fell at the feet of Audora in a puff of Shalimar perfume. From the tile floor, Cassie raised a greeting hand, smile unshaken, lace-rimmed legs flailing to regain grace and composure. "I'm Cassie. I'm a dance major."

7

"What's neemunmarkis?" asked Cassie, rising to her feet.

Audora cocked her head and arched one eyebrow. "What?"

"Neemunmarkis. You said we'd be blackballed quicker than you can say 'neemunmarkis.'"

"Oh, you mean Neiman-Marcus. It's a fancy department store in Dallas. They've just branched out with a new store at the North Park Mall. Father says it's a bad move. That you shouldn't mix cream and crass. He used to be one of their vice-presidents, but he got in on the ground floor of a company called Texas Instruments. They make silly little electric calculators. Have you seen them? He's says they're going to replace the slide rule some day. Ho-hum."

Amy knew she was supposed to be impressed, but she wasn't.

Audora entered the tiny room, while Cassie joined Amy on the edge of one of the twin beds.

After her huge eyes had scoured the chamber, Audora said one word: "Primitive."

Amy gave Cassie a wink as they both turned to Audora, waiting for more.

The princess strolled down the skinny aisle between the beds, then to the windows that formed the crossbar of the "T" living space. Built-in study desks were crammed between sleep and fresh air at each end of the crossbar. Audora moved with cautious grace, sliding her forefinger along a graffiti-riddled white pine desktop, then inspecting the tip of that same finger as if gauging the amount of dust. Turning, pausing, hands to hips like a runway model, she said, "Yes, 'primitive' is the right word. Or Spartan. Or better yet, ascetic. It would be *so* wrong to call this crude. And worse to call it filthy. This is just the right ambiance, a quiet place from which to tackle the riddles of life."

Amy felt herself drifting to the edge of the bed, where she was sure she was about to splatter onto the floor. What sort of loon was slinking around their room?

"Alas, I'm sure Father and the Pointer will nonetheless be unable to appreciate this domicile."

Cassie arched her back and clasped her hands between her legs as if she were a little girl again at the movies, back when the cartoon would introduce the feature. "Who, or what, is the Pointer?" she asked.

Before the answer came, Amy heard a man clear his throat in the hallway. Cassie scrambled to cover her pettipants with the blanket.

"Audora, I see you've made some friends already," the gray-coiffed gentleman said.

The words were stiff and forced, coming from a man with a scary, callous look, like the sort of fellow who backhands his wife while stroking the head of his prized retriever. Then, squeezing between this imposing gentleman and the doorway came a five-foot ball of bleached hair, makeup, and screaming red fingernails. She was about the right age to be Audora's older sister, but there was no resemblance.

"Eee-gad, this room is *filthy!* Davey dear, you *cannot* let your daughter attend this so-called university." The woman approached Audora as she continued, "Audora, please, for the last time—everyone we know has their kids in SMU, or back East. For God's sake, your SAT scores let you go anywhere you want. Are you *sure* about this?"

Amy watched Audora stand still, unmoved by the show. Audora's eyes grew even larger as she stared at the little woman whose broad red headband couldn't hold back the wild strands of peroxided hair that were trying to escape their roots.

Audora's reply was so soft that Amy felt herself lean in tandem with Cassie as the bewildered girls moved closer to hear: "We've already had this conversation, Madge. More than once. Time for a memory check."

And with those words, Madge's stiff right arm lifted with a forefinger pointed at Audora. And at the tip of that forefinger was a long red nail. "I may only be your stepmother, Audora, but someone's got to watch you. Lord knows your father won't." As the fingernail drew close to Audora's nose, the wayward girl stood her ground, then crossed her eyes when the red point came within an inch. Amy had to hold back the laughter as Audora, cross-eyed, focused on the tip of Madge's finger. Audora's pupils hovered over the bridge of her nose like two UFOs making a landing.

"Put on some makeup. And get some rollers in that hair. For god-sakes, if you're going to be a Kappa like the rest of the women in your family, then you'll have to get rid of that beatnik look." Madge dropped her hand to her side, and Audora relaxed her eyes to dead-on straight.

As Madge retraced her steps down the aisle to join Davey, Amy noticed the back zipper of the woman's white skirt was halfway down, with the tail of her leopard blouse pooching out the hole. Audora gave Amy a subtle smile, letting her suite-mate know she'd just been initiated to the inner circle of Pointerhood.

"Allow me to introduce myself," said Davey. "I'm David Winchester, Audora's father. And you've already met Madge, sort of."

Audora was still by the windows, Davey and Madge were at the doorway, and Amy felt that she and Cassie were watching a tennis match as they tried to capture every return to every serve. Audora looked at the ground when her father spoke.

After several volleys, Amy interrupted the tension by introducing herself, then said, "And this is Cassie St. Clair. She's here on a dance scholarship." When there was no response, Amy continued, trying to fill the horrible void. "She's from a little town called Two Blinks. Now you see it. Now you don't. I thought I was from a little town, but—"

"Davey, we *must* check out Audora's room next door," said the Pointer as if she were the only voice in the room. "We have to make sure they got rid of that second bed, so we can go ahead and ship your mother's antique armoire for the rest of the wardrobe." Madge pulled Davey down the hall to the next door.

Amy's jaw froze in mid-sentence. She tried to close her mouth, but she couldn't. She wasn't prone to cursing, but the words "you rude bitch" were jostling around in her throat, and she so desperately wanted to let them fly. After a moment, she turned to Cassie and saw that her lips were still parted by shock as well.

Audora leaned down between Cassie and Amy, then whispered, "Save your questions for the end." Audora gave them a mischievous grin that made Amy feel as though their suite-mate might be of a different mold than the money seemed to imply. And as Audora left the room to join Davey and Madge, she wiggled her hips with such an exaggerated sashay down the runway of the "T" that Amy started chuckling. Cassie laughed as well, while she put on a skirt in case they returned.

Through sieve-like walls, Amy and Cassie listened to the rantings of Madge, having to imagine that fingernail pointed at Audora. Davey was silent, at least too silent for words to pass through drywall. Madge's nagging about comportment at college included a minor soliloquy on the dangers of those "newfangled" birth control pills, prompting Amy and Cassie to plaster their ears against the wall. "Madge, the pill has been out for seven years now. They've got to be safe," Audora said. "Safe is not what I'm talking about," Madge replied, "and you know it. I'm talking about you keeping a vice around your knees."

The subject switched to the Kappa sorority as Madge's voice grew louder. The Winchester party was making its way back through the common bathroom, so Amy and Cassie scrambled to their original, innocent positions on the bed.

"Oh, dear. I cannot—no, I *will* not—picture you in this bathroom. Just look at those fixtures. The rust is *so* . . . *so* . . . and the stain on that shower door. Why, it's . . . mildew . . . ee-gad, this is aw—Oh, it's you two. I was just reminding Audora how rush week is a mere formality for her. After all, her mother was a Kappa, her grandmother a Kappa, two sisters, and two aunts. She's a multiple legacy, and Kappa will be lucky to have her. Of course, the Kappas at SMU are simply delicious. I don't know about *here*."

Cassie perked straight up. "We don't have the slightest, Mrs. Winchester. We'll be lucky to get bids anywhere, coming from nowhere and all. Y'all heard of a one-horse town? Well, Two Blinks is a one-outhouse town. There aren't any strings being pulled for us during rush week."

Madge looked stupefied. "My dear," she said to Cassie, "have you ever heard of Highland Park?"

"No, m'am."

"Would you know what I was talking about if I said that Audora was a Dallas debu—oh, never mind. Da-vey! We really must be going. Audora, it's not too late to stop the nonsense. The Mexicans haven't left yet. They can still load your belongings back in the truck."

Amy couldn't remain silent. She stood up, towering over Madge, and announced, "I don't think you'll have to worry, Mrs. Winchester, about this university or Audora. I'm pre-med, so I think Audora will be in pretty good company."

"Pre-med? Oh, *really*. Well, my dear, that'll end up being pre-nursing—that is, until some cute intern puts you in a family way. But I'm sure Audora can help you with your studies, all the same. She's never made a B in her life."

"If a cute intern puts me in a *family way*," said Amy, "number one, he'll already be my hubby, and number two, I'll just make history as one of the first pregnant interns *ever*." Amy gave Mrs. Winchester her unflinching, beauty queen smile.

The Pointer began flicking her scarlet talon with her thumb, as if sharpening for the attack. Amy felt herself preparing to cross her eyes should the waggling finger strike. "Oh, very clever, my dear. Davey, I think it's time for us to be off."

Audora showed her parents out, nodding to Amy as she passed. Phony pleasantries were exchanged, and just before the door was shut, Amy spotted Audora pull away from her father's intended kiss. Finally, they were gone. The room became remarkably quiet.

"Father married the Pointer two months after my mom died of cancer. I was twelve at the time. I'll never forgive him."

As Amy sat back down with Cassie, Audora collapsed in the opposite bed, legs spread to the limits of her black skirt, her silky hair fanning across the bed. "Thank heavens I won't have to see them until Thanksgiving." She lifted her legs to the point that Amy thought she was about to begin Cassie's bicycling exercise. Then she used one foot to pry the shoe off the other, launching the pump like a grenade where it hit the wall above Amy and Cassie. The two girls covered their heads to avoid the fallout. Then the other shoe smacked the wall above them. Cassie grabbed the high heels and held them in her lap.

"So, how did you girls like my bullshit entry this afternoon? Wasn't that a pisser?"

"What do you mean?" asked Cassie.

"Ah, come on. You know, the pretentious snob act."

Amy and Cassie looked at each other, confused.

Audora unbuttoned her jacket, revealing a lime green bra with silk panels and exquisite lace, the likes of which Amy had never seen before.

"Wow. Where do you buy green underwear?" asked Cassie.

Audora laughed. "You haven't seen Vassarette before? Oh, Cassie dear, I have so much to teach you. I love bright colors. It can be such a dreary world, and I think you should use every opportunity to color your dreams."

Amy was astonished as Audora continued to strip to matching panties and bra. She had never known a girl so free of modesty. And for some reason, Audora's phrase 'color your dreams' resonated with Amy so much that the memory was banked.

"There. Now I'm cooler. That bitch gets me so overheated I can barely stand it." Apparently recognizing the befuddled look on the two girls' faces, she continued. "In fact, I came to this university to get away from the very so-called friends that Madge wants me to join at SMU. Just a bunch of stuck-up snoots from high school that she thinks are the *right people* for me to be around. I have nothing in common with those husband-hunters. I'm a philosophy major, and this school supposedly has a great department."

"Philosophy? What do you do with a degree like that?" asked Cassie.

"The question is not what *I'll* do with *it* . . . but what *it* will do with *me*."

As they continued to chat, Amy found it hard to focus on the conversation while Audora was shining in her neon lime lingerie. Eventually, they returned to the subject of sorority rush, where Amy admitted she had barely paid attention to the process.

"I'll guide you through," offered Audora. "Rush week is terribly phony, but I think living in the sorority will be a blast."

Cassie said, "Too bad we'll not all be in the same house."

"What do you mean?" Audora asked.

"You know. You'll be pledging Kappa, but Amy and I don't have those connections. We'll be somewhere else."

"Oh, my dear Cassie," Audora said as she leaned forward, crossing her legs, "you don't understand me at all, do you? I'm sure the Kappas are lovely girls and all, but Satan will shit ice cubes before I pledge Kappa. Let me introduce myself again. My name is Audora, and I like high heels, wet kisses, and half-mad men."

8

Rushees swarmed over the lawn in front of the dorms at Crim Center searching for their chosen fraternity flags, planted near the street where the boys could rally 'round.

Chipper was smug in his silence that his courageous and brilliant strategy had worked—indeed, Peachy had received a Sig Zeta bid, and Peachy had accepted. They were pledge brothers now.

As he and Peachy approached the flag bearing the Greek letters ΣZX where a school bus waited for boarding, Chipper was startled by his friend's howling whine: "Dammit, I'm de-pledging. I knew I should have gone Deke."

"What are you talking about?" Chipper asked.

"Look at our scum-sucking-piece-of-shit pledge brother," Peachy said, pointing through the crowd to another new pledge who was rolling his ΣZX-emblazoned T-shirt over his head.

"Oh, my gosh," said Chipper, disappointed, as he recognized Monty Guilford, jerk-of-jerks from Castlemont private high school. They had played golf against him for years, but Peachy had gone 36 holes with Monty in the state tournament, man-to-man, insult-to-insult, before El Viento pulled out the championship in an upset over Castlemont. The victory was in no small part due to Peachy's miracle round of 77 on the final 18, where his subliminal torture techniques had rattled his foe, Guilford, who sank to the crass low of not-so-subliminal cursing at Peachy en route to an 84 and the team loss.

"I think I'm gonna puke," Peachy said. Then he fumed, glaring at Guilford who was now ricocheting through the new pledges, glad-handing each of them.

"Hello, brothers," came Monty's smarmy voice as he threw one arm around Chipper and the other arm around Peachy, grinning at both of them through thin lips. "My name's Monty Guilford. Right on, Sig Zeta, eh? So, how 'bout you guys? What're your names?"

"What are our names? WHAT ARE OUR NAMES?" yelled Peachy. "Guilford, you sorry sack of shit, you know damn well what our names are!"

"Sorry, lads, though you do look a bit familiar. The pleasure's mine, though," he said as he tried to give them both the secret grip.

Peachy pulled his hand away. "You asshole, are you honestly going to stand there and pretend you don't know us?"

Chipper thought that the jerk-of-jerks was contorting his face with mock sincerity, struggling hard to pretend to remember what he forgot. During these facial gymnastics, Chipper's enthusiasm for pledging Sig Zeta plummeted 50 stories.

"Don't tell me. It's coming to me. Did you lads play any sports?" Guilford's too-large teeth were glistening as he smiled, his straight black hair flip-flopped by the wind.

"You lowlife pissant mutherfuggin' piece of rat shit," began Peachy, "why don't you go stick a 2-iron up your ass and see if that won't tickle your memory?"

"That's it! I remember now. You played golf for El Viento. Wow, what a performance you lads put on last spring. You sure waxed our fannies." Monte tapped Chipper on the shoulder with a closed fist.

"And another thing," said Peachy, "what's this 'lads' shit? We ain't your kids. Are we supposed to call you 'pop?'"

Chipper thought Peachy was on the brink of a swift punch to the nose, so he jumped in to mediate, playing along with Monty's phony amnesia. "We've met before, Monty. I'm Chipper DeHart and this is Peachy Waterman . . . *junior.*"

Peachy gave Chipper a scowl, denoting strong disapproval of Chipper's annoying habit of peacemaking.

After Monty moved on to work the crowd, Peachy couldn't stop repeating, "Do you believe it? Do you fuggin' believe it?"

Chipper said, "You know, when you think about it, we only saw half the rushees who were considering Sig Zeta on Two-party Day. Half our pledge class is going to be brand new to us."

"Hell, they're all new to me. Remember? I was in the basement. But I can assure you, I'd like to see a lot less of what I've seen already, starting with that banana-nosed bastard."

"College is a new leaf, Peachy. A new start for all of us. Maybe we should give the guy a chance."

"Don't start in with me, *lad*. I ain't pledging this place so's you can preach to me for four years. If I'm gonna hate the mutherfugger, then that's damn well what I'm gonna do."

Chipper and Peachy were nearly last to board the yellow school bus, driven by one of the Sigma Z Actives who wore a World War I flying cap and goggles, a comic who was doing his routine over the microphone while a sea of pledging arms extended across the aisle in brief introductions.

Chipper trailed Peachy to an empty seat at the back, counting rows as he went, multiplying four pledges per. It looked like there would be about 35 pledges altogether.

Before sitting down, Chipper saw Peachy reach across the aisle to thump a guy on the head with his palm. "Hey, Twohatchets. Told ya' we'd make it. Everything's copacetic, just like I said."

Chipper saw a broad-shouldered Indian who turned and delivered a halfhearted grin, while vertical slits formed in the skin between his scrunched eyebrows.

"Chipper, meet my Polack friend, Larry Twohatchets."

"Nice to meet you. I think I know . . . didn't you play golf for Anadarko?"

"Yup," interrupted Peachy. "Polack City, U.S.A."

Drawing from his memory of the rush manual, with composite photos for each and every fraternity, Chipper couldn't recall a single full-blood in the entire frat scene. He hoped Larry Twohatchets could smile more convincingly than now because he looked like a wolf baring its teeth.

As he took his seat, Chipper was pleased that Monty Guilford was at the front of the bus. This was going to take some adjustment. He couldn't imagine ever calling the guy 'brother.' At least there wouldn't be any bullies in college like there were in high school. Jerks, sure, but no bullies. Scanning the new faces, he still sensed a wonderful adventure. Adios, El Viento. Hello, Universe.

"Okie dokie, brothers," the World War I flying ace at the controls said. "This bus is going to the Sig house, 558 University or bust, courtesy of Interfraternity Council regulations. For about three seconds. Then we're going to Grady's Pub so y'all can get shit-faced."

A cheer shook the bus as the Active-driver closed the door.

"Wait a minute!" someone hollered. "There's one more."

A short, squatty guy with long arms and a crazy cowboy hat was strolling up to the bus, in no hurry at all. Stringy yellow hair poured out from beneath the brim of the hat that was trimmed with a rattlesnake band.

Chipper and Peachy turned to each other in such a state of shock that it seemed their mouths were competing to form the perfect O.

The cowboy paused on the first step of the bus and struck a match on the rattlesnake band, then lit his cigarette.

"No smoking on the bus, brother," said the driver, generously dishing out the word 'brother' that was held in reverence only for initiated members.

Chipper buried his face in his hands. "Oh, my gosh. It's Smokey Ray Divine. I never dreamed he'd go through rush, much less pledge Sig Zeta."

"Hell, who'd ever thought he'd go to *college*?"

"Oh, don't kid yourself," Chipper said. "He's smart. Maybe too smart for his own good."

Smokey Ray Divine was a championship golfer from Pottowattomie, a town El Viento had played against regularly throughout their high school years. Chipper thought of Smokey Ray as a friend to keep at arm's distance, for the guy seemed to enjoy spawning calamity for the sheer pleasure of staring trouble back down again.

Smokey Ray eased to the second step when the driver repeated the message, "Sorry, brother, no smoking on the bus."

Chipper found the Active to be amazingly polite. After all, it was a member's right to humiliate a pledge. Perhaps the hazing stories were nothing but rumor.

All eyes in the bus were fixed on Smokey Ray, then those pledges at the back started to rise out of their seats to get a better look. Smokey Ray scrutinized the busload with his wry smile. And without using his hands for the cigarette between his lips, he waggled his tongue to twirl the cancer stick so that the burning end was pointing inside his mouth. As he closed his lips around the fiery tip, smoke started billowing out his nostrils.

A curious silence spread through the new pledge class as Smokey Ray seemed to gulp. The smoke stopped pouring out his nose. Still without using his hands, he twirled the cigarette around again and held it with his lips, the burning end extinguished. Smokey Ray took his place in one of the few remaining seats.

"He's a friggin' god, I'm telling you," Peachy said. "This is going to be so cool."

9

Chorus-lined pledge brothers, linked by arms around shoulders, sang in unison: "And our love becomes a funeral pyre . . ."

"Helluva song," Smokey Ray said to Chipper. "Fell outta number one slot this week, but I'm betting you dime to dollar that Jim Morrison is the friggin' Second Coming."

Chipper cringed at the sacrilege as he eyed Smokey Ray hovering over the jukebox, an eerie glow from the machine's lights reflected in the shrewd face of his new pledge brother.

Grady's Pub was a closed party for the neophyte Sigma Zs. The aroma of the stone-walled tavern was new to Chipper, and it blended with the cigarette smoke in a nearly nauseating fragrance, tinctured by spilt beer marinating for decades in the cracks of oak tables.

"This is an antique, a 1953 Wurlitzer," said Chipper, "first model to have over a hundred plays. A hundred four to be exact. Before that, forty-eight was—"

"Creepers, cowboy," said Smokey Ray. "Are you still with that same muchacha? Amy, was it? The Wurlitzer girl?"

Peachy was standing with his back to the jukebox, beer cup to lips. "Two letters are all you need for Chipper, Smokey Ray—P and W," said Peachy. "No, I take that back. You can't be PW'd if you're still a virgin. He's just plain W."

Smokey Ray looked up from the selection of songs and stared at Chipper, the way Smokey could do where his eyeballs just roll right through you. "Still a virgin? Damn. Hard to believe." Seemingly bored, Smokey Ray turned back to the spooky light coming from the Model 1550a Wurlitzer.

Chipper wanted to strangle Peachy for making him feel like a peanut.

"Look at that sorry sonuvabitch," said Peachy, distracted from their engaging conversation. "Old banana-nose Guilford is bouncing around the room like a fuggin' politician, the way he's shoving his hairy palm into every conversation."

"He *is* a politician," said Smokey Ray, without looking up from the 104 selections.

"Whaddya mean?" asked Peachy.

"He's running for office. Pledge class president. He's promising the family lodge on Grand Lake for the brothers to shack up in, he's bragging about his father the big alum, and his grandfather the bigger alum—a founder of this chapter of Sigma Zeta. I heard his bullshit earlier."

"He's what?" Peachy yelled. "Over my dead body." And he faded into the smoke.

Chipper felt a little sick inside. If he were to be the President some day, he should probably consider pledge class president now. On the other hand, did he really want to draw attention to himself? Wouldn't the pledge class president be a lightning rod? Besides, getting elected by strangers was no easy feat, especially if campaign promises included hideaways for shacking up. The beer helped squash his shyness, and he thought about working through the crowd. But he was torn because he didn't want to bounce around the room like bootlick Guilford. The rise from small town obscurity might be harder than he thought.

"Wow, what got into the Peach?" Smokey Ray asked.

"He can't stand the guy. I mean, who can?"

"It's a dog's life and Guilford is nothing but a flea. Who cares? He's a total BSer to anyone he talks to, probably losing one vote every time he opens his choppers."

Pledge Trainer Ted Boone, the only Active at the party, joined Smokey Ray and Chipper at the jukebox. Ted's spindly arms dangled from the generous sleeves of his Sig Zeta T-shirt where, as a member, he was allowed to wear the golden cross crest in addition to the Greek letters.

"Congratulations, brothers," said Ted. "Welcome aboard." As Boone and Smokey Ray shook hands, it seemed to Chipper they were sizing each other up as the Pledge Trainer continued. "I look forward to some engaging discussions at our pledge meetings. Your pledge class is unique, and I hope to take you well beyond the pledge manual."

Smokey Ray looked at Boone without a trace of expression. Chipper had seen those beady eyes stare down men twice Smokey Ray's size, but this was not the stare-down look. Then, one corner of Smokey Ray's mouth twitched upward in a semi-smile. "Well," began Smokey, "the truth is . . . I pledged just to make sure I had quick access to good poon-tang, but if you want to jawbone about the mystic meaning of life, I'll be right there with you." His smile extended to the other corner of his mouth, forming an impish grin.

"I'm sure you will," replied Ted who then turned Chipper's way. "And Chipper, I'm counting on you to run for office. You know we elect officers next week at our first meeting."

"Well . . ."

"Hell, he's already got one foot in the White House," answered Smokey Ray. "He's a sucker for that sort of thing." Smokey Ray turned back to the jukebox to punch out another song: "There's something happenin' here . . ."

Boone began stroking his chin, smiling, as if toying with a thought when, in fact, the thought was already strapped in the cockpit and ready for blastoff.

"Chipper, I'd like to see you run for—" began the Pledge Trainer.

Chipper felt a hand on his shoulder. "Brother, my name's Ernie Dumas." Chipper turned around to face a guy taller than his own six feet. "Firssst of all, I can whoop anybody at chuggin' beer." As he chugged his glass, spilling at least half around the edges and onto the floor, Chipper was struck by Ernie's peculiar eyebrows. While the lower half of his brows were red like his curly hair, the top half of each brow was pure white, providing two-tone streaks above each green eye. Maybe it was just the strange light of the jukebox, thought Chipper. Surely his eyebrows weren't *that* white.

Ernie slammed his glass on the table to punctuate his skill. "Your buddy over there's tellin' us you're gonna be preshhident of the Preshhident's Leadership Class."

"Well, for the first term, to be fair." Chipper beamed as he remembered the phone call from the president of the university, appointing Chipper last spring, while still in high school, to the honor. PLC was a group of the outstanding high school graduates, one from most every school in the state. And here he was, handpicked for this crucial role in student leadership, though he fought a feeble inner voice that reminded him he'd done *nothing* of importance to deserve the honor.

"Shhhit, that's good enough f'r me," said Ernie. "You oughta be our pres, just like that pissant Peachy-fella over there's tellin' everyone."

Ernie's wild eyes seemed to flash as he spoke, opening so wide that Chipper could see around the green centers, tree-topped by those crazy white stripes as if his eyebrows were painted on in chalk.

Chipper studied Peachy crisscrossing through the crowd with more fervor even than Monty Guilford, collaring pledge brothers, pointing in Chipper's direction, yucking it up as he most assuredly described Chipper as the chosen ruler of the free world.

Ernie Dumas was starting to sway as he chugged another.

"As a matter a' fact," said Ernie, "why wait 'til next week? Let's fuggin' elect the pres right now!"

"Uhh . . . you guys might be just a little too tanked," began Pledge Trainer Boone.

"Bullshit," said Ernie as he grabbed a spoon from a nearby table, then a glass. "Gennelmen, gennelmen, can I have your tenshun, pleeeze?" Ernie was wobbling now, pushing Smokey Ray out of the way as he braced himself against the jukebox, trying to clank the glass with his spoon. "We've decided to elect pledge the class pres tonight. Do I hear nominashunns?"

"Kyle 'Chipper' DeHart for president," yelled Peachy from the far side of the tavern.

After acknowledging the nomination, Chipper stood on one of the wooden chairs that matched the oak tables, introduced himself to all, then presented his platform, which was, in brief, nothing.

"Damn straight. Well put. Do I hear any other nominashunns?" asked Ernie.

Chipper looked at Monty Guilford whose frantic eyes were groping for support among his brethren. Monty even began elbowing a few of the lads nearby.

"I nominate Monty Guilford," said Smokey Ray.

Chipper turned to his quasi-friend, startled.

"They'll roast the asshole," whispered Smokey to Chipper. "I'm just leading the turkey to the oven."

Monty gave an extended campaign speech, beginning with his enriched and sacred birthright, moving on to the pleasure and freedom that money allows, concluding with his towering benevolence whereby all pledges would benefit, perhaps even financially, simply by touching the hem of his garment.

Chipper won the vote, 35 to 1.

Smokey Ray didn't even vote for his own nominee. Peachy returned to the home base jukebox, yelling back across the room to ease the tension, "Uno vote for brother Monty—his own! I dub thee from now on—Uno . . . Uno . . . Uno . . ."

Peachy's Uno chant gained momentum while pledges took turns slapping Uno Guilford on the back. And in a strange twist, it seemed that Uno was made part of the group in the role of Reject Supreme, gaining a spectacular acceptance that would otherwise have been foreign. Pledge brothers were all smiles as they surrounded Uno to congratulate him on being a good loser.

But Uno was not smiling. He wasn't even struggling to smile. He was dagger-eyed, glaring across the room at Chipper where a larger group was shaking hands with Mr. President. Chipper ignored him.

In the commotion, Smokey Ray plopped another quarter in the jukebox: "We skipped the light fandango . . ."

"Hey, Dumas," said Smokey Ray, "Pretty big claims you make about being a champion chugger."

Ernie scowled at first, then grinned. Choosing a large paper cup for weaponry, he filled it from a pitcher, then downed his Coors in three seconds flat (though a stern judge would have disqualified Ernie for the streams that poured out each corner of his mouth). After his final gulp, he threw the paper cup into an empty stone fireplace that looked as though it hadn't hosted a fire in years. Ernie put his hands on his hips, his chalk-stripe eyebrows almost glowing in the dark.

Smokey Ray took a full pitcher—fivefold the amount in Ernie's cup—and hoisted it in the air. "Veni, vidi, vici," he said, then he put his lips to the glass edge and consumed the entire pitcher in seconds, without so much as a swallow, literally pouring the liquid into his stomach as fast as it would empty, without spilling a single drop. Then he said, "A lion among ladies is a most dreadful thing; for there is not a more fearful wildfowl than your lion living."

Chipper and Peachy exchanged a knowing look, learned from their shenanigans with Smokey Ray back in high school. "Shakespeare," they said together, nodding.

Ernie Dumas was squinting, his chalk-stripe eyebrows angled sharply. Chipper thought he could see, in the shadows of the tavern, a nervous smile on the second-best chugger in the pledge class.

10

"*Opposition candidates charge that the South Vietnamese elections were rigged in favor of the Thieu-Ky military slate. However, 22 prominent Americans served as election observers, walking away satisfied with the process. And today, Secretary of Defense McNamara announced plans to build a fortified barrier just south of the DMZ, to curb the flow of arms and troops from North Vietnam to the South. General Westmoreland opposes the McNamara Line, contending that surprise attacks inside the DMZ are more effective . . .*"

Al Marlowe twisted the noise away until the radio knob clicked off. Law school would protect him for a while. But if required to serve his country, he would do so with manufactured pride.

As he traveled the empty hallway to chair his first chapter meeting as President, Al dredged the sewer of memories from his own pledge-ship, perhaps as a test for some vestigial emotion. Worksessions ("What do you know about me, pledge?"), Going Around the Table ("What do you know about me, pledge?"), and on and on. There were good times, too, he supposed. The pledge class walkout, football, the parties, the takeout of the most hated Active. And finally, Initiation. Al thought about his golden career as a Sig Zeta, from quarterback on the intramural field to his current leadership role. He was this year's Mister Sigma Zeta Chi. And as he recalled hoisting the Spring Bash trophy in the air as Head Coach of the Pi Phi team . . . as he thought of his upcoming nomination for the province Aegis Award . . . as he flashed through it all . . . a terrifying realization grabbed his heart in a choke-hold—he didn't care.

He knew certain feelings, both good and bad, should escort these memories, but the emotions were gone. Perhaps he knew something was wrong back when his high school team won the state football championship. He was a sophomore starter, and he noticed then that the victory seemed to mean more to the others—even for the kids who didn't play.

And with each passing year, the sun seemed to slip more and more behind the horizon. Sadness was not really the ogre on his back. He could always laugh at a good joke. It was emptiness—a void that reduced him to robotic ritual.

Later, midway through the chapter meeting, after his lifeless arm had pounded the gavel at least 50 times, President Marlowe called, "Is there any new business?"

Black Jack DeLaughter rose slowly from his chair, one of 60 Actives with their backs to the wall as they formed a square at the periphery of the Chapter Room. A salmon terrazzo floor formed a central rink, so slick that stockinged feet could glide 30 feet after a good run on new wax.

Marlowe's ears captured a few groans and moans that rumbled around the room like distant thunder as Black Jack took center stage. From his elevated station, a throne-like podium, the President looked down on the cantankerous Active, wishing he could make Black Jack vanish.

When Black Jack reached front and center, he faced the chapter members first, then turned slowly, looking upward, squarely, at Marlowe.

Black Jack's close-set eyes pinched the bridge of his nose, looking downright silly on his triangular head that gave an illusion of extra brains at the top. His pointy chin aimed the triangle to a middle-aged profile, complete with sloping shoulders and beer belly. Long dark hair combed forward in spikes was not enough to cover a billboard forehead.

Al fought to remember that they had been pledge brothers and were now bonded in Sig Zeta.

"Yeah, I got some new business," said Black Jack, stroking his day-old whiskers. "How the *fuck* did Peachy Waterman and Injun Joe get bids when I blackballed both the bastards? Answer me that." He stared at the President like Bigfoot being told he didn't exist.

As a defensive tackle, Black Jack could penetrate a stonewall line. In fact, he held the unofficial intramural school record for all-time quarterback sacks. However, as a spokesman for any cause, Black Jack could alienate the entire chapter in a breath.

Al pulled the words from somewhere and spoke in a forced monotone. "First of all, Jack, you're fined five bucks for using the f-word in the Chapter Room. Second, we're not sure exactly how it happened, but remember, we might have lost the DeHart kid without Waterman. And please don't forget that Brother Burton is pinned to Ayita Conrad . . . Larry Twohatchet's half-sister."

From the corner of the room, Brother Burton stood up, placing one foot on the seat of his chair, leaning forward to rest his crisscrossed arms on his knee. President Marlowe gave Burton the floor.

"You're pushing the limits on this one, Jack," said Burton. "And let me remind you that we've got 10 card-carrying brothers on the Indian rolls in this house. In fact, I wouldn't be surprised if there isn't some Indian blood in you, what with that dark skin of yours, and that straight black hair." Brother Burton smiled.

Black Jack took a few steps toward Brother Burton as if to add to his quarterback sacks, then he pointed. "Listen, *brother*, we damn sure don't have any full-bloods in this house. Twohatchets is a *full-blood*. Your pinmate gets by 'cause she passes for white."

Then Jack spun around to President Marlowe, his finger still outstretched and threatening. "For years I've put up with your shit-doesn't-stink attitude, Marlowe, and I'm sick of it. Just 'cause you're the President doesn't give you the right to veto my blackballs."

"Jack, calm down," Al said, "I'm not exactly sure what happened, but they're both good guys —"

"Good guys? Good guys! Kiss my ass, good guys. The Waterman kid is a fucking dough —"

"Another five dollar fine," said Al as he banged the gavel.

"And Injun Joe looks like he just escaped from the reservation."

"Times are a-changing, Jack," called Brother Burton from the back of the room. "And for you, it's time to get your fat ass back in your chair."

Defiant catcalls and laughter echoed Brother Burton, taunting Black Jack. Each brother would have shriveled and quaked in a one-on-one with Black Jack, but the unity of brotherhood extended an invisible arm, well-muscled.

Jack began to spin, pointing at various brothers joining the ridicule, then he stopped, facing the President, and approached the lofty podium. Marlowe was glad to be flanked on his right by Vice-President Woolman, and on his left by Secretary Rector. The three members of the tribunal were mute as Black Jack fumed and glared.

Then Jack spoke. "I will guaranfuckingtee you this, Marlowe —"

"Five more dollars." The gavel crashed again.

"You can bet your goddam ass that I'll run off both those spooks in six weeks. I'll goddam guarantee it. The two of them will be squealing for their mommies in six weeks. And I won't lay a hand on 'em. Won't even let the door hit 'em on the butt on their way out. I'll . . ."

The President looked at the lunatic before him with scorching condescension. But in truth, Al Marlowe didn't even care.

11

Three glasses, raised high, touched gently with a clink that was barely audible above the drone in the dark pub. The Split Onion was a place college kids could drink as long as someone in the group had an ID, and Audora had a fake. Swirls of bubbly Coors threatened to top the glass rims as Cassie gave the toast. "Here's to the three musketeers."

"Or muskerettes," said Amy.

"How about mousquetaires? From the French?" added Audora.

Amy sipped, Cassie gulped, and Audora chugged.

"I think it's so neat we all pledged Beta Chi Omega," continued Cassie, wiping the foam from her lips.

"I hope you two are happy with Beta Chi," said Amy. "When I found out how many activities they have with the Sig Zetas . . . well, you know my boyfriend pledged Sig— "

"No need to feel responsible," said Audora. "We're big girls. Mistresses of our own fate. And my fate is a family that will never speak to me again." Audora laughed as she hooked the edge of her silky black hair with her forefinger and draped it behind her ear.

"How did you tell them?" asked Amy.

"I simply told them I pledged."

"And?"

"And that's all I said—literally. I said I pledged. My two sisters and my aunts started screaming on the other end of the phone. They didn't even let me finish my sentence. They just assumed it was Kappa."

"So what happened when you corrected them?" asked Amy.

"I didn't."

"What?" squealed the other two.

Amy set her glass on the table, waiting for an explanation, as she and Cassie exchanged looks of astonishment.

"Won't it be a real kicker when I tell them it's time for initiation? They'll come from all over the country, expecting to live their Kappa dream all over again."

"You wouldn't," said Cassie.

"Audora, that's awful," Amy added.

Audora fiddled with her necklace, then she slipped them a mischievous grin. "Oh, I suppose I'll tell them eventually."

From her purse, Audora pulled a gold cigarette case, prompting looks of fascination from Amy and Cassie. But rather than light the Camel that she took from the case, she laid the cigarette down carefully after drying the wooden tabletop with a napkin.

Fumbling through her purse, she pulled out a silk handkerchief trimmed with white lace, containing something precious. Audora held the treasure with both hands, easing it like an egg onto the table where she daintily peeled back the folded layers of silk.

Inside, Amy saw a small brick, army green mixed with ugly brown, that looked not too far removed from a cubed cow chip.

Audora smiled at both girls before touching her fingernail file to one corner of the brick, shaving a kernel, then tapping the tiny rock into the end of her cigarette.

"What—?" managed Cassie.

After a light and a long drag, Audora held her breath until her nose turned purple, then she raised her puckered lips to the overhanging lamp and sent a stream of smoke to mingle with the light bulb.

She cocked one eyebrow and smiled. "Hashish," she said, chasing the word with a swallow of Coors.

From their corner table, Amy checked the rest of the pub to make sure none of the other kids could see the contraband before her. She had worried about Audora, but her concern had been some sort of amorphous blob. Tonight, Amy's concern began to take shape.

12

Chipper pressed Amy against one of the adolescent trees that lined the parkway near the towering new dormitory. Tonight, her hairspray had mostly crumbled, so he was able to stroke through her frosted flip without his hand becoming lodged in the curl. As he moved in for the kiss, he saw that the streetlight had changed her green eyes to gray. Or maybe it was the moonlight, weaving through the swaying branches of the trees in rhythm with her eyes, which turned from gray to green then back again. Then he kissed her.

"Do you think we'll be able to wait four years 'til we're married?" Amy asked as she pulled away, breathing with a depth that Chipper had come to crave. Not every kiss made her gasp for air, so he knew to charge on.

"I hope not," he said as he guided his embracing fingers down the middle of her back until they eased onto her full and luscious fanny. She pulled him into a below-the-belt vice that signaled a four-year wait was a long shot.

"You know Jacob and Kelly are probably doing it right now," she said, referring to their best friends from high school.

"I know." Chipper was bathing in the moment. Amy was his dream come true, his missing half, and the only person on the planet with whom he could drop the mask and be himself. And now they were on their own at last, sort of, destined for a hunch hut of their own some day, loving life, here at college. Hometown El Viento seemed 500 miles away.

Chipper was born to be a college man. He had studied the art for years by reading through his parents' yearbooks, by observing room decor of the older brothers of his friends (yes, a parachute to decorate the ceiling would work just fine), but mostly his image of college was defined by one album recorded in '58 by the Kingston Trio—"... *from the Hungry i,*" popular when Chipper was twelve.

Even the name of the nightclub where the trio was recorded live— Hungry i—was cool. But it was clear that the trio was much more than a simple folk group. They were driven by the human plight. They sang of rioting in Africa, strife in Iran, and mushroom-shaped clouds. His parents never considered such things. Yet these college men, so studly in their vertical-striped shirts, seemed to appreciate a larger world, a world that needed deep thought and close attention.

Yes, the Kingston Trio were the ultimate college men, and Chipper was excited beyond description that he would be surrounded by others of like mind. Sophisticated folks. The intelligentsia (a word he had embraced). At last, he had found a home where his insightful thoughts and perspicacity (his "new word" of the day) could be nurtured.

"Chipper, look!" Amy cried, pushing him away. "Some girl is go-go dancing at the top of the Beehive. It looks like she's naked. And the guys are pouring out of the dorms."

The Beehive was the new 12-story cylindrical dorm where cookie-cutter windows made the rooms look like cells from the outside. Originally, the windows could open, but an escapee from the nearby mental institution had tested the limits of 12-story gravity with a grisly splatter just weeks before school started, forcing the windows to be sealed.

And on the top floor, with clever backlighting that turned her into a nude silhouette, a girl with waist-length hair was doing the Pony and the Frug for a mushrooming crowd standing outside the base of the Beehive.

"Let's get a closer look," said Chipper, thrilled that Ivory Tower intelligentsia was going to include the luxury of dancing girls. And maybe this would require some . . . perspicacity.

Amy smacked him teasingly on the arm with her fist. "We better stay back here," she said. "Those guys are getting a little rowdy. Besides, I have to get over to the Beta Chi house in a minute. We're getting our big sisters tonight."

"I hope you have better luck than I did," Chipper said. He had mixed feelings about his big brother match—Al Marlowe. Of course, it was an indicator that Chipper was on track to become President some day. Train under a Master and all that sort of mishmash. And

Chipper couldn't deny that Al had charisma, in a Jake Chisum movie star sort of way. But it turned out that Al was every bit as mute as last summer when he had ignored Chipper during rush. Chipper's Big Brother was more of a Big Icebox.

"My gosh," said Amy, "I've never seen so many people gather so quickly."

"Look at all the guys with coolers passing out beer."

Because the dancing girl was behind glass, there was no music. Only the roar of the crowd. She was doing the Watusi now, alternating with the Jerk.

"I bet there's 200 guys over there," said Chipper.

"Look. They must be calling their friends. The boys are coming out of Crim Center. And down the street, look. More from the Bass Building."

"And Bentley Plaza," Chipper added.

"I'm starting to get a little scared," said Amy.

"Don't be silly."

As the rivers of molten lava flowed from the dorms to the base of the Beehive, Chipper saw a game emerging—King of the Hill. Guys were jumping on top of cement planters, rooting others into frenzy. Once pushed from the planter, a new orator would take his stand. And as Chipper listened, it seemed that the Kings of the mob were calling out sorority names.

Transistor radios started blaring a hodgepodge of songs. Through the cacophony, Chipper could hear wisps of lyrics, fading in and out, overlapping: *"I don't care how much money I got to spend—All you need is love . . .* dum-dum-da-da-dum—*To Itchycoo Park, that's where I've been."*

The parkway filled with bodies until the perimeter of the mob edged within 20 feet of Chipper and Amy.

"This isn't hundreds of guys, Chipper, this is *thousands*. We better get out of here."

He was starting to agree.

Beer cans were flying, shirts were coming off, and the cuss words were changing from the deplorable to the unthinkable.

"Oh, no," said Chipper.

"What's the matter?"

"I think that's my pledge brother up on the planter leading the crowd."

"Who? Where?"

"Ernie Dumas. Right in front of us. You remember, the crazy guy that tried to out-chug Smokey Ray on the day we pledged."

"Redhead?"

"Yeah. Blondish-red. You can tell it's him by the way he twitches his head around, like a hawk," said Chipper. "I guess I should do something. This wouldn't look good for Sig Zeta."

"What can you do? You can't get near him. Even if you could, someone like him is not going to listen to you. Not now."

As the air was filled with the touchdown-roar of young men leaving their mark on the world, more sorority names could be heard above the melodious hum of a riot—the way "Kill the Ref" can be heard above the boos. Then two words jumped out of the crowd— "Panty Raid"—with so much power that the thousands began to unify into an organized legion.

Like a fire-breathing dragon weaving between buildings, the cast of thousands vacated the parkway and headed in the direction of Sorority Row. The base camp at the bottom of the Beehive was empty within a minute, though the sound of the dragon steamed in the distance. In a way, it seemed to Chipper that the noise was scarier when you could no longer see the source.

"I've gotta get to a phone," said Amy. "Cassie and Audora are already at the Beta Chi house."

Chipper looked to the top floor of the Beehive. The dancing girl was gone.

13

As the bare-chested animal broke through the door, Cassie let out a shriek that was neutered by the riotous noises outside. Guys yelling. Girls screaming. Doorjambs busting. She was by herself to face a lone threat that had emerged from the swarm.

She cowered, hunkered into a ball on the bedspread of Bettyann, the Active she hoped would be her Big Sis here at the Beta Chi house.

"They're in the drawer. Take all you want," she said, pointing the wild-eyed monster to the panty stash.

He laughed through clenched teeth as he shut the door behind him.

"I don't take panties out of drawers," he said. "I go for the source." And he reached for the top button of his faded blue Levis.

Cassie shut her eyes and screamed. And screamed. And screa—

His huge hand sealed her mouth. "One more peep out of you, and it'll be your last. I'm not kidding, bitch."

The horror was too real, too quickly. He was instantly on top of her, trying unsuccessfully to use his free hand to lift her skirt above her waist. She could almost taste his hot, stinking beer-breath.

"Now when I let go of your pretty little face, you better be as quiet as a goddam mouse."

Audora was in the bathroom down the hall, where she had fled moments earlier, along with two Actives, Jane and Kathleen. Upon realizing the magnitude of the mob attack, they had decided to fill their old party mugs with scalding water, allowing a crude defense—a boiling oil approach to the raid on their castle. *Where are they?* thought Cassie. *Where are they?*

The brute lifted his hand from her frozen mouth, then raised to his knees, unbuttoning his jeans. She was too frightened to scream again. He leaned forward with a sickening grin, sliding both hands up her legs while raising her skirt. Then, Cassie saw his ferocity melt with bug-eyed curiosity.

"What the hell are those?" he said, apparently shocked at her pettipants that held such chaste design.

And in that divine moment so opportune, Cassie struck like a snake with her two python thighs coiling around the neck of the varmint. She locked her legs and squeezed until his face was the color of his reddish hair.

She knew she would never forget the sight of the detached, fiery head lodged in her crotch as she squeezed tighter and tighter until he seemed to be choking. His arms were flailing, but she wouldn't let go. In the struggle, her skirt slipped down over his face as his body fell to the ground in an effort to free his head. From Cassie's view, it looked as though she were giving birth to a six-foot two-inch linebacker.

Audora charged through the door, a steamy mug of scalding pain in each hand. "You let her go, you goddam asshole!" she yelled, in apparent confusion as to who was holding whom. Audora doused the assailant on his bare back with the blistering water. Muted screams rose from the head beneath Cassie's skirt.

Jane and Kathleen followed Audora into the room, pouring out more of the steaming water. Cassie wouldn't let go. The attacker tugged at Cassie's thighs, pulling her to the ground with him in a pas de deux.

From the ground, Cassie could see Jane and Kathleen run out of the room, yelling a promise of quick return with Beta Chi party mugs filled to the brim with more scorching water. Audora started to follow but turned instead, heading for her purse on Bettyann's bed.

Cassie was merely an observer now. Her legs were ratcheted shut and locked tight. Dampened threats were rumbling beneath her plaid skirt, but years of plies in ballet had given her pliar-like thighs, and her tormentor was now a prisoner, locked in pettipant hell.

Audora pulled a bottle of Joy perfume from her purse and said, "I *told* you to let her go, you sonuvabitch."

The beast's legs were kicking and his hands were groping at Cassie's thighs as he tried to free himself.

Audora poured some of the liquid into her palm, then lifted Cassie's skirt to reveal the hideous head underneath. "Fresh from

Neiman's, you asshole," she said, as she smeared the perfume into his eyes, rubbing with vigor to force the alcohol inside the eyelids.

When he began to scream, Cassie let go.

He rolled onto his hands and knees, then crawled toward the door before jumping to a run. Audora chased him to the hallway, heaving the bottle of Joy his direction as an exclamation point. Then, as if transformed back to debutante, she tapped behind her ears with the pads of her fragrant fingers.

Cassie crawled back to the edge of the bed, angry, hurt, dirty. Most of all, she was mad that her memory would forever be soiled by the hideous face between her legs. Those pop-eyes hooded by bizarre two-toned eyebrows, white on top, red on bottom.

Audora sat down and put her arm around Cassie who was too shamed, too dazed, too outraged to cry.

14

As he took his seat on the U-bench for pledge class meeting, Chipper beamed at the new Wurlitzer Model 2600, fortified for 200 plays. Though Peachy was trying to take full credit for the new jukebox in the basement, the name on the fraternity's collective lips was Amy Valente, a *pledge's* girlfriend, and Chipper hoped this small victory might shield him from anticipated hazing now that Grace Week was over.

Pledge assignments had been made at their first meeting last week. Chipper had already memorized "The Rickel Standard" and "My Shield." Over the next week, he would learn the Greek alphabet and something about the Two Founders.

Later, the pledges would face hellish memorization, or so they said, of excruciating minutiae on the history of the local chapter. For now, though, bio sketches on the Actives were far more important in preparation for the cross-examinations that tended to open with, "What do you know about me?"

Each pledge had drawn his own room chart—first floor architectural plans on the front, second floor on the back—with the name of every Active living in every room. Over the next few months, individual pledges would corner the members one-on-one, force a meaningful conversation, then get a signature on the room chart to document that the seeds of brotherhood had been sowed.

Chipper was proud of his system for centralizing the data, a validation of his presidential nature. In addition to the mandatory scoop— name, major, hometown, class, girlfriend and girlfriend's sorority—the bank of pooled information would be dynamic, adding personal tidbits gathered by pledge brothers so that a dazzling and detailed sketch could be recited on demand by all pledges at Worksessions and at meals while Going Round the Table. And if everyone performed well, kudos to the pledge class president. And for Chipper, kudos meant personal immunity against attack, an alleged perk for the president.

He scanned his murmuring pledge brothers gathered around the U-bench as they awaited the arrival of Pledge Trainer Boone. As his eyes skipped from face to face, Chipper scrolled through his rote accounting of each, reminding himself to check his crib sheet and fill in bio blanks later. And, as if given names were some sort of hideous parental error, nicknames sprouted and grew, seemingly blessed, and pledges were christened: Peatmoss, Twobits, C.C. the Dwarf, Einstink, Kong, and on and on.

Peachy was, of course, just "Peachy." But nicknames ricocheted off Larry Twohatchets like a racquetball. Both "Polack" and "Chief" had been tried. Both failed. "Grumpy" was suggested by Dumas, but Peachy nipped it in the bud. One thing for sure, though, "Twohatchets" was too hard to say. It would never last.

Smokey Ray Divine was seated in the back row. That is, Smokey Ray *was* the back row. He had forged his solo spot well behind the U-bench, on a barstool by the jukebox.

Pledge Trainer Boone entered the room with a curious stroll, his black bushy eyebrows angled more sternly than usual. His gait was always peculiar in that his moose-antler hipbones seemed to be the leading edge of his body, with his sunken chest coming in a distant second. In fact, his necktie hung loose from the knot, so far away from his shirt that you could pass a fist through the space without touching yellow shirt or navy club tie.

"Well . . . well . . . well," said the Pledge Trainer, each "well" a few notes down on the musical scale. "I hear that some of you might have been involved in a wee bit of mob hysteria last night."

A few exchanged snickers signaled the guilt of many, including Chipper, who possessed extrasensory culpability just by being *near* trouble. News reports had indicated a crazed crowd of 2,000, property damage yet to be determined, and a few minor injuries. The campus cops had been overwhelmed and city police slow to respond, but both forces had issued pleas for informants. It was rumored that not a single college kid helped them out, and no one complained, at least not to the cops. A local newspaper editorial also made a plea to equip police with riot gear, given the chaos brewing "back East" and "out West," though admitting that those riots had political agendas that were unlikely to make it inland.

"Well . . . well . . . well. Rest assured I have no intention to pry from you the names of those involved, because, in a way, all of you must share the disgra—"

"I think the guys that destroyed stuff should have to pay for it," interrupted Ernie Dumas, his hand in the air like a grade school snitch.

"Whoa, Dumas, you dumb ass," Peachy hollered from across the U-bench, "I saw your ugly mug there. So'd Chipper. You were one of the ringleaders. What kinda crap you tryin' to pull on us?"

"Screw you, Peachy Pie, I didn't destroy nuthin'."

Neither Dumb Ass nor Peachy Pie would probably stick as nicknames, though such witty repartee was often the genesis for monikers.

"Hush, hush, children," Boone said.

"Yeah, listen to Mother," said Smokey Ray from the back of the room.

"Mother" would stick.

"I want you to look at a much bigger picture," continued Mother. "Ask yourself at what point does harmless fun cross the line? When is your sport someone else's misery? More importantly, what does the panty raid tell us about personal strength versus mob rule? We don't fall reluctantly into screwball behavior. Or even violent behavior. We do it willingly. Gleefully. Bewitched in our enthusiasm. Why? Why? Why? . . ."

Chipper lost count of the number of times, in different musical pitches, the Pledge Trainer said "why," but each time the word shot out, Chipper felt he was being impaled.

"Why? Why? Why?"

Ernie Dumas raised his hand again. "Maybe we do it just to get the girls' panties in an uproar."

The feeble-minded joke landed on the floor like a flapjack. Ernie yucked it up all by himself, trying to generate support and erase the silence. It was pathetic, and Chipper fought a voice of ill-will inside.

"The worst damage was at the Beta Chi house," said Mother Boone, bringing a stillness beyond silence to the room. "I don't know if you realize it or not, but we do a lot with the Beta Chis. Functions, Homecoming floats, and Varsity Sing. I think it would be a nice gesture if the Sig Zeta pledge class sent the Beta Chis a peace offering. After all, as I understand it, the mob last night was made up mostly of freshmen pledges from the dorms."

Chipper was ready to bet that a slew of Actives poured out of the houses on fraternity row as well, since fraternities and sororities were all located south of campus on a looping avenue. All the houses, save one, that is. The Sig Zeta house, at 558 University Boulevard, was located all by itself north of campus. The sequestered locale was a major deterrent to the rush effort, and word had it that tough alums were clinging to their memories and would not allow the house to move south, even though the Sigma Zs felt themselves to be in crippling quarantine.

Chipper watched Ernie fidget behind the U-bench, hanging onto the support pole that rose to the ceiling. He didn't sit with the other pledges. Rather, he stood behind the bench, twitching his head around like a hawk with each comment, scrutinizing the room to identify support, or prey.

Uno Guilford, jerk of jerks, was seated in the center of the U, and it seemed that he had been nodding in agreement with Ernie, trying to interject. Finally: "I'm with Dumas," he said. "This is why *Playboy* named us the number one party school in the country, with numbers two through ten pale by comparison. You're making too big a deal out of this, Ted. After all, they're just girls. Screw 'em." Uno crossed his arms and smiled at Mother Boone, daring the Pledge Trainer to push him any further.

Smokey Ray rose and balanced on the first rung of his barstool. *Oh, no*, thought Chipper, *this could get out of control in a jiffy. If anyone's ready to pounce on the bones of innocent girls, it's Smokey Ray. I hope he doesn't make Ted mad.*

"Gentlemen," began Smokey Ray, "I don't think you want to talk about the future mothers of your children like that. Each of you in this room wants kids someday. Well, those sons and daughters will be molded by the girls you now mock. Love the woman. Fear the woman. But the devil will have his due if you *mock* the woman. Your needles are but weapons for those who have no other." And he sat back down.

Peachy was seated next to Chipper, at one end of the U, and the Peach whispered to the president, "I can't figure that peckerwood out, even after all these years. He's been inside more panties than Inspector Number 55 at the Sears and Roebuck factory. I would've never figured him to say something like that."

An uncomfortable hush lasted eight seconds, at least. Realizing that Smokey Ray had soothed, or perhaps stunned, the crowd, Chipper felt the need to stand and demonstrate his natural talent for leadership, picking up where Smokey Ray had left off. As he spoke, he began to realize that Smokey Ray had already made the point with a striking economy of words, some of which were probably borrowed from Shakespeare. In the end, Chipper felt like a total idiot, and he sat back down.

"Impressive," sneered Peachy.

An hour later, the meeting broke ranks. Mother Boone had handed out the homework assignments and, with painstaking care, had tutored the group in what to expect during their first Worksession this coming Saturday night.

On the way up the basement stairs, Dumas pushed a few pledge brothers out of the way to reach Guilford. Ernie cackled as he spoke, those crazed eyes with their two-toned, bouncing eyebrows. Chipper could see their conversation turn private when Ernie pulled the jerk-of-jerks to the side. Both of the pledges bent forward, gripping their bellies in wild laughter.

As Peachy walked by Chipper, he whispered, "B.F."

"B.S.?"

"No, B.F.," Peachy said. "Both those guys are B.F.—Buddyfuckers. You know, the kind of brothers who'd rather spread cheeks than spread cheer."

15

The living room lights at the Sig Zeta house were off, only a corner lamp broadcasting a creepy glow that seemed more dark than bright. Thirty-nine pledges filled the room, some on the mile-long couch beneath the front window, most sitting cross-legged on the blue shag rug that spread out like a lake over much of the salmon terrazzo floor.

Chipper tried to remember his Saturday night date with Amy that had ended only moments before, though it seemed like another year on a different planet. First, they had gone to the free concert at the Student Union where the Strawberry Alarm Clock had performed their current hit, "Incense and Peppermints." But the songs that followed were grating and irritating, the crowd muttering something about "acid rock." So they left for a movie. Amy had wanted to see "Up the Down Staircase," but Chipper won out with a gander at blood-soaking "Bonnie and Clyde."

As he scanned the waist-high stone planter that separated the living room from the dining room, it reminded him of a giant birdfeeder, this notion reflected by the 15 or so Actives perched on the ledge, swigging their quart bottles of Coors, drying their mouths with the backs of their hands. Ornery blue jays gawking at the pledges. Chipper thought back to that machine gun ambush where Bonnie and Clyde found themselves pushing up daisies to welcome the sun and the morning dew.

After the House Manager issued ground rules for the Worksession, it was Chipper's turn. His authority buoyed by the clipboard in hand, Chipper called out assignments that would ensure the chapter house would be spic and span before sunrise. Peatmoss and Twobits would tackle the upstairs head, Einstink and Kong would strip and wax the downstairs hall, and so forth. And the job of the pledge class president? Why, Chipper would supervise, coordinate, and orchestrate, all while enjoying the perk of immunity. As Chipper understood the official protocol, the president took flak for the whole group, but rarely would the hazing be directed at him personally.

The front doors blasted open, cracking against the wall and driving a gaping hole in the plaster where the knob hit. Black Jack DeLaughter lunged inside, threw his quart bottle back out to the dark night, then screamed, "Where's the fucking pledge class president?"

Chipper melted and froze simultaneously.

"I *said*—'Where's the fucking pledge class president?'"

Chipper held his clipboard high in the air, hoping that his tremor didn't show.

Black Jack DeLaughter lumbered toward the president until he was face-to-smelly-face. "Give me the goddam clipboard," he said.

Chipper obliged.

Black Jack tried to look over the names and the assignments, though his eyes looked crossed and confused.

"Where's your name on this list?" asked Black Jack, his head weaving, but eyes riveted on Chipper.

"I'm not on there."

"And why the fuck not?"

"I'm . . . I'm . . ." Chipper looked to the House Manager for help. *Wasn't the role of the pledge class president clearly understood by all? Before Perry Crane left for Harvard Law, didn't he tell this gorilla about the top rushee? The once and future President?*

"You're what? Go ahead and say it."

"I'm . . . I'm the supervisor," Chipper said, his words barely squeaking out.

Black Jack threw the clipboard on the floor and jammed his finger against Chipper's chest. "Let me tell you something, fuckjaw. When I was a pledge, your big brother Al Marlowe walked around the house with his goddam clipboard giving orders, and I didn't like it then any more than I like it now. Supervisor, my ass, you get on your hands and knees with your pledge brothers, do you understand me, you sorry sack of shit?"

Chipper had miscalculated his personal level of immunity. In fact, his calculations were so far off he thought he might best serve humanity as a Greek-less independent.

"I've got my own assignments to make," said Jack. "There's two pissant pledges that need special instruction." Then he turned to scan the crowd, and Chipper could see multiple pledge-eyes turn away as Black Jack's triangular head moved like a radar screen across the room. "Peachy Waterman and Larry Twohatchets. Where are you? Get your asses up front here with the *supervisor*."

Peachy was wide-eyed with a runaway look Chipper knew all too well, but Larry Twohatchets was calm, shoulders straight, chest out, as he moved to the front. And once again, Chipper saw Larry's sneer that seemed to bare razor sharp teeth.

"You two are hereby assigned to the Puke Pit for your entire pledgeship, which I estimate won't last very long. And Mr. Supervisor, you go with 'em and do your *supervisin'* from the Pit."

The Puke Pit was the bottom cesspool of an outside stairwell that served as a back entrance directly into the basement. The inside door was located between the pool table and the new jukebox, close to Smokey Ray's barstool. An eight-inch concrete threshold kept water from pouring into the fraternity house when the drain at the bottom of the pit was plugged, which was almost always. But it was not the vicious Oklahoma storms that usually filled this reservoir at the bottom of the stairs, but various bodily excretions, most commonly plain old puke. The pledge class had agreed beforehand to rotate assignment to the infamous Puke Pit, but the best laid plans . . .

"Before you get to work, fellas," interrupted Gary Hortense, the House Manager, "do any of you know how to fix holes with drywall?" Gary seemed a kindly sort, yet when he turned to Black Jack, his eyes turned stern as he said, "Jack, you're fined 20 bucks for the hole, by the way."

Black Jack swaggered over to the hole where the doorknob had rammed, then he took his fist and plowed it into the wall at the edges of the hole repeatedly, gouging a cavernous defect. "Now, the rule says 20 bucks per hole, right brother Hortense? So I got these last ones in for free." Then Jack disappeared into what seemed the bowels of the dimly lit chapter house.

Gary Hortense shook his head in a way to let the entire pledge class know that Jack was not a fair sample of the whole. "As I was saying, anybody know how to drywall?"

Larry Twohatchets, standing near the House Manager, raised his hand. Gary laughed and put his arm around Larry's shoulders. "Now, come on, son. The Puke Pit ain't that bad."

"No," Larry said. "Really. I know how. I *want* to fix it."

Chipper didn't understand. Larry had looked ready to strangle Black Jack.

Gary the House Manager paused, then delivered a cautious smile. "I'll show you where we keep the stuff. Some idiot is likely to pull that crap most every weekend. You're in charge for the whole year, my friend. Fix the holes during Worksession, then come back and paint on Monday. The Puke Pit usually takes just a few hours at most. You should be able to do both."

A few hours? Why would the Puke Pit take a few hours? But when Chipper saw the black lagoon at the bottom of the pit, he understood. Six inches of foul fluid, broken beer bottles, and at least three smashed Wellers bottles with glass everywhere. The shards and slivers extended up the concrete stairs that were carpeted with barf, emitting a stench that made a visit to stadium restrooms seem like a romp in a field of lilacs.

Chipper and Peachy (and later Larry, after he cut and plastered the drywall patch) worked at the mess for over two hours, though Chipper had to leave periodically and presidentially to check on progress at the various stations. The House Manager had prepared a long list of chores for each site, and failure to complete a task meant Worksession could last through Sunday afternoon. For example, when the terrazzo wax team was finished downstairs, they had to be shuttled to the kitchen for pot and pan duty, and so forth. Skillful orchestration was the key. Yes, leadership had its administrative burdens.

After the glass had been swept from the Puke Pit, the drain unplugged, the solid matter disposed of, and the concrete steps mopped as clean as a plate, then the threesome deemed the Puke Pit a fait accompli. Chipper assigned Peachy to help with the front yard cleanup crew, while Larry returned to sand his drywall repair. And the president was able to resume his true role as Mister Supervisor.

Chipper decided that beyond supervising, he should encourage, befriend, all while nurturing excellence in housekeeping. So he stopped to talk to C.C. the Dwarf who was in charge of the TV room, a character-building task that included the dusting and polishing of trophies dating back to the 1920s. Such a chat carried a wee measure of danger since Actives were scattered about the house, quizzing the working pledges: "What do you know about me? What? You don't even know the basics? Why haven't you been around to meet me?" Pledges either worked or answered questions. You did not lollygag.

But no Actives were in sight when Chipper joined C.C. Chastain in the TV room. And when roaming Actives did stroll by, the General camouflaged his intent to mingle with the troops by dusting token trophies. C.C. was from Tulsa, pre-med, girlfriend Kathy pledged Chi O, but his claim to fame was playing keyboard for a rock band—the Velvet Lizards—which was a rival band to a so-called talented cat named Leon Russell whom Chipper had never heard of, limiting the power of said claim.

Still, C.C. loved Sigma Zeta Chi. His father was a surgeon (Chipper's was a doctor, too), and his godfather was a Sig Zeta (Chipper's was, too). C.C. buzzed around the room as if in fast motion, his tousled blonde hair flying as he talked about his dreams to become a doctor/songwriter and his deep love for the principles of Sig Zeta. Chipper was astonished that C.C. had already memorized next week's assignment to the hilt. He not only knew about the Two Founders, but also such minutia as Founder Clovis Rickel's dying in the Civil War, leaving Cofounder Thatcher Bell to carry on. What's more, C.C. already had 27 signatures on his room chart. Chipper only had eight. After they chewed the fat for a while, Chipper had a whole new perspective on the guy. He decided that the pledge class should drop 'the Dwarf,' leaving a drab C.C. in exchange for someone who was clearly bigger than his size.

Moving on, Chipper pretended to scrub toilets in the ladies' head with Mitch Addison, a black-haired, blue-eyed face man who was from a small town in Kansas. Mitch was in the J-school and he planned to be a photojournalist, maybe a newscaster. He was instantly likeable but aloof, as if on stage at the news desk already. He joked his way through the ladies' grime and talked a lot about his dates so far in college, all of them with "ballll-shakers." As he cleaned the mirror, he began to imitate his future dates as they primped at future parties: "Oh, my dear, have you seen my date . . . Mitch Dreamboat? He can tickle my toes in bed anytime he wants. Or, for that matter, he can tickle my—"

"LINE-UP!" yelled someone just outside the door to the ladies' head. Chipper's heart twirled until it came to a complete stop. "Line up! Everyone in the dining room for Line-up."

Within minutes, the pledges were standing side-by-side, shoulder-to-shoulder, with a steady succession of Actives pacing in front of them delivering sermonettes for half an hour on what it means to be a Sig Zeta pledge and, maybe, with some luck, a member. Chipper noted two possibly conflicting themes emerge. The first was "unity," and it was clear that the pledges were to think and act as one, *always* supporting each other. The second theme—respect for individuality?— came with the repeated reference to a document called "The Heart of Sigma Zeta Chi" that was meant to capture the origins of the fraternity and included the phrase, "sharing one standard . . . while possessing *different* gifts and convictions."

Chipper had read enough of the history of the fraternity to know that Sig Zeta was a splinter from another fraternity. Before the Civil War, the two Sig Zeta founders had refused to vote for their own "brother" who was running for Golden Mean of the Aristotle Society because he didn't know diddly about philosophy. The Two Founders were charged with treason. And in a dramatic moment before a mock tribunal, one of the rebels, Clovis Rickel, pulled off his pin, tossed it on the table and pronounced, "I didn't join this fraternity to be anyone's pawn." Thatcher Bell did the same, and Sigma Zeta Chi was born.

Chipper looked at the dining room clock. It was 3:30 a.m. As the various members spoke, he recalled his "hot box" where the outgoing President had told him that they were using this new pledge class to return to the original ideals of Sig Zeta—men of different gifts and convictions—and that the transition back to origins would not be smooth.

The Active pacing in front of them now was a senior, a former Pledge Trainer. "The members are calling this class the New Breed," he said, "and I'm not so sure that's fair because quite a few of the *members* consider themselves New Breed, and that's why the decision was made last spring to focus on men of different gifts and conv—"

"Except— *except*, there's such a thing as being *too* different," interrupted Black Jack DeLaughter who rounded the corner for his first appearance at the Worksession since his welcoming fist at the midnight start.

Chipper thought he could hear the entire pledge class in a collective groan.

"And that's why they call *us* the Dying Breed," Jack said.

Brother DeLaughter delivered a scowl to the preaching ex-Pledge Trainer, then he took center stage as the new drill sergeant. "And speaking of *too* different, I want Peachy Waterman and Larry Twohatchets to step forward."

And at that moment, Chipper realized he might have made an error in working so cleverly to get Peachy a bid to Sig Zeta.

Both pledges took steps forward and remained at attention. Black Jack approached Peachy first.

"What do you know about me?" he said in a voice that did not particularly invite familiarity.

Peachy became a statue. His tiny eyes were widening by the second, and he struggled to nudge his glasses back to the bridge of his nose.

"I said . . . what do you know about me? Name, class, major, give me the basics."

"Black—ahem, Jack DeLaughter. Senior. From Muskogee. Majoring in . . . in . . . marketing—"

"Let me tell you something, you friggin' little piece of shit. You've never talked to me once. How dare you start with your bullshit when you've never had a conversation with me?" Black Jack scowled as he scanned the lineup. Chipper cringed at the thought that he had been avoiding Jack as well, saving him for dead last on his room chart.

"The only pledge in this class who's come to talk to me is C.C. Chastain. So where in the hell are the rest of you?"

How did C.C. do it? He was everywhere. Learning the history, learning the Actives. He virtually lived at the Sigma Z house, even though freshmen were confined to the dorms.

Black Jack moved again within an inch of Peachy's nose. "Let me ask you something, Waterman. How is it that you drive a fancy red Corvette, but you dress like you steal your clothes from the Salvation Army? And your friggin' haircut . . . what is that? What do you call that shit you do to your neck?"

"It's called 'blocking,' *sir*. I have my hair blocked in back. It's a London look."

"A London look? A *London* look? You're in friggin' Oklahoma, you piece of shit, and if I see that silly crap again on your neck, I'm gonna take you down and buzz the back of your head myself."

Chipper was sick inside, and he could only imagine what Peachy felt. The Peach did not like to take lip from anyone. At the same time, Peachy sported a major league yellow streak, so it was difficult to predict if Peachy would wisecrack, duck, or run in a situation like this.

"And another thing, Waterman. I know your type. I've seen you around here, and I've heard your smart-ass mouth. You're cocky, son. I don't like cocky. This is fair warning. I'm gonna break your goddam back. Now get in line."

Chipper was starting to lose the fine line between mental hazing and physical hazing. He was drawn to Sig Zeta because they boasted endlessly about "no physical hazing," but he began thinking that a hundred push-ups was paradise when compared to such pointless humiliation. And those rumors didn't seem so bad about the varsity athletes being initiated into the O-Club only after crab-walking on their backs, carrying marshmallows in the crack of their butts, being stunned with cattle prods, and having to eat the marshmallows if they dropped them.

"And you, Mr. Larry Twohatchets, what kind of friggin' name is Twohatchets, as if I have to ask?"

"Do you?" muttered Larry through barely parted lips.

"Do I what?"

"Do you have to ask?"

Chipper couldn't believe that Larry was smarting off.

"Listen, wiseass, I do the talking here. What kind of name is that?"

"Indian. I'm Kickapoo. The name has a musical sound when spoken in our native tongue."

"Now see what I mean?" Jack said, rubbing the back of his head with his paw, seeming to soften. "That's exactly what I was talking about earlier. About being *too* different. I don't think you oughta be talking about 'native tongues' when you're in a fraternity. Do you get my drift?"

"No."

All noise seemed to suck from the room, leaving dead air.

Jack put his hands on his hips and began to shout: "I'm sayin'—if you want to be in a fucking tribe, then get the hell out of this house, and don't let the door hit you in the butt on your way out!"

Jack was fuming, but Larry Twohatchets didn't budge. Chipper couldn't detect a single twitch, other than Larry's jaw muscles that seemed to be knotting beneath the skin. Jack seemed to get angrier by the second when he couldn't get a reaction out of the Indian.

Chipper stole a glance down the row at Smokey Ray Divine, and their eyes met. Smokey Ray had demonstrated a knack for dealing with such bruisers in their high school days, and Chipper could almost see the wheels churning in the mastermind of Smokey Ray. But Ray Divine didn't send any smoke signals back Chipper's way.

Black Jack said, "Best I can tell, everyone in this pledge class has a nickname, but you, Injun' Twohatchets. So *I'm* gonna name you." Jack stared at the pledges as if they were to take notes and burn in hell if they didn't follow his direction. "And if I catch anyone calling Twohatchets here anything else, then they'll get the same treatment as . . . as . . . *Pocahontas*." Jack smiled like the mean kid who's just squashed a horny toad under his shoes during recess. "That's right. From now on, your name is Pocahontas. Got it?"

From somewhere deep inside, perhaps fueled by a special sense that liberation was hatching at this very moment in Smokey Ray's brilliant brain, Chipper took the boldest step in his young life. And that step was exactly one foot forward, followed by: "He already has a nickname, sir." Chipper stared straight ahead, fearful that eye contact would make him wither.

"Oh, give me a break. It's the fucking *supervisor* coming to the rescue." Jack moved his triangular head directly in front of Chipper, and it seemed to Chipper that every spike of black hair on that large forehead was a dagger aimed at his heart. "And just exactly what *is* his nickname?"

Chipper's mind was racing. *Chief, Polack, Grumpy, anything... think!* He looked through the dining room, over the planter and its phony plastic greenery, and to the front door where Larry Twohatchets had patched the hole in the wall hours earlier. "It's ... 'Drywall,' sir."

"Drywall? Drywall!" Black Jack glared at Chipper, as though stunned by the folly of desperation.

Without saying another word, Jack turned from the pledge class, walked into the living room, and rammed his fist repeatedly through the freshly repaired patch of drywall that Drywall had fixed. "That's what I think of Drywall," he proclaimed. Then he walked back to assume charge of the lineup.

"The basement looks like crap," he said, changing subjects to the astonishment of Chipper. "Start over, all you sonzabitches. Redo the study hall, wax the basement floor again, clean the fireplace, and ... I think you'll find that the Puke Pit needs a little touch up." Then he pulled out two toothbrushes from the back pocket of his jeans, one brush to Peachy and one to Drywall. "Do a better job on the Puke Pit this time, *gentlemen*."

House Manager Gary Hortense appeared in his bathrobe, giving Chipper the impression that one of the Actives had roused him from bed. "Jack, this is their first Worksession, and things look pretty good to me so far, so I'll take over from here." Black Jack backed his way to the planter.

Gary turned to the pledges. "Now most of the house is done, so half of you follow Chipper down to the basement and redo it like Jack says. The other half come with me and we'll figure out what's left. Break it up. Back to work."

Actually, the basement looked pretty good, and Chipper could tell that Gary's support of the redo was simply to save face, covering for Jack DeLaughter. But when they opened the downstairs door to the Puke Pit, Chipper saw that someone had trashed the area with more broken bottles and who knows what else.

At first, Chipper thought he was losing his mind when he heard the strum of a guitar echoing in the Puke Pit. Then another. And from the outside concrete stairs, stepping into the basement through the open Puke Pit door, the Roy Orbison look-a-like, joke-of-the-Actives, leader of the spook patrol, appeared. Ty Wheeler's black hair was combed in the Roy pompadour, and he was adorned with sunglasses, black clothes, and a guitar. Chipper exchanged quizzical looks with Peachy and Drywall.

Wheeler went straight to the jukebox, plopped a coin and punched a tune.

As the song, "Working for the Man," began, Chipper was struck that Wheeler's strumming on the guitar blended nicely with the tune, but as for the voice—Ty pantomimed.

16

Drywall Twohatchets stopped scrubbing a pockmarked concrete step in the pit with his toothbrush, then raised his head slowly to view a rectangular glimpse of the night sky, framed by the mouth of the stairwell. Dawn was still an hour away so he could still see fragments of constellations as they hovered above this doorway to hell, seeming to look down and mock him as he worked. At midnight, Pegasus had been gazing at his humiliation, but now Orion was starting to peep into the rectangle for a good laugh.

"I'll guaranfuggintee ya'," said his friend Peachy, "there's no way that Ty Wheeler has anything to do with us bein' back in the pit. He's nothin' more than a weirdo spook that thinks he's Roy Orbison. Doesn't know shit from shinola. Haven't you seen how the other Actives just laugh at him like he's the village idiot? No, we're in the deep doodoo for some other reason. Just remember, if *we* go, so do the jukeboxes. Trust me, Wheeler's not the problem."

Drywall didn't respond to Peachy who was nose-to-the-drain picking up pieces of glass at the bottom of the stairs. With a last name of Twohatchets, he needed no explanation as to the hazing. There was no mystery. He had seen the lily-white faces of fraternity members during rush week. He had seen such faces and their subtleties his whole life—faces where the glare narrows upon eye contact, faces that wait for eye contact just to have the pleasure of looking away, stern faces that shake back and forth in a nearly imperceptible 'no' for no reason at all. And even though the very name Oklahoma came from two Choctaw words meaning "red people," there were no red people in this odd world of Greek gods and goddesses. No Indian fraternities. Yet there were three Jewish fraternities. And was the rumor true that a Negro fraternity was applying for a charter?

"We've got to plan a takeout on that sumbitch DeLaughter," Peachy said. "Maybe that'll shut the bastard up."

"A takeout?"

"Yeah. The entire pledge class breaks into his room in the middle of night, then we haul his naked ass off to Pringle's Pool and throw him in. It'll be really cool."

"I know what a takeout is, but what the heck good does it do?" Drywall could feel his friend's eyes on the back of his head as he continued to stare at the hunter Orion.

"The purpose? The purpose, my friend, is to teach the asshole a lesson."

"But he expects it. The takeout is tradition. For scum like DeLaughter, he'd consider it a compliment. Twisted minds have twisted honor. He needs to feel shame. He needs to feel it down to his fu—friggin' bones."

"Well, it's lookin' like our only other option is to de-pledge," said Peachy. "They say five or six guys de-pledge after the first Worksession anyway. It would be a little on the chickenshit side, but—"

"No de-pledging for Drywall." He couldn't believe he was referring to himself using the ridiculous nickname. "I must honor my sister. She's why I'm here. I wish it wasn't so."

"Honor, schwommer," said Peachy. "Our lives are gonna be fuggin' hell the longer we stick around. I'm not believin' I actually connived our way into this."

"Don't take any blame, Peachy. My sister's as tough as shoe leather about the Kickapoo giving up their fight and joining white society. I'm my sister's hope. Do you get it? Frankly, I could give a—."

"No offense, Drywall, but it seems to me like all you Polacks are a little on the proud side. Or maybe it's just that you're quiet. That's what I figure. Proud or quiet. Who knows what you're really thinking?"

Drywall Twohatchets went back to work with his toothbrush, perched on his knees, midway down the stairs. "The Kickapoo have been fighting to be our own nation for a heckuva long time." Flashing through Drywall's mind were all the stories that the Elders told of fighting on the British side in both the Revolutionary War and the War of 1812. About fighting against Texans from settlements based in Mexico. About refusing to take either evil side in the Civil War.

"You know how we're s'posed to be learning 'bout the history of Sig Zeta and all, back to 1855?" Drywall continued. "Well, at the same time that stuff was happening, the Kickapoo got sick and tired of bein' force-fed the white way of life, so they moved to Oklahoma, then on to Mexico where the original Kickapoo still are. But some got tricked into coming back to Indian Territory so's to keep them from buggin' folks at the Mexican border. Then, some white squatters forced their way onto protected land, so the Okie Kickapoo tried to move back to Mexico to join up with their old tribe. No dice. The Mexican Kicka-poo considered my ancestors *contaminated* by white culture, so they kicked our behinds out. Our branch had to return to Indian Territory, now Oklahoma."

"I give up. What's your point? That you've memorized 1885 for the start of Sig Zeta, and I haven't?"

"It's 1855, you moron."

"So who gives a rip fart? 1885? 1855? What does it matter about the Kickapoo a hundred years ago? Or Sig Zeta a hundred years ago?"

Drywall smiled inside at his offbeat friend, though he didn't dare let the amusement show on his lips.

"It matters 'cause my family's been contaminated. Kickapoo do not marry out of the tribe, much less out of the race. My mother's full-blood, but she up and married a white minister and had my sister. When the preacher was killed in Korea, my mother she comes back to the tribe and marries my full-blood father, but that don't cut it. She was still contaminated. My sister watched the curse it brought our family, and she laid down the law that says we outcast Kickapoo gotta cross the bridge between the races."

"Let me guess, Mr. Lamb-of-the-Month, you get to take heap big shit whenever it's slung, all for your sister's cause. No offense, Drywall, but this all seems pretty easy for your sister to say. About blending, I mean. I've seen her. She's a damn good-looker. And she's got a great bod'. And you—well, hell—you're not bad yourself, for an Indian I mean, but you're . . . you're. . . ."

"Straight from the reservation?"

"Well, let's put it this way, if you were to go to Hollywood. . . ."

"I owe my sister everything. I got into a s-load of trouble as a kid. In court, she swore to the judge she'd watch over me. Kept my rear end out of jail."

"I knew I liked you the first time I saw you. What kind of trouble?" asked his new friend whose eyes glistened as he said the word "trouble."

"A scumbag white man made moves on my sister at a football game. She was sellin' Cokes up and down the aisle, you know. He'd been sittin' there givin' my friends and me dirty looks the whole game whiles he looks up her skirt every time she heads up the aisle. I was just thirteen, but getting madder and madder. Then, the a-hole orders two big Cokes for hisself, and while she's got both her hands busy jugglin' his drinks, he wraps his friggin' hands around her . . . her . . ."

"Bazookas?"

"Yeah. So I took out my knife, put it up his nostril, then slit him up right. Not a big cut, but enough to get the blood flowing. Truth is, I'd a liked to have cut his nose clean off. I'm still not sorry." And as he admitted his lack of remorse out loud for the very first time, Drywall realized it wasn't idle railing against whites. Sometimes, it took all his strength to keep his verbal blade in its sheath.

Drywall's friend fell silent. "Cool," Peachy said, after an apparent moment of thought.

"I never did cut a guy again, but it was my sister what saved me from jail. My parents were no help at all. By that time, both of 'em were gutter-drunks. My sister, in her way, became my mother, too. Convinced the judge she'd be responsible."

"I guess you Kickapoo know how to kick a few," said Peachy, grinning. "I ain't particularly from the right side of the tracks myself. My old man's a wheeler-dealer. Used to run some snazzy nightclubs where there was hidden gambling rooms and all. Really neat stuff. But he's moved up big-time now. He's in Las Vegas mostly. All sorts of business deals, but he knows everyone. Meets movie stars, rock stars, you name it. He even played poker once with Jake Chisum."

Drywall sensed his friend shifting the course of their conversation. Perhaps he should not have talked so much. After all, it was not the Kickapoo way. In fact, he'd never opened up so much to a white. Maybe his verbal excess was due to the fact he was still bleeding inside from the wounds delivered by Black Jack.

After a few more spit-shined concrete steps, the silence was broken by Peachy as he finished plucking the last fragment of glass out of the drain. "So I gotta ask, what are you doin' going to college and all? I mean, isn't that gonna make it harder to stay a real Kickapoo?"

"Maybe. But one of the Council of Elders pulled me aside when I was young. Said I was the smartest Kickapoo he'd ever seen, and he *arranged* for me to go to public school. Others in the tribe made a big stew about it since they educate their own. I was an experiment, I guess. I was the only full-blood Kickapoo there. Then, the only Kickapoo to play golf, of course. Now, the only one to go to college. And you can be dang sure I'm the only Kickapoo in the history of our tribe to ever pledge a fu—friggin' fraternity. There's no going back for me, and no de-pledging, no matter how much Black Jack makes my blood boil. I got both the Elder and my sister countin' on me to act right, talk right, and be right. I think I'm gonna do law school, then I want to help my tribe even if they think I'm contaminated."

Peachy had refused to use his toothbrush. Since Black Jack had gone back to bed, Peachy used every other tool available to scoop up glass, and he was now mopping the floor around the drain. It bothered Drywall just a smidgen that while he was committed to playing by the rules, apparently Peachy wasn't.

Peachy, resting with both hands folded atop the mop handle, said, "You know, once they forced us to read a short story in high school called, 'The Man without a Country,' or some such rubbish. You kinda remind me of that."

"Never heard of it. But the Kickapoo have lived so long all across the U.S. and Mexico that the authorities can't figure out where we should be citizens. The Kickapoo, of course, could give a—. In our minds, we're citizens only of the Kickapoo Nation. But all of us officially have dual citizenship."

"Dual citizenship?"

"Yes. We can live on either side of the border, crossing back and forth whenever we want."

Drywall saw a curious look on his friend's face at the bottom of the pit. Peachy set the mop against the concrete wall of the Pit and began massaging his hands together, as if preparing to deal at poker.

"And when you go back and forth across the border . . . what about taxes? Tariffs?"

"Hah, I'm startin' to see why you look so funny. No, there are no taxes."

Peachy walked up the steps to join him midway. Then he held out his hand to shake. "Here's to a long and prosperous friendship, my blood brother," said the Peach.

For the first time in a long time, Drywall's heart seemed warm. His world was so small, so contracted, he hadn't really made a new friend since childhood. And here was this crazy misfit, a smart-aleck white for gosh sakes, who could make him open up and bare his soul.

Drywall felt some sprinkles on his face. *But how could it be raining? I just saw the starry sky two seconds ago!* More water splattered on his face. And Peachy was brushing away drops from his face as well.

When Drywall looked to the top of the stairs, he saw Black Jack DeLaughter proudly poised, pissing on the two of them. And laughing.

17

Chipper, leaning on his driver, watched Peachy address the ball by assuming his signature Quasimodo pose. Long pause. Club head makes a cross with a circle at the top. Wiggle to the left. Wiggle to the right. Backswing brings club shaft within a hair of twisted head. Downswing. *Crack.* The obligatory "Awshit." Master's pose.

It was the ugliest swing in the history of golf, but Peachy's triumphant contribution to last year's state championship team had given him a new level of confidence. Peachy's drive, with only a remnant of his flatbelly slice, pierced the blue October sky and sailed about 220 yards to the right side of the fairway.

"Fuggin-A," he said, snatching his tee from the ground and strutting toward the other players.

Peachy seemed to be staring directly at arch-asshole Uno Guilford as he spoke. The pledge class golf team was playing together for the first time, and Chipper hoped that Peachy would stay muzzled. Peachy possessed a boldness that sprouted in camaraderie, and most certainly the Peach counted Chipper, Drywall, and Smokey Ray as his comrades. But not Uno. Not by a long shot.

"I suppose that's a good play, or shot, or whatever you call it," said Mother Boone, composing the gallery of one. Ted had joined them today, Chipper figured, to boost the pledge class morale that was running snake-belly low due to the ongoing abuse by Black Jack DeLaughter. And to make matters worse, the Actives were ignoring the abuse, or worse, copying it.

Ted Boone was dressed in houndstooth slacks, yellow shirt and club tie, while his Sig Zeta pin, a golden cross, was located near the corner of his pocket, tilted slightly to aim over his left shoulder. He made for an oddball on the golf course. However, during these first few weeks of easy schooling and hard pledgeship, Boone had earned the trust of the pledges, and they treated him as one of their own. No words were spared in front of the Pledge Trainer when it came time to drag Black Jack through the mud.

Drywall took his stance and hit a smooth drive up the middle that rolled well past Peachy's. Chipper saw that Drywall's swing was lackluster, but in a good sort of way. All golfers, it seemed, had quirky spice in their swings that flavored the individual. But Drywall's form was so bland that Chipper wondered if he was witnessing what some called "the perfect swing." Drywall's borderline scowl didn't alter one bit after the fine shot.

"So, Ted," said Peachy in the interlude of tee shots, "what the hell are we doing wrong? Three screwups in three attempts. We ain't nowhere close to taking that sumbitch out."

Ted Boone clasped his hands together, fingers interlocked. "Well, first, you've got to get organized. It doesn't count unless every single pledge is present, and you confirm it with a roll call witnessed by the Active being taken out."

Chipper interrupted. "Ted, I can barely keep up with who the pledges are. We've had about five guys de-pledge after each Worksession so far. Others de-pledge after having to go 'round the table just once. But somehow there's a constant stream of new guys pledging. My roster changes daily. Trying to get everyone together and have an accurate roll call is tough."

"That'll die down soon enough, all the pledging and de-pledging, that is," said Ted. "It's worse at the beginning."

"And we also gotta lay down the law and tell guys they can't go runnin' home to their mommas every weekend, either," said Peachy. "That's your job, Mr. President. We ain't gonna get a hundred per cent roll call if the same weasels are out of town come every Friday."

Chipper saw that Peachy was staring at Guilford as he spoke, and it was clear Uno wasn't going to stay silent for long.

"Shut your trap, Peach-pie," Uno said, "I go home when I want to go home."

"Listen here, Ricky Retardo—"

Chipper broke in to referee. "Okay, in order to get a hundred per cent on roll call, we'll try the next takeout on a week night. All right with everyone?"

"I have no problem skipping classes if we're up half the night," said Peachy. "Come to think of it, I *never* have trouble skipping classes."

Smokey Ray had been strangely silent, not just today on the golf course, but ever since that first lineup where Black Jack made his intentions clear. Chipper thought back to the time in high school when Smokey Ray had dished fair revenge to Chipper's tormentors. And it wasn't just on one occasion. Smokey Ray had gifts beyond normal guys, and even though Peachy thought these talents heaven-sent, Chipper had never been able to figure good from bad when it came to Smokey Ray.

Smokey Ray took his turn at the tee box. Wearing his cowboy hat, he flicked his cigarette to the ground just beside his teed golf ball, the smoke spiraling upward on this rare calm day. No practice swing. No hovering over the ball. Smokey Ray simply smacked it close to 300 yards up the left side of the fairway.

"Nice shot, Smokey," said the entire group, almost in unison.

"Smokey Ray, what do *you* think?" asked Chipper. "We've had two takeout attempts where we couldn't get everyone together, and one where Black Jack wasn't even in his room. You've got to have some ideas on this."

Without taking his eyes off his white speck of a ball in the distance, Smokey Ray said, "When you girls are through with your sissy games, I'll let you know what I think." Then he trapped his grounded cigarette between his shoe and the head of his driver, lifting the cig up a few inches before kicking the sparkles toward Peachy. Smokey Ray laughed as Peachy's body curved into a C to avoid the butt as it flew by. Peachy tried to laugh as well.

"One thing for sure," Pledge Trainer Boone added, "you've got to keep your plans secret. On that last try, Black Jack heard that a takeout was scheduled, and that's why he wasn't in his room. It's going to take trust and unity in your pledge class to make it happen."

Smokey Ray walked off the tee box as if he didn't hear one word that was being said, like he didn't even care. Chipper tried to read him, but felt foolish at the thought. Smokey Ray was beyond scrutiny.

As Uno teed his ball, Peachy stood out of direct view, though Chipper could see that Peachy was firing a subtle bird at the banana-nosed bastard, the Peach's middle finger stiff as it nudged the bridge of his glasses back in place. Peachy had a way of enjoying his own private pleasures.

They couldn't deny that Uno was a crackerjack golfer. And though the pledge class tournament next spring would not count for points in the overall intramural race, they knew that next year, the Sig golf team would make a difference. Sig Zeta had never won the Intramural Trophy, nor had they ever won Fraternity of the Year, but the wheels in Chipper's head were already turning.

"Nice shot," said Chipper after Uno's drive.

"Great shot," said Mother Boone.

"Eat me," whispered Peachy.

As Chipper prepared to tee off, he recaptured the thrill of his final round in the state tournament last spring when he shot 71, capped by his now-legendary final approach, popping the ball from beneath a tree root, through a tiny opening in the forest, up to one foot from the cup.

After the victory and after graduation, Chipper had taken the summer off from golf. But then, recess became respite, which evolved to reprieve as he realized that golf had consumed his life for years. Five months had passed without a swing. It was time to resume the sport now as a hobby rather than an obsession. He couldn't wait to feel the sweet crack of the ball, free from the grueling pressure of competition.

Chipper duck-hooked his drive out-of-bounds.

* * *

By the sixth hole, Chipper was 10 over par. Drywall was helping him hunt for his ball in the forest after Chipper's sixth errant drive was sucked in by the trees. Chipper was starting to feel ill. The first few holes he had attributed to rust, but things were not getting any better. Boone was in the short rough about 20 feet away helping them look, pinching his slacks above the knees and holding the hems out of the weeds.

"By the way, Drywall," said Chipper, trying to resurrect a subject to divert from his golf game, "rest assured we're gonna finally get Black Jack. He's just gotta be stopped. You know, my Big Brother is Al Marlowe, and I've talked to him about it." Chipper hoped that this hollow boast wasn't obvious, given that his Big Brother had not promised anything.

Chipper looked to see if Boone had heard this claim. Indeed, the Pledge Trainer gazed in Chipper's direction, but without expression. *Complaining to Al Marlowe was like pissing in the wind*, thought Chipper. *Even the Pledge Trainer's look says so.*

On the 11th hole Chipper was again looking for his ball in the woods. He was 16 over par, and the only word that came to mind was "catastrophe." Guilford snaked toward Chipper's direction for a moment, as if to help him search, but then he veered away again as a simple phrase slipped from the corner of his mouth: "Hit another."

On the 16th hole good friend Peachy was helping him search for his ball in the woods, providing words of solace: "Man, you are on your way to the Hacker's Hall of Fame. I mean, gimme a break. I thought you just needed a few holes to loosen up. But it's not just a matter of spraying your shots—to be honest, you never were that great off the tee—but your short game! What's happened to your chipping? You either dub it or blade it. It's the damnedest thing I've ever seen. I mean, if you don't get in the groove pretty quick, I'd say your game is pretty well shot to hell."

"Thanks, Peachy."

"You're welcome. No offense intended, Chipper, my boy. Say, listen. On this takeout deal. I've been thinking. Let me and Drywall organize it. You've got too many other things going on, like running for Student Senate and all that other ridiculous crap you do. Me and Drywall, why we're the ones that gotta get even. We're the ones that got pissed on. And no one pisses on the Peach.

"Sure. Fine."

On the final hole, a par 5, Chipper bladed his 5-iron approach shot into the woods. If he could salvage a triple-bogey on this hole, he'd break a hundred—a goal he'd originally set and achieved at age 12.

As he looked for his lost ball he was comforted by the cool shade from the crooked tree limbs overhead, and the leaves starting to wither with autumn. This cloistered station in the forest, housing his errant shot, provided a tranquillity that took the edge off shame, and he welcomed the solitude.

The voices of his pledge brothers and Ted Boone seemed far away, so he was startled when he looked up from the ground to see Smokey Ray Divine standing in the clearing, tipping his hat, the speckled shade moving over his face like shifting spots of a leopard.

18

"I'm dead, Smokey Ray," said Chipper, embarrassed by his own whining sound.

"Not at all," Smokey Ray replied, "Now, Woody Guthrie, he's one dead sucker, as of today."

"Woody Guthrie? Who's that?"

Smokey Ray's eyebrows lifted in surprise, then he shook his head in disgust. "Dean of American folk music? Father of the protest song? Born in Okemah? Given the Okie pink slip because of his Red persuasion?"

Chipper knew his own face was blank, so he tried to force some semblance of recognition.

"Opposed all copyright laws on songs, including his own? Wrote 'This Land Is Your Land'?"

A resonant chord struck Chipper. "Hey, I thought the Kingston Trio wrote that."

"They sang it. Didn't write it. But I'm not making my point. And my point is this—Woody Guthrie came, made his mark, and he left today. And you, Chipper, you're not dead."

"Well, my golf game is dead."

As they made random circles while hunting for his ball, Chipper anticipated worthless riddles from Smokey Ray that would be intended as inspiration.

"You may be right," said Smokey Ray. "Your golf game might be dead."

"What?"

"If you're a believer in existentialism, you might have had your defining moment last spring at the state tourney. After a defining moment, all that follows is futility. At least in that area of your life. Maybe it's time to move on. Forget about golf."

This wasn't exactly the halftime speech that Chipper needed right now.

"Forget golf? You've got to be kidding?"

Even as he spoke these words, his heart wasn't backing him up. His magical 7-iron had been nearly pretzeled when he broke the tree root to lead El Viento to victory. His avoidance of the golf course thereafter had been semimysterious, a fact Chipper refused to discuss with himself.

"What's existentialism?" Chipper asked. "Some sort of religion?"

Smokey Ray took a final drag on his short-stubbed cigarette, then twisted the butt into the forest floor with the toe of his cleated shoe. At the sound of Mother Boone in the distance, both boys reared their heads to the edge of the trees where they could see him headed their way.

"It's a philosophy, not a religion," said Smokey Ray. "You arrive on earth, then you leave, like two pieces of bread in a sandwich. The defining moment is the meat in the middle. The good part is, as humans, we get to pick the meat. The bad part is . . . we *have* to pick. Most people waste their lives on the mayonnaise and the tomatoes, and never think about the meat. But some people search for a moment that will explain why we're caught in the middle of this sandwich. Sometimes, though, you don't have to pick—the moment picks you. The moment is the meat."

"So that's it?"

"In a nutshell."

"Certainly not much room for hopes and dreams," Chipper said, "which looks to be the case for my golf game now."

"You had a once-in-a-lifetime shot last spring," Smokey Ray said, a twinkle in his eye that made Chipper feel proud. "That's not to say you might not have other defining moments in other areas, if you go for existentialism, that is." Mother Boone was within earshot now as Smokey Ray continued, "Chipper, have you ever heard of Kierkegaard?"

"Another folk singer?"

Smokey Ray delivered a look of hopelessness, putting fingertips to forehead as if to burn the patience to suffer fools deep into his brain.

"No. How about Jean-Paul Sartre?"

"Nope. Who are these guys?"

"Some of the key players in existential thought. How about Nietzsche?"

"Nietzsche is not an existentialist, Smokey Ray," interrupted Ted Boone.

"Not in the classical sense, no. But you've got to read his original works."

"I've read quite a bit," said Ted, "and people confuse the 'God is Dead' shtick as a default endorsement of existentialism. Nietzsche was very much into personal development, merging compassion and strength, a blend of traditionally feminine and masculine virtues."

"But when you speak of the Superman in *Thus Spake Zarathustra*," Smokey replied, "where Dionysian and Apollonian traits come together, the development of the Ubermensch is not exclusive of the existential position."

"So you would support the Ubermensch, the Superman?"

"Don't look at me, Ted, with those 'you're a facist pig' eyes. When they carted Nietzsche off to the loony bin, it was his weirdo sister that twisted his writings."

Chipper checked the earth beneath his feet to make sure he was standing on the same planet as these two card-carrying members of "the intelligentsia." Next, Chipper looked at the tee box behind them to make sure no players were shaking their fists at these lollygagging sloths. Smokey Ray had quit searching for Chipper's ball to lock himself into this unintelligible dialogue with the Pledge Trainer. Neither debater was aware that Chipper was in the same forest—or the same universe. He was not a part of their discussion, nor did he want to be. He simply wanted to mourn the death of his golf game.

Chipper found his ball buried in a tuft of grass, and he punched it back to the fairway with a 6-iron. Smokey Ray and Mother Boone didn't even notice.

By the time he hit his next shot, spraying it into the opposite rough, the two Platos in the woods noticed Chipper was missing from the landscape, and they emerged from the trees. Ted moved ahead to join the others who were standing near the green, waiting impatiently. Smokey Ray hit his next shot near the flagstick, then joined Chipper in a new tongue of the same forest.

"What the heck was that all about?" asked Chipper. "Abalonian? Dyineesian?"

Smokey Ray grinned and adjusted the brim of his cowboy hat. "Apollonian, as in the God Apollo. The penultimate Greek god. Inventor of medicine, master musician, Mr. Cool, but most important . . . the god of light, not the sun per se, but light in general. On the other hand, Dionysus was—"

"But why do you guys care about that mumbo jumbo?"

"We spar for fun," Smokey Ray said. "It's a game for original thinkers."

"Original thinkers?" asked Chipper, feeling that this tête-à-tête was headed for a deep, dark hole.

"Why, we're the people who thought we had original thoughts until we discovered that there aren't any original thoughts."

"Oh."

"I've known since I was a little kid that I think differently. If the other boys saw an ambulance go by, they'd hop on their bikes to follow the flashing lights, and the depths of their thoughts were simply, 'Gee whillikers, an ambulance.' Not me. I'd stay back, wondering whose life was going to change, how that change might ripple, and could such a ripple alter the course of humanity? And that was me in grade school."

Chipper stayed mum. Never had Smokey Ray revealed himself in this way. Usually, Smokey Ray spoke like a rapid-fire deejay with a peppering of cuss words, but Chipper felt like he was in Sunday school now.

"My parents were loony-tunes, but my teachers saw early on that I was different. One of them took me aside, the summer after the second grade, and started teaching me Greek and Roman mythology. Later, philosophy and literature, especially Shakespeare.

"What I eventually figured out was this—all my weird thoughts were not original at all. The great writers and philosophers *had done thunk 'em*. And the only thing that made these guys famous was the clever way they wrote down those thoughts. There are a lot of folks scattered out there, original thinkers, many sitting on proverbial back porches, whittling their lives away."

"So why aren't you majoring in philosophy rather than psych?"

"Philosophy major? Dead end. I don't want to end up in the ivory tower where a bunch of pseudo-intellectuals sit around in a circle-jerk, conniving to get their pompous asses in print, just to get tenure, so they can tell the world what they *really* think. I'm in the Intro course now, and the pissant GA hasn't taught me anything new. I'm not sure he even understands what he's teaching. No, I'll stick with Psych. Psychology is just applied philosophy. Besides, I've got to earn a living. And the great majority of people, I believe, walk around in a fog. I kind of like the thought of lifting the fog to make a living."

Chipper remembered some fog-lifting in high school. He thought back to Smokey Ray's home brew and his admission to hallucinations (source unknown); he recalled avenging the bully Tucker Doogan with resultant property destruction and a trip to the emergency room; and he remembered a romp onto the property of one Chief Crazy Hawk where Chipper and Peachy almost lost their young lives while Smokey

Ray vamoosed unharmed. So Chipper had to wonder if the world was safe with a fog-lifter like Smokey Ray Divine.

"Well, then, apply your psychology, or philosophy, to this," Chipper said as he checked his ball's lie in the forested right rough. "You've watched this Black Jack thing for almost a month now without saying a word. Surely you've got some ideas."

Smokey Ray lifted his cowboy hat and smoothed his long yellow hair back underneath the brim.

"First," he said, "define the problem."

"Huh? The problem?" Chipper asked in disbelief. "Jeepers, the problem is Black Jack DeLaughter."

"No. It's not. And that's why your fixation on this takeout bullshit will doom you to failure."

"What are you talking about?" asked Chipper, sorry he'd asked Smokey Ray for his opinion.

"The problem is not Black Jack. The problem is the fraternity."

Smokey Ray's face had always reminded Chipper of a snowman, pie-round with those coal-black eyes. But it seemed now that his eyes were squeezing into a squint, ever watchful for weakness.

"How so?"

"There're Black Jacks all over the world, and most of them surround themselves with their sycophantic stoolies. But their power is limited to a small territory. Remember how Tucker Doogan always had Homer and Eddie by his side?"

"Yeah," said Chipper, reminding himself to look up the word "siccofantic" when he got back to the dorm and to make it his word-of-the-day.

"Well, bullies are actually weaklings caught in their own straightjackets. That is, until they are tolerated by an organization, be that a club, an institution, or—a fraternity. Institutional tolerance of evil—and I say each of these words with capital letters—works like scissors, allowing the bullies to escape their restraints. If any other member of Sig Zeta had pissed on Drywall and Peachy, he'd likely have his pin jerked. But because it's Black Jack, because the Actives are cowards at heart, they say, 'Oh, it's just Black Jack. He doesn't mean anything by it. That's just him. You've gotta learn to live with it.'"

Those were Al Marlowe's exact words when I complained about Black Jack, remembered Chipper. *Al said, "He doesn't mean anything by it. That's just Jack."* He was spooked that Smokey Ray could be so dead-accurate.

"It's amazing, isn't it," continued Smokey Ray, "that a fuckjaw like Black Jack gets more freedom than anyone else? More than anyone in the chapter? What gives? Well, he does it through . . . consistency. By being a consistent asshole every goddam day, he numbs his fraternity brothers into accepting his behavior as the norm. By being consistently vulgar, he emerges victorious, with the liberty to piss on anyone he wants. And why? Because they let him. The root of the problem is the passive Actives, my friend, not Black Jack."

Chipper felt jittery, and a little nauseous, just thinking about the implications. Perhaps Smokey Ray was right. "But what are you suggesting? That we pull a takeout on the whole fraternity?"

Expecting a guffaw from Smokey Ray to indicate the lunacy of such an idea, Chipper was shocked to the core when Smokey Ray responded, "In a sense . . . yes."

Chipper looked to the ground, embarrassed that the great Smokey Ray Divine could be so out of touch with reality. "And just how—" he began.

"No plan yet," said Smokey Ray, smiling. "I'm working on some of those original thoughts."

Chipper lifted his head and saw that a bar of sunlight had pierced the forest canopy, slanting onto Smokey Ray and fueling the coals of the snowman, where his eyes began to look like embers just before a flame pops up. Chipper replied, "Well, if you come up with a way to lift the fog off this entire fraternity, maybe that will be *your* defining moment."

"Easy does it, my rookie sage. You misunderstood. I never said I endorsed existentialism for myself. I kinda think existentialism is just a highbrow way of saying you're really pissed off at life. No, I study such things to avoid slipping into them. I don't want a defining moment. I want enlightenment. If anything, I'm a transcendentalist."

Chipper was rapidly losing his infatuation with the word "intelligentsia." He knew that he didn't have a clue what Smokey Ray was talking about.

"You're something, Smokey Ray."

"Ah, cowboy, don't try to scrunch me into a single word, and certainly not an impotent word like 'something.' A sentence isn't enough. Or even a paragraph. I don't fit inside a nutshell. Are you still planning on writing books someday?"

"Maybe."

"Then you'll need an entire book for me. Even then, I doubt you can handle the whorls and curlicues."

From the green, Peachy's voice rang out, echoing: "Hey, fuckjaws, get the lead out of your britches! We ain't got all day!"

19

"Apparently, some of you ladies have simply tossed out the pledge rules," said the pledge trainer, a snooty pedagogue who, Amy thought, was more interested in an iron hand than a soft touch. "Remember, you are *never* to be seen drinking an alcoholic beverage, and you should smoke *only* if there's a roof over your head and a seat under your bottom. You will *never* see a Beta Chi member smoke while standing up, so . . ."

Amy turned away from their trainer and whispered to Audora, "I see members smoking all the time standing up. Don't you?"

"I wonder if those rules apply to hashish," Audora replied. "Just to be safe, I'll make sure my butt's always in a chair when I light up a joint."

"Shhhh," cautioned Cassie who was sitting on the other side of Audora, the three of them positioned like spokes on the far side of a wheel-shaped couch in the Beta Chi living room. Having to peer through a jungle of green plastic elephant ears and bamboo in a planter at the hub of the couch, they felt comfortably veiled from sorority edicts.

"Now that everyone's turned in their Activity List for the year, I'll be doing calculations later tonight," said the pledge trainer. "Remember, three minor activities per semester, or one major. If you have a job, then the requirement is adjusted accordingly. At first glance, I can see some problems already. Amy? Amy Valente?"

"Here I am, on the couch," said Amy, raising her hand.

"Amy, I see that you've listed 'golf team' as an activity. There *is* no women's golf team."

"That's going to be one of my activities," she said, trying hard not to sound smug. "I plan to organize one."

"Sor-ry. Doesn't count."

Amy fumed quietly. She had already been denied working status in her efforts to reduce her activity requirements. Distributing juke-boxes didn't have defined hours, and without said definition, it simply wasn't a job.

"And what's this Association of Women Students? I've never heard of it. I mean, no one *I know* is part of that."

"They're trying to organize a Women's Week this year, bringing in famous women to speak."

"Okay, if you must. I'll let it count as a minor."

After nixing approval on three or four other girls, the pledge trainer gave Cassie a big fat F for her request to count judo as an activity.

Cassie had described to Amy, in detail, on at least three occasions, about the intruder the night of the panty raid, so judo made perfect sense. Cassie's anger and hurt were the same each time she told the story.

The pledge trainer droned on and on about activities, phone duty, study hall, campaigning for queen candidates, until the meeting finally came to an end. As the girls began to scatter, the sorority house door-bell rang, and a delivery boy brought in a box of Dreamy Donuts, set-ting the large cardboard container on a table near the entry. Thirty curious Beta Chi pledges crowded around the package. On the front of the box was a note that read: "Expressing our deep regrets over the recent panty raid—from the pledges of Sigma Zeta Chi."

Amy was so proud of Chipper. All her pledge sisters knew her beau was president of the Sigma Z pledge class, and as soon as they read the message, they began to fawn over Amy, commenting on Chipper's classy style. And as they tore into the box and began to munch on the creamy smooth glazed donuts, they discussed other Sigma Z pledges whom they wanted to date and how they needed to have more functions with the Sig Zetas. More eager arms groped their way into the box.

After Amy took her donut, the pastry melting in her mouth, she watched Cassie grab two of the golden rings from the bottom layer. Cassie bit into the first, but after a few chews, a quizzical look flushed across her face. Still staring at the remaining donuts in the box, Cassie pulled out several more, stacking them to the side.

Amy hesitated on the final bite of her donut when she saw Cassie's curious expression change to disgust. Cassie had pulled a small paper square from the bottom of the donut box, then her eyes widened and donut particles shot from her mouth like fireworks as she let loose with an earsplitting scream.

Thirty girls rushed to her aid, but she could only hold out the small white square at arm's length, pinched between the tips of her forefinger and thumb like a dirty diaper. Each girl stared at the white square for several enlightening seconds, then they spewed pastry chunks in a mixture of screams. Then the same thing started all over again with another grouping of girls as the white square passed from hand to hand. In short order, the girls migrated into clusters, plucking donut shrapnel from each other's hair, cursing the pledges of Sig Zeta while pleading for others to stop eating the donuts.

Amy was stunned. Cassie was wiping out the inside of her mouth with the sleeve of her blouse. Then, to Amy's surprise, Audora took a gander at the white square and immediately chomped a big bite out of her donut, unfazed, followed by a smile where the crumbling dough replaced her teeth.

When Amy finally captured the square, she realized it was a black-and-white photo taken with the new Polaroid Swinger camera. And what she saw in the photograph sent chills up and down her spine. But chills soon turned to burning, and she couldn't remember a time when she was angrier with her boyfriend, Chipper DeHart.

With photo in tow, she ran to the house telephone and called Chipper at his dorm room.

"Chipper, I can't believe it. I can't believe you would do such a thing. It's the most disgusting thing you've ever done. This was Peachy's idea, wasn't it? *Wasn't* it? How could you?"

"Wait a minute, Amy. What are you talking about?" came the disgustingly innocent voice at the other end.

"The photograph. The donuts. How could you? Especially after what happened to Cassie?"

"What donuts? What photograph?"

"Oh, don't pretend. It's too late. The girls are so . . . so . . . I can't even think of the word. I doubt we'll ever do anything with the Sigma Zs again."

Amy walked Chipper through the horrible sequence, right up to the moment when the photograph was discovered.

"Amy, slow down. You keep talking about a photograph. What's in the picture?"

"As if you have to ask. It's your pledge class, Chipper. Naked, for god's sake, with your heads cut off so we can't identify you. But whoever took the picture goofed. I can see the lower half of Kong's face, and I think I can tell Twobits and Peatmoss, too."

"How many are in the picture?"

"Twenty or so. What does it matter? I hope for godsakes you're not one of them."

Chipper's dumb act was wearing thin. It would be better if he'd just 'fess up.

"Amy, calm down. I don't know anything about it, but it's certainly not all of our class. We must have over 40 pledges right now. Are you sure you recognize Kong and the guys? And really, is it that big a deal? To be honest, you're sounding half-crazed over this."

Amy wanted to crawl through the phone, travel along the copper wires into Chipper's dorm, then choke him until his forked tongue turned blue.

"Chipper, your pledge brothers are standing side-by-side in the buff, with each of their . . . their . . . dammit—their pricks are sticking through the holes in the donuts!"

She couldn't tell from the silence if Chipper was still on the line.

Fall Snippets

20

The lineup during the next Worksession was considered the most ferocious in recorded history. The Donut Orgy, as it came to be known, drew screaming wrath from many of the Actives, especially those who were linked to Beta Chis by drop-necklaces, pins, or engagement rings.

Black Jack took a back seat to the army of Actives who bellowed during the first part of the night, initially in the lineup, then with continued one-on-one rantings as the Worksession continued.

Chipper noted a confusing theme throughout the belittling profanity—*the lack of unity*. That the Donut Orgy was a vulgar act seemed to slip behind the more serious transgression that only 20 of the pledges were in the photograph. The twisted message thus emerged that if the pledges had been *unified*, poking *all 40* peckers through the pastry, then reasonable accolades might be in order. Chipper pondered this tangled morality until it made more of an impact on him than the Donut Orgy itself.

Confessions were extracted from Ernie Dumas and Uno Guilford, the smug organizers of the prank, and Chipper believed his authority had been severely undermined by the covert maneuvering. And to boot, Chipper knew Amy's forgiveness would be slow.

Donut reprisals gained momentum during this post-Western Party Worksession, and two more lineups were called, each with expanding scope. Donuts and lack of unity were forgotten while a greater agenda emerged—the belief that the membership had erred with this so-called New Breed Pledge Class—that the Sigma Zs would have been better off pledging jocks and hellers, as was the reigning standard. By

5:00 a.m., a handful of Actives were still blasting away when Black Jack took the spotlight.

Just before sunrise, Jack pulled a stunt that sent chills through the entire pledge class. Moving the china cabinet away from the wall in the dining room, he unscrewed the wallcover of the sizable return air vent, then he ordered Peachy and Drywall to crawl inside and clean the vents. This ultimate act of "mental" hazing was legendary, not because of any inherent brutality—after all, the vents were far cleaner than the Puke Pit—but due to the sheer humiliation of the whole affair. "Cleaning the vents" was known to be the final measure of hazing prior to a formal de-pledging mandate by the Active chapter. Many men de-pledged of their own accord, but to *be* de-pledged was singular in its disgrace. So it was with sardonic smile that Black Jack screwed the wallcover back in place, then shifted the cabinet so that it would block even the tiniest slits of light.

And with the tainted solace that comes when communal threat is diverted to the misfortune of a few, Chipper hung his head in silent shame, noting at the same time that none of his pledge brothers could look each other in the eye. He wondered if the others felt like chickenshit candy asses, too.

For Peachy and Drywall, who experienced the next hour in claustrophobic darkness, it was a terrifying turning point. The joking was over. The game was over. When House Manager Gary Hortense discovered the imprisonment, he let the two condemned men out of the labyrinth immediately. Peachy and Drywall emerged with a mission. Drywall didn't even attempt his makeshift smile. Within hours after the Worksession ended, Drywall and Peachy held the first of many clandestine meetings with Smokey Ray Divine.

* * *

Peachy and Drywall had no patience for Smokey Ray's long-winded ruminations, so during the ensuing months, the two of them planned three more takeouts on their own. All three failed. On the day they planned to intercept Black Jack en route to class, their target was shielded by an entourage of secret service Actives. On the night they broke into his room to whisk him away to Pringle's Pool, he had hand-cuffed himself to his own bed, and the pledge class stood there like the helpless fools they were. By the third attempt, Black Jack had built a barricade to his room, using metal brackets and two-by-fours that slid into place at three different levels on his door in the downstairs senior wing. Total humiliation was cast on the entire pledge class when they couldn't even make a dent in the door.

Never in the history of pledgedom had a class failed to achieve a successful takeout after so many tries. Promises of reprisals by the Actives for pledge class failures escalated, while sympathy for the pledges waned. What idiots they were! Couldn't even pull off a simple takeout. But boy howdy, they sure knew how to screw unity, splitting the pledge class so that only half of them stuck their dicks through donuts. Black Jack's followers actually grew in number, and soon they were wearing T-shirts that proclaimed themselves The Dying Breed.

* * *

The next major party was the Baby Bawl, conceived as a slick trick to get the girls to parade in their baby doll nighties under the guise of "just another dance." Clever costumes included two-piece diapers and pajamas-with-feet, but the winner of Best Costume was Audora Winchester, Smokey Ray's date, who wore drop-seat PJs that revealed the Greek letters ΣZX emblazoned on her undies when she lowered the trapdoor.

Smokey Ray had teamed with Audora after Chipper suggested that Smokey seek her out in philosophy class. Smokey Ray said he didn't believe in heaven until he saw Audora's long legs revealing the stairway, and the two were inseparable after that. It seemed a straightforward match to Chipper.

During one of the band breaks, Peachy groused about the no-name groups that were playing at the parties, in sharp contrast to the headliners they were promised during Rush Week. He began to boast that his father was entering the big leagues of entertainment, and if improvement wasn't on the horizon, well, the Peach might have to intervene.

Later, an odd thing occurred. During the band's last break, President Al Marlowe took off his baby bonnet and stepped to the microphone where he announced that last year's All-American varsity football player, Travis Dunn, had just been killed in Vietnam. Partygoers froze for maybe 10 seconds before some of the girls placed flattened palms to their cheeks in shock. Then some of the more soused partygoers began muttering about the timing of the proclamation. Others admitted the tragedy, but after the no-name band resumed, Travis Dunn's name was not spoken again. Travis was a legend all right, but he had lived at a comfortable distance. He wasn't a Sig Zeta.

* * *

A week later, after a pledge meeting, Chipper found himself in the
TV room with Smokey Ray watching Secretary of State Dean Rusk
explain that the bombing of North Vietnam was critical for the peace
process. "Without bombing, where would be the incentive for peace?"
he asked. Then Senator Fulbright countered, accusing Rusk of a
"McCarthy-type" crusade against war critics.

"This is going to be big, my friend," said Smokey Ray. "Beyond big.
Huge." Indeed, within days, there were 50,000 people demonstrating
in Washington D.C. against U.S. policy in Vietnam.

For Chipper, the country was defined by a solo fraternity on the
north of campus, isolated at 558 University Boulevard, along with Grady's
Pub and Danner's clothing store. Foreign travel consisted of jaunts to the
Sooner Theater or the Wallaby Drive-In. However, within this tiny
radius, directly across the street from 558, he had recently been noticing
a one-story, pueblo-style apartment complex, white stucco, with log
beams protruding. On occasion, he could catch a glimpse through the
front gate at the bustle in the courtyard. Hippies roamed wildly within
the confines, and rumor held that the leaders of the S.D.S. had made it
their headquarters. But so much for campus radicals and the counterculture—for rumor also held that the Establishment was sending in rein-
forcements to unite America in the Vietnam cause. It was said that Sigma
Z Supreme-o, Brother Jake Chisum, was filming a galvanizing movie that
would have America scrambling for flags to rally 'round.

* * *

Ignoring a voice from his past that preached caution against
superficial pursuits, Chipper won his race for Student Senate, making
Top Ten Freshmen a realistic goal. However, he was losing the battle
for honor on the home front. Pledge brother C.C. Chastain, the pre-
med musician from Tulsa, had committed to memory the entire pledge
manual, not to mention having rounded through all the Actives'
rooms, not just once for the room chart, but often—because he *liked*
it! C.C. was a shoo-in for the Outstanding Pledge Award it seemed.
Chipper hadn't even completed the initial signatures on his room
chart, dreading the interaction with the likes of Black Jack, not to
mention weirdos like Ty "Roy Orbison" Wheeler who still serenaded
the pledges every week during Worksessions, seemingly content in his
jukebox world of masquerade.

* * *

Amy didn't flinch when told "no" by the Athletic Director after she requested a girls' golf team. The reason—no money—seemed weak in this time of football stadium expansion. She offered a deal with the university whereby Panhellenic rules would be relaxed with regard to proprietary jukeboxes in sorority houses. Then, after placing a Wurlitzer in each, she would donate half her profits toward establishing a girls' golf team. When the AD's reason switched to "no coach," Amy discovered an ex-L.P.G.A. player living in town who agreed to coach for free. Amy needed the jukebox money to help pay for college, but placing boxes in all sororities at once was a master coup with mutual benefit for her and her golf team. As usual, Chipper was astonished at his girlfriend. Amy dusted her clubs and began practicing on weekends, though never to the neglect of her grades. She was a for-real pre-med.

* * *

Consumed by his passion for retribution against Black Jack and the hours of plotting that went with it, Peachy's early college grades were pitiful. Drywall, on the other hand, scored nothing below a B. Late night strategy sessions, organizing takeouts, calling the 40 or so pledges with each effort, then the post-mortems to discuss what had gone wrong—all of it left Peachy with a predicted GPA hovering close to failure in meeting the initiation requirement of 2.00.

In response to the GPA crisis, Peachy investigated the art of Dempster Dumpster Diving for cold copies of exams, where the orphaned mimeograph masters lay begging for adoption. His first night out, however, he found the Betas had occupied the waste receptacles behind Woolman Hall, the Phi Delts had filled the dumpster behind Bentley Hall, and the trash bin behind Woodward Hall was teeming with Sigma Nus.

Undaunted, Peachy organized a small group of Sig pledge commandos and outfitted them in Army fatigues, including caps and black beneath their eyes. With toy weapons, they developed a presence in the trash lanes on university campus by practicing drills, complete with chants, until the pansy frat boys were too frightened by the military presence to wallow in the trash any longer. Within three nights of starting his drills, Peachy and his squadron had complete access to the long row of empty dumpsters. This maneuver was repeated throughout the year at test time, and Peachy (with friends) realized a corresponding rise in their GPAs.

* * *

Amy said that Audora and Smokey Ray were a match made in Purgatory. Smokey Ray was spending nights with Audora in the dorms, and the paper-thin walls introduced Cassie and Amy to high-decibeled lovemaking. Worse, the smell of hashish oozed its way through the bathroom on a regular basis, and Amy wondered if she weren't getting high herself.

Cassie took the arrangement with less grace, finally confronting Audora about the next-door shenanigans that had the potential to get them all expelled. "Not to worry," said Audora, "I'm going to start working nights."

Audora explained that, while she didn't need the money, she had joined the graveyard shift as an aide at the nearby insane asylum to be with Smokey Ray. For Smokey Ray, it was a must-do to finance college, but he was having "the time of his life" working as an aide on the experimental ward where, currently, all the schizophrenics were taken off their meds, so that the shrinks could experiment with new drugs. "I'll be gone four nights a week, at least," she said. "Smokey Ray's having such a good time at the loony bin."

"I miss Audora," Cassie would say on occasion.

"I do, too," Amy would reply.

"Maybe I'm just kinda jealous. Not so much jealous of the time she spends with Smokey Ray, but I wonder how it would be to feel so free about everything. After what all I've been through in my life, I just don't know if I could ever be that free."

Amy would remember their conversations about Ernie Dumas, and how Cassie felt she was getting angrier and angrier rather than better. Then Amy would think about Chipper's resistance to the notion that Ernie had been the attacker. Cassie knew it. Amy knew it. And Chipper pretended not to know it.

* * *

C.C. Chastain was not only setting world records for pledge performance, but he'd also organized a house band. They called themselves "The Rickel Four" after the Sig Zeta founder, and they weren't half-bad. Amazingly, it was C.C., a *pledge*, singing and playing keyboard, while Actives played bass guitar, lead guitar, and drums. Mother Ted Boone helped out as a songwriter, of sorts, so they even dabbled in original tunes. Ted's strength, however, turned out to be Broadway stuff, not rock, so the Pledge Trainer and C.C often spoke of combining their talents someday to create a musical for the stage.

Chipper (who knew his place as a pledge) was not a member of the band, but C.C. told him to get on deck, especially given his track record in the Oklahoma Junior Symphony. C.C. spent a fair amount of time teaching Chipper to apply his marimba skills to the trap set so that Chipper could someday replace the Active drummer who would graduate. The transition to rock drumming was not easy. Chipper knew some rudimental drumming, but flam paradiddles offered little in the way of getting to the guts of rock. C.C. was a short-fused instructor, and would usually scream, "Goddamit, Chipper, this ain't 'March Grandioso.' Get rid of that freaking cadence crap and turn on. Rock, man, rock."

Slowly, Chipper tried to rock.

* * *

Chipper sat with Amy in the T-bird, parked in the Beta Chi parking lot, one hour before the start of Worksession. Over the course of pledgeship, he had grown increasingly despondent in the hours prior to housecleanings on Saturday nights. The leather seats in the back of the car were for necking, but the couple was in the front bucket seats now as Chipper's dread outweighed all.

Amy was Chipper's only confidante. He could share things with her that he wouldn't think of telling Peachy or any of his pledge brothers. And she had proved in high school that her compass was stronger than Chipper's. In times when they had broken up, Chipper had been too easily swayed toward shenanigans, and he had learned his lesson the hard way. He had come to depend on her support and advice. More than that, it didn't seem that he was a whole person without her. And for him, this halfness that he felt without her defined his love. In fraternity affairs he missed her presence every minute, and he sought her counsel at every opportunity.

"I never woulda thought that I'd say this," Chipper confided, "but I'm not sure I should have pledged at all."

"And why not?"

"Teamwork is everything to me. You know that. In high school, I had my hands full just keeping the golf team working together. Now, I've got almost 40 pledge brothers, and it's more like crowd control."

"You can't hold yourself responsible for everything," Amy said.

"No, but I could do better with pledge class unity. I can't seem to get everyone on the same side. Last week, I even convinced Peachy to go with me to Grady's to drink beer with Uno and Ernie. We've *got* to get those two into the fold. I spent an hour on the phone getting everyone to agree to sit down together. Told 'em we needed to form a committee to plan a successful takeout on Black Jack."

"Is that when Peachy and Uno got into the shouting match?"

"Yeah. I thought the beer would mend fences. Boy, was I wrong. But it's not just that. It's everything. I understand that we're supposed to get unified by Actives yellin' at us and stuff, but I don't think that ought to be the center of unity. It makes initiation good only through the old deal of how good it feels when you stop banging your head against the wall. And they say that every pledge class swears they're not going to do it to the next class, yet they *all* end up doing it anyway. Isn't it crazy how that keeps going?"

"Pretty typical for guys, I think," Amy said. "Not that there's anything admirable about it. Just typical."

"I don't mind getting yelled at by most of the members. It's like an act, and you can tell they'll like you after initiation and all. But some, the ones that hang around Black Jack, they're mean. I'm talkin' mean to the core. They get their kicks out of digging as deep as they can. You know Peatmoss? You know how his mom died just a few months right before we all pledged? Well, one Worksession lineup, one of Black Jack's flunkees was yellin' at Peatmoss until he finally cried. Not a boo-hoo. Just one puny tear sneaked out, but it was cryin' all the same. Now, they're working on him unmercifully for being a crybaby. That's what I mean by 'mean.' That stuff *has* to stop, or I don't know if I can be a part of this."

"Have you thought of de-pledging?" she asked.

"Not seriously, but yes, I've thought about it. Can you imagine? A pledge class president de-pledging? It's unheard of."

"Well, personally, I think you should stick it out," Amy said. "Overall, I think it's a good place for guys to learn to work together. Lord knows you need it. I think the Greek system builds lots of folks up, but it tears others down. If you can make it, I'd stick with it. I think you're one of the ones it builds up. And you should be one of the ones that changes the system—so it quits tearing others down."

"Well, I can make it. I think. But I'm wearin' down. I was so excited at the first of the year, caught up in the thought of being President and all, but now it's all so dark and gloomy. I don't give a crap about being President anymore. I bet they told a whole bunch of the rushees they'd be President if they pledged. Prob'ly had them lined up, giving them the same old line of BS. I'm just tired of being yelled at. They say the same guys yellin' at us now will be our best friends later. I doubt it, Amy, I really do. Not the regular yellin', but the mean stuff. It hurts. And that dang Peachy can let the insults run off his back like water off a duck. I don't get it. Even Black Jack. For Peachy, if we throw Black Jack in the drink, he'll be all square. I never thought I'd admit that Peachy is better equipped for life than me, but when it comes to the Worksessions and stuff, he's pretty much oblivious."

"You're sensitive, Chipper. That's good for a lot of reasons. A lot of reasons that I happen to love. But it can be deadly, if you don't watch it. You've got to ask yourself if you've got enough energy for both you *and* the fraternity. Because I know you, and you're not going to sit by and watch the status quo after you're initiated."

Chipper's forehead was resting on the steering wheel when Amy reached across and pulled him toward her with the palm of her hand. Then she kissed him. "It's only months away," she said. "I'll bet you make it."

As much as Chipper shared openly with her, he had not told her of the pissing incident in the Puke Pit, nor any other comparable events. He was too ashamed to admit the gross stuff. If Amy knew the details, she might reverse her opinion. And as much as he daydreamed about tossing down his pledge pin and walking out, he didn't really want that.

* * *

The pledge class walkout whisked the group away to the rundown Adolphus Hotel in Dallas. Peachy and Drywall spent the entire weekend arguing plans for the successful takeout of Black Jack, begging for advice from an aloof Smokey Ray.

On Saturday night, top floor, in a dusty ballroom with ripped curtains and splattered ceiling, the boys gathered for "the stripper." This tradition was an integral part of pledge class walkouts, and for many of the pledges, represented the first full exposure to the female anatomy.

Mitch Addison, male model and chaser-extraordinaire of 'ball-shakers,' shocked the other pledges in the circle — the stripper dancing to Aretha's "Respect" in the center — when he jumped out of his chair and dropped to his knees, face to G-string. Then, face to nothing. Wide-eyed Chipper had never seen anything like it before.

Mitch passed out drunk shortly thereafter, and he was still puking the next day on the bus ride home. Ernie and Uno were muttering about Mitch on the bus—something about an incident on the way to Dallas. Their discussion was meant to be private, but Chipper found it unsettling the way they kept looking over their seats as they scrutinized Mitch, whose head was buried in a barf bag.

As the bus began its ascent into the hills called the Arbuckle Mountains, Smokey Ray Divine dragged Peachy and Drywall to the three-seater at the back where the trio engaged in a two-hour conversation that began with Smokey Ray proclaiming, "Cowboys, I've got a plan."

21

Nothing could meld fraternity factions, Chipper believed, like song practice, a solemn preparation for sorority serenades. Hellers and bookers and lookers and jocks, all seemed to come together in song. But the most notable, and most improbable, fusion was the one between Actives and pledges when the first notes of the fraternity standards rang out.

Singing took place on Monday nights after dinner, before chapter meeting, with Ted Boone, or even pledge C.C. Chastain, playing the grand piano in the living room. But the fraternity often practiced without the piano crutch because serenades were performed outside in the wilds of Sorority Row.

Pledges had been given extended grace to memorize words and learn the tunes, but Chipper sensed the grace coming to a close when, on a dreary day in November, President Al Marlowe tapped his spoon against his water glass to make an announcement: "We're cutting chapter meeting short tonight, so that we can get to the Beta Chi house for a serenade at nine o'clock." Chipper sunk in his chair, knowing that the serenade was another attempt to repair the donut damage. The President scanned the dining room until he found the Pledge Trainer. "Ted, are your pledges up to snuff? Do they know the songs yet?"

Before Boone could answer, catcalls began popping out of the crowd:

"Hell, they oughta have 'em memorized. All these New Breeders ever do is study."

"Shit, they can't even pull off a takeout. How d'you expect 'em to learn the songs?"

"They sure know how to stick their dicks through donuts, though."

"Only half of 'em. Remember? Prob'ly only half of 'em can sing."

"Ted, get your friggin' New Breeders up here in a group, and let's hear 'em."

Ted Boone sauntered to the brick wall at the far end of the dining room, his necktie bouncing against his sunken chest as he walked. "Come, children," he said, as the pledge class, scattered and interspersed with the Actives at 12 tables, rose and followed Ted.

While they were accustomed to singing softly with the Actives for these past few months, they had never performed as a group. Mother Boone stood in front of their coalescing semicircle, his back to the Active chapter, conductor fingertips poised, then he whispered: "The Sweetheart Serenade." And they started the Intro:

> *When dreams fade away*
> *As they sometimes do*
> *And you've lost the light in your heart*
> *And yearn you may*
> *For a brighter day*
> *And a love that will never part . . .*

By this point in the song, all eyes were scouring the group to find the source of an astonishing tenor. Even the pledges didn't know. Why hadn't they heard this voice before? As Chipper sang, he looked first to the crowd of members exchanging glances, then to his own pledge brothers who all had quizzical looks. Chipper turned to Peachy whose head was twisting like an owl in search of the Voice.

> *Then close your eyes*
> *Bid sadness farewell*
> *Light the fire 'neath your shrine of dreams*
> *And dream the face of your Sweetheart there . . .*

Then, Peachy fired his index finger into the face of the culprit, the one whose soothing, yet powerful, voice was gingerly flavored with a tremolo—Larry "Drywall" Twohatchets.

After the membership realized it was Drywall with the Voice, they seemed mesmerized. And when the chorus ended, Chipper had time only to hear Peachy say, "Damn, I never knew a Polack that could sing!" before the audience applause began. Struck by such a staggering confirmation from the Actives, Chipper looked at the smiles of his pledge brothers, all of whom were riding the coattails of Drywall Twohatchets. And for the first time, Chipper felt the bonds of Sigma Zeta Chi. Men of different gifts and convictions—sharing.

Ted Boone walked into the crowd of pledges and grabbed Drywall's hand, holding it in the air. And the Active chapter rose to its feet in continued applause.

But in the far corner, at a table near the china cabinet, one figure stayed seated. There was no applause from Black Jack DeLaughter.

* * *

Hours later, Drywall was still in a daze. The Actives and pledges were gathering around him as they grouped in front of the Beta Chi house, hoping that his strong voice would lift their own weak efforts. Social Chairman Wesley Schofflin rang the doorbell, then throngs of girls poured out the door and filled the front porch behind white columns, under the stars. Drywall had never seen anything like this before, and he suddenly felt way too conspicuous, yet at the same time, all alone.

"Fraternity Forever" by the Sig Zetas was countered by the angelic chorus of Beta Chis, proclaiming their belief in sunshine, working hard, having fun, the scarlet, the olive green, and sisterhood. Drywall was so enraptured by their melodious sound he thought he was living a dream. "Marching to the Blue and Gold" was next. Drywall had been coached to sing softly, holding his secret weapon for the end. The Beta Chis responded with a catchy tune about their someday-dreamboat. Drywall's throat wrenched another notch tighter when he realized it was time for the grand finale by the Sig Zetas—"The Sweetheart Serenade."

Drywall warbled the Intro. And as he listened to his own voice, loud and proud, his mind drifted away to his hometown where his entire world was other Indians, and it seemed that this moment, though wrapped in magic, had a centerpiece of betrayal to his people. Yet he sang on, in silent denial of any brotherhood whatsoever to the men standing about him.

At first, his voice was accompanied only by the sound of the few leaves still clinging to trees as they rattled in the chilly wind. But then, he heard squeals—the unmistakable sound of feminine delight brought forth by the likes of Elvis, then the Beatles. It didn't make sense. It didn't seem possible. Why the big deal? And as the chorus began, he was joined by the entire chapter, both the Actives and the pledges.

When Drywall's eyes met Cassie's, the evening sky shrank to just one star. The white columns were gone. The crowd of beautiful girls on the porch disappeared. The rattling leaves were silenced. Just one face beamed at him, her eyes with sparkling rays of light that clearly were intended to shine on him and him alone.

And the starlight streams
On the girl of my dreams . . .

Drywall couldn't hear the applause, nor could he feel the slaps on his back, as the little girl with squinty eyes and unruly hair bounced down three steps from the porch by first rising to tiptoe with her arms locked behind her back, then hopping down to the next level. And as she drew close to him, her full-face freckles seemed to invite a child-like playfulness he had never known.

"Your voice is beautiful," she said. "Here it is Novemberish, and I've never met you before. My name is Cassie St. Clair. I'm a dance major."

22

Yes, Smokey Ray Divine had an aura, but Chipper knew there was a sharp distinction between aura and halo. Peachy, on the other hand, had never been able to tell the difference.

And it was Peachy who had made all the arrangements for the clandestine formal dinner tonight, where Smokey Ray would divulge his plan. At the last Worksession, Peachy and Drywall had been assigned to polish the silver, so four ornate candelabra and fine linen tablecloths had been smuggled to adorn the battered tables in the private clubroom at Doyle's Steakhouse.

Doyle's was a one-story, flat-roofed, windowless restaurant at the outskirts of town where it was said that secret panels led to rooms that brought a little bit of Las Vegas to Oklahoma. Because of the quasi-legality of the establishment, college kids were not allowed for fear of rumor and more exposure than desired. Peachy's well-connected old man, Peach Waterman Sr. had somehow intervened for the boys so that they could cloak their intentions from the Actives in this private world of low ceilings, red carpet, fog-thick smoke, and geezers middle-aging with their highballs and slot machines. As each underage pledge entered the restaurant, he simply had to utter the password—"black-jack"—and he was led to the clubroom.

In their exclusive station, the long tables were arranged in a square, concentric to the walls of the room. The pledges were seated facing the center, and each other. Technically, there was no head table allowed by the square, but everyone knew that Smokey Ray Divine determined the head, with Peachy and Drywall seated to his left and

Chipper to his right. One three-armed candelabra for each side of the square offered flickering light just as dim as the recessed lamps above.

Dinner was strangely sparse—steak, salad, and a glass of water for each of the 34 pledges (down from 37 just one week prior). When questioned about the menu, specifically the lack of baked potatoes, Peachy answered, "No starch just yet."

Smokey Ray followed with, "Gentlemen, this is our last dinner without respect. As we rise to our place, we will use a single stone to kill two birds—both the oppressor and the cloud of cowardice that hides him."

Chipper knew the plan already, so he was a bit confused. One bird, yes, assuming the clever plan worked. But cloud of cowardice? After all, the ultimate goal was drenching the one bird—Black Jack—in the freezing December waters of Pringle's Pool.

Throughout supper Chipper silently studied the crowd, wondering if each man would be up to his assignment. No more chaos, as with earlier attempts. Every single pledge had a specific task for the takeout. When Chipper looked at Drywall it seemed he was surveying the crowd as well, with his usual stoic style, while Peachy talked nonstop with Smokey Ray.

Chipper had tried to make friends with Drywall, but the kid was intensely private. Only Peachy had been a pal to the Indian. And now, two weeks after the Beta Chi serenade, Chipper was bothered that Drywall didn't seem to have the nerve to ask Cassie for a date. Amy was pressing him hard to get Drywall to move, but so far, not a twitch.

The pledges would be holed up tonight at Doyle's until the start of Worksession, and Chipper hated to miss a date night with Amy. While most of the girls would be huddled around the TV this evening trying to hear news clips about the wedding of President Johnson's daughter, Lynda Bird, Amy said she'd be trying to find out all she could about some chap in South Africa who had transplanted a human heart. Fearing undue wear and tear on his own heart from the Master Takeout underway, Chipper's roaming thoughts circled to "the plan."

Smokey Ray had insisted that the pledges be held in congregation from the moment he revealed his plan, on through the actual takeout, as he was convinced there was a traitor in the pledge class leaking plans to Black Jack. He also claimed he would uncover the traitor tonight, then stick like glue to the bastard during Worksession to make sure destiny was fulfilled.

The after-dinner speech was delivered by Peachy who succeeded in stirring the crowd through reliving every "goddam, stinking, motherfuggin', shitass" stunt that Black Jack had ever pulled. Peachy molded the group like putty in his hand, and if there'd been torches and pitchforks present, they'd have stormed the castle. Then he yielded the floor, walking to the skinny exit door where he turned down the rheostat so that the only light for Smokey Ray's speech would come from the flickering candles. Three-fourths burnt, the white candles were dripping onto the linen tablecloths where some of the pledges sculpted the hot wax as it cooled.

Smokey Ray stood, leaving his cowboy hat resting by his plate. His floppy blonde hair had been stretching south this semester, far longer than any of the other pledges. Actives had been grumbling about it, but never to Smokey's face. And it seemed to Chipper that, every day, Smokey's sideburns were a tad bit longer. Usually, his eyes of coal registered either detached bemusement or grave cunning, but tonight his eyes were both.

"Once more unto the breach, dear friends, once more," said Smokey Ray. "Or close the wall up with our dead Sigma Z bodies."

Chipper wasn't exactly sure what "breach" was supposed to mean here, but he had learned to recognize when Smokey Ray was borrowing, or stealing, from Shakespeare.

"We have failed, time and again, my friends, *not* because of lack of will or want," said Smokey Ray, his eyes scavenging the dead looks of his defeated brethren, "and *not* because I think one of us is a traitor, squealing plans to Black Jack—"

"Hold it right there," shouted Ernie Dumas, jumping to his feet. The dancing candlelight gave his chalk-stripe eyebrows a quivering glow. "You don't know that for a fact. Where do you come off with an accusation like that? Where's your unity?" Ernie was at the opposite point of the squared tables. Seated next to Ernie was Uno Guilford who seemed bored, at least to Chipper's eye.

As Ernie lowered a defensive fist, Chipper expected something from Smokey Ray about "protesteth too mucheth," but Smokey Ray didn't flinch while crazy Ernie Dumas continued to stare.

"Be seated, *brother*," said Smokey Ray with a chill in his voice. "I'm not standing here to badger, nor to humiliate, nor to expose. I'm trying to prepare a place for us where we will no longer be mocked. It is a station of self-respect, a place of dignity, a seat of honor."

Smokey Ray glared at the loudmouth until Ernie shriveled back into his chair. Then he continued with a rhyme:

> "A windward sail may bring delight,
> Unconscious of our own true plight,

It's leeward where the shore is bright,
Kindled by our deadly fright."

Chipper noticed that Peachy was beaming, as if he had one iota as to the meaning of Smokey Ray's circle-talk. But Chipper understood the rhyme, considered it cool, and resolved to try his hand at a poem someday. Chipper guessed the poem was original Ray Divine, for Smokey had a peculiar speech pattern when he was quoting others, sort of a pompous British windbag for Shakespeare and company. But when he was speaking from the Divine heart, Smokey Ray had a Tom-Joad-Okie twang that could pop a banjo string.

"The reason we have failed—as I started to say—is because we have been thinking small. We have feared thinking big. After all, Black Jack's mind is a tiny kingdom, and a very quick tour reveals the landscape. He believes himself armored, so the key is not hammering away, but luring him out of his suit of steel."

For the next 30 minutes, Smokey Ray outlined the details of the takeout planned for the Worksession tonight. Peachy stood by Smokey Ray's side with a Big Chief tablet, calling out assignments, as each step of the elaborate scheme was unveiled. Chipper had some concerns. It seemed too complicated. Too far-fetched. But every time Chipper was about to point out a flaw, Smokey Ray described the contingency plans.

"After that, we're home free," Smokey Ray concluded. "However, key point—we don't want to wake the Actives since we're not taking Black Jack directly to Pringle's Pool. So, a gag in the mouth covered with duct tape will come at the beginning. Kong, you're gonna have to hold on for dear life. Since Black Jack lives at the end of the downstairs hall, I think we can get him subdued and out the back door within 30 seconds."

"But what if he's handcuffed to the bed like before?" someone asked.

"Remember, he's going to come to us. But in case we have to resort to brute force, Peachy and Drywall went to Ace Rentals this afternoon, and they've got an arsenal of weapons, including a sledge hammer and a cutting torch."

Step by step, the group rehearsed their roles. During the next hour, they repeatedly acted out the attack in the center of the squared tables, with Drywall playing the role of Black Jack. The choreography was set. After the final run-through, Drywall stood up and left the room. It was 11:30 p.m., half an hour 'til Worksession.

When Drywall returned moments later, he was accompanied by the owner, Doyle, followed by two waiters pushing carts.

"Back to your seats, men," said Smokey Ray.

Chipper felt like a lost soul. He had no idea what was happening. He was not their leader tonight. Smokey Ray was president.

As they scrambled for their seats, the waiters pulled white cloths from the carts, revealing countless quart bottles of cold beer beneath. Waiters then put two quarts in front of each pledge around the square. A final cart, loaded with loaves of bread, was parked near Smokey Ray.

"Drink these bottles of Bud, remembering all that has happened, especially to Peachy and Drywall. As your bladders fill after the Worksession starts, seek to restore your level of personal comfort in the Puke Pit. Peachy has already plugged the drain."

When the waiters left the room, Peachy stood and walked over to the bread cart and began passing out loaves.

Smokey Ray continued. "Do not drink more than two quarts, then follow it with the bread to keep sober. We want full bladders, not drunk pledges."

"What about the smell?" asked C.C. Chastain. "The Puke Pit stinks even when it's clean."

"Hey, I've got it!" yelled Ernie Dumas, who had converted sharply to Smokey Ray's side, given the sheer brilliance of the vulgarity. "I've got my grandpa's World War I gas mask in my Big Brother's room at the house. During the Worksession, I'll get it from him, and we'll share."

Smokey Ray acknowledged the idea and nodded okay, then he leaned over to look at Peachy's watch. Smokey Ray gave the start signal, and each pledge gulped two quarts.

The candles were down to nubs when Smokey Ray suggested they end their last night as cowards with the anthem, "Oh, Brotherhood." The song had a haunting hymnal sound, and Chipper felt a vague impiety knowing he had tucked away two quarts of Bud. But the odd sense of irreverence went beyond the Bud, and he couldn't really define it, nor did he intend to. Their final dinner as failures was over.

His bladder was already feeling the pressure as they filed out of Doyle's and headed for their cars. Chipper was driving his old Thunderbird, Smokey Ray was shotgun in the leather bucket seat, while Peachy and Drywall were in the back.

"So who's the traitor?" asked Chipper. "Ernie?"

Smokey Ray laughed. "Are you kidding? That nitwit isn't smart enough to be a traitor."

"Who do you think, then?" asked Peachy.

"I wasn't positive," said Smokey Ray. "Until tonight. But I've noticed over the semester that Black Jack never, ever, gives Uno Guilford any shit whatsoever. And if there was ever a guy that needed to be given shit, it's Uno."

"No shit," said Peachy.

"Then tonight, while I mentioned the possibility of a traitor, I sent my peepers darting around the room, while everyone stared back at me all bug-eyed. When I targeted old Uno, well, the asshole couldn't look down fast enough. Guilty as hell. The whole time dumbass Dumas was standing there shaking his fist at me, I was looking at Uno. He'd never look back at me."

"Damn," said Peachy. "What a buddyfucker."

"No matter," said Smokey Ray. "I'll watch him like a hawk tonight. He's too scared to do anything now."

As each light on Main Street turned green without his having to slow, Chipper saw it as an omen that the rendezvous with revenge was a go. And as the beer went to his brain and bladder simultaneously, the fear of reprisals subsided. After all, this was a takeout to beat all takeouts.

"Hey, Smokey Ray," said Peachy. "You know, Black Jack has never given you any shit either, for that matter. Maybe you're the traitor."

Chipper cringed, hoping that Peachy was kidding.

"For that matter," continued Peachy, *"no one* gives you any shit. What's the deal?"

Smokey Ray laughed in one loud burst. Chipper couldn't recall such a guffaw before, not as long as he'd known Smokey Ray.

"I'm not sure I should cast my pearls before swine," said Smokey, "but you clowns oughta learn something tonight. And that would be, simply this—when you meet someone new, the relationship is established in the first five seconds. Chipper, let me tell you, when you meet someone new, you give 'em that big grin and you stick out your hand to shake. Well, that's just like a dog that comes up waggin' his tail with his butt twisting around sideways. Yeah, a lot of people are gonna pet the dog, but others are gonna see an opportunity to kick the dog. Where there's kindness, they see weakness. And you'll fight that the rest of your life if you don't change.

"Peachy, when you meet someone new, you've got a cardshark grin on your face that says, 'if you give me an opening, I'll pick your pocket in a heartbeat.' Folks seem to have radar that picks right up on that, but radar just spots the outside, so they don't bother to look what's underneath. They turn against you, right off the bat.

"And Drywall, pity your poor soul, you don't mean to, but you can be scary. I'm not just talking the color of your skin. I'm saying that you're one hatchet away from a scalp with that sourpuss scowl of yours. You breed fear, and fear breeds hostility. And woe to us all when hostility joins authority Black Jack style."

"Hey, man," said Peachy, "so much for the Freudian crap, Mr. Psych 101, you've not answered my question. Why don't the Actives pick on you, Smokey Ray?"

"Because, Peachy, when I meet someone new, my face goes flat and *my* eyes penetrate *his* soul. I don't care what he thinks about me. I'm too busy seeing him for what he is. My look cuts through his façade. I see my own reflection in his pupils, but he can't see himself in me. If he tries to scrutinize my face in return, it's beyond his comprehension, so there's just one message a-comin' his way. And that message is— uncertainty."

Clearly, the aura was a few notches below a halo, and Chipper could never put his finger on the reason he felt both oafish and nervous in the presence of Smokey Ray Divine.

23

Apathy was a disease endemic to Actives. Pledges were untouched. Like children observing their parents, pledges studied their forebears with curious wonder as to when the transition took place. Sophomore year? Junior year? Indeed, the dominant theme of pledge meetings was Active Apathy. What was the power of its grip? Why did so many succumb? Always, the deliberations would end with boastful declarations that this new pledge class would be different.

Tonight, however, Active Apathy would work to their advantage. With Christmas break approaching and no final exams until after break, with House Manager Gary Hortense out of town for the weekend, with Mother Ted Boone substitute-teaching the Worksession, with Actives growing weary of ranting until 3:00 a.m—with Apathy on their side, the New Breed Pledge Class, ignoring the crags and crevices of earlier attempts, would finally climb to the mountaintop. They would taste the glory of righteous revenge at last. Things were different now. Previous takeout plans had not included the wily genius of Smokey Ray Divine.

As a unified workforce, the New Breed attacked the Worksession as a model of efficiency—strip, wax, buff, drywall patch, paint, replace smashed doors, upstairs heads, downstairs head, ladies head, all spic and span. As various chores were completed, workers were reassigned to other tasks with orchestrated brilliance for which Chipper took full credit. Tonight, there was one small difference, though—*all* were assigned to the Puke Pit.

Black Jack DeLaughter made his drunken debut through the front doors early, at 2:00 a.m., just as the last TV show was broadcast for the night. One of the remaining Actives in the TV room flipped the switch, short-circuiting "The Star-Spangled Banner." Black Jack joined the last of the night-owl members as they disappeared into the living quarters of the house. Conclusion of television broadcasting was a pivotal point in the Worksession. Most of the Actives went to bed, so it meant the start of relative peace where the pledges could get their work done.

But tonight, the post-television silence was broken by whispers that traveled through the halls, into the kitchen, back out to the dining room, the living room, the upstairs heads, and even the ladies head, like a wind without trees, where the only evidence of wind at all is the quiet roar against your ears. And the whispers said: *Black Jack went straight to bed. His barricade is up. Downstairs hall crew has confirmed that the two-by-fours slammed into place.*

Chipper felt his heart begin to thump, trying to hammer its way through his breastbone. They had contingency plans out the wazoo, and they could already start chucking some of the backup strategies. Such as, what if Black Jack inspected the Puke Pit? What if he didn't go to bed at all? What if . . . what if . . . what if?

Knowing glances passed from pledge to pledge when a worker would excuse himself for a moment to the Puke Pit. Chipper had relieved his two quarts of Bud earlier, but other pledges were sneaking to their cars where more Bud kept the water flowing. Whispers held that the stew was now halfway to the top of the concrete lip that protected the Puke Pit from the inside basement floor. Those who continued to make trips to the Puke Pit were whispering that you couldn't make it down the stairs anymore without using Ernie's grandfather's World War I gas mask because, in fact, Ernie and others had puked in the pit.

The last Active sighting took place at the room of wandering minstrel Ty Wheeler whose room was located in Senior Hall, only two doors down from Black Jack. Like a cuckoo emerging from the clock to announce the time, Wheeler cracked open his door at 3:00 a.m., scaring the bejeesus out of C.C. Chastain who was scrubbing the baseboard nearby. And with his own personal jukebox blaring in the background, Ty "Roy" Wheeler took a few steps into the hall, and pantomimed his usual Worksession selection, "Working for the Man."

Chipper was on his way down the stairs, following the noise. And when Ty looked up toward Chipper, the cuckoo smiled and backed into his hole, shutting the door.

C.C. Chastain tiptoed up the stairs to meet Chipper near the top. "Do you think he knows?" he whispered. "I mean, why would he come out just to sing the part about 'I oughta kill him, but it wouldn't be right'?"

"Naw, he can't know. Come on, he's just a nut case. Remember, Smokey Ray knows who the traitor is, and Smokey's stuck to him like glue. Trust me, it's still top secret."

C.C. didn't appear convinced, but he retreated to the baseboards and resumed scrubbing away the scuffmarks.

Almost one hour later, Drywall and Peachy emerged from the utility room in the basement carrying a door-sized slab of plasterboard like in those old comedy films where the two-man team carries a sheet of glass doomed for breakage. And as they paraded up the stairs and through the house, each of the bystanding pledges stopped their task and stood still out of great respect for the duo that had suffered so much.

On cue, Chipper traveled through the house with the okay sign to let everyone know that the sequence had been launched. By the time he finished his rounds, ending up at Senior Hall, Chipper saw that Drywall and Peachy had the premeasured slab in place covering Black Jack's doorway, and they were sealing the edges with plaster.

Chipper thought the scene Poe-esque, and it seemed that Peachy's eyes fit well with Vincent Price's arched eyebrows that had frozen all of them in their cinema seats as kids. Peachy and Drywall silently smoothed their work, while Black Jack was entombed on the other side, perhaps with his wine casks.

Another hour allowed the mortar to set, at least enough to hold the plasterboard in place. Pledges began migrating toward stations, coalescing into small groups, where the quietude held fast. Every step, every duty, every motion was calculated.

Although Black Jack was deemed too large to escape through his window, pledge Mitch Addison stood as sentry on the outside lawn, equipped with a cattle prod and whistle. Equipment managers held lockbelt and wristlets, duct tape, cutting torches and the like. Limb teams crept into position near Black Jack's door, arm guys in front, leg guys behind. And standing directly in front of the drywalled doorway was man-mountain Kong. Though he had played freshman football at Notre Dame, sophomore Kong made the decision he'd rather carry beer kegs under his arm than a football, so he had transferred back home.

Smokey Ray Divine waltzed through the scene, tipping his hat to the men as he passed down Senior Hall toward the pay phone at the front of the house. Senior Hall was the original fraternity house, built in '28, all one-man rooms on the ground floor, reasonably secluded from the new wing, built in '57, where most of the members lived. Chipper followed Smokey Ray to the main living area where the pay phone rested in the alcove between the living room and the TV room. For the scheduled fireworks, Chipper had been demoted to serve as Smokey Ray's assistant.

Smokey Ray squinted his eyes and gave a wink to Chipper, then he plopped a dime in the phone and dialed. As each number on the dial ratcheted back to its starting point, Chipper felt his insides twist tighter and tighter.

"Jack? This is the Sig Zeta pledge class giving you a wake-up call."

Eternity passed for Chipper.

"I said, 'a wake-up call.' The poet said it best: 'So free we seem, so fettered fast we are!'"

Smokey Ray covered the mouthpiece and turned to Chipper. "Robert Browning," he explained to his ignorant friend.

"No, I'm not a mutherfuggin' sumbitch. I'm your conscience telling you that you are a prisoner of your own choosing. You cannot escape your room any more than you can escape the hideous hole you've dug for yourself, a hole most eager to greet you."

Smokey Ray's eyes widened, and he turned, nodding to Chipper. The fish was on the line.

"That's right. I said you can't escape. We've sealed you in your room. Jack? Are you still there? Jack?" Smokey Ray calmly placed the phone back on the receiver.

"Let's go, cowboy," said Smokey Ray. Chipper trailed the master-mind down the hall where at least half the pledge class was positioned. The rest were out the back door forming a gauntlet that turned the corner of the frat house, leading to the outside entrance to the Puke Pit.

As the twosome joined the others, Chipper could feel the silence about to explode.

"Listen, he's pulling back his deadbolts," said someone from the left leg team.

Chipper couldn't believe it. Just like Smokey Ray had predicted— the sound of a two-by-four sliding through metal brackets. Then, the sound of another sliding bolt. Spies had indicated there were three of them, but Chipper might have missed the first. Then came the sound of the Black Jack's door opening to the inside.

"What in the fucking hell?" came a muffled sound within. "What in the goddam—"

A huge fist ramrodded through the drywall and blasted shards and debris everywhere, but Kong pounced on the protruding arm like a defensive tackle about to recover his first fumble for a touchdown. Knute

Rockne beamed from above as Kong yanked the arm and its owner through the crumbling drywall into the hall where a Full Nelson turned Black Jack into a pretzel, and the upper limb teams went to work latching the wristlets. Smokey Ray stuffed a sock into Black Jack's choppers to stop the cussing, then sealed the foul mouth with duct tape.

Black Jack's legs were the problem. He was thrashing and kicking so powerfully that the limb teams were thrown from their positions several times like sailors trying to ride the tail of Moby Dick. The hope for a silent brawl, to avoid waking other Actives, caved. Black Jack could still generate a primitive, guttural sound. Recognizing the threat of Actives to the rescue, Peachy dove through the hole in the drywall, retrieving Black Jack's pillow. It covered the ugly triangular face quite nicely. But the banging of legs against the walls continued, mixed with grunts of struggling pledges, and strained whispers of instruction. Kong held on tight in this battle of the mutes.

Peatmoss and Twobits had the left wrist clasped in a jiffy, then Einstink and C.C. followed with the right wrist. After the lock belt was placed, the arms were brought down like rusted levers as Kong eased his Full Nelson. Smokey Ray Divine locked the wrists to the waist. After Kong released, he helped both leg teams strap the locked anklets, then they mummified their prisoner with duct tape.

Hoisted like a wriggling carpet, they passed Black Jack down the gauntlet, in the air, out the door, around the corner, with the original attack team racing around to the front of the line where they served as pallbearers easing Black Jack down the stairs to his watery grave.

Chipper stood at the top of the concrete stairs, nearly overpowered by the stench from the Puke Pit below. Even in the dark of early dawn, he could see the radiant white of Black Jack's eyes in the Pit. Like a giant silver caterpillar wrapped in the duct tape, Black Jack was positioned by the team so that his butt was seated in the sewage, while he was propped up against the concrete wall, knees drawn to chest, nearly fetal. The remaining pledges gathered at the top of the stairs to gawk. And when the core team was finished, they left Jack alone in the Puke Pit and closed the storm door above just long enough to give him the feel of pitch black vents and how it must have been for the two pledges he'd held prisoner.

When Smokey Ray opened the mausoleum door, each pledge had the opportunity to visit their quarry and deliver their rehearsed lines of choice, all under the blessed anonymity of Ernie's gas mask. Peachy led the way, looking half-man, half-praying mantis in the gas mask as he delivered a brilliant recitation of obscenities to the silver caterpillar at the base of the stairwell. When he returned to the top of the stairs, he handed the mask off to the next in line, whereupon most pledges followed suit, one by one, all of them protected by the World War I technology that allowed Ernie's grandfather to escape the dangers of mustard gas.

"Makes you wonder if the revenge is worse than the original crime," said Chipper to Smokey Ray as they watched the dawn breaking. But Smokey Ray replied:

> "One man's the aggressor,
> 'cause he feels he's right.
> The second says 'No,'
> and now there's a fight.
> When the blood is spilled
> and the second man's blamed,
> at least Number Two
> knows he's suffered no shame."

"Who's the poet?" Chipper asked.

"Smokey Ray."

"Well, eye for an eye is Old Testament, you know."

"And?" questioned Smokey Ray, cocking his head.

"And . . . gee, I dunno. It just bugs me that we have to stoop to the same level as Black Jack to make a point." Chipper thought it odd that all the pledges were zeroed in on the creature below, but Ernie Dumas was standing close, supervising the use of the gas mask, clearly eavesdropping and keeping one eye centered on Smokey Ray.

Smokey Ray put his hand on Chipper's shoulder. "Chipper, my boy, we're speaking the only language that Black Jack understands. When we face the rest of the chapter, we'll speak with a different tongue."

"Rest of the chapter? What do you mean?"

"I'll explain it later, 'cause I'm counting on you to come up with the language." Smokey Ray turned to the group, and said, "Okay, guys, let's wind it up and move on to Pringle's Pool. Anyone else want to—"

"One more," said Drywall Twohatchets as he broke through the crowd. He rebuffed the gas mask being handed to him by Ernie Dumas. "No mask for me," he said. Drywall stood tall as he slowly walked down the stairs of the Puke Pit. The entire pledge class huddled near the mouth of the opening above to watch, warmed with excitement such that the freezing December air was left feeble, barely a chill.

A few steps above the sludge at the bottom, Drywall stopped and raised his finger toward Black Jack. "A word of warning to you, my friend. You've mocked my name. You've mocked my ancestors. So let me tell you something—the name Twohatchets comes from my great-

great-grandfather whose left hand was as good as his right. So he wore two hatchets on his belt. It is said he could scalp a man with either hand. And so I say to you now—if you so much as look in my direction again, I will take the hatchets of my fathers, and I will scalp one of your ugly eyebrows with one hand, and the second with my other hand, and I'll feed them to the pigs, for you are nothing but a piece of fucking garbage!"

Chipper, leaning over the brim of the Pit, paralyzed with shock, thought he was about to slip in the pool of slime. He couldn't believe it. No one could. He scanned his pledge brothers, and all were saucer-eyed and speechless. All except Smokey Ray, that is, who betrayed a grin at one corner of his mouth.

Drywall Twohatchets stepped out of Puke Pit, a new man in all of their eyes.

"Evacuation team . . . load the bastard up," shouted Peachy.

A crew marched into the pit and lifted the silver creature out of the lagoon. Black Jack's jockey briefs were indistinguishable from his bare skin, even though the early morning sunlight was threatening to break up the scene. The droppings of debris flipped off Jack onto the evacuation team's clothes, making Chipper appreciate his supervisory role.

Smokey Ray, spotting the revulsion, said to Chipper, "A man should never put on his best trousers when he goes out to battle for freedom and truth."

"That must be from Smokey Ray Divine."

"Wrong again, cowboy. Henrik Ibsen, playwright and poet."

* * *

At Pringle's Pool, located on the outskirts of campus, Kong's '53 white convertible Cadillac Eldorado backed up slowly to the edge of the water. When Chipper joined the crowd at the bank, most were disappointed that the water was not frozen, as they had hoped to toss Black Jack through the ice. Peachy and Drywall were in the front seat with Kong, and as they parked at water's edge, Chipper noticed that Kong tossed his keys to Peachy as they emerged from the car.

Peachy opened the cavernous trunk, revealing the writhing duct-taped body of Black Jack DeLaughter. In a way, Chipper was glad it was almost over. *Remove the duct tape and the nuthouse restraints, throw the sumbitch in the water, then get the hell out of Dodge.*

When it looked like all the cars had arrived, and all pledges were gathered, Chipper started roll call. And as he read through his list of names, he saw that Peachy, Drywall, Smokey Ray, and Kong were scooting Black Jack into the shallow water near the shore. *Odd*, thought Chipper, as he continued reading names.

When he called out the name of Uno Guilford, and a sickly "Present and accounted for" returned, Chipper tried to detect a double-crossed stare from Black Jack, but he couldn't see Jack's face very well. Smokey Ray was standing knee-deep in the water, repeatedly dipping into the pond and pouring it over Black Jack's head. *What in the world?* Chipper could barely get through the list as he struggled to holler all of the names, craning his neck trying to understand why his pledge brothers were toying with Black Jack in the water.

"Hundred per cent," shouted Chipper. "We're all here. Now let's throw him in."

Smokey Ray stepped from the pond, while Peachy and Drywall balanced Black Jack, one pledge holding onto each shoulder. Kong stood as sergeant-at-arms. Whatever the ritual had been, Black Jack's skin was white again, in fact blanched and glistening to the point it looked as though a thin sheet of ice was forming. Black Jack was shivering to beat all, and Chipper hoped it was fear rather than the cold.

Smokey Ray joined Chipper in the center of the pledges on the bank. He touched the brim of his cowboy hat as he spoke. "My brothers, we have used one stone, and we've killed one bird. But the great bird remains. Drafted into league with Peachy and Drywall to avenge the injustices imposed on them, I took it upon myself to dream noble purpose 'lest a mundane drenching in Pringle's Pool be remembered in terms too small. Now it's time for the great bird."

Chipper felt his heart sinking. Any plans beyond this point were new to him.

Kong slipped his arms under the freshly cleaned armpits of Black Jack and lifted him off his rear, whereupon Peachy and Drywall grabbed the feet. Sagging in the middle, they hustled the body back into the trunk of the El Dorado and slammed the lid shut. Peachy took the keys from his pocket and sat down in the driver's seat. Drywall rode shotgun.

"What the hell is going on?" asked Chipper of Smokey Ray. "Why didn't you tell me about this? Where are they headed?"

Smokey Ray turned to Chipper, lifting his cowboy hat only long enough to smooth his hair. "Now, let's go back to the dorms, and I'll explain the rest of the plan."

Chipper shuddered.

As Kong waved a sad good-bye to his car, Peachy carved a dough-nut into the dirt with the spinning El Dorado. Then, as he and Drywall peeled away with their cargo in tow, Peachy stuck his head out the window and shouted, "Adios, amigos!"

24

Peachy found it hard to believe that in the past few days, he had traveled from Joe College to a stint with the Kickapoo tribe in the state of Coahuila, Mexico. He could still feel the sinewy strings of fire-roasted jackrabbit between his teeth from their open-fire dinner last night in the wigwam. And now, they were on the road back. Before all this, his only notion of the Kickapoo was based on the Joy Juice from the Li'l Abner cartoon strip. Drywall had been just another white guy with dark skin.

"Say, Drywall, I gotta admit, I was pretty shocked you could speak Kickapoo."

Drywall laughed as he was driving. "My friend, you're an exception. You really don't see our differences, do you? I'm just a Polack to you."

"I guess so. I never really thought about it. Maybe 'cause I grew up surrounded by Indians in El Viento."

As they drove through the Mexican border town of Piedras Negras, Peachy spotted a department store that fueled a lingering thought he had since his first night in the Puke Pit with Drywall.

"Hey, pull in to that store," Peachy said. "Let me see what they got." And within 10 minutes he was hauling a stereophonic sound system into the back of the Cadillac. "Dirt cheap. Lower than wholesale in the U.S. Now let's see if that dual citizenship stuff works."

Drywall took the El Dorado through the border gate, declaring the stereo set and flashing his Kickapoo tribal card. No taxes. No tariffs. Peachy felt a rush of excitement, knowing that this simple act could mark the beginning of a prosperous adventure.

"Do you see the possibilities?" he asked his friend.

"No."

"Today, a stereo. Tomorrow, stereos for all. Refrigerators for all. Blenders—maybe air-conditioners—and on and on. And not just in the Sig Zeta house. I know you could use the wampum, my friend, college expenses and all that."

Drywall didn't agree, not right off. But he asked Peachy logistical questions, which held no challenge whatsoever for the Peach, who had done his homework in a flash simply by creating the vision. Across the border, they were back in Eagle Pass, Texas.

"What did you call those wigwams back at the reservation?"

"Wickiups."

"And there you have it. Wickiup Enterprises International. Copresidents Peachy Waterman Junior and Larry 'Drywall' Twohatchets."

"I'll give it some thought."

"What's there to think about?"

"Not to change the subject," Drywall said, "but I sure hope that Smokey Ray is closing his end of the deal with the chapter. I don't know how long the tribe will put up with Black Jack. I told them to have him at the bus station day after tomorrow. I hope they make it, 'cause there ain't no phones anywhere else."

Somewhere between San Antonio and Austin, Peachy asked, "Say, Drywall, when are you gonna ask that cute little Cassie St. Clair on a date? I'm tellin' ya', man, by the way she was salivating at the serenade, she wants to jump your bones."

"I'm not."

"You're not what?"

"I'm not going to ask her out."

"Are you nuts? Why the hell not?"

"I'm planning to marry within the tribe."

"Hell, I didn't say marry her. Tribal loyalty don't plug up no holes."

25

Chipper concentrated so hard in the chilly night air of El Viento that he didn't know if he was hearing his own thoughts, or if he was talking out loud:

"Doc Jody? It's me, Chipper. I guess you know I pledged Sig Zeta. Well, I'm in a bit of a pickle, but I suppose that's old news for you. Or maybe it's not.

"Sorry I haven't been back since the funeral. Looks like the Bermuda has grown right up to your headstone and all. S'posed to snow tonight, they say. Sure feels cold enough. Jacob and Kelly are doing fine, I guess. Without Jacob pledging with me, though, Peachy sorta became my best friend, but now he's buddied up with another pledge brother, and I'm kinda alone, which is sort of weird for a fraternity. Thank goodness for Amy.

"I gotta get back to school tonight for a big meeting. I mean a *really* big meeting. I came home to talk to Dad, but you know he wasn't in a fraternity, so he doesn't really get this stuff. But I saw your picture on the wall at the Sig Zeta house, back when you were President. Pretty neat.

"They told me I'd be President some day, so I pledged. I'm startin' to wonder, though. I thought I wanted to be President to build something really neat, to get all the guys pumped up for things like Fraternity of the Year. To change things, too. But then, sometimes I think I want to be top dog just for the helluvit.

"What I'm getting to is this. I thought being pledge class president was a matter of running the meetings and supervising the Worksessions. And now, all of a sudden, I'm in the middle of some really big trouble.

"You see, we pulled a takeout. I don't know if they had those in your day, but we take out Actives we don't like and throw 'em in Pringle's Pool. Only we didn't exactly throw our guy into Pringle's Pool. We . . . uh . . . to tell the truth, he's on a Kickapoo reservation in Mexico. Only they've got him at the bus station now, waiting for my phone call to tell 'em the coast is clear and to ship him back.

"Now, I know that sounds crazy and it's a long story, but just to get to the real problem, let me tell you that our plans didn't work out like we thought.

"We went back to the Actives and said we weren't going to release Black Jack—that's the guy's name—Jack DeLaughter. That is, we weren't going to release him until we had a promise he'd never bother any pledges again. Mainly, we were talking about two pledges. Peachy Waterman and Drywall Twohatchets.

"I know, I know, but Peachy didn't really deserve it this time. And the other kid didn't either. I don't get it.

"There's a rumor out there that the two of them got pledge bids by mistake, but I know that isn't true. I pulled a slick one to make sure Peachy got his bid.

"So anyway, when we tried to bargain with the Actives, they told us to kiss off. Then, we threatened to de-pledge—the whole pledge class. Things got really nasty. The Actives are arguing among themselves. Some say give in, some say to let us de-pledge. It's been five days, and everyone's about to leave for Christmas break. The Actives have threatened to go to the police, but we don't think they will. Awful bad publicity if we have to explain why we took Black Jack out in the first place.

"Problem is, tonight we're facing off at Pringle's Pool. Actives versus pledges. And I'm supposed to speak for the pledges. And this is where I get my dander up a little. This whole Kickapoo thing was Smokey Ray Divine's idea. You remember him, I bet. First man on the Pottawatomie golf team. I shoulda known better than to turn it over to Smokey Ray. Sometimes, he seems like a genius, then you turn around and he's got a screw loose.

"Anyway, now that we're down to a face-off, where's Smokey Ray? He's masterminded all of this, every step of the way, then he tells me that *I* should be the one to deliver the Liberty Address, as he calls it. I've been working on it for three days now, using a dictionary, a thesaurus, and everything. Then I memorized it so as to look like the words were coming out of my head, just like when Smokey Ray talks. But to be honest, I've never been so scared in my life.

"Also, my pledge brothers are starting to chicken out. They say we've done enough, that we need to bring Jack back. Smokey Ray was pretty smart, though. Only a few of us know where Jack is, and we're not gonna cave in.

"But what if during the standoff tonight, while I'm out front saying we're all united and we'll de-pledge together unless Black Jack is barred from the pledges—what if some guys weasel out, give in, and leave me standing there? What if the Actives say 'fine—don't let the door hit you on the butt on your way out'?

"I wanna get initiated, so I'm wonderin' . . . what in the heck am I doing? How'd this happen? How did it mushroom like this? We kept screwing up the takeouts, so I turned it all over to Smokey Ray. He says the problem isn't Black Jack. It's the apathy in the members, so here we sit smack-dab in the middle of a civil war with my neck on the line and Smokey Ray standing behind me like a long, tall Texan—all hat, no cattle, but plenty of bull.

"You always taught Jay and me to do what's right no matter what the price. And that bugs me a little bit because it doesn't always work. Like the time you told us it was our decision whether or not to play on that all-city baseball team when our pitcher was 13 and the age limit was 12. We didn't play. We did the right thing. But the team won state, and we weren't part of it. I know I'm supposed to feel good about doin' right, but every time I see the picture of those guys with their trophy, I gotta wonder. There were other kids who knew, and their fathers knew that Rusty Woodhead was 13, but they all let him get away with it. If crime doesn't pay, then why are they all sittin' around that four-foot trophy smiling, still bragging to this very day, believing their own lie?

"Part of me wants to call the whole thing off, go get Black Jack, and move on. I mean how bad can three more months of him be before initiation? But the other part of me hears Smokey Ray talking about higher principles and stuff like that—and the next thing I know, I'm writin' a speech!

"I know you can't answer me. Not out loud anyway. So I thought maybe I'd come here and listen, sorta. I don't guess college was so complicated back in your day, back when the big deal was swallowing goldfish. But man, is it ever crazy today.

"I brought you these flowers. I mean they're fake and all, but I remembered from the funeral that the headstone had one of those little deelyboppers to stick flowers in. I see a few snowflakes coming down, so I'm gonna get on back now. Thanks for talkin' with me, Doc Jody. I'll let you know how it turns out. Then again, maybe you already know."

26

As Chipper stepped forward on the fresh snow, he felt the crunch of frozen grass needles beneath the powder, a winter cake layered by rain first, frosting second.

Brushing shoulders as he eased to the front between Peachy and Drywall, he glanced to his left, confirming that Smokey Ray was near. Behind him, 34 pledge brothers. In front, a horde of Actives, maybe 70 strong, salivating, just itching to lynch. And as Chipper prepared to speak, he could feel the rope tightening around his neck.

The city lights coming from beyond the members cast the Actives' faces in silhouette, though President Al Marlowe, front row and facing the pledges, seemed to have a bluish glow, perhaps from the moon, over half his face. The two armies were bordered on the west by cedars growing heavy with snow, on the east by Pringle's Pool. Pledge Trainer Ted Boone stood between the two groups beneath cedar branches, a referee of sorts.

Chipper felt the snowflakes sizzle as they landed on his burning cheeks. Then his voice cracked the still air:

"Over a century ago, our founders were dedicated members of another fraternity—dedicated, loyal, honor-bound, and votive. As all present know so well, when one of their brothers was nominated to serve as the Golden Mean in the Aristotle Society on campus, two members refused to support him for they knew he lacked any knowledge of philosophy. Instead, they favored the opponent. The fraternity was split down the middle, and when an alumnus was brought in to settle the matter, he passed judgment against our founders after hearing only one side of the story. And that is when Clovis Rickel pulled off his fraternity pin, threw it on the table, and said, 'I didn't join this fraternity to be anyone's pawn.' Of the 20 members, only Thatcher Bell followed suit. Thus, Sigma Zeta Chi was founded by these two individualists who would not buckle, cave, fold, or capitulate to the pressure of 'our fraternity right or wrong.'

"How far we have come. How far indeed. But in the wrong direction. From 1855 to 1967, we are no longer in a fraternity-splitting debate over the leadership of a philosophical society. We are locked in a debate, an affray, a donnybrook over a member micturating on the pledges—"

"Speak English, you fucking twerp," someone yelled from the crowd of Actives.

Another Active joined in: "Us dumb Dying Breeders can't understand your high fallutin' words, so cut the egghead crap and talk like a white man, you pissant!"

Chipper wanted to burrow all the way to China. He felt like an idiot, a dolt, a ninnyhammer. Perhaps he'd overdone it with the thesaurus.

He continued, his red face masked by the cold:

"Well, in words more suited for the moment—instead of the Golden Mean, our battle began the moment that Jack DeLaughter peed on Peachy Waterman and Drywall Twohatchets."

Chipper could hear some Actives snickering with the crystal clarity of mountain air. But he continued:

"As a result of our founders choosing to root themselves in principle, they were dubbed 'The Insurrectionists'—an insult they embraced as a badge of honor. Tonight, we resurrect the words of founder Clovis Rickel who said, 'I didn't joint this fraternity to be anyone's pawn,' as we, the insurrectionist Sig Zeta pledge class of 1967 proclaim: 'We didn't pledge this fraternity to be anyone's fool.' "

And from the rear, in loud pledge chorus: *We didn't pledge this fraternity to be anyone's fool!*"

The echo shocked him. A humongous lump swelled in Chipper's throat as he knew nothing of the unison, planned most assuredly by Smokey Ray, the only living human who had a sneak preview of the Liberty Address. Fearful that he was speaking for a fractured, bickering pledge class, Chipper was so stunned by the outpouring that he hesitated to proceed and thus betray his tearful relief in the form of a crackling voice.

He gulped several times, then continued:

"We will take the heat when we screw up. Yes, you can chew our butts if we don't know our stuff. When it comes to knowing about all the members, for memorizing the Rickel Standard, and especially our national and our local history, we—are—accountable. But we will not be pissed on while an entire chapter stands by and does nothing. 'Complacency' and 'complicity' are two words distinguished by only a few letters, yet their meanings are vastly different. But when evil slimes its way onto the scene, the distinction is lost, and the two words become one, gentlemen. Complacency *is* complicity."

Oh, help me now, Lord, thought Chipper.

"For the return of Jack DeLaughter, two conditions must be met. First, the chapter must agree that Jack has lost his right to interact with pledges in any way. If he so much as speaks to a pledge, the chapter is to initiate the formal jerking of his pin. Failing this, you will find all of our pledge pins in a pile, and you will be sifting through the rubble, looking for a strand of hay in a needlestack, trying to stay on campus and explain what happened to the alums and the folks at national."

Chipper couldn't believe his own lips were letting these words pass.

The catcalls started promptly. Black Jack's stooles encouraged the pledges to drop their pins on the spot, articulating their retort with verbiage that could have been dipped and drawn from the stew in the Puke Pit.

In the snowy silence that followed, President Al Marlowe took a few steps out of the front row, then turned to address his flock: "The pledges are right. And I'm the first to take blame. Jack has been out of line for a long time. But no one had the courage to stop him. I suppose sometimes it's the children who teach the parents."

Then Al turned and faced Chipper. Without a trace of expression or emotion, he offered his hand to Chipper and they shook, little fingers interlocked. "I give you my word and the word of the chapter— Jack will be silenced."

Chipper's arm went limp as the President pumped it up and down. He couldn't believe what he was hearing.

"And now, what's the second condition?" asked his Big Brother.

"Huh?" asked Chipper, giddy at the victory.

"You said there were two conditions to end all this. What's second?"

"Oh." *No time to chicken out now.* "In view of the entire chapter's complicity in the reckless behavior of Jack DeLaughter, we declare a total chapter takeout."

"A what?" asked the President.

"Each and every member must toss himself into Pringle's Pool. Only then do we promise the rapid return of Jack DeLaughter."

The Actives started to roar, some with laugher, some with disbelief, and some with contempt. But the crescendo of their barbaric cries peaked and ebbed while Al Marlowe smiled ever so slightly at Chipper then walked slowly to the edge of Pringle's Pool—and, by golly, the President jumped, crashing through the paper-thin layer of ice.

Chipper felt his eyes a-poppin' as he turned to locate Smokey Ray who tipped his cowboy hat. Then Smokey Ray delivered a secret sign to Chipper, a gesture that crafty pledges always managed to discover from the ritual before initiation.

One by one, the Actives followed their President into the chilly water. And as the freezing cold took their breath away, they began to laugh and shout, converted to kids in the summer, splashing and dunking. Within minutes, all the Actives had joined the fun, frolicking in the icy pool.

Something didn't seem right to Chipper. Where was the remorse? *These guys are having fun!*

Smokey Ray stepped up to Chipper's side.

"Why are they acting like that?" Chipper asked.

"It's a defense mechanism," replied Smokey Ray.

"Oh." Chipper pondered the answer for a moment. "What's a defense mechanism?"

Chipper felt a body hurl by, knocking both Smokey Ray and him aside. By the time he regained his balance, Chipper saw that Smokey Ray had grabbed Ernie Dumas by the arm and was locked face-to-face, with Ernie a full head taller than Ray.

"What are you doing, Ernie?"

"Let go of me, Smokey Ray, I don't want to hurt you," replied Dumas as he pulled his arm away. Then Ernie turned to the pledge class and yelled, "Come on, guys, let's all jump in with the Actives. It'll be fun, freezin' our butts."

Smokey Ray reproached Ernie in a low, scary tone: "Ernie, don't go in the water. You do not understand the dynamics going on here."

Ernie lifted one corner of his upper lip into a snarl, his chalk-stripe eyebrows pinching together above his nose. "Screw you, Smokey. I do what I want."

As Ernie twirled away to charge for Pringle's Pool, Smokey Ray danced a judo jig, intertwining his legs with Dumas, sending Ernie sprawling to the ground.

When Ernie lifted his face from the snowy earth, he twisted his neck to look back at Smokey Ray. The powder on his face made his eyebrows disappear, leaving two dark, menacing eyes peering out of the white. "I'm keeping score, asshole, and you can be damned sure that payback day is coming."

Smokey Ray didn't flinch.

Winter Tales

27

After safe portage back to Oklahoma, Jack DeLaughter was lost in legend. Within 24 hours of his arrival, Jack moved out of the Sig Zeta house and flat disappeared. Or so it seemed. For the pledges—whose entire world was boxed by the dorms, the campus, Danner's Clothiers, Grady's Pub, Sorority Row, and the Sigma Z house—Black Jack ceased to exist.

Several sightings on campus suggested Jack was still attending classes, but the pledges who claimed to have seen him only reported they were pretty sure it was him. These dubious accounts were largely discredited because Jack's triangular head was unmistakable.

As for the Actives . . . a plague of global amnesia: "Jack who?"

But Chipper noticed something far more significant than Jack's absence. The collective mood of the pledges rose. Rote memorization of fraternity ideals lost the "rote" and gained fresh meaning. Even the Actives (most of them) seemed to be enjoying a renewed spirit of cooperation. During the reign of harassment, it had seemed dreadful only when Jack was nearby. But now, in retrospect, Chipper realized the entire year had been gloomy so far. Black Jack's cruelty had stained everything—even the fun of pledge football and parties and functions. The fraternity songs hadn't rung true. The Rickel Standard had seemed a lie. Joy came only when Black Jack was stopped for good. So the full significance of the words in the Liberty Address came gradually to Chipper, long after the events at Pringle's Pool. It was a new and bright world, as if a fog had lifted.

* * *

One week after finals, Peachy burst through the door of Drywall's dorm room shouting, "I did it. I friggin' did it."

"Did what?"

"Made my grades. A friggin' two point even. No sweat, Sherlock."

"I thought you were getting a big red flag in Biology. How'd you pull out a two point?"

"Aced the final."

"Aced the final? But you had straight Fs going into the test."

"I studied. Studied my butt off, as a matter of fact."

"Studied? I didn't see you crack a book all semester, you moron."

"Drywall, my friend, the word 'study' can have a broad definition. If one is allowed to focus on what's *really* important, well . . . the powers of one's mind are friggin' amazing."

"You crazy sonuva—. You landed a cold copy, didn't you?"

"What *is* this? The 64,000-dollar question? I didn't have no answers."

"Maybe not answers. But you dang sure had the questions! You lucky S.O.B."

"Ain't no luck involved. As the old man always says, 'The jackpot favors the shrewd mind.' I told you last fall everything would be copacetic."

***

In addition to devouring the pledge manual and book-length biographies on each Active, superpledge C.C. Chastain managed to organize a campus-wide talent show, composed of singing, acting, dancing members of all the Greek houses, men and women. He was assisted in this first-ever endeavor by Mother Ted Boone who was simultaneously winning every BMOC award on campus his senior year.

The talented cast played to the university audience first, then toured Ft. Sill, Altus Air Force Base, and Perrin Air Force base in Sherman, Texas, dubbing themselves the "Greek Review." Troupe members described standing ovations lasting 10 minutes and "the time of their lives."

Chipper was semi-miffed that C.C. had not chosen him as the percussionist. C.C. explained that he wanted the orchestra composed entirely of music school students, Greek or not. Chipper had reminded C.C. of the DeHart track record, serving a stint as first chair percussionist in the All-State Orchestra . . . *and* that he had declined a music school scholarship . . . *and* that the orchestra pit should be filled with Greeks, just like the performers.

C.C. replied that while Chipper might be world-class talent when it came to classical music and useless instruments like the marimba, he "lacked the knack when the clock said rock." Indeed, after Chipper's tryout for Greek Review, C.C. had peppered the rejection with: "Rock, dammit, Chipper. This isn't the freakin' *Polyvetsian Dances.* Rock!"

* * *

With all the pressures of college life, Chipper found respite in memories, and his most cherished recollection was last year's state championship golf team. Peachy and Buster Nelson had been cat and dog for years, but when Buster broke his hand slugging his brutal father's jaw, and when precarious Peachy shot his miracle 77 by listening to ballet music on cassette, and when Buster showed up in his cast to caddy for Peachy on that final day—well, it just sort of choked Chipper up. In fact, sometimes this final harmony between the two enemies meant more to Chipper than the championship itself. It seemed to have a lasting glow that would not tarnish.

So Chipper was not prepared when the rug of such sentimental comfort was ripped from beneath his feet. He stood in the lobby of his dorm near the postal boxes as he read the first paragraph of the letter from his mother:

"I heard today that the boy who used to play on your golf team, Buster Nelson, was killed in Vietnam. They say he was a hero with the Marines at Khe Sanh, but I'm not sure I know what a hero is anymore. His wife was left with a year-old son. Study hard because they're drafting more and more . . . "

Chipper couldn't read anymore. The letter must have dropped from his hand for he never saw it after that. He called his old teammates. He called Amy. The war was now in their own front yard, gobbling up their friends. Amy summed it up in the fewest words of anyone: "Stop the madness." Chipper wrote a letter to widow Carol, describing the good things about Buster that Chipper would keep inside him to his dying day. And, as Chipper had learned in his youth, his letter-writing was intended for emancipation—his own.

* * *

On a strangely warm day in early February, Chipper lingered on the front lawn of the Sig house after Monday night meal, talking with pledge brother Mitch Addison who had just announced a major coup being named principal model for Danner's Clothier. The chicks would be flocking now. Mitch could ramble on forever about himself.

Chipper changed the subject with his own self-indulgence, bragging how well he'd "gone around the table," naming names, pin-mates, majors, hometowns, and other stuff that reflected a veneer of brotherhood, drawn from personal chats with the Actives.

"So have you got everyone's signature on your room chart?" asked Mitch.

"All but one. Ty Wheeler. It's pretty hard to nail him down."

"I know. I bet half the guys in our class haven't talked to him yet. I can't believe the Actives let him hang around. I mean, shouldn't someone who thinks he's Roy Orbison be locked up in the nuthouse, or something?"

"Maybe," Chipper said. "But he sure seems harmless."

Chipper's gaze drifted over Mitch's shoulder to the white adobe apartments across the street, the alleged nucleus of the radical left. And through the tiny portal provided by the front gate, Chipper caught a glimpse of a cowboy-hatted hippie with a black-haired girl who was every bit as tall as the guy's hat.

Chipper tried to remember if Smokey Ray had been at the Monday night meal.

* * *

As each pledge handed in his Sig Zeta final exam, Mother Boone snapped a Polaroid to send to "nationals." Glued to the test, the photo would be graded at headquarters (along with the answers, of course) where it could be assured that the "men of different gifts and convictions" all had the same color of skin.

Drywall Twohatchets did not pass the Polaroid Purification Test on the first try. Even after four tries, one could still make the claim that he was half-Negro. The distinction was critical. On the fifth try, Drywall combed his silky black hair onto his forehead, while Peachy held one of the living room lamps, shadeless, near Drywall's face to help blanch the skin. And for an extra touch, Drywall smiled.

"I've never seen you smile like that before," said Mother Boone.

"Never had reason to," replied Drywall.

The fifth photo was a keeper.

"The smile made the difference," said the Pledge Trainer.

* * *

At the next pledge meeting, a communal groan filled the basement when Ted Boone passed out a *new* pledge manual for memorization. This time, it was the history of the local chapter.

While this final task meant they were in the home stretch for initiation, no one was excited at the prospect of memorizing another boring 55 pages.

Chipper sat on the U-bench, crowded with the likes of Einstink, Twobits, Peatmoss, Kong, C.C., Peachy, and Drywall. The rest of the class—including Uno the Buddyfucker and sidekick Ernie Dumas—were seated, or standing, in concert formation. Except for Smokey Ray, of course, who was perched on his barstool next to the jukebox.

"Surely we don't have to learn this junk as good as we did the real stuff, do we?" whined Peachy.

"And why isn't this 'real'?" asked the Pledge Trainer.

"You know what I mean. Just look at the el-cheapo cover on this thing. I don't have time to fiddlefart with this crap."

"Chapter history has to be freshened every year, so there can't be a permanent manual. It's the job of the Historian. I think you'll find it interesting reading, Peachy. Who knows? Maybe some day you'll end up running for Historian."

"Fat chance," replied the Peach. "But while we're on the subject . . ."

Peachy stood and faced the group. "Let me take this opportunity to put in a word for myself as Social Chairman next year. My old man could get us some big name bands—"

"Shut up and sit down, Peachy-pie," interrupted Uno Guilford. "The Social Chairman has to be cool, and believe me, you ain't it."

"Fuck you, Uno. You gonna try to buy your way into Social Chairman, too? We all know you're damn sure to get *one* vote."

"Okay everybody, cool it," said the Pledge Trainer. "Peachy, you sit down. Read the manual. Study the manual. Ignore the el-cheapo cover."

As Chipper leafed through the typewritten pages, another burden joined the other boulders on his back. Information such as: "The bronze cross on the front of the house, emblematic of the Gold Cross, was dedicated in 1951 by the Tulsa Alumni Club. It weighs 746 pounds and is made of an alloy of 80% copper, 15% tin, 3% lead," was present in minutia on pages and pages.

Then Chipper saw the lists: "Years in Which Sigma Zeta Chi Won Intramural Football—1925, 1935, 1948," etc. It was trivia to boggle the mind.

But when he found "Past Ten Winners of the Outstanding Pledge Award," and he spotted Big Brother Al Marlowe's name listed three years ago, his rancor began to lose its edge. And then, "Past Ten Presidents."

Having recently questioned his Presidential destiny, Chipper was warmed at the thought that his name might appear for pledges to memorize for the next 10 years. It was a small measure of immortality—about 10 years' worth, as a matter of fact.

* * *

Audora Winchester bought engraved invitations announcing her upcoming initiation into Beta Chi Omega, then slapped one of the new 6-cent stamps on each and mailed them to her four living Kappa relatives—two Kappa sisters and two Kappa aunts. The past six months had not offered a particularly opportune moment to share her joy at pledging Beta Chi.

Kappa chaos followed.

One aunt screamed, one cursed. One sister cried, one vowed never to speak to Audora again. But the Pointer said it best: "I am so glad your mother is dead so that she doesn't have to witness this."

* * *

Near midnight, Al Marlowe pulled off the pavement in his 1956 Mercedes gullwing coupe, steering the silver car onto the dirt road toward the banks of the South Canadian River. He parked close to the spot where two fellow students, lovers intertwined in secure ecstasy, had been murdered a few months earlier.

With the side of the car parallel to the river, he raised the door and swung one leg outside, resting it on the sand.

"Hello darkness, my old friend," he whispered to himself. "I've come to talk to you again."

Four days earlier in South Vietnam, President Thieu had granted amnesty to 500 Vietcong prisoners, in honor and celebration of Tet, the Vietnamese new lunar year. Then today, in loving return, the Vietcong launched the largest offensive of the so-called conflict, attacking 30 provincial capitals and marching to the center of South Vietnam's seven largest cities.

But Al Marlowe didn't care. As a matter of fact, he found peace in the starry night where he could appreciate the smothering insignificance of a single human being when compared to an overpopulated world and an incomprehensible universe. He was just as likely to be murdered here on the banks of the South Canadian as in the jungles of South Vietnam.

By the light of the full moon—a prying heavenly eyeball—he surveyed the riverbed, sandy dry, meandering like Dust Bowl entrails. Too weary even to make a noise, he mouthed the words: "Are you there, God?"

28

Amy was on her bed in the dorm, sitting cross-legged in her terry-cloth robe, when Cassie appeared in the doorway, beaming.

"I'm so excited, Amy. I just can't believe it," said Cassie, her two clenched fists vibrating at waist level.

"What?" replied Amy, hoping that Drywall had finally called.

"I've got one of the leads in 'The Juggler of Notre Dame.'"

Amy didn't hesitate to admit her ignorance. "The what?"

"'The Juggler of Notre Dame.' I'm the juggler. One of the leads."

"Oh. Your dancing stuff. I get it. Congratulations."

Cassie threw her purse on her bed, then pranced into the bathroom where she began striking poses. "It's a yearly tradition. Orchesis puts it on—the dance club—and I've got the lead. I just don't believe it." She began sucking in her cheeks as she stared at herself in the mirror. "I'm supposed to be a poor, starving entertainer—the juggler, that is. But my cheeks are *so* fat."

"Use some dark blush to hollow them," offered Amy, "but I bet you steal the show, and your cheeks won't really matter much."

Cassie trotted over to Amy and hugged her at the neck, while Amy reached up with both hands to steady the mega-curlers that forged her flip. "Oh, Amy, you're such a good friend. Thanks. You *will* come, won't you? To see me?"

"Of course. Wouldn't miss it for the world. I may have to go with Audora, though. I don't think I could drag Chipper."

Cassie sat down across from Amy on the edge of her bed, her legs bridging the chasm between the two, her shoes off and toes pointing.

She watched her nylon-covered toes flex and extend as she spoke. "That would be good. I hope Audora will come. You never know about her anymore."

"I know what you mean, but she'll be there with bells on her toes."

"She's terribly preoccupied, especially since initiation," Cassie said. "Have you noticed how Smokey Ray and her seem to have these inside jokes that make them giggly? They even have their own language almost. Sometimes, it's like she doesn't want to talk to us because we don't use her crazy new words. Admit it, Amy, don't you think Smokey Ray is a bit of a fruitcake?"

"Maybe, but I've got to admit, Audora is a pretty good match for him. She's got a few bolts loose herself, and I don't mean that in a bad way. I love her to death. But, Cassie, she was listening to a different tune the day we met her."

"I suppose so."

Cassie grabbed one foot in her hand, and with knee locked, she rolled to her back where the leg-arm fusion pointed to the ceiling, moving in circles and arcs, weaving like the mast of a ship blown by the wind.

Softly, Amy heard the haunting simplicity of her new favorite song, "Love Is Blue." She scrambled from her bed to the radio in the bathroom where she twisted up the volume, then returned to find Cassie dancing between the two beds and the small study area. She was swaying, spinning, pausing, with the music.

Amy joined in, and the two began a minuet of sorts, with Amy holding a pointed finger outstretched, Cassie spinning beneath.

"This song is the first instrumental to go number one in years," said Amy. "So far, it's kept 'Green Tambourine' and 'Sittin' on the Dock of the Bay' in the number two spot."

Cassie lowered into a sweeping bow, then straightened again. "Gosh, Amy, how do you keep up with all that?"

"I'm a jukebox junkie, remember? I've got to keep track of which 45s need to go on my boxes out there. Fourteen boxes now, and climbing."

"Wow," said Cassie, pirouetting. "This song really makes me want to dance. You too, huh?"

Amy loved the Hully Gully, the Swim, and especially the Bird, where she liked to shake her tail feathers. But as for free expression of modern dance, or the calculated grace of ballet . . . no.

"Actually, Cassie, this song *doesn't* make me want to dance."

"Oh?" Cassie stopped spinning when she realized her minuet partner was standing still.

"More than anything, it makes me want to cuddle with my guy."

Amy noticed a crinkle in Cassie's smile, giving her a wistful look, and though Amy didn't want to ramble on and on about her boyfriend to a boyless girl, she was puzzled by the charm this song held. Each time she heard the instrumental, she found herself lost in thoughts of going all the way with Chipper—rose petals surrounding the bed, flickering candles perched around the room, and white satin sheets with lace trim. And with each repetition of "Love Is Blue" over these past few months since the song's debut, Amy's fantasy sprouted more and more details, so that the sequence was already choreographed in her mind.

29

"I ain't doing this again," said Peachy.

"Fine," answered Drywall, knowing Peachy's absolutes were relative.

"We look like two friggin' homos here on the back row."

"Like I said, just this once."

"I mean, what if somebody sees us?"

"Quit your bellyaching, moron. I thought you told me your mom once danced with Maria Tallchief."

"Hey, that doesn't mean diddly-squat where my ass is concerned. And my ass is sittin' in a friggin' auditorium watchin' a friggin' ballet with a bunch of friggin' peckerwoods."

Drywall let his friend's prattle sing harmony with the background music. Eyes riveted on the stage, Larry Twohatchets watched the "juggler," Cassie St. Clair, drift and glide and sway and leap. He had never been so spellbound by anything in his life.

"Peachy, do you see her grace? Do you see how she stands out from the rest?"

"You bet your sweet bippy, I do. The juggler's jugs are so big you can see 'em from beneath that elf costume she's wearing. I know exactly why they call her the juggler."

Drywall lowered his forehead into the basket of his outstretched fingers. As he kneaded the skin in frustration, he said, "Watch her closely. Look how every muscle in her body is perfectly coordinated, right down to her fingertips that curl like a cresting wave to the music."

"A cresting wave? Giminy Christmas, you are one sick puppy. Drywall, the only reason those fingers need to curl are so they can wrap themselves around your ying and give it a yang until you bang."

"SHHHH," came the disgusted hiss of a wrinkled woman sitting in front of them as she turned to scowl at Peachy. The back of her seat was draped with a fur, and her black hair was squished into a tight bun penetrated by three knitting needles.

After she returned her glare front and center, Peachy shot her the bird, almost touching his middle finger to the back of her bun. Then, it looked as though he was about to flick one of the knitting needles, so Drywall grabbed his arm and nixed him with one look.

Although stifled for the moment, Peachy returned his signature smirk as he slowly undressed a stick of Juicy Fruit, tossing the wrapper on the floor.

Drywall whispered, "There's more to a woman than the size of her boobs, my friend."

"Gee, maybe you *are* a homo."

"When the lights go out, it all comes down to her scent. Love blooms in the dark."

Peachy let his gum dangle on the ledge of his lip before using the palm of his own hand to close his mouth. "I get it. Polacks sniff out their women just like tracking wild animals in the woods. Which scent do you follow exactly? Beaver?"

Drywall gestured to Peachy to lower his voice. "No. Each woman has her own fragrance," he said. "Maybe it blends with perfume, but she has a certain smell."

"Uh-huh."

"The night that Cassie walked down the steps at the Beta Chi house, I caught her fragrance. It was like some sort of incense. It did something to me."

"Uh-huh."

"I can't seem to get her out of my head. I want to get another whiff."

"Uh-huh."

"But I can't."

"Why not?"

"You know. Too much trouble. Races don't mix."

"Let me tell you something, my friend. You can't smell her from the back row. We might as well be in Timbuktu."

"SHHHH," came the steamy sound of the high-toned woman in front. When she turned around this time, Drywall saw makeup so thick it was cracking in places. Heavy rouge turned her cheeks into apples. She stared first at Peachy, but his friend's incriminating finger was pointing that guilt lay elsewhere, so the lady shifted her glare to Drywall instead. He smacked Peachy's shoulder with the back of his hand.

About 45 minutes into the production, in a rare moment while the juggler was stilled, Drywall scanned the backs of heads throughout the crowd. "Hey, that looks like Audora down there to the left."

"Yeah, you're right. And she's with Amy."

"You told me they weren't coming," Drywall said.

"No, I told you that Amy asked Chipper to come, but he said no. I didn't say anything about— "

"We gotta get outta here," said Drywall, rattled. "I don't want them to see us. They'll tell Cassie we were here."

"Calm down—"

Peachy continued to talk, but Drywall was near panic. He stood, bent at the waist, and stole his way to the aisle, stomping on the art-loving toes of the audience in his row. When he looked back, he saw that Peachy was only now following his lead.

Drywall checked the lady with the pancake and apple makeup and the tight bun on the back of her head. Horrified, he saw a glob stuck on the end of one of the knitting needles. It was a wad of Juicy Fruit, shish kebabbed onto the point.

* * *

"Amy, sweetheart, don't look now, but they slipped out," whispered Audora.

"So you think they spotted us?"

"Probably. So much for matchmaking. Another blossoming romance stuck in the bud."

"Dealing with those two is like trying to catch Heckle and Jeckle."

30

Chipper managed a sheepish grin as he entered the shadowy world of Ty Wheeler. Wheeler was the elusive final name on Chipper's room chart, now that the DeLaughter named had been erased.

A quick glance around the room confirmed what his pledge brothers had said: black walls, black bedspread, black throw rug, black leather chair, and black clothes hanging in the open closet. The walls were decorated with black-and-white photos of Mr. Roy Orbison. The only color in the room came from the corner jukebox, courtesy of Amy. Well, not exactly *courtesy*. Peachy had funded the box for reasons he would never discuss with Chipper.

Ty Wheeler stood at his mirror, combing his black pompadour, black-rimmed sunglasses in place. Black shirt. Black pants. Black shoes and socks.

"Come in, son, have a seat." Chipper picked the black chair as opposed to the black bedspread.

"Mr. Orbison has recently made the decision to comb the hair down on his forehead, but I'll be sticking with this wave for a while, until I see how he's finally remembered."

"You kinda like Roy Orbison, don't you?" said Chipper, recognizing the stupidity of his words were like the bong of a chime that won't quit ringing.

"Oh, it's much more than that."

Ignoring the lead, Chipper tried again, "I'm sorry it's taken me so long to get around to your room and all—"

"Say no more!" Ty Wheeler said, boldly spinning to point his finger at Chipper. "I know you pledges are scared of me."

No, actually, we think you're one weird duck whose sole contribution to the fraternity is commandeering the spook patrol during rush week, thought Chipper as he fought back nervous laughter.

"Actually, I'm not as strange as you might think. Unlike everyone else, I simply know my destiny. How much different would all the so-called *normal* members behave if they had seen their own future through a crystal ball?" Wheeler faced back to the mirror to continue primping.

This loon was not going to let Chipper pursue a normal conversation. Ty didn't seem to understand that this visit was simply to add more biographical information to the "basics"—name, class, home-town, major.

Ty continued, "But back to your business at hand. What do you know about me already?"

Chipper was ready with the basics. "You were born in Vernon, Texas in 1936, but you moved to Wink, Texas early on and you consider that your hometown. You went to North Texas State in Denton before transferring here, and you're a super-senior majoring in music." Chipper rattled off the data without skipping a beat.

"So, if I was born in 1936, that would make me . . . 32?"

"Yeah, I guess so."

"How do you explain that, son? What would a 32-year-old man be doing in a college fraternity? Do I look 32?"

Chipper thought Ty's pudgy cheeks were already drooping into jowls, and with that receding chin, his age was anybody's guess. *Yes, he could pass for 32.* "No, you don't look 32," he said.

"Then how do you explain the basics you just gave me?"

"It's what we were given. We have a crib sheet we put together. During the first week, each pledge got the scoop on two or three Actives, then we compiled—"

"I know what you did. The crib sheet wasn't your idea. It's been a tradition for years. So what would you think if I told you I tricked the first pledge, your scout, and that I gave him Roy Orbison's biography?"

"Uhhh . . ."

"You spooks have been giving Roy's basics every time you go around the table, every one of you. Every time you're in lineup at a Worksession, and on and on, you've been telling us about 32-year-old Roy Orbison."

"But . . . the Actives. They just sit there. They don't say a thing."

"They're in on the joke, too."

"But, why? And later, when my pledge brothers started coming in to have you sign their charts, you just kept telling them Roy Orbison's basics?"

"My first message to you is, 'when you're laughing at someone, just remember, they might be laughing back at you.'"

Chipper was scrambling for something to say, ashamed, but at the same time, irritated that he'd been tricked by such a squirrel.

"So why'd you pick me to tell the truth to?"

"We tell everyone after initiation. It's not fraternity ritual in the traditional sense, but it's a local ritual, just for fun. I'm different. I know that. You might say it's my way of being 'one of the guys.' Since all the Actives in the house were fooled as pledges, they get a kick out of watching you guys fall for it, too."

"You were around when all the Actives were pledges?" *Maybe this guy really is 32.*

Ty Wheeler set his comb on the black surface of the dresser, then pulled his guitar from the closet and began strumming chords.

"I'm giving you the scoop before initiation because I understand your girlfriend is responsible for this jukebox that pledge Peachy got me. I'm real grateful for that, 'cause it's not just *any* jukebox, it's not the ugly chrome boxes of today. It's a Wurlitzer 1400, made in 1951, the last model to have an arc-en-ciel border."

Chipper thought he heard the French word for rainbow, but he let it pass. "Uh-huh," he replied.

"I'm from Leadville, Colorado. My daddy left home and my mama died before I was old enough to remember any of it. Was raised by my mama's brother, a wealthy old coot, a bachelor whose ranch in the high plains of Colorado was worth almost a million when he died, right before I went to college. He didn't have kids, so I inherited it all. I'm set for life. But I don't have any family. Came here and pledged Sig Zeta 'cause that's what my uncle was. I didn't really fit in, even from the start. But summer after I was initiated, I had a vision."

"A vision? Like you saw something that wasn't there?"

"No. I saw something that *was* there." Ty strummed another chord.

"Oh."

"I was driving that summer along a highway, with both sides of the road bein' part of my uncle's spread. It was the day that the estate sale of the ranch was finalized, and I knew I'd probably never come that way again. Horrible thunderstorm was passing over the mountains and dumping rain on the plains. Weirdest cloud formations I'd ever seen, like pillars of smoke that finally enclosed the plains between the mountains like a palace of doom. As the storm ended, I saw a triple rainbow. You ever seen three rainbows at once?"

"No, can't say as I have."

"Well, there were three of 'em. And not just three ordinary rainbows. The brightest and the closest was so real you could touch it, but the most amazing thing was that one end of this bright rainbow was planted on the ground in front of the mountains. You could see the actual end of the rainbow! It was a sight to behold, every bit as real as the colored bars on this jukebox where they touch the floor."

Chipper had never stopped to consider the particulars of rainbows, so his interest in this story was fading fast. And when a yawn tried to expose him, he kept his lips closed.

"The other cars on the highway saw it, too. So much so that they were all stopping and taking pictures. I still had my stuff from freshman year in the car, including my new color camera, so I decided to stop and take a picture. But then it happened. This large black Lincoln in front of me stops, and out gets Roy Orbison. I'm not shittin' you. The real Roy Orbison. I introduce myself, and we talk about the rainbow and stuff. He tells me that 'rainbow' is a stupid name, meaning there's no rain when you see one, and there's no bow, either. Think about it. A violin bow is straight, an archer's bow is barely curved. A rainbow isn't a bow. It's an arch, an arch in the sky. Roy tells me that the French have it right—their word for rainbow is 'arc-en-ciel,' an arch in the sky. Finally, I get this lady from the car behind me to take a picture of Roy and me and the ground-touching arc-en-ciel with my camera."

Ty walked to his closet where he pulled out a black leather photo album. And when he opened the cover, there was only a single picture inside to show to Chipper—Ty and the real Roy Orbison with a rainbow in the background. Ty explained that the two fainter rainbows didn't show very well. Just the one that reached the ground. Chipper looked closely at the photo, and yes, it did seem to be Roy Orbison, and yes, it did seem that the rainbow touched earth.

"Then comes the strangest part," continued Ty. "As we start back for our cars, Roy turns around and sticks out his hand, saying, 'Pleasure to meet you.' We hadn't shook hands until then. And he goes on to ask, 'Son, anyone ever tell you that you bear a resemblance to me?' And I hadn't thought of it until then. I'd always looked funny, and kids teased me the whole time I was growing up, to the point I'd cry myself to sleep. But it had never occurred to me that I looked so much like Roy Orbison, probably because my hair was sort of a dusty brown. Now that it's dyed black, what with the pompadour, it's damn amazing, isn't it?"

Chipper agreed. It was eerie. "That's quite a story," he offered.

"Yeah, but that's not the vision. That's what the casual observer would have seen that day, but that's not all that *I* saw."

Chipper felt his eyebrows rise a notch as he waited for the next installment.

"When I was shaking hands with Roy, and we both realized how much I looked like him, there was a lightning strike directly behind him. And from my view, the lightning bolt came from the heavens, branched into fingers that struck Roy right on the pompadour. Then I felt his hand turn cold in mine, like it was dead. And as the thunder rolled, I knew God was going to call Roy home soon. Too soon. And I realized in that instant that it would be me that would carry on.

"I had a vision. I could see an assassin's bullet take Mr. Orbison down and out. A crazed fan will kill Mr. Orbison in front of a hotel, and he'll sing no more. But I—*I* will continue to sing his great songs. A sort of impersonator, you might say. And every ugly duckling kid in America will scramble to impersonate him, but I'll be the first in line, ready to carry the torch. I saw a country full of Roy Orbison impersonators that day, son, but it was Ty Wheeler's destiny, my role in life, to be the premier of them all—to be the real thing.

"So you see, this is no joke for me. I pretend it's a joke, but it's not. I'm in training for my day in the sun. As I let go of Mr. Orbison's hand, I saw myself on stage, spotlight beaming down on *my* hands, strumming *my* guitar. It's been six years since I had that sure-as-the-world vision. I switched my major from business to music right afterward, and I'm pretty salty on this here guitar." He strummed another chord.

Chipper was mute. He knew that Ty Wheeler couldn't carry a tune, so he was at a loss to explain how a dream could be so far removed from reality. But he had to ask: "I notice you pantomime most the songs you sing around the house, during Worksessions and all."

"Yeah, therein lies the problem.

"I've got a pretty good voice, but it doesn't really sound like Mr. Orbison. Of course, *no one* sounds like Mr. Orbison, so I haven't figured out that angle yet. That's why I'm hanging out here, still in college. I'm majoring in vocal music, not the guitar, and—well, I've met with lots of advice to move in other directions with my career. Lots of Fs in my vocal classes. Lots of repeated courses."

"So why don't you get a degree, then continue voice lessons?"

"Son, you don't understand a thing I've been saying, do you? It's the vision I saw. Present circumstances don't matter after you've seen a vision. It's going to happen one way or the other. If I have to stay in college 20 years, I've got to get ready for the day when Mr. Orbison turns it over to me. I don't have to work. I don't need a degree. I pay my house bills. All I need is to learn to sing. And frankly, I need the guys here in the house to let me practice, to be my perpetual audience. New recruits every year. Always turnover. Always a new crowd. Don't you see? I might be living my vision right now.

"Son, have you ever noticed how hit tunes are on the radio only as long as they're popular? Then you never hear them again? Well, it's been over 10 years since the rock 'n roll revolution began, so those first songs will have historical significance soon. Very soon. We will start to pine away for the days of old, and the songs of old. And I'll be right there, for the rest of my life, reminding everyone about the great Roy Orbison."

"Should I keep this to myself 'til after initiation?" asked Chipper, groping for a conclusion.

"Yes. Initiation is around the corner. You can reveal everything after that. Then the initiates can share the secret the next year. And the year after that. And the year after that. I'm here for the duration."

Then Ty Wheeler strummed again and began singing off-key, "You won't be seeing rainbows anymore . . ."

Maybe rainbow is a bad word, thought Chipper, but it sure fits into songs a heckuvalot better than 'arc-en-ciel.'

31

While the ritual of initiation was sacrosanct, the Sigma Zeta Chi tradition of Reflection Week, as opposed to Hell Week, was public information (to anyone who cared). In fact, the concept of Reflection Week, remaining speechless for the duration, had appealed to Chipper in his original decision to pledge. Still, he was greatly surprised at the elaborate efforts of the Actives that greeted the pledges as they moved into the fraternity house for the week and assumed a monastic pose for seven days.

It was a time for contemplation, a time for austerity. It was both joy and terror, courage and fear, isolation and unification.

Communication was through the written word, usually a pocket notebook each pledge was required to sport. However, in a special document—a two-way journal—meant only for the eyes of the Pledge Trainer, each pledge was charged with soul-searching, diving into pools of doubt and dread from which Mother Boone would spring forth with solace or rebuke.

Chipper was astonished that Ted could retrieve all 29 journals of the proposed initiates each night, then return them the next morning, presumably with responding paragraphs in all of them. Boone wrote one page of feedback per night in Chipper's journal, and Chipper was struck by the power of Ted's words in the transcribed dialogue.

At first, Chipper wrote about the changes he'd like to see in the fraternity. Ever troubled by the fact that 77 pledges rotated through his initiate class over the year, some lasting only a few days, it was perplexing to Chipper that only 29 made it all the way to initiation. And, of the 29, only 16 had pledged at the time of Rush Week. He wrote about a stronger, more lasting, Rush. He wrote about measures to avoid a repeat of Black Jack. He wrote about Fraternity of the Year some day. But more than winning trophies, he wrote of the "slippery simplicity" of encouraging each other in teamwork, a trait Chipper thought scarce.

But after a few days, he was writing personal stuff—his waffling about going into medicine, about his luck in finding Amy, about his concern that if he didn't go into medicine, Amy would be the bread-winner while he floundered as a penniless writer. In short, his fear of the future. And even more, his fear that his passion for teamwork might be just a cover for being petrified at the thought of facing the world alone.

And in reading Ted's responses, Chipper felt he came to know the man more in the first few days of Reflection Week than he had all year. He read compassion, he read sincerity, he read honest caring from the words of the Pledge Trainer. And he took note when Ted wrote that "insight" was a gift granted to Chipper.

On the fourth day of Reflection Week, Benny Taylor died.

Benny Taylor was the older brother of Chipper's high school golfing friend, L.K. Taylor, the power-hitter on their state champion team. Benny had been born with muscular dystrophy, and he began wasting away just a few years after birth. Although his body became a tangled mass of meatless bone, he had survived for 23 years. L.K.'s father was a ferocious man who wouldn't have anything to do with his crippled son. Chipper felt a crowning moment in his own life had occurred one year earlier, watching the father melt into a sea of forgiveness when he carried Benny onto the trophy stand to join his brother L.K. who had won top individual honors in state golf, in addition to El Viento's team trophy.

Chipper was devastated at the news, and he wrote to be released from Reflection Week for the funeral. *"Too close to initiation,"* came the written reply. *"We only excuse candidates for family emergencies, not brothers of friends. Sorry."* The note came from his Big Brother, President Al Marlowe.

Chipper was seething. Everything he had come to appreciate and love about Sig Zeta seemed to vanish in an instant. He wanted to tear down the walls of his Reflection Week chamber, but he held himself in check. He had to do *something*.

He took his journal and began to write. Inspired by Smokey Ray's penchant for limericks, Chipper decided on a poem to describe that moment of the trophy presentation when L.K. handed his trophy to Benny, the moment when the three Taylors—the two boys and their father—huddled in conciliation. The title of his rhyme would be "No Rhyme." And he surprised himself at the liquidity of the words as they flowed into his journal:

No rhyme or reason can explain a life
That from dawn to dusk is yoked with strife.

Did Heaven's touch leave fingerprints to maim?
Or did Vapor from Below cause you to be lame?

Friends grew strong while you grew weak
Then of your name no one would speak.

You viewed the world between bars of pain
Yet somehow smiled through drops of rain.

The cause of suffering remains unseen
Above, Below, or In-Between.

But when we say, "It's just God's will"
To you, it seemed so awfully shrill.

We know it's love that wins the gold
That faith is second, we're also told.

As you hoped to walk on legs of faith
No rhyme or reason explains your fate.

But love did seek and shield the cold
And drank you well from a cup of gold.

A trophied image now seems like mist
Your father's knee replaced the fist.

And in that twinkle of primal joy
Love made man become the boy.

You previewed Heaven on that golden day
Something few on Earth can ever say.

My sorrow now is full and rife
For no rhyme or reason can explain a life.

Chipper wrote at the end: "Ted, would you please tear this page out of my journal and mail it to the Taylor family?"

Mother Boone responded in his note the next day: "I did more than that. I made a copy for myself (and you) and took the original to the Taylor family in El Viento. Your parents directed me to their home. The Taylors are lovely people. L.K. said 'thanks' and to tell you 'hello.' His short game at golf remains superb, thanks to you. They plan to read your poem at the funeral. By the way, a bunch of guys were there, and they told me they would be wearing red jeans to the funeral, whatever that means.

"And now I want to tell you something. Remember my writings a few days ago, about your 'insight'? I was wrong. I should have said 'uncanny insight.' Your poem could be molded for anyone born with a handicap, be it physical or mental, and I suppose all of us have some sort of mental handicap, at least. I can't say much for the sophistication of your poetic structure. You're not far removed from doggerel. However, you have a talent with words—a gift that must be nurtured. Some are great sculptors of words that persuade, or words that illuminate, or words of commerce, but your talent is quite specific—you bundle words so that they transmit feelings. You shouldn't worry about making words rhyme. Claim it, nurture it, and bring those words to their fruition."

Chipper was overwhelmed at the response. He knew the Taylors would appreciate the poem, but it never occurred to him that the only bona fide member of the intelligentsia that he knew, with the possible exception of Smokey Ray, considered his words to have a measure of importance.

And a tiny miracle occurred—Chipper's resentment at missing the funeral disappeared. It didn't simply vanish; rather, it was replaced by mystical warmth. He had only felt this warmth once before, when Doc Jody's widow told Chipper after the funeral that of the hundreds of letters she received after Doc's death, Chipper's was the most memorable, the most comforting. Stuck in the narrow confines of Reflection Week, it was emancipating.

* * *

In preparation for initiation, the candidates were blindfolded in the basement near the U-bench, then Chipper could sense they were being arranged one at a time into an ordered single file. He could hear the muffled sobs of relief from some of his pledge brothers behind him as the line was formed. Then came the voice of Mother Boone, "My pledges—and I call you that for the last time—we're ready to move forward now. Put your hands on the shoulders of your brother in front of you."

Chipper groped the air, but there was no one in front of him. *Maybe C.C. is so short I can't find his shoulders.* And when he reached lower to find C.C., small hands from behind dug into the flesh of his own shoulders, holding him in place. Chipper then recognized the tearful sighs at his back were from C.C. Chastain, though half the pledge class was blubbering at the moment.

In the darkness, Mother Boone's voice again: "Follow me."

And Chipper felt his arms being lifted and secured onto the shoulders of the Pledge Trainer as they stumbled forward, blindfolded, somber, mute.

Spring Yarns

32

Names were linked to numbers, perhaps forever. As Outstanding Pledge, Chipper was initiate number 1401 in the chapter. C.C. Chastain, heavily favored for top spot, would instead be known as 1402. Smokey Ray claimed 1407, while Drywall was 1408. Since GPA figured into the equation, Peachy had to settle for 1425, which would have been A-okay if it weren't for the fact that Uno Guilford was ahead of him at 1419. And dead last? Ernie Dumas, of course, at 1429.

Chipper felt guilty in the number one spot. Not so guilty as to return the diamond-rimmed gold cross fraternity pin that he would wear until passing the prize to next year's winner, but guilty enough to offer semisincere condolence to C.C. Chastain.

"You really deserved it," he said. "I honestly don't know why Ted put me number one."

"Hey, man. It doesn't make a shit to me," replied C.C. "This is the happiest day of my life. I'm so glad to finally be a Sig Zeta that I couldn't care less. I'm in, and that's all that matters."

* * *

Wickiup Enterprises International was officially launched three minutes after Initiation. Neither Peachy nor Drywall had Sig Zeta relatives at the reception, so they entertained each other with visions of wealth as their glasses of champagne clinked in the air.

"We have to anticipate the market," said Peachy. "We can't wait for trends. We have to set the trends."

"Like how?" asked Drywall.

"Like, for instance, ever notice that every guy in the fraternity has a fan in his room? Used to be just to keep cool, but nowadays all the long-hairs stick their heads in the breeze when they get out of the shower."

"And . . . ?"

"Think about it, brother 1408. It takes for friggin' ever to dry your hair that way. So listen to this—when I was in that department store when we were in Mexico, I saw those handheld dryers that girls have had, but now they have 'em for guys."

"How's a guy's hair dryer any different?"

"There *is* no difference, don't you see? They stick a guy's picture on the box and call it manly. Hair dryers for us studs are a trend waiting to happen. And easy as hell to import. Small, lightweight, cheap. I figure we can bring back three or four hundred to start with. Sell the bastards to every frat rat on campus who is just now realizing that the wet head is dead. Criminy, sell 'em to the Independents. We set the trend."

"How we gonna haul so many boxes?"

"My old man has a big motherin' truck he ain't got no use for. Used to be for bootleg whiskey back when Oklahoma was dry. He's moved on to the big time now, so the truck just sits there at my house, rusting. We'll fix her up and we'll be in business, just as long as you stay a card-carryin' Kickapoo."

"You think my stripes are changin'?"

* * *

Promotions for employees at the insane asylum were rare in times of budgetary crisis, yet orderly Ray Divine was given laudatory comments in the letter that proclaimed his 60-cents per hour raise:

"Mr. Divine has consistently demonstrated intuitive skills beyond his years in dealing with some of our most troubled patients. Our schizophrenic population in Building 19 has had all psychotropic medication withheld for the past six months in preparation for a randomized controlled trial of a new agent, so our aides have been unduly burdened with this increasingly agitated group. Mr. Divine's work with these individuals has been exemplary, and he is hereby promoted from Psychiatric Aide I to P.A. II."

Smokey Ray cut the letter into eight rectangles, then placed one of the papers into a contraption he had pilfered from Building 19—a cigarette-rolling machine. After gauging the margins of the letter snippet to be perfectly set within the red metal framework, he sprinkled some weed into the trough at the bottom. With a downward pull on the lever, his laudatory communiqué became a joint.

"The trust of simpletons is indeed a treasure," he said, as he lit, inhaled, and held.

* * *

"So, I've decided to go to law school," said soon-to-be-ex-President Al Marlowe.

"That's good," replied Chipper in one of their typically stilted conversations. "I guess you'll be coming over to the house for meals and all. That'll be nice. And, of course, you can hope Vietnam is over by the time you're done."

"If I have to fight, I'll fight."

Chipper felt a rush of guilt, as if he'd just tried to paint a yellow stripe down Marlowe's middle while his big brother sat behind the huge presidential desk.

"But I doubt Vietnam will be an issue then," Al continued.

"Really? Why not?"

"Didn't you hear the news today?" he asked, pointing to the poster above his head, the one in which the former President was shaking hands with Robert F. Kennedy. "The man in the photo just announced he's running for *The* Presidency."

"Perry Crane?"

Al Marlowe didn't seem to get the joke.

"No. Kennedy. I'll bet he wins the nomination over Johnson, then he'll be a shoo-in. He's already launched an attack on Johnson's Vietnam policy. He'll be going for peace right off the bat. He says U.S. involvement is like sending in a lion to halt an epidemic of jungle rot."

Chipper thought it odd that Al was sounding like a dove. The only sure-fire dove Chipper knew was Smokey Ray.

"By the way, Chipper, I've never really taken the time to tell you that I thought it took a load of courage to do what your pledge class did last winter."

Chipper nodded in silence, figuring any words he mustered would be a step down from the ambiguity of quiet.

"It taught me a lesson," Al continued. "And I hope your pledge class is able to hang onto that spirit of brotherhood, at least during your careers here at Sig Zeta."

Chipper watched the President as he spoke. Not a facial muscle bothered to move, save the corners of his mouth that curled sparingly.

His bristle-blond hair was thick and rigid as a scouring brush. Eyelids blinked slowly, but only after long intervals, like curtains announcing intermission.

This guy is untouchable, thought Chipper. *It just cracks me up when he uses the word "brotherhood." He is one cold fish.* Yet Chipper couldn't deny that Al Marlowe was a born leader—a mix of poise and power. Chipper even felt a little jealous that he didn't have Al's instant command of a room when he entered. Al didn't have to glad-hand the crowd; the crowd came to him.

* * *

Beta Chi was not a high priority for Amy. Sure, she loved all the girls, but first and foremost, she had to concentrate on a dazzling GPA (a puny 7% of med school admissions were girls). *Almost* foremost was financing her extended education—80% came from her jukebox enterprise, now with 19 units placed; 20% came from her mother's job as a salesclerk at Rita's Discount Haute Couture in the tiny town of Pocasset, near El Viento; and 0% came from Amy's father who had vamoosed years ago, in tow with the original Rita who had abandoned her promising career as a high fashion clothier.

And then there was the girls' golf team. Three informal matches this spring, not sanctioned by the university. But then again, their opponents weren't sanctioned, either. Transportation? Gratis, per the unpaid coach who drove her own car. Amy had been medalist in two of the three matches.

With her mind buzzing over so many things of gravity, Amy was caught off guard by her own silly sentiment one night. She dripped a joyful tear at her candlelight ceremony, as the flame was passed in the sorority circle three times until she blew it out (to the squealing delight of her Beta Chi sisters), proclaiming that she had just received the diamond-embroidered pin of the Outstanding Sig Zeta pledge.

And as she looked at the smoking wick of the candle with its pin-point ember still aglow, she thought it odd that the girls celebrated the ritual of pinning by extinguishing a flame.

* * *

"I'm tellin' ya', this is the last time."

"Okay, I won't ask you to do it again."

"You either call this muchacha on the phone, or give it up."

"Okay."

"I ain't sittin' on the back row, lookin' at no more friggin' ballerina crap, with every chick in the place thinkin' we're a couple of homos."

"But dagnabit, what if she won't go out with me?"

"She will. Trust me. I seen the look in her eye. And the look said, 'Drywall, baby, sock it to me.'"

"Maybe I'll just wait 'til next semester. Heck, the year's almost over anyway."

"Drywall, you're giving a whole new meaning to the term 'pussy-whipped.' You're whipped into a friggin' bowl of Jell-o just thinking about it. For chrissakes, put some starch in that spine of yours."

"Maybe next year, dang it, maybe next year."

"You lily-livered, gutless, spineless . . ."

* * *

The New Initiate golf tournament was an informal rematch of the fall groupings. The match did not count toward the Intramural Trophy, but the Sig Zeta crew walked away with top honors just as they had done earlier in the year as pledges.

Peachy was proud of his 84 on the tough, tough university course, but the outing was spoiled by the fact that Uno Guilford had taken medalist honors with a 71, one shot better than Smokey Ray.

Drywall shot a 78, then remarked that if the new initiates had been playing A-team golf for actual points last week in real intramurals, they would have tied the Betas for first place.

Chipper had caddied for Peachy.

* * *

Pledge Trainer Ted Boone was named Yearbook Man of Distinction. There would be a full-page, full-length photo; hopefully, he would not be photographed sideways lest he look like a question mark. Since no Sig Zeta had ever captured this honor, Kong was quick to announce that Ted Boone was the "biggest stud in the history of the chapter."

But the words on everyone's lips rang something like this: "How's he going to avoid Vietnam? The only thing a degree in Letters puts in your paws is an M-16 rifle, effective for mowing down gooks at 400 meters."

No one could have guessed it in a million years . . .

"He's what?"

"He's going to graduate school. In drama."

"What? Like to become an actor?"

"No. He plans to be a playwright."

"You've got to be kidding."

"I'm serious."

"Beats killing gooks in the jungle."

"Boy, that's an understatement."

* * *

Spring Bash was the biggest party on campus, or so it seemed to the Sigma Zs. The week-long gala culminated in sorority competition in the backyard where tall cedars provided an enclave such that the neighboring homes couldn't steal a view of the Sweatshirt Balloon Carry, the Broom Handle Push-ball Race, the Egg-in-Panty Slingshot Contest, or the Pole-Riding Pillow Fights. And finally, the Miss Venus Contest, where sorority girls whose bodies beckoned lusty eyes, wore brown paper bags over their heads, while judges picked the winner based on sub-neckline curves.

The Grande Finale each year was the Spring Bash Dance, with Sig Zetas and their dates dancing to a big-name band. Whereas it may have been traditional to "stretch the truth" during Rush Week about big-name bands at *every* party, the Sigma Zs did indeed try to land a big one for Spring Bash. Last year, it had been the McCoys with their Hang-on-Sloopy-fame, and this year, it was to be Herman's Hermits.

But sometimes, Fate reaches down with giant knobby fingers and twists the course of human events.

Ten *days* before the Spring Bash Dance, Herman's Hermits canceled.

Rush Chairman Paul Sherman nearly murdered Social Chairman John Rockwell. At least 80 high school seniors were scheduled to attend this year. Total humiliation. The Sig Zetas would look like outright spooks with the house band playing, no matter how good the Rickel Four were, no matter how loud C.C. Chastain could squeal soulfully at the keyboards.

Just as the sun is always shining somewhere, it chose to angle its beam during this critical juncture on the one and only Peachy Waterman Junior.

In rescue of near-tragedy, Peachy contacted his old man in Las Vegas whose big-name contacts were thought to be classic examples of Peachy's bullshit. But as things played out, *Peachy's bullshit* became known as *Peachy's miracle*.

Although the band didn't set up until 10:00 that evening, no one cared. Horns blaring and jive dancing, the Ike and Tina Turner Review turned the Sig Zeta house upside down. More Sigs gatored on the floor than stood upright. More beer sloshed out of paper cups onto the floor than was actually drunk. And many dancers who slipped on the wet terrazo simply decided to stay on the floor and gator. Later, there were "gator piles" where recumbent bodies, boys and girls, formed squirming human mounds, six and eight people deep, with more revelers flying in from the sides, often bouncing off to the floor, where a new gator pile would form. If it wasn't Sodom, it was damn sure Gomorrah.

The night served itself up as a dish of folklore, and the man responsible for it all—Peachy Waterman Jr.—was canonized as Social Chairman for Life.

Chipper took movies of the festival with his father's 8mm camera, planning to use the footage in a rush film—Great Moments in Sigma Zeta Chi History. Amy served as assistant, opening flat yellow film boxes and helping Chipper thread the camera. The journalistic bent in making this documentary worked well for Chipper, as he really couldn't picture himself (or Amy) in a gator pile, but he found great merriment in the piles of his brothers. But he also felt something more ill defined—a curious comfort behind the lens.

* * *

Chipper had never seen the TV room at the Sig Zeta house so full. Thursday night should be the "Batman" crowd, but the series had ended a few weeks ago. He squeezed into the back row and whispered, "What's going on? Why's everyone watching the evening news?"

"Martin Luther King's been shot dead."

"Uh-oh."

"No shit. Riots everywhere, in over a hundred cities. Twenty thousand federal troops called in. Twice as many National Guardsmen. People gettin' killed all over."

"No time to be white in those places," said Chipper as he eyed the TV with its surrealistic reflection of a foreign world. Negroes smashing windows, smashing whites, all the horror encased and fishbowled by the plastic TV screen.

Hours later, still glued to the television but worming his way to the couch by virtue of crowd attrition and rotation, Chipper was sitting with Smokey Ray Divine when the front door banged open and Ernie Dumas with Uno Guilford rushed in, huffing and puffing.

"You guys, switch to channel four," said Ernie, "you're not gonna believe the spook that's on the Johnny Carson Show. Hurry. We caught the first of his act just now across the street at Grady's."

When no one moved, Uno Guilford charged to the built-in TV, nestled among the trophy shelves, then switched to channel four.

There, strumming a ukulele, was a weirdo with a banana nose strikingly similar to Uno's, but this guy's repulsive face was surrounded by long, tight coils of black hair lubed from a crankcase, eyelids fluttering to roving eyes, in a screeching falsetto, singing, "Tiptoe through the Tulips."

"Have you ever seen a fucking freak like that before?" shouted Ernie in absolute delight over the importance of his discovery. "What a goddam freak! Calls himself Tiny Tim."

For once, Ernie was right. Chipper had never seen anything like it. He was mesmerized. In fact, he barely noticed Smokey Ray rise from the couch and walk slowly to the television. One minute Chipper was looking at Johnny Carson applauding his new discovery, with the oddball Tiny Tim swishing bashfully in deference to "Mr. Carson," then with a channel flick, Chipper saw an angry Negro smashing in the windshield of a car with a baseball bat as a terrified white driver clutched his bloody face with one hand and shifted into reverse with the other.

"Turn it back, Smokey Ray," ordered Ernie Dumas with a trace of self-doubt in his voice. "This Tiny Tim guy is the craziest sumbitch I've ever seen on television. It's historical, man."

Smokey Ray glared at Ernie in apparent disbelief. "Martin Luther King was assassinated this evening. Did you know that, Ernie? Uno?"

Uno Guilford said, "So, what's the big deal about one dead nig? People die every day."

Ernie laughed as they exchanged brotherly glances.

"I'm never sure why you two compete for Imbecile-of-the-Year, but let me tell you something. It's *not* one dead man. People may die every day, but that's not what happened here. It was a Dream that was killed. And it is very, *very* dangerous to murder a Dream."

Caught between novelty and consequence, Chipper felt that Tiny Tim deserved more than 30 seconds of Sig Zeta airtime since they had been watching the assassination fallout for hours. Still, with the riots on the TV screen again, something tugged at Chipper to lift the B-team football trophy off the top of the set, reach inside the TV bowl and swirl his hand with the angry fish in the water. But he didn't. Instead, Chipper heard himself blurt out: "Aw, c'mon Smokey Ray, let's turn back to Johnny Carson for just a minute."

33

"I can't believe I let you talk me into this," Chipper said, checking his watch as he steered his Thunderbird down Main Street. "What time did Smokey Ray want us to be there?"

"Six sharp. It's two minutes 'til," Peachy replied.

"Why didn't Drywall come with us? I thought you guys did everything together these days."

"Drywall's as straight as they come, man. You know how Polacks have an itchin' for the firewater. Well, Drywall won't touch the stuff. So he's damn sure not interested in watchin' a girl drop acid. He won't go near nothin' if it ain't certified legal."

"Can't say as I blame him. This *is* semi-crazy, you know?"

Peachy grinned as he spoke, "Yeah, but I been thinking this girl might go down if she's high, so what's there to lose? And with a nickname like Window Wizard—"

"What's that about?" asked Chipper.

"She's an old friend of Audora's, but now she's one of those antiwar radicals at Boulder. Smokey Ray said she trips every weekend, and that she keeps her supply of LSD in little gelatin squares called window panes. So, she's the Window Wizard."

"I've heard of sugar cubes and little squares of paper, but never that," said Chipper. "Didn't they make LSD illegal last year?"

"I think so."

Chipper pulled into the Holiday Inn parking lot then drove to the back row of rooms until he found number 16. With his hand on the wooden gearshift knob between the bucket seats, he eased his T-bird into a parking spot. Only a few other cars dotted the alleyway between the motel and the stockade fence that separated commercial from residential.

The Room 16 door opened and Smokey Ray appeared, tipping his cowboy hat, smoking a joint. Chipper made a quick glance around the property for witnesses and, finding none, waved with one finger and a twist of the wrist to Smokey Ray.

"So, did you cowboys both finish your finals today?" Smokey Ray asked.

"Aced 'em all, Smokey," said Peachy whose dumpster marvels were now legendary.

Audora appeared at the doorway briefly, only to grab Smokey Ray's arm and pull him back inside where the weed could be safely enjoyed.

Peachy gesticulated to Chipper with a repetitive pumping action of his loosely cupped fist near his crotch, elbow chicken-winged—sign language for: *'Smokey has banged her three times already this afternoon and if I'm lucky I'll be humping away soon on the Window Wizard, driving her acid-soaked brain all the way to a Land Called Honalee and back again.'*

Inside, Chipper and Peachy plopped into beige-coated armchairs, separated by a formica-topped table. Chipper hardly noticed the paraphernalia on the tabletop in deference to the sight of Audora stretched out on the rumpled bedcover, wearing a long dress made of purple fishnet over some flimsy black fabric that barely knew how to keep a secret.

"Hi, guys," she said, before taking a drag on her own joint. "How's Amy?"

"Fine."

"Peachy, has Drywall ever asked Cassie out?"

"Nope. He's pure chickenshit."

Chipper saw that Peachy's eyes were trying to penetrate Audora's dress as well.

"Hardly ever get to see you guys anymore," she said, exhaling.

"Nope," they both replied.

"Chipper, Peachy, take a hit of this," said Smokey Ray, offering a communal puff of weed. Both boys took a drag apiece, acting as if pot was as routine as a shower and a shave, not wanting to appear like the callow country boobs that they were.

"I tried it once before," said Chipper with feigned nonchalance. "Couldn't even feel it."

"So where's the Window Wizard?" asked Peachy in a raspy voice that indicated that he, too, was about to betray a novice's choke.

"She's going to be a little late," said Audora. "Her flight out of Denver was delayed."

"So, she has money to fly?" asked Peachy. It seemed to Chipper that Peachy was almost drooling.

Audora laughed. "Plenty of money," she said. "More than me."

"Cool," said fantasy-soaked Peachy.

"But you'd never know it. She does her dope, of course, but she uses her daddy's money to finance the antiwar movement. At the University of Colorado mostly. She's one of the few women driving the protest movement nationwide."

"So, a real live celebrity, huh?" said Peachy. "Well, we just won't talk politics then, 'cause I think we should just drop the friggin' Big One on those gooks and get this damn deal over with."

Smokey Ray smiled and handed Peachy his own personal joint. "Here, Peachy, you need this more than you can possibly know."

"In a minute," said Peachy, setting the joint back on the table where the clutter included, oddly, some flower seed packets. "I don't want to get too stoned. After all, I gotta get a load of this Window Wizard when she drops acid."

"I've got a tip for you, then. Don't mention your views on Vietnam. Her brother was killed there, and she's not very tolerant of the folks that keep the war going."

Chipper wasn't sure this discussion of the Not-Really-a-War War should exclude him. "A-bombs aside," he said, "don't you think it would be better, like Peachy says, to go in with full force rather than let them pick our guys off like sitting ducks?"

Audora sat up on the edge of the bed, and Smokey Ray eased to her side, letting his hand fall into her lap. Chipper noticed that her long legs spread just a twitch to invite Smokey's hand to nestle.

"Chipper, don't tell me you really think we're over there fighting Communism?"

"Well—" Chipper had been raised in right field, just shy of the foul line where John Birch sat in the cheap seats. And for the past five years, he had convinced himself that this was a holy war. After all, Brother Jake Chisum, movie star, had been quite explicit publicly about the need to win in Vietnam, and his new movie would explain it all. "I realize you guys are doves, and that's okay and all. I mean after Kennedy is elected, I guess we're gonna be pullin' out anyway."

"Kennedy, schmennedy," said Audora, "he's just another establishment puppet who'll say anything to get elected. The only way to get out of Vietnam is if McCarthy wins. You know McCarthy got 31% this week in the Nebraska primary, compared to Kennedy's 52%. And that's

Nebraska, for gosh sakes. We're hot on Kennedy's tail. We've just *got* to get McCarthy in the White House."

Chipper was stupefied. McCarthy was a card-carrying Communist, and he ought to be shot as a traitor. At least that's what his hawk-world taught. "Maybe we just shouldn't discuss it. You guys go on bein' doves, and Peachy and I, we'll—"

"I'm not a dove," said Smokey Ray, strangely silent while his girl-friend had taken the podium.

"What?" said Chipper, puzzled.

"I'm not a dove," he repeated. "A dove is a pacifist. I'm no pacifist. I'm against this particular war is all. Something's wrong when we grow numb to nightly body counts on the news and our fearless leaders tell us we're not at war—that it's just a 'conflict.' This past week had the highest toll yet, 562 dead. The grand total is almost *twenty-three thousand* now, and those goddam liars tell us it's a *conflict* because we haven't *declared* war. Gimmee a friggin' break. I'm no dove, Chipper. I'm a scissortail."

Chipper and Peachy exchanged mystified looks.

"The Scissortail is a beautiful bird that loves its territory," continued Smokey Ray. "Never the aggressor, it lives and does its flycatcher thing within its boundary. But heaven help the dove or the hawk that tries to horn in on its territory. It will attack any bird of any size that crosses the line."

Chipper nodded to reflect some small measure of understanding. He had never crossed or challenged Smokey Ray, and he didn't intend to start now. The "domino theory" popped into his mind in defense of the nonwar, but somehow the scissortail concept had a ring to it. Nervously, he felt himself fiddling with the flower seed packets on the table that were mixed with odd-shaped brass hash pipes, baggies full of grass, a package of Zig-Zag cigarette papers, and a peculiar cigarette-rolling device.

"What are these for?" asked Chipper, latching onto one of the flower seed packets.

"They're my present to you both," said Audora. "I picked them up at TG&Y on my way over. They're morning glory seeds."

"Let me guess," Peachy said. "You'd like us to plant a garden right here in this avocado green shag carpet."

"In a manner of speaking, yes," she said, with a strange coolness. "They're not just any morning glory seeds . . . they're Heavenly Blues."

"And?" said Peachy.

"And—while we're waiting for the Window Wizard to get here, I thought you guys might like to get a little buzz going first."

"Are you saying you can get high on morning glory seeds?" asked Chipper, a veteran of the great Banana Skin Fraud of '66 where, in spite of Donovan's cryptic prophecy of electrical banana as "a sudden craze . . . the very next phase," there was zero banana buzz from the peels, and mellow yellow turned out to be tutti-frutti. He and Peachy, in their naive younger years, had researched saffron as well with no luck, but were completely stumped in their quest for "fontine," until they learned that Donovan's word was actually "fourteen."

"Yes, but only with a few types of morning glories. Heavenly Blues are the next best thing to the original Mexican variety. I bought you both three packs apiece."

Chipper and Peachy fought the seductive spell of Audora who explained the experience as a mild rush while she licked her full lips and crossed her long legs so many times that Chipper thought he might need the Heavenly Blues simply as a bromide to secure his allegiance to Amy.

Before he understood what had happened, or why their naive younger years had suddenly returned, he and Peachy opened the packages, crushed the seeds with the back of Audora's silver compact case (following her instruction), then each placed his portion in a Holiday Inn glass filled with water to allow the elixir to brew for 30 minutes before swallowing. *How could it be bad if it came from TG&Y?*

"After Wendy gets here—that's the Window Wizard's real name—we're joining some other protest organizers tomorrow from Madison as we plan some antiwar strategies on our way to the folk-rock festival in Santa Clara," Audora said. "Smokey Ray says when he was at Monterey last summer, they dropped a hundred thousand orchids out of an airplane onto the crowd."

Smokey Ray took his turn: "A lot of the same people will be in Santa Clara that I heard last summer. It was mind-blowing. The Doors, Animals, Big Brother, Youngbloods, Jefferson Airplane, Taj Mahal, Electric Flag, Country Joe . . ."

"Whoa, whoa, whoa. You lost me there," said Peachy. "I was with you all the way up to Taj Mahal. Who the heck is Country Joe?"

Smokey Ray replied, "Peachy, I'm surprised you don't know. Now Chipper here, a guy who's glued to the radio listening to Bobby Goldsboro sing 'Honey'—well, I ain't expectin' him to know, but *you?*"

"Never heard of him," insisted Peachy.

"That's probably because his music is banned on Oklahoma radio. Most folks here aren't too hip to hear the 'I-Feel-Like-I'm-Fixin'-to-Die-Rag.' "

"'Be the first one on your block to come home in a wooden box,'" sang Audora, giggling as she struggled to carry a tune.

Chipper began to feel like he and Peachy were being left out of a huge joke.

Smokey Ray spoke about the songs of unknown musicians, like Tom Paxton's "Lyndon Johnson Told a Nation," and Phil Ochs' "I Ain't Marching Anymore," and Jimmy Cliff's "Vietnam," and Chipper thought that Smokey talked with so much passion that he didn't really belong in Oklahoma, that perhaps he should just go to Santa Clara or Monterey or Berkeley or Madison wherever, and just stay there, where he would be among his own. Audora, too.

Audora looked at her watch. "It's time." She hopped from the edge of the bed and skipped, literally, to the glasses of Heavenly Blue where she swirled the water, then stuck her nose to each edge and whiffed. "Your Kool-Aid is ready, boys."

Peachy chugged quickly, but he still gagged as the dark and bloated seeds at the bottom of the glass trailed into his throat. *What the heck,* thought Chipper, whereupon he did the same, with the seeds feeling like mutant oatmeal as the clumps crawled down the back of his tongue.

Smokey Ray rolled another joint and turned up the radio so that he could hear "White Rabbit" by Jefferson Airplane. Audora clasped her hands in her lap with a look of smug satisfaction that left Chipper feeling tingly. *Or was it the seeds?*

Peachy suddenly ran to the bathroom and puked, his stomach now scoured and scrubbed, purged of Heavenly Blues.

And Chipper, sensing no nausea whatsoever, began to feel terribly alone.

C.C. Chastain was wrong. "White Rabbit" was backed throughout by rudimentary drumming in a military cadence. No rock rhythm whatsoever!

34

Audora scooted Chipper's chair to face the edge of the bed where she sat, elbows on thighs, knees apart, allowing his knees to touch the draping hem of her dress. As she spoke, her wrists flopped, and her fingertips danced back and forth from her knees to his:

"No one is exactly sure, Chipper, but Schwaller de Lubicz showed that the Zodiac of Dendera in the Temple of Hathor was actually a time clock used in 100 B.C., measuring the procession of the equinoxes from the Age of Pisces back to the Age of Taurus. Then, by working forward, he estimated the Age of Pisces to begin near 60 B.C. That would make the Age of Aquarius begin around 2100 A.D. Others disagree, but the range is from 1905 to 2160. I believe we're passaging to the Age of Aquarius now. Children of the light all over the world are having the same dreams and visions. *Fish* for the Age of Pisces and *water* for the Age of Aquarius. Fish and water. Same thing over and over—fish and water. Why, just last night I dreamed I was a fish swimming in a giant fishbowl, and all of us sad, gray fishies knew something wonderful was about to happen. Suddenly, the glass broke and the water carried us to a river, then down a beautiful waterfall, and when we landed in the lake below, all of us turned golden, only now we were angels. Radiant angels. Bathing in the water, replenished by the mist from the waterfall, the shining sun filtered into rainbowed colors."

Chipper felt his heart racing as he remembered his own vision (more or less) of the fishbowl just weeks ago in the TV room at the Sig house, where a different world was knocking on the television screen in response to the King assassination. Audora was starting to scare him with her crazy talk, but the thought of that foreign image in the TV room made him look deeply into her dark eyes where he could see his own reflection. This was not the Audora he had known for the past school year. This was not the Audora of Highland Park. This was a siren casting a spell.

"I think that astrology stuff is a crock of bullshit," Chipper heard Peachy say, ever so faintly, as if he were in another room, talking through plaster walls.

From the corner of his eye, Chipper could see Smokey Ray pushing the final thumbtack into a poster on the opposing wall. As Smokey stepped away, Chipper moved his eyes from Audora to look at the poster's design. A large orange sun rested in the middle with radiating spokes against a purple background. A thin white rim framed the rectangle.

Smokey Ray joined Audora on the bed, facing Chipper. "You know, cowboy, I told you once I was seeking enlightenment," said the Smoke. "Well, I believe I've found it. One thing for sure, you don't go searching for light with a candle in your hand. The wayfarer must extinguish the candle first, in order to discover light where there is no sun. Remember, too, that there is no light without shadows, so on your journey you must explore whether you are standing in the shadows, or if you're casting the shadows."

Chipper was at the point of full-fledged heebie-jeebies as to why Smokey Ray and Audora were teaming up on him. *Why aren't they talking to Peachy? Aren't we all here tonight to watch the Window Wizard?*

Jets of water spurted into the sides of Chipper's mouth, and he felt himself starting to sink into the chair. The free fall into dreary beige vinyl was so fast and so powerful that he grabbed the wooden arms for support. But he was puzzled why he was still even-eyed with Audora. After all, he was falling, falling, falling, and the pit seemed bottomless. He was plummeting to his death. He would be crushed on impact. Sweat began to flood his face. Spittle oozed from the corners of his mouth like a toilet overflowing. And in the distance . . . a strange mix of bells and sirens and whirling wind.

Audora put both palms onto his knees, her fingers drumming on his thighs. "You see, Chipper, you must die first. You must experience total and complete darkness before you can see the light."

At the sound of the word "die," Chipper felt fingers of a ghostly hand around his throat as a hideous realization dawned on him. *Audora and Smokey Ray were evil missionaries from the drug world!* He'd known it all along, and now they were recruiting him into their sordid lot, hoping to whisk him away to a never-never land.

"Peachy! Get me out of here!" he heard a voice say. Perhaps the voice was his.

Audora moved her face so close to his that Chipper could only focus on one eye, so close that he could see her eye wasn't really black, so close that the iris displayed multicolored striations radiating from his own image in the pupil. "Goodnight, sweet prince," he heard Audora say as she kissed one of his eyelids, then the other. "You may come down, but you'll *never* be the same," came her chilling words as he opened his eyes again to see one large eye staring back.

"Peachy! Get me out of here!" said the stranger's voice again.

The large eye blinked slowly, the radiations in the iris now orange and purple. Then the eyelid was gone, leaving only the globe. Audora was gone. So was Smokey Ray. The room was black, but the large orange eye was glowing. No, it wasn't an eye—it was a sun. Then he saw that the sun had a cartoon face—eyes, nose, and mouth—and it was talking to him. More accurately, it was struggling to talk to him in primitive animation, as if this embryonic sun was formulating its very first words. The bells and sirens and whistling wind were getting stronger.

The fear seemed to be melting. The falling had stopped. How strange. The funny sun with its grimacing mouth began to ooze garbled words, sounding as though a 45rpm record were being played at 33. The unintelligible words almost made Chipper laugh. Indeed, he heard laughter, and since he was alone, he figured it was his.

Then Chipper saw the sun as part of a poster, and the four white corners were starting to peel away from the wall. The white points of the frame bunched into four tiny fists with rhythmic pounding of the fingers as if they were miniature pistons. But a sticky glue held the four corner-hands against the wall. The corners would try to pull their way forward toward Chipper, one at a time, as if intending to grab him, but then they would snap back against the wall. Finally, Chipper understood why the cartoon mouth of the sun was growling—it was struggling to get free from the wall!

The fists developed wrists, and with each pull away from the wall, the white hands came closer and closer to Chipper. The dripping goo that held the poster to the wall touched the floor as the hands reached across the room. Bells, sirens, whistles were so loud now that Chipper felt his eardrums vibrating, shattering. Then, with its comic book eyes furrowing into evil slits, the sun's mangled words through the animated mouth became crystal clear: "I've been waiting for you. I am the Great and Powerful Sand-Oz." And when Chipper felt the white hands in a stranglehold on his neck, plucking him out of his chair, it was over.

Perfect silence. Standing on the vast orange beach, Chipper was struck by the mystic calm of the purple ocean where gentle swells of water seemed choco-

late-thick, unable to muster a wave. The sea was barely distinguishable from the sky, also purple, with a bright orange sun punching a hole in this mono-chromatic vista. When Chipper turned around, he saw a white, rectangular frame flapping its gull-wings in the distance, the poster that he'd just passed through, getting smaller and smaller, until the white dot disappeared.

> *"Thrown like a star in my vast sleep*
> *I open my eyes to take a peep*
> *To find that I was by the sea*
> *Gazing with tranquility."*

Chipper heard the music and turned to find the source. Twenty yards away, stuck in the sand, a hand organ was being cranked by a crimson monkey with a cream-colored face. But no one was singing the words, which seemed to be coming out of the wooden music box:

> *"'Twas then when the Hurdy-Gurdy Man*
> *Came singing songs of love."*

Chipper dragged his leaden feet through the orange granules that possessed a rich mint aroma stirred by the plumes of sand he created. The monkey appeared robotic as it cranked, and as Chipper drew close, he saw that the animal was every bit as mechanical as the hand organ. The wooden music box was decorated in each of its squares with mother-of-pearl fish, arched so that the four fish on each side seemed to be dancing on their back fins. Then, Chipper realized he had been watching them dance for hours. No, days. No . . . years.

The monkey disappeared, yet the hurdy-gurdy still stood, a wooden knob at the end of its crank looking strangely familiar. He stepped forward and grabbed the knob to make sure the music continued.

In a blink of an eye, it was over, and Chipper found himself in the comfort of his own car, passenger side.

"Keep your hands off the friggin' gearshift knob. I've told you 10 times now. Sit back and let me drive."

Why is Peachy driving? "What's going on?" managed Chipper.

"I've told you about 10 goddam times now. Will you listen? Smokey Ray and Audora gave you some bad shit. We're driving to the city to get some Thorazine. Smokey Ray says that's the antidote."

"Oh, I remember now. It was those seeds, wasn't it? Damn, Peachy, you wouldn't believe this place I went. Purple sky, purple sea, a hurdy-gurdy played by a monkey, then all these fish that—" Chipper felt his heart race with excitement.

"Listen, asshole, I'm gonna tell you once more. You've already told me this story."

"I have?"

"Yessss."

"And did I sing the song? Did I tell you the words?"

"Yessss," said Peachy, exasperated. "Remember me telling you that it was Donovan's new song, and you claimed you'd never heard it, and I said 'bullshit' because you were giving me the words verbatim."

"Oh. Well. Gawd, it's hot in here. Turn on the air-conditioner. Wait a minute. I remember now. I already said that. I remember turning on the air-conditioner, then my mouth gets so dry I can't . . . I can't . . . there it is again. I can't even talk my mouth is so dry."

The realization was grotesque and horrifying—Chipper was trapped in a repeating cycle from which he would never emerge. He was brain-damaged now, permanently. The cycle was fixed forever. He couldn't stop himself: "Gawd it's cold in here. Turn on the heater, Peachy. Oh crap, there goes that saliva again, I'm drooling all over the place."

Thoughts raced as if his mind were thumbing through pages fast enough to create a breeze. His reputation was ruined. His Outstanding Pledge pin would be ripped from Amy's chest and sent back to national headquarters where they would mount it on a Plaque of Shame, hoisted for all Sig Zetas to see—a forever reminder of the evils of sin. The worst Sig Zeta to ever wear the gold cross. Amy would toss him in the dumpster. Who would want a brain-damaged nincompoop for a pinmate? Or a husband? The fraternity was history. No more friends. No girlfriend. *Gawd it's hot.* "I can't even talk my mouth is so dry." *Gawd, how'd it get so cold?* "Jiminy, I'm drooling all over the place." Ruin. Disgrace. No chance at med school. No chance at any school. His life was ruined.

Chipper felt a firecracker explode in his head, surely atomizing millions of brain cells, and it was over. Finally. Peace. Total, wonderful peace.

"Gosh, I can't believe it, Peachy. That was awful. At the very end there, my thoughts were flickering so fast, going lickety-split. But it's over now. Thank goodness. Something popped in my head, a real loud sound, and now I feel fine. Normal. It's just the right temperature." He licked his lips to make sure the moisture was even. He wiped his brow . . . no sweat. He let his head fall back on the leather seat to rest. "Won't be needing any Thorazine after all."

"Uh-huh."

His relief was overwhelming, exhilarating, and after a few quiet minutes, Chipper heard music from the radio: *Histories of ages past*

... unenlightened shadows cast ... down through all eternity ... the crying of humanity. "There! There! That's the song I was telling you about, Peachy. On the radio. That's the song I heard while I was in that other world."

"The radio ... is *not on*, Chipper. I've been trying to tell you."

"What?!" The panic struck again. "Stop the car, dammit Peachy. Something is really wrong here. I mean really, *really* wrong." Chipper reached for the wooden knob of the gear shift, intending to throw the car into park even though they were traveling at full speed.

"Keep your hands off the friggin' gearshift knob. I've told you 10 times now. Sit back and let me drive."

Why is Peachy driving? "What's going on?" managed Chipper.

"I've told you and told you and told you. Will you listen, dammit? Smokey Ray and Audora gave you some bad shit. Goin' to the city to get some Thorazine, remember? Smokey Ray says that's the antidote."

"Oh, I remember now. It was those seeds, wasn't it? Damn, Peachy, you wouldn't believe this place I went. Purple sky, purple sea, a hurdy-gurdy played by a monkey, then all these fish that—" Chipper felt his heart race with excitement.

"Listen to me, asshole. You've already told me this story."

"I have?"

"Yessss."

"And did I sing the song? Did I tell you the words?"

"Yessss. Why can't you remember me telling you that it was Donovan's new song? And then you claim you've never heard it—about 10 friggin' times—and I say 'bullshit' because you're giving me the words verbatim."

"Oh. Well. Gawd, it's hot in here. Turn on the air-conditioner. Wait a minute. I remember now. I already said that. I remember turning on the air-conditioner, then my mouth gets so dry I can't ... I can't ... there it is again. I can't even talk my mouth is so dry."

35

Amy buried her head in her hands and told Chipper she never wanted to hear the story again. Then she buried herself in summer school, in her golf game, and in her precious jukeboxes that needed constant replenishing with new 45s.

* * *

Privately, Chipper couldn't shake the other world. It had been every bit as real as the fairways on his hometown El Viento golf course. His preoccupation was damning because his parents suggested he drop his plans for summer school and spend the summer doing penance in hard labor.

The night of horrors had ended with Chipper's parents discovering all. The emergency rooms in the city had been jammed, so Peachy had driven Chipper to El Viento where none other than Chipper's physician-father delivered the antidotal Thorazine. The horrifying circle for Chipper ended after 12 hours, though consequences of the night promised to reverberate as he could hear Audora's words still ringing in his ears: "You may come down, but you'll *never* be the same."

* * *

Peachy was forlorn. The rules of mind-alteration were well-established—alcohol openly encouraged and approved by all; marijuana privately okay, not approved by all (and overrated); hard drugs a no-no in any setting. Smokey Ray had always been the embodiment of "cool." But the events at the Holiday Inn had blurred the picture. Heavenly Blues didn't necessarily mean that Smokey Ray was a bad person. After all, unpredictability and adventure had always been part of Smokey's aura, but somehow the ambush on Chipper (if indeed it had been an ambush), *and himself,* for that matter, had given the mystery a dark undercurrent. In order to convince himself that Smokey was still the same old Ray Divine, Peachy spent long hours refreshing his memory of each and every daunting Smokey Ray victory over the years—most importantly, the annihilation of Black Jack DeLaughter.

But when he would join Chipper to talk about the awful night, perhaps fueling each other in their recounting, they decided that they would never have to deal with Smokey Ray or Audora again. Not after the twosome had exposed themselves as full-fledged, psychedelic, acid-popping hippies. And had there ever *been* a Window Wizard? Or was the whole nightmare staged as a way to snare Peachy and Chipper into their drug-infested world? When all the excuses in support of Smokey Ray and Audora had been exhausted, Peachy and Chipper decided that the two hippies were no longer the people they used to know, and it would be best if the two acid-heads just stayed in California. Surely, they wouldn't dare show their faces next fall.

* * *

Concern over their altered son prompted Chipper's parents to figure that they'd somehow failed in his upbringing. Somehow, they'd left out *something*. Or perhaps it had been the leisure and privilege that they had permitted to pathetic extreme. After all, man was not created to spend his life on the golf course. Chipper had weaseled out of every character-building opportunity at manual labor since he was old enough to carry his own clubs. The golf course had stolen him away from productivity, from enrichment, and from appreciation for right and wrong (this latter deficiency augmented in part by Chipper's life-long friendship with Peachy Waterman Jr.).

It was this conclusive reasoning that led Dr. DeHart to call in favors from the town folk in securing Chipper's venue for the summer, a job that would allow his son to get a little better grip on old terra firma. This was a job that, in the words of Chipper's mother, would take Chipper "back to the land," a job that would allow him to scoop the soil with his hands, letting the dirt sift to the ground, forcing her wayward son to stare heavenward, shake his fist, and proclaim, "As God is my witness, I'll never go seed-popping again."

* * *

In the same abrupt fashion that the white-framed poster had yanked him into Otherworld, Chipper landed butt-first on the second story seat of a monster combine, facing a summer wheat harvest. (He had been too embarrassed to admit to the fact that he barely knew how to drive a standard shift. The T-bird *looked* like a standard, but was actually a 'cutting edge' console automatic.)

Not only did the combine have a standard transmission, but also the same clutch worked forward motion *and* the gizmo that emptied the grain from the combine's bin. And then, there was that tiny lever that raised and lowered the cutter bar. Chipper didn't bother to learn any of the names of these controls. He focused only on the avoidance of fooldom as he joined Farmer Stone and one son in mowing the world's largest lawns. Farmer Stone had four machines (for him and his three sons), but two of the sons were down and out with a rare summer flu. This unfortunate mini-epidemic brought Chipper to the iron seat he now occupied, along with a dim-witted fellow in combine #4 named Horace who, after 27 years on the farm, had finally been promoted from the wheat truck—manned by women and children—to the combine.

As he looked over the sea of shimmering gold wheat, with grain heads bent as if to slurp one last drink before execution, he wondered how many more times he was going to be jerked to strange worlds.

Shouldn't I have had more than five minutes of instruction? Especially since I still lurch out of first gear in Peachy's Vette?

On Day One, Chipper drove too fast into a luxuriant growth of wheat, clogging the entire combine mechanism, forcing Farmer Stone to become Plumber Stone who then shouted fanciful cuss words as he cleaned out the bowels of the combine. From this rich array of cursing, Chipper's ears were assaulted by a recurring thematic phrase—"damn city boy."

On Day Two, Chipper inadvertently wandered into a patch of barley ("Golly, it looks pretty much the same"), mixing the grains and prompting Farmer Stone to reprise many of the choice expletives he had plucked from his repertoire the day before.

On Day Three, Chipper emptied his grain into the wheat truck, but forgot to disengage the grain tank auger before driving back to the field. As a result, the piddly little nothin' amount of grain that was left in the bottom of the bin continued to empty onto the cab of the truck, then trailed Chipper's fabulous combine, pouring onto the ground in a long golden streak. The bone-chilling screams of *Mrs.* Farmer Stone drew Chipper's attention to this minor faux pas, and when Chipper turned over his shoulder (speeding in third gear) he could see the women near the truck on their knees, scooping the precious grain from the earth with their bare hands, wailing. Mrs. Farmer Stone held one clenched fist in the air toward Chipper as if to say, "As God is my witness, I'll never hire a *city boy* again."

On Day Four, Chipper mastered the art of combine cruising. With deft manipulation of the cutter bar, he no longer allowed the blade to plow the ground—instead, Chipper adjusted the bar to guillotine the grain heads just like a pro. He could make the fine color distinction between barley and hard red winter wheat. He knew when to down-shift through thick growth. He knew when to speed through the thin sections to maximize cutting time since the setting sun was an enemy when one considered the next day could always bring rain delays.

In fact, the ho-hum harvest was so automatic that he could drift into reverie as he drove. And as the hours passed, he began to dwell on a pervasive force, an altering mood, a shifting climate, summarized by the song that said, "Everybody's talkin' 'bout a new way a-walkin'." Along with the plumes of dust and wheat chaff, he was getting a whiff of a new way to interpret events in the world. Politics were being reborn on college campuses and, without explanation, this revolutionary view was linked to brain chemistry and the potential manipulations therein.

Otherworld lost a little of its power daily, less and less like a true beach, more and more like a vivid dream. But it made Chipper wonder about the porous borders between what he knew to be true and what might really be true. And nothing was starting to bother him more than the scuttlebutt surrounding Southeast Asia.

As the Vietnam controversy crept like jungle rot into his mind, he wondered if Brother Jake Chisum was in the right, trying to pull the country together by filming a super-hawk movie. Where were the great patriotic victories? How did they even define a victory? Buster Nelson had been his first close friend to die. Who was next?

His own thin skin wanted no part of jungle rot, but he kept his anti-American thoughts to himself. And he thought about the poster. Not the orange sun poster, but the poster back at the Sig Zeta house, showing the former chapter President shaking hands at a podium with Robert Kennedy, the current shoo-in for the Democratic nomination and, likely, the real presidency. Perhaps the poster had been an omen for him—a message to open his mind to the liberal nonsense of King Kennedy. Perhaps RFK was the pathway out of Vietnam, returning the country to harmony. But heaven forbid he should openly endorse Kennedy, and deny Brother Jake Chisum.

On the last square of virgin wheat, Farmer Stone and his son peeled off to let Chipper and Horace finish. Just as he and his best friend Jay had done years ago mowing lawns, the two remaining combines cut concentric squares in an ever-shrinking dance.

Several ways occurred to Chipper to avoid hand-to-hand combat in Vietnam. The most practical approach would be a medical school deferment, but his lukewarm passion for medicine was still a puzzle for him. He loved science, but yanking tonsils from the back of a throat? Or carving an appendix?

And what if the war dragged on? The only sure way to avoid hand-to-hand combat was to sign up for the Berry Plan where doctors could enter the military as doctors. That way, he could finish med school and residency, the drawback there being a first-class ticket to Vietnam (though as a medical officer in hand-to-bloody-body combat).

But what if Robert Kennedy did indeed snag the presidency? The war would scale down, and pretty soon it would fizzle. Would that occur before, *or after*, he was already waist-deep in the Berry Plan? Would there even be a point in going to medical school if the war ended? After all, wife Amy could earn the big salary while he wrote great novels. These thoughts so enveloped him that he felt like he was part of the golden sea of wheat rippling with the gentle breeze. The drone and roar of the combine mimicked the surf, while Chipper worried that his evolving politics were, in fact, the politics of cowards.

The hideous clash of metal on Day Four short-circuited his musings. The collision knocked him from his iron seat onto the driving platform as the combine spun to a stop. From his knees, he saw another combine just a few feet away, both monster machines with stiff-armed augers now hanging limp, swinging in silence, nearly amputated by the crash of titans when these outstretched limbs jousted on the final strip of wheat.

Amazingly, Chipper was saved from certain death by Horace who absorbed the full force of Farmer Stone: "Horace, you f___ing imbecile. God d__n your hide. You've been on a farm your whole god d__n life and you pull a f___ing stunt like that. D__n your hide. I'd expect something like this out of the god d__n f___ing city boy standing there with his citified thumb up his city boy butt. But you? You sonuvaf___ing bitch, you'll be paying for this for the rest of your f___ing life. We've got a s__tload of wheat to get cut, maybe 50 bushels an acre this year, and you leave me with two god d__n f___ing machines? I'll tear your god d__n hide a new one, I will."

Chipper was much obliged to Horace for serving as the magnet for Famer Stone's steely barbs, though it was hard to determine exactly which one of the two imbeciles was at the lowest point in the shitpile. Chipper was given a farmer's pink slip ("Get your f___ing ass off my property and go back to your god d___n country club."), so his parents came to believe that perhaps Chipper should, indeed, return to summer school. He promptly enrolled in Philosophy 202 — Comparative Theology. Girlfriend Amy was already deep into Comparative Anatomy.

On June 5, in the Ambassador Hotel in Los Angeles, Sirhan Sirhan assassinated Robert F. Kennedy.

* * *

Two weeks later, Chipper watched TV film footage of antiwar demonstrators picketing the Warner Theater in New York City during the world premiere of Brother Jake Chisum's gung-ho, win-at-all-costs war movie, "Silver Wings upon Their Chest." One demonstrator's sign read, "Yo, Chisum, we don't want your fucking war."

Sophomore Year (1968–69)

36

As the Actives began migrating back into the chapter house during Work Week, Chipper noticed creeping, crawling changes from last spring—ears were disappearing beneath unruly hair, cheeks were shrinking under sideburned growth, and eyes were hiding behind wire-rimmed glasses. But the new look was mostly clean and groomed, not the radical leap from Beatle mop to Sgt. Pepper's that was infiltrating the non-Greek campus and, for that matter, campuses nationwide.

Initiation numbers dealt rank to otherwise disorderly greed, and room assignments were made accordingly. Outstanding pledge #1401 didn't mean squat when 52 juniors and seniors had lower numbers than Chipper, but he managed to corral the top three-man room for himself, Peachy, and Drywall.

The "best" number in the house was, of course, super-duper senior Ty Wheeler, now in his seventh or eighth year of Orbison-inspired education, lodged in Senior Hall, where a row of one-man rooms lined the old wing built in '29 as the original chapter house.

And, as Chipper expected, shaman Smokey Ray Divine had the prudence to remain discreetly absent, maybe lost, never to show his face at the Sig Zeta house again.

In spite of the forecasted thrill of melding within the walls of brotherhood, Chipper felt a peculiar emptiness. Somehow the bonds did not completely moor him as he had anticipated. Perhaps it had been his brief and abrupt departure to another world last spring.

On the afternoon before the start of Rush Week, while the sophomores joined in drink and raucous song with upperclassmen—once tormentors, now mentors—at Grady's Pub, Chipper slipped out a back-door to Rickhoff's bookstore across the alley where he browsed for an hour before buying *Man's Search for Meaning* by Frankl, *Irrational Man* by Barrett, and *Great Religions of the World* by a great many authors.

* * *

Rush was a great success, with 41 signees. However, the week was marred by a different sort of draft—fifth-year senior Terry Hardemann who had gambled on last spring's marginal GPA would now be strolling waist-deep through rice paddies holding an M-16 rifle over his head.

Chipper found it disturbing that a college kid could be walking along a path, then suddenly drop into a pit where bamboo spikes laced with human excrement could inoculate gangrene and turn knees into knobs.

But the drafting of Terry Hardemann had local implications as well—a rare vacancy in a one-man room.

And with a sixth sense for opportunity it seemed, Smokey Ray Divine showed up one full week after classes started, absorbing the 50-dollar fine for missing Rush Week and stumbling into the vacancy. Private First Class Hardemann's quarters thus became Smokey Ray's crash pad.

Smokey Ray was not easily recognizable. The cowboy hat with the rattlesnake band was gone, and his flat yellow hair touched his shoulders, roped to his forehead with a beaded headband. A full beard, muddy brown, fanned out from his mouth like crabgrass, and his glasses were not just standard issue wire-rims, they were octagonal and filled with pink lenses. Wearing some sort of white pajama top, with a divot out of the neck, Smokey Ray looked to be sporting—a necklace! A row of tiny white shells circled his neck.

"Hey, cowboy, good to see you," Smokey Ray said to a stupefied Chipper.

"I—I didn't really think you'd come back here," managed Chipper, bordering on speechless.

"What?! Why not?" Smokey Ray looked puzzled as he slipped Chipper "the grip."

"Well, do you happen to recall a little incident at the Holiday Inn last year?" Chipper was trying his best to stay calm, but he punctuated each word as it left his mouth like a string of pop beads breaking away one by one.

"Sure, but what does that have to do with my not coming back?"

"Smokey Ray, I didn't do so well with that stuff. Are you aware that those seeds contain a form of LSD? That they soak 'em in a poison that makes you throw up so idiots like me can't eat 'em?"

"Hey, c'mon man, you're not gonna lay that gig on me are you? I didn't see anyone twisting your arm. Heavenly Blues are child's play, Chipper. They're sort of a starter kit. If you didn't like it—don't do it anymore. I don't make anyone do anything they don't want to do. I told you once that I'm a fog-lifter. Sometimes you need a friend like me to take you to the edge of a cliff to get away from the fog. Then, it's your decision. Either enjoy the view from the cliff, or jump off and see if you can fly. Besides, Audora *real-ly* wanted you to turn on."

Chipper started to launch into his own version of the events surrounding psycho night, but it was obvious that Smokey Ray had a completely different perspective. No deceit. No misrepresentation on his part, nor Audora's. And no recruitment into the dark underbelly of campus life in a drug-infested world full of SDS radicals high on LSD getting ready to sell short the USA to the Commie USSR by destroying everything wonderful and good and bright about Our Country 'Tis of Thee. Nope. For Smokey Ray, it was just another day. And last spring was just another exercise in fog-lifting.

Before Chipper could open his mouth to offer pitiful protest, Smokey Ray walked deeper into the heart of the Sig Zeta house, carrying his clothes in one hand, books in another, and a sneaky grin on his face. "Where's that shithead, Peachy Waterman?" yelled Smokey Ray. "I never thought I'd ever miss that old douche bag."

Chipper's feet were stuck to the floor. He couldn't believe that Smokey Ray actually had the nerve to come back. He turned slowly and stared for a moment at the lighted portrait of Brother Jake Chisum hanging by the entrance, where the hero sported a wry grin that seemed to say, "I ain't dead yet, pilgrim."

* * *

Wickiup Enterprises International, with world headquarters located in Room 17 of the Sig Zeta house at 558 University Boulevard, enjoyed such success with its first product launch—hair dryers for men—that copresidents Peachy and Drywall were able to paint the old bootlegging truck blood red, emblazoned on both sides with the Wickiup logo (a wigwam with a golden cross in the doorway), and to stockpile a daunting supply of working capital.

The hair dryers enjoyed staggering market penetration, with 83% saturation at the Sig Zeta house, 61% at the other fraternities on campus, and 12% of the independents and pledges in the dorms. All told, 1,692 heads would be dried with greater efficiency at a 12-dollar profit per macho machine. After expenses, Wickiup was sitting pretty, so Peachy and Drywall laid out a strategy to blanket all the colleges in the state and the Big Eight, focusing on Greeks where there was a clear premium on the dry look.

Spotting a sidekick to hair dryers for men, Peachy zeroed in on hair spray for men as well, another example of a woman's product repackaged for the illusion of difference. Crates of the stuff were ordered for the second run to Mexico. "What a racket," said President Peachy, "I oughta stick pretty boy Mitch Addison's face on a box of Tampax and market the suckers as albino cigars."

On calculations derived from shipping capacity and their Mexican distributor's stockpile, it appeared that the two Wickiup founders would be making every-other-weekend runs south of the border. And during these long excursions, it would be inevitable that the two chief executives would drift into discussions concerning additional product lines. After all, one of the basic tenets of capitalism was the fact that finite growth forced infinite imagination.

*　*　*

C.C. Chastain, runner-up as Outstanding Pledge, had been boasting that his closest friend from high school would be the next knock-'em-dead rushee. Potential pledge John Tatum had skipped Rush Week to serve as a Presidential Scholar at the White House during the summer. C.C. maintained that Tatum had a 4.0 GPA, was All-Conference quarterback, All-City (Tulsa) in basketball, and All-State shortstop. What's more, Tatum was a pre-med face man with a National Merit Scholarship.

The buzz began weeks before the anticipated dinner where C.C. would introduce Tatum to the Sigs. And what began as "Sounds like a great guy," grew with the passing days until it seemed that the very viability of Sigma Zeta Chi hinged on whether or not John Tatum pledged. Rumor held that he was having dinner at the Beta house every night, that the Delts were fixing him up with coeds every weekend, and that he had, in fact, already pledged Fiji.

But C.C. had an entirely different reason for wanting Tatum to pledge. John Tatum was a bona fide prodigy on lead guitar and had been in C.C. Chastain's high school rock band. C.C. claimed the guy could play professionally anytime he wanted to, so John Tatum was a *must* for the house band—the Rickel Four (hopefully . . . Five).

The active chapter could almost hear the Tatum guitar licks by the time that rush dinner rolled around.

Chipper, Peachy, and Drywall left Room #17 as a squad, marching downstairs, late for meal. As they rounded the corner, Chipper was struck by an eerie quietude that rarely, if ever, graced the dining room. Ordinarily, the room buzzed like a scene from a prison movie, just before the con jumps to his feet and yells, "I ain't gonna eat this slop anymore!"

Peachy was leading the threesome when he suddenly stopped short and blurted, "Jumpin' Jehosephat! John Tatum is a jigaboo!"

Even Kickapoo Drywall froze in his tracks. Integration had occurred most everywhere a few years back, but never in the known history of any fraternity had a Negro darkened the doorway.

Chipper could barely catch his breath, but when he saw the empty seats at the Chastain/Tatum table, plus the palsied heads at the other tables bobbing in silence to get a good look, he was embarrassed at his own shock and marched toward John Tatum to extend a hand.

Peachy beat him to the punch.

"My name's Peachy Waterman, and this here's my Polack brother, Drywall Twohatchets. My other friend here is Chipper DeHart. Welcome to the Sig Zeta house."

The threesome joined C.C. and John Tatum, halfway filling the table.

"So you're friends with C.C.?" continued Peachy. "Was he just as much of a sawed-off peckerwood in high school as he is now? There ain't nobody in our pledge class what can play tunes like the little hobbit, though. I figure a guy like C.C. is so full o' friggin' music in his head he's got transistors for brains. And speakin' of transistors, did you know that . . ."

Never in Chipper's long friendship with Peachy was he more grateful for his friend's ability to spew vocal garbage than now, when an entire fraternity was held in captive silence, prisoners of change.

". . . and I read the other day that those new beanbag chairs have 120,000 beans in 'em," continued the Peach. "And another thing, if vegetarians just eat vegetables, what do humanitarians eat?" And the lullaby went on and on.

* * *

After C.C. Chastain read John Tatum's chock-full bio at the chapter meeting following rush meal, the room was gripped by a disconcerting realization—John Tatum, a Negro, probably had more talent in his guitar-picking fingers than any 10 men in the room. And this revelation brought forth two reactions: hatred and awe. Hatred flanked one side of the chapter room, while awe flanked the other.

Drywall Twohatchets sat in Awe.

As C.C. Chastain launched his filibuster, issuing a charge to Sig Zeta (specifically this chapter) to lead the country in fraternity integration, Drywall ran his eyes up and down his hairless brown arms, afraid to make eye contact with the opposite side of the room. His full-blooded ass had received a Sig Zeta bid through the cunning subterfuge of the current Social-Chairman-for-Life and copresident of Wickiup Enterprises International. The taunts being thrown at C.C. from the hatred side concerning dark skin could just as easily land on his back, albeit sprinkled with a pinch of amelioration.

Yes, a full-blooded Indian stood taller than poor light-skinned John Tatum whose African ancestors would likely be bug-eyed at John's white mix. This slightly higher stature of the Indian was never more evident than when Goose Driscoll became the first Negro footballer at the university 10 years earlier, prompting a plethora of jokes ending with the same punchline: "Look at that Indian run!"

As the wisecracks and shouted interruptions speared C.C. Chastain, Drywall noticed that the little guy didn't waiver one bit. It was as though he was being smacked in the face with rotten tomatoes every few seconds, undaunted. The supreme idealist. A man who truly understood the full meaning of Sigma Zeta Chi—men possessing different gifts and convictions.

"I'm here to tell you," said the idealistic C.C., "that when John Tatum received the Outstanding Graduate award last year, he got a standing ovation. This wasn't some punk high school. I'm talkin' over a thousand graduating seniors. And you want to know who *didn't* stand up? Who sat there stony faced while the whole crowd was cheering? The black kids. *His own freakin' people* just sat there pissed off at Uncle Tom. Do you assholes understand what courage this man has? What sacrifices he is making by building bridges? How by himself he is, caught between the races?"

Drywall nodded silently.

"Martin Luther King had a dream and they killed him for it. But I'm telling you it's like those broomsticks that Mickey Mouse chopped up in *Fantasia*, for every one they strike down, two will rise in his place—"

"Sit down and shut up, nigger-lover," yelled a former disciple of Black Jack DeLaughter, usually muted by the embarrassment of his former life as Jack's toadie.

C.C. aimed his finger at the ex-toadie. "And I, too, have a dream. I have a dream that blacks—and let me inform everyone here tonight that it's not *nigger,* never has been . . . it's not even *Negro* . . . and it's not *colored* . . . the proper term now is *black*—and in my dream, blacks and whites walk together in harmony, and they do it through music. It's not gonna happen through sports like everyone thinks. You don't smooth over years of hatred by placing men in competition with each other. It's the arts that's gonna do it, specifically music. And John Tatum is just the sort of man to stick on lead guitar and make it happen. I pray and I plead—*do not* blackball this man."

C.C. sat down, ignoring the muttered jokes about John Tatum already having two black balls.

Drywall felt the urge to stand up and second the proposal to pledge Tatum, but why commit social suicide when you walk around with a loose noose around your red neck anyway? It only took one black ball to keep someone out, and C.C. was squawking from another planet if he thought Tatum had a snowball's chance. And as he stayed glued to his seat, Drywall realized he had not been given one iota of credit for building bridges between the races. No, he would stay put.

The vote tally—58 for Tatum, 19 against.

While mind-boggling that 58 members were willing to be the first chapter in the country to break the color barrier, the fact remained that no serious candidate proposed for pledgeship in local history had ever garnered so many black balls.

In the silence after the vote was announced, Drywall sniffed various aromas—a fragrance of relief, essence of fear, even a bewitching perfume of confusion.

Then the stench of hatred filled the room when the toadie shouted once again: "C.C., why don't you take your nigger-lovin' ass, pack your bags, and move in with that new nigger fraternity, Alpha Phi Alpha?"

Before C.C. could answer, Drywall sprung to his full six-foot-two-inch frame and raised both hands with palms outward to imply 'I will speak in peace, but only for the moment.' Then he said: "The next son-of-a-bitch who utters the n-word again is going to wonder why the circle of my hands is so much smaller than his neck, and why his fucking eyeballs dangle from their sockets."

"Amen, brother," yelled Peachy. "That's the way to let those words fly."

* * *

"Good morning. My name is Dot Turco, and I'm pleased to be teaching this inaugural course in Women's Studies. We're getting a late start in the classroom due to my short leave of absence to help the New York Radical Women in their history-making protest of the Miss America Pageant last week in Atlantic City. I hope everyone has finished reading our main study guide for the course, Betty Friedan's *The Feminine Mystique*, the book that led to the formation of the National Organization of Women two years ago."

Amy sat at her desk, cross-legged, bouncing her foot. She was mesmerized by, but leery of, this frizzy-haired woman of 40 or so, lips pale and chapped, forehead wrinkled as if by an additional two decades of worry and anger.

"We are at a crossroads today in the new wave of feminism, and we will explore this critical time in our history with great scrutiny during our time together. Our sisters in the Civil Rights movement and those in the New Left, I'm speaking of the SDS, are all starting to realize the horrible truth—even the enlightened men, allegedly our brothers, so astute in their critique of our society in general, have failed miserably to establish any consciousness whatsoever with regard to women."

As Dot droned on, Amy considered her motives for enrolling in the new course. And her interest was not so much political as personal. She wasn't one to wallow in self-pity, nor hoist a chip onto her shoulder, nor was she easily swayed by mind-bending rhetoric. Amy quite simply had been overwhelmed her entire life by one word as it regarded women—*missing*.

Women were missing. They were missing from science, from government, from business, but of great concern to Amy, they were missing from medicine.

In fact, women were missing everywhere. Chipper had pointed out to her once that there wasn't a single female philosopher of import, but this didn't mean diddly. Amy figured that the wives of the great philosophers were too busy imparting wisdom to their children while their lollygagging husbands smoked cigars, sipped brandy, and pontificated on the obvious to the point of obfuscation. As a matter of fact, Amy sometimes grew weary of Chipper's idle ruminations about "the meaning of it all."

Her view on life was a simple triad: develop given talent, earn a living, and inspire your husband and children to do the same. She considered the raising of children the most critical role, also the most difficult. As for the first two—develop talent and earn a living—a "man's world" caused a blockade. And that's why she was here now, though having second thoughts as she listened to Dot brag about how she crowned a sheep Miss America last week in Atlantic City.

Women had been *missing* in high school (no golf team for girls), and she had been shocked to discover the same at college. Not this year. It was official, and the other Big Eight schools were following suit with women's golf. But Amy's greatest concern was that only 5% of the new medical school class each year were women. Whereas her pre-med friends (all males) were moaning daily about the rigors of becoming one of 140 accepted, Amy knew she would have to be one of seven.

And why were women excluded from such a genteel profession? Would not a great seamstress make a good surgeon? Would not a bright midwife make a good obstetrician? Yet identical talent had been regimented into false difference by "a man's world." Something was missing.

As she sat there—wearing a dress and tinted hose, her black pump dangling from the toe of her bouncing foot, and Chipper's Sig Zeta pin on her chest—she began to scrutinize the other girls in the class. Only a handful were in regulation sorority threads, while the remaining 30 or so wore jeans or slacks with their T-shirts (grubbies), clones of Dot Turco. In fact, it seemed that Dot singled out the sorority girls with her eyes as she spoke, offering an unspoken condemnation of their long, smooth legs.

Amy regretted her choice to sit on the front row. It was a bad habit she'd have to learn to break. Growing up in small town El Viento, the front row allowed her to focus on the teacher rather than class clowns. It appeared, though, in college, the front row placed you dangerously close to the gateway of dogma that you may or may not want to enter.

From the rear of the room, the scraping sound of a wooden chair across the linoleum floor was like fingernails on a blackboard. Amy watched the face of Dot Turco melt, then saw her classmates turn their heads like 30 kittens following a ball of string.

A straggler student plopped into the back row and smiled. A male!

Amy buried her head in hands when she realized it was Monty "Uno" Guilford.

"M. Guilford, I presume," said Professor Turco.

"Yes."

"I have to admit that when I saw the class roster I presumed M. Guilford would be a female. Now see, everyone? See how insidious our sexism can be? How dangerous our suppositions . . ."

Amy couldn't believe it—at first. Then she anticipated the scam. After class, Guilford would stand by his Porsche like a spider in its web, waiting to snare coeds as they streamed from the building. And what greater conquest could there be than a "liberated" woman?

No—she was being too harsh. She would not let herself be swayed by Peachy's nonstop diatribe against Uno. No one is as foul as the Peach maintained.

* * *

"I told you before, I ain't doin' this again," said Peachy, his nagging wasted on Drywall's plugged ears. "I ain't sittin' in this back row like two homos. This is the last time for a friggin' ballet, you understand? I'm going to write Cassie's number on the backside of our door at the house, so's that every time you walk out the room you remember what a yellowbellied, lily-livered chickenshit you are. Are you hearin' me? Drywall? Knock, knock. Anyone home? Drywall?"

* * *

Audora lived in the one-story, white adobe apartments across the street from the Sig Zeta house. And, of course, she also lived in Smokey Ray's private room, though slippage through the outside window was a maneuver of the night, due to a silly punishable-by-death rule imposed by hopelessly square alums stating "no girls in the rooms—ever." This placed the one-man, ground floor rooms at a premium, given the easy expansion into one-man-one-woman. And the oddity of sophomore Smokey Ray landing such a room did not escape notice, though no one complained.

Amy was disappointed in Audora. A girl who began college as an amusing, renegade-debutante seemed to be taking an inexorable march toward hippiedom in the truest sense of the word. And it wasn't so much the "turn on" or even the "tune in." It was the "drop out." Audora had been clever and charming just one short year ago, her sterling silver exterior forming a thin plate over a heart of gold. But now she was secretive, sly, and she made her old friends feel backward with her smug condescension of their "bourgeois middle-class American values" while extolling the virtues of the counterculture. Amy quietly held Smokey Ray responsible for the decline. Audora was the only sophomore who didn't move into the Beta Chi house with her pledge sisters. Indeed, the old Audora was missing.

Chipper was too consumed with his personal scrutiny of Smokey Ray and Audora to worry about the self-destructive potential of the duo. Smokey Ray continued to dazzle the Sigma Zs in chapter meetings with his "baffling bullshit." In spite of a few Actives grumbling that Smokey Ray was possessed by reefer madness, most thought of their resident hippie as a Sig Zeta guru of sorts, as he often incorporated the fraternity ideals into his soliloquies.

As for Audora, she made Chipper nervous. Ever since the seedy event of last year, she acted hurt and disappointed that Chipper had not taken the opportunity to expand his mind—that instead, Chipper would sink so low as to actually accuse her of trying to do him harm. Realizing, and reflecting on, his own volitional contribution to the brain-wreck, Chipper still felt a bubbling resentment in his partially potted mind where Audora had dabbled with her witchcraft. For what truly bugged him was the *sanctimony* of the trickster Audora who seemed so proud of her craft.

And when Smokey Ray wasn't looking, Audora would stare at Chipper with those dark, nonblinking windows that would say: "But you'll *never* be the same." Then those shrouded portals would go on to proclaim: "No matter how long it takes, I'll be waiting, sweet prince, to escort you back to Otherworld."

* * *

Peachy never dreamed of such rapid success. Equanimity, though, was not to be—for each new rung on the ladder led him to a station where he could see more rungs, more clearly.

As Social-Chairman-for-Life, he secured talent from the second tiers on the pop charts (with the help of his well-connected father living in Vegas, New York, and now L.A.), even for the lesser parties, while other fraternities continued the perpetual struggle to book local bands. For the Sig Zetas, it was the Hondells for Western Party, the Zombies for Baby Bawl, and Left Banke for the Sweetheart Gala. Chipper, who was recording the entire year on film for Rush Week, always included a clip of Peachy at the party, twirling, gyrating, occasionally doing splits, in the center of the room, his once-only date flung to the periphery, a mere ornament for the trademark dance spectacle.

With bands and parties the primary lure for rushing high school seniors, fate gifted Peachy a potent currency—he was, in fact, becoming more valuable to the fraternity's future than the Rush Chairman.

And Peachy's wealth was not limited to the symbolic. Wickiup Enterprises International scored so heavily in the Big Eight region with their next product launch—the minifridge, choice of sizes: two-6-pack or four-6-pack—that the Board of Directors (Peachy and Drywall) voted to go legit, sort of, by forming a limited liability company. This strategy allowed a certain degree of cash flow to be channeled onto the books, creating both deductions and a dollop of taxation upon themselves, all the while limiting the liability that they might go to jail courtesy of the IRS.

In addition, the Great Avalanche of minifridges that poured out of the back of the truck onto Big Eight campuses raised so much working capital that Wickiup purchased a second and third truck. Now, the runs to Mexico required the help of a third Sig driver (usually Kong) as well as representatives from the Kickapoo Nation.

The Sig caravan drove twice a month to the suppliers in Mexico, where they were joined by card-carrying Kickapoos. The helpful Indians would then ride across the border from Piedras Negras to Eagle Pass, flashing their Kickapoo credentials to border patrol, allowing safe and nontariffed passage back to the States, where the Indians would hop off and return home. These tribal employees of Wickiup were compensated a fair and fixed percentage of that portion of revenue that was recorded in the liability-limiting books by the chief accountant—Peachy Waterman Junior.

Growth was exponential, and Peachy could see no end in sight to his great fortune.

"Drywall, have you ever considered the fact that about half the people in the world are women?" asked Peachy.

"No," answered Drywall as he rolled his eyes, "I'm not a deep thinker like you."

"Well, consider this—we need to extend our product lines to women. Don't you agree?"

* * *

While Sig Zeta officers might have been the official undergraduate governing body, it was the House Corporation that made the real rules. And they held their semesterly meetings center stage in the dining room for all to see. For if the undergrads ever deluded themselves into believing omnipotence in their Greek world, the rugged alumni members of House Corporation were easily capable of injecting humility, twice a year.

Interested Actives, mostly aspiring officers, sat in a circle around the House Corporation to watch their beloved President and Treasurer get pummeled, and to offer halfhearted support of their mighty leaders if the beating ever got too bloody. Chipper studied the names of the men—Grimes, Riley, Shoplin, and Vandeleer—wondering if someday he would be facing them center stage.

But it was the president of the House Corporation that held Chipper's attention, a bulldog named Brewster Stone who had a pro wrestler's head on a halfback's body and who looked like the sort of scowling man whose best smile can't reverse a fixed, downward arc, especially on the more droopy side where it was said he'd had a slight stroke. Brewster dominated the meeting, articulating poorly as he balanced and bobbled a short, stubby cigar at the nadir of his crooked mouth.

In listening to the financial report, Chipper was surprised that, while gross revenues from Active house payments were impressive, so were expenses. The chapter barely broke even. How shocked the House Corporation would be, thought Chipper, if they knew Wickiup Enterprises had greater total revenues than the chapter, and a far greater net.

When the three-hour meeting came to an end (2-1/2 hours spent in strategy to keep the rickety house in shape to pass code—and probably to preserve memories of the alums), the center table broke ranks, and the corporation members began to mingle with the Actives.

Chipper was startled from his observational comfort when Brewster Stone charged directly toward him, coming to a screeching halt, it seemed, with his warrior face uncomfortably close. Chipper could feel his own heels scooching backward.

"I hear you're planning to be head Rush Chairman next summer," growled Mr. Stone. Chipper could only see two rows of yellow teeth through thick lips, tobacco-stained in one corner.

"Well . . . uh . . . I haven't been elected yet, sir. Most guys know I'm planning to run. You know how guys talk way before actual elections. Usually, it's sort of decided be—"

Chipper felt Brewster's forefinger press against his breastbone. "My son's coming through rush next year. He gets a bid . . . *period*. You understand?" Mr. Stone poked him again.

"Yes, sir."

Chipper wondered if his decision to run for Rush Chairman had been a bit hasty.

* * *

To the extreme annoyance of his roommates, Chipper worked to become a bona fide drummer using a hard rubber practice pad, hoping someday to win the approval of maestro C.C. Chastain. This year's Greek Review would again tour the military bases, offering bon voyage to soldiers destined to stamp out Communism by firing M-16s at puffs of smoke in the jungle.

C.C. seemed grouchier than usual at tryouts this year. His best friend from high school, John Tatum, ended up pledging the new black fraternity, Alpha Phi Alpha, and C.C.'s heart was broken when Tatum refused to play lead guitar for C.C.'s musical review.

"Chipper, I've told you a thousand times, you're too stiff. This ain't rudimentary drumming. Forget the cadences. We ain't playing John Freakin' Sousa for these guys. Take your drumsticks, go buy a copy of the Doors' 'Break On Through,' listen to it one hundred times, play along with it five hundred times, dream it, live it, breathe it, then bring your sorry ass back here next year and try again. Rock, dammit, rock!"

* * *

Al Marlowe stewed over torts and contracts, without the least bit of interest. Since graduating last spring and entering law school, he had not graced the Sig Zeta house even once. He knew that his absence was noted. After all, he was a former President, still on campus, and there was an expectation that the "old guys" return, on occasion, to provide inspiration for the Actives, even if said uplift was illusory.

Vietnam was tugging at Al, and he considered dropping out of law school to enlist. Not because it was his patriotic duty. Not because he believed the war was effectively halting Communism as presented by Brother Jake Chisum. And not because he thought he could help.

Al was at a complete loss as to the origins of his melancholy (if that was even the correct word). His life had gone very well, exceptionally well to be more honest, but an inborn error seemed to have caused a huge hole in his heart. Oddly, he felt a color to his perennial mood—sort of a blue-gray. And he began to fear that the color would soon start oozing from his pores, then drip, drip, drip to the ground where it would seep from beneath the crack at the bottom of his door allowing the whole world to see a pool of grim blue-gray.

So it wasn't truly Vietnam tugging at Al Marlowe.

When his phone rang, he almost didn't answer. Usually, he just let it go. *If it rings more than seven times, I'll pick it up*, he thought.

"Hello," he managed after the tenth ring.

"Is this Al? Al Marlowe?"

"Yes."

"My name is Ross Loveland. I'm a Sig Zeta from Florida, on staff here now with Varsity Voyagers. Wondered if you'd like to go to lunch some time?"

"Who? What?—What is Varsity Voyagers?"

* * *

Mitch Addison was the perfect addition to Wickiup Enterprises. As vice-president of the newly formed Women's Division, Mitch simply had to stand at the open end of the Wickiup truck and pass out booty and rake in the coin from the girls on sorority row, then the dorms, then the rest of the schools in the Big Eight.

Mitch tried to maintain his stock in traditional fashion and accessories, but with each passing month he found it more and more difficult to keep up with the demand for loose tunics, embroidered caftans, granny shawls, East Indian overblouses, flared bell-bottoms, hip-length vests, safari handbags, crocheted bikinis, microminiskirts, maxi coats, ponchos, wide leather belts, and the first allergy-tested line of cosmetics (Clinique), not to mention a roaring demand for the new rage—pantyhose.

Whether it was the product line, low prices, or Mitch's gorgeous kisser, it didn't matter. The money flowed. Mitch was able to quit his job as a model for Danner's and work full-time for Wickiup.

And with his new exposure to the fair and gentle half of the population, Mitch's boasts of one-night stands reached epidemic proportions.

* * *

Ernie Dumas decked Mitch Addison with a closed fist, and the details were squelched at the highest level—the President. Dumas was fined the highest amount allowed ($100), and all involved were ordered never to speak of the incident again. Most believed the skirmish was over a girl.

But Ernie and pal Uno Guilford spent a great deal of time in provocative hallway conversations, and they infiltrated the nightly poker game at the round table in the center of the dining room, muttering innuendoes all the while.

Chipper found factions within the house disturbing, but physical violence was unthinkable. No one could remember serious fisticuffs between members in the house. Not ever. And when Chipper tried to learn more about the incident, there were only two responses: ignorance and feigned ignorance.

* * *

Another swarm of pledges was duped by Ty Wheeler whose Roy Orbison shtick became fodder for their freshman jokes, only to find out after initiation that the joke was on them. Each and every pledge had recited Roy's bio during inquisitions, all of them proudly stating info from their crib sheet, nonsensical if anyone had taken the time to do the math. Or, if anyone had taken the time to have a real conversation with Ty Wheeler.

As always, the revelation that Ty Wheeler's bio was a joke was double-edged—while each new initiate realized they had been the butt of the whole fraternity, they also realized that, in reality, brother Ty Wheeler was very much a loon.

And this latter realization kept Ty in a cage by himself, a novelty with whom no one dare form the true bond of brotherhood. Ty's place (and thank goodness he knew it) was leader of the Spook Patrol during Rush Week, a likeable embarrassment for the whole chapter, and a great relief for all when he chose not to participate in fraternity functions so as to not sully the name of Sigma Zeta Chi.

So, in a way, the joke came back to rest on harmless, partially pathetic, Ty Wheeler, existing in an ill-defined space where mystery generates invisible walls and no exits.

But to his credit, Ty Wheeler had no attributes. Though fair on the guitar, he had no real talent, no looks, no wit, no smarts, no glib B.S., no athletic skills, no identifiable attributes. And without attributes, Ty Wheeler had no enemies. So in a twisted sort of way, without anyone saying words to confirm, there was a silent and persistent cheer in the fraternity for Ty Wheeler, always rooting him onward and upward, aimlessly.

* * *

Amy signed up for a second semester with Dot Turco. The man-hating theme in the sociologist's agenda seemed to mellow after the adrenaline was gone from the sheep-crowning ceremony in Atlantic City. But a different factor piqued Amy's enthusiasm for another round with Dot—Uno Guilford was *not* in the class this semester.

Much to the annoyance of Amy, Uno had dominated the course first semester. He seemed able to read the mind of the radical feminist professor, offering the perfect answers as a "liberated man," completely tolerant and understanding of the "liberated woman." And he did it with a sparkling smile. To make matters worse, Dot Turco's voice lost its edge when she dove into dialogue with "Monty," and her staunch dignity vanished, giggling like a little girl at Uno's weak jokes.

To Amy, the phoniness was suffocating, and she was incredulous that Professor Turco couldn't pick up on it. Even more amazing was the fact that Uno's Porsche strategy had worked—he had dated several girls in the class. Plus, the sorority grapevine suggested a host of others, all lapping up his lies that ranged from being an orphan, to having terminal cancer, to suffering excruciating loneliness after losing his fiancee in a fatal car wreck. And when the grapevine confirmed the lies, confirmed that Uno regularly told different girls different things, it became a marvelous display to Amy of the power of the Porsche as Uno headed out every weekend to his love nest at Grand Lake with another conquest.

* * *

A visit by the Grand President (Grand Poobah for the entire fraternity—undergrad and alums) was every bit as rare in Oklahoma as a visit by a U.S. President. The historical event was heralded by such chapter anxiety that Actives actually helped the pledges at the Work-session, right down to the spit and polish on the fine silver.

Song rehearsals were held nightly, three weeks in advance, with everyone excited that Drywall would be featured soloist for the opening of the most famous fraternity song of all time—"The Sweetheart Serenade." Actives still marveled at the resonant, slightly nasal sound that came from the Kickapoo when he warbled the lyrics: "When dreams fade away . . . As they sometimes do . . . And you've lost the light in your heart . . ."

Since the Grand President would be attending a chapter meeting, the proceedings were scripted, making sure the wisecrackers and monkeyshiners would be held at bay.

But from the moment of his arrival, Chipper felt uneasy. The Grand President had a sour expression, and it seemed to Chipper that when Drywall the Kickapoo belted the opening line—"When dreams fade away . . ."—the Poobah squinted and squirmed, without a trace of a smile.

Then, during chapter meeting, when the Grand President delivered his speech, there was one long, sustained note that served as background for a medley of tunes—and that note was the *preservation of the status quo, at all cost, unyielding to societal pressures.* As for the medley, it seemed that the Grand Jukebox tested one play after another, each song more bold than the last. As long as he generated laughter and applause, his wry observations concerning mixing of the races became gentle mockery. Then a few tunes later, the whole room was laughing about a Sig Zeta chapter "back East" that had tried to hide their "darkie pledge" from him when he visited. "Yes, they had little black Sambo down in the basement—"

C.C. Chastain rocketed from his sophomore seat and, with hands jammed onto hips, then arms flailing wildly, he interrupted the Grand President to everyone's shocked silence: "I can't believe—I simply can't believe, that as the representative of a national organization, you are traveling around the country, spreading your bigotry and your prejudice with statements like that. But I'll tell you this—you will rue the day you walked into *this* chapter to do your deed."

In the aftermath, C.C. Chastain was shocked at the chapter's response to his outburst. After all, C.C. had truly been the Outstanding Pledge, and everyone knew it. No one served the standards of Sig Zeta more. No one lived more truly by the Rickel Standard. C.C. had worshiped the fraternity and every one of its high ideals as a pledge.

Believing himself to be carrier of the torch of righteousness, C.C. fell into deep despair when he realized that, in a "little ol' three-minute tirade," he was the new black sheep of the chapter, one notch lower than Ty Wheeler. To attack the Grand President was clearly an unforgivable sin, worthy only of fraternal shunning, spitting, and denigration.

Within the month, C.C. moved out of the house and swore he'd never return.

When word of C.C.'s tongue-lashing of the Grand President made it to the local alumni chapters and the House Corporation, whisperings of a "pin jerking" rolled around like thunder, eventually reaching the sophomore class, who vowed to fight for their pledge brother.

* * *

The Sig Zeta A-team golfers—Smokey Ray, Uno Guilford, Peachy, and Drywall—walked away with the intramural trophy, adding three points toward the overall intramural championship.

In fact, Peachy pointed out that if they had been playing as a college team in the Big Eight, they would have placed third on this very same university course where the varsity tournament had been held a week earlier.

But their three puny points toward the overall trophy were almost meaningless. Major sports counted 20 points for first, all the way down to badminton where one point was given for first, a half-point for second. The intramural golf tournament was the last event every year, and the three points for first-in-golf this year gave the Sig Zetas fifth place in the final intramural standings.

The highlight of the tournament, though, was hippie Ray Divine in his shoulder-length hair and full beard, wearing his Hang Ten surfer jams, as he shot a two-under 70 to win the medalist trophy.

* * *

Drywall didn't understand why Peachy had been so agreeable this time. What's more, Peachy had purchased the tickets for the ballet himself. What a friend. And as they sat down on the back row, Peachy didn't once start cussing, nor did he snivel about being called a homo.

But as Drywall scanned the program with his forefinger, he couldn't find Cassie's name. He checked again.

"Hey, what's going on, Peachy, I don't see her name listed."

Peachy twisted the corner of his mouth around so that he could speak while staring straight ahead. "She's not in this one."

"Not in this one? Then what the heck are we doing here?"

"Look to your right." And with that, Peachy stood and walked out to the left.

Drywall shifted slowly in his seat until his eyes met the most beautiful creature in the world, sitting right next to him. He gulped, realizing he'd never been so frightened in his life.

"Hello, Drywall. Long time, no call. Remember me?"

"I . . . I . . ."

"Sit back and let's enjoy the ballet. I had to drop out of this one. Missed a bunch of rehearsals due to one horrible sunburn I got in Padre. I'm okay now, though. It all turned tannish afterward, even though I did lose chunks of skin. Boy, I'll never do that again. It was so . . ."

He didn't hear a word she was saying. He kept staring into her cheerful, squinty eyes, while wanting to touch and count each of the darling freckles on her nose and cheeks.

As the ballet began, Cassie took his breath away by groping for his hand with hers until they locked in her lap. He was struggling for air. *Remain calm. Relax. Breathe deeply. Don't let her know how scared you are. Relax hand. Relax fingers. There. Grip is relaxed, but firm, I think.*

His eyes fixated on their two forearms lying side by side, not much difference at all in the color, especially with her recent tan, and in the dim light of the theater.

Drywall put so much effort into relaxing his hand that it went numb. In fact, he couldn't tell if his hand was frozen stiff, or if it had turned into a bundle of five noodles. Was he hurting her with his grip? Or was it so loose she'd think him a weenie? And for two hours, Drywall sat—fingers curled into a crab's claw or sponge, he wasn't sure— while Cassie did all the talking, and he fell so deeply into a spell that he couldn't remember a life before her.

* * *

Peachy usually kept the Wickiup checkbook under lock and key, so the day he left it on his desk in Room #17 presented Chipper with a temptation he couldn't resist.

As he lifted the cover, Chipper saw the latest figures from the new divisions—Men's Apparel and Wholesale Groceries. But it was the "To Do" list folded neatly in the checkbook that Chipper found fascinating:

Expand cold copy business with more dumpster teams (use pledges)

Wrestle bookie business from Phi Delts

Have Mitch check out wig craze, order commercial tie-dyes, double the textured hose order, quadruple last month's pantyhose order

Call Miguel to order 1,000 blenders, 400 more room fans, and 250 popcorn poppers

Check out the new countertop Radarange and do microwave market analysis

Find cheaper distributor for the new Sony Trinitron portable color TV

Strike deal with Army surplus for combat boots, camouflage pants, and paratrooper jackets

Consider Nehru jackets for Men's Division—first do market analysis

Secure shipment of Rod McKuen books—"Listen to the Warm" and "Lonesome Cities" (consider normal books as well)

Study legal loopholes on tequila imports (and cigarettes)

Approach Amy about taking over her Wurlitzer distributorship (avoid hostility)

Take control of the pork belly trade from the Fijis

Buy two more trucks and have DW recruit more Kickapoos

Increase staff and drivers (Twobits? Peatmoss? Einstink?)

Formalize into Divisions for each Big Eight school, with Sig Zeta contact at each serving as a Vice-prez in charge of Distribution, and one truck per school

Next step: Infiltrate Southwest Conference with a Sig bro at each Nation-wide Sigma Z network.

When Chipper lifted the "To Do" list from the record, he was startled to see a $30,000 check made payable to Peachy Waterman *Senior*. The notation said, "Booking of the Hondells for Western Party." And the scheme became perfectly clear. Peachy was financing his own legendary status on campus. Through a para-economy to Sig Zeta, he was booking the top name bands in the country through Wickiup profits. And Peachy's old man didn't come cheap.

Members thought that Peachy's connection to Peach Senior was a remarkable father-son relationship wherein the fraternity was the lucky beneficiary. It had been assumed that band managers and booking agents owed Peachy's dad unspoken favors. All had grown accustomed to Peachy's miracles. No one would have dreamed that Peachy Junior was paying Peachy Senior the going rate—top dollar—the big bucks—for the big bands.

Sig Zeta parties, in one short year with Peachy at the helm, had garnered attention in high schools across the state, and seniors no longer waited for Spring Bash, showing up for *all* the parties. The fraternity had become a thriving legend, all thanks to Wickiup.

With summer about to begin, and Chipper the newly elected Rush Chairman, it was almost ho-hum that Peachy had already arranged for Archie Bell and The Drells to play at the statewide party to be held at the Bud Ramm Mansion in Oklahoma City (one of the founders of the local Sig Zeta chapter, long dead). Peachy had made Chipper's job easy.

And it was all legal, for the most part.

* * *

A celestial convergence brought Chipper and Amy to the full consummation of their relationship, or nearly full.

Two Sig Zeta rush parties, Amy's golf tournament, and the Moon Landing all connected in a most remarkable way to plop Chipper and

Amy together in pledge brother Steve Brindley's bed in Lawton, huffing and puffing, sweating and snorting, writhing closer and closer with
no intent by either party to slow down or stop. Chipper couldn't
remember Amy ever being so eager, or so hot.

"Lower, baby. No, Chipper, you're in the wrong spot."

"Where? What?"

"Here, let me help."

"O-gawd."

Neither of them could have predicted the moment. Chipper had
been in charge of two rush parties, both regional events with throngs
of rushees begging to become Sigma Zs, largely due to the tales of
musical prowess provided by Wickiup Enterprises International.

Who would have imagined over 50 rushees for a small afternoon keg party earlier in Hobart, Oklahoma? But they came from as
far away as Altus, plus closer towns like Gotebo and Lone Wolf.
Maybe half of the attendees were actually going to college, and
some were truly going through rush. But all wanted a piece of the
Wickiup-Sigma Z magic. In the home of Active brothers Drake and
Kelton Mahoney, the entire group watched TV in amazement, sip-
ping their brewskis, as they heard Neil Armstrong say, "The Eagle
has landed."

"Slower, baby, slower. Try to go in circles."

"Like this?"

"Slower . . . there, that's better. Oh, yesss . . ."

And who would have guessed that there would have been such a
long period of time between the Eagle touching down on the moon surface before Neil and Edwin would actually take their earth-shattering
stroll? Or, that there would be enough time to travel to a nighttime rush
party in Lawton where brother Brindley offered his home (parents
touring Europe for the summer) for an astonishing 72 rushees, many
following in caravan from Hobart?

And who could have figured that Amy would claim the championship trophy in her flight at nearby Duncan in their first-ever
Women's Invitational, then still have time and energy to join Chipper
in Lawton where the mostly-male party was in progress, with the
Rushee:Active ratio 6:1, all revelers crowding closer and closer to
the television screen, waiting for Neil Armstrong to emerge?

"Yes, that's more like it."

"I want you, baby."

"I want you, too."

"All of you."

And who could have predicted that while Chipper gave Amy a tour through the Brindley mansion, they would stumble into his pledge brother's bedroom where, of all things, a Paul Mauriat album would be lying on the bed—the one with the naked girl sitting one leg outstretched, the other tucked, viewed sideways with a flower vine tattooed up her side and onto her face *and* containing the hit single, "Love Is Blue"? Who could have predicted the effect on Amy of that dreamy hit single after she began playing it on Brindley's stereo?

No, these things were not predictable. They were not anticipated. Not at this particular moment in time when the moon was in the Seventh House and Jupiter aligned with Mars.

And now, with Neil Armstrong posed for the most remarkable event in the history of the human race, Chipper and Amy were seconds away . . .

"Here, let me help."

"O-gawd."

"Yes, that's it. I feel you so deep."

"Oh, you feel sooo . . . good."

"So do youuuu."

Chipper climaxed just as the bedroom door banged against the wall, rattling the room. Startled out of his wits and his position, he creamed Amy's stomach and the bedsheets.

Kong stood in the doorway, blocking the hallway light. "Chipper, you're gonna miss it. Armstrong just stepped out of the capsule. He's on the ladder now. Hurry." Then Chipper heard both Kong and Brindley going down the hall, banging on all the bedroom doors so that no one would miss this historic occasion.

"Coitus interruptus lunaris," said Amy.

"Sorry."

"That *wasn't* how I'd dreamed it. *Kong* wasn't in my vision of how it would be."

"This was un—unfor—un-something, Amy. We don't *really* have to count it as the first time, you know. Let's not."

Chipper dressed and hurried into the TV room where he saw The Foot touch dust and heard Armstrong say, "One small step for man . . . one giant leap for mankind."

Amy was a little slower in dressing, so she missed the first moon step, but she caught the rest, including President Nixon's live phone call to the moon where he offered some mumbo jumbo to the space crew (and 500 million viewers) about the moon landing being in the

Sea of Tranquility, so perhaps Earth will follow suit and enjoy world-wide Peace and Tranquility hereafter.

Chipper turned to Amy and said, "Poor Michael Collins."

"Who?"

"Michael Collins, the guy who has to sit there in the Eagle, never touching ground. No one will ever remember he was even there."

Amy looked at Chipper like she sometimes did, apparently wondering just how weird her moondoggie really was.

Junior Year (1969–70)

37

Fortunes of war, aptly called spoils, extend long and gnarly fingers from the front lines toward home. When the Sigma Z gang returned for Work Week, President-elect John R. Webb was missing from action. Indeed, President Webb had been so inspired by Brother Jake Chisum's war movie that he'd traded in his gavel for a green beret mission that rifled him near An Loc, a few miles away from the Cambodian border.

The scramble to fill the President position was confusing due to the honorary (perfunctory) status to which the vice president had been reduced, as evidenced by number-two-man Brad Wahl's response to the news: "Hell no, I ain't gonna be President. I just ran for vice prez so's I could sit up front at chapter meetings and help the President yell at everyone to shut their friggin' traps."

Given the dearth of enthusiasm for the thankless throne, eyes began to roll and twist to a most unlikely candidate, a junior for godsakes, someone so blindly trusting that the seniors could still manipulate the office and launch the important decisions from the poker game at the roundtable in the dining room.

And as the caucuses convened in the hallways and heads, the vitriolic objections to a junior occupying the esteemed station were squelched; the Dying Breed protesters were silenced; and the endorsement of one Chipper DeHart as the the new President ushered the Reign of the New Breed—disciples of quirky Pledge Trainer Ted Boone—taking spurious control of the house at 558 University Boulevard.

As for Chipper, long-buried habits began to assert themselves once again—he started nibbling his fingernails as he'd done in grade school; he began popping his knuckles as a warm-up for the fingernails; and, as a prelude to the popping, he found himself drumming his fingers on the monstrous desk in the President's room where he now lived—all alone.

* * *

"I'd like to hear your response to the death of Ho Chi Minh last week," said Amy, one of the judges for this year's university beauty pageant. Amy had lobbied for screening interviews to be added to the selection process, so here she sat, looking at a gorgeous redhead gulp and sweat and wiggle in her chair to the question.

"I guess I didn't hear that he had died. I'm sorry."

"Yes. Die he did. What do you know about him?"

The hapless girl began to toy with the ski-jump flip of her lacquered red hair.

"I . . . I've never heard of him."

After 32 interviews, Amy tallied the numbers. Four candidates correctly identified the newly dead President of North Vietnam; 25 offered "I don't knows," most accompanied by "I'm sorrys"; two reasoned that Ho Chi Minh was a dish to be relished at a Chinese restaurant; and one broke into tears upon learning of the death, believing that Ho Chi Minh was the name of the clown that had performed at her birthday parties when she was a little girl.

Amy was mortified.

* * *

Drywall and Cassie St. Clair's lives became so enmeshed, so euphoric, and so whimsical that the real world outside their celestial sphere became the dream. Like faraway echoes, the aftermath of Woodstock and daily updates on the Manson murders were barely heard by the lovers. And when the whole universe believed Paul McCartney was a goner, Drywall and Cassie didn't even play their Beatles records backward to listen for "Paul is dead." Drywall didn't seem to care when 89 American Indians occupied the island of Alcatraz, claiming the site as their own, squatting for the duration. And neither paid much attention when homegrown Steve Owens won the Heisman Trophy.

Their hands were always locked, their eyes were only on each other, and their lips were pressed whenever possible. Even apart, each pretended the other nigh.

Close friend and matchmaker Peachy Waterman never regretted his ploy. He didn't mind Drywall's splashing in a sea of love, for it relegated the starry-eyed Kickapoo to a "figurehead," allowing the true mastermind to rule Amalgamated Wickiup Enterprises and Subsidiaries, International.

* * *

Chipper and Peachy carried a hip pocket offering of a bid-to-pledge as they entered the off-campus dorm (flophouse) of Brewster Stone Junior, son of the House Corporation president who had barked the bid-order last year. Yet, Brewster Junior had skipped summer rush entirely.

"Man, this place is a dump,"said Peachy as the delegation of two entered the creaky screen door of the three-story tan brick building. "Why in the hell would this joker live in a dive like this? Isn't his dad rich? This ain't even approved university housing."

"Beats me," said Chipper. "Let's just hope the guy's decent 'cause he'll be one of us."

When there was no reply to their knock on Room #4, Peachy took the bold step of twisting the tarnished knob and opening the door. A large sprawling room came into view, no furniture, wall-to-wall mattresses. And in the center, sitting cross-legged, hands touching as if in prayer, an old, bearded hippie (at least age 30) sat in a white linen frock of some sort. Candles lined the two windowsills where their flames were premature at dusk. Plunky sitar music played from a source unseen and a sweet musty odor spilled out the doorway. The hippie kept his eyes lowered to a cluster of candles that were balanced on the mattress near his feet.

Chipper looked at Peachy to verify that his friend's eyes were as wide as his own. "Uh . . . excuse me," began Chipper. The hippie didn't move.

"I think he's dead," whispered Peachy.

"We're here to see Brewster Stone. Are you him?"

Slowly, the hippie's right arm began to float until one finger pointed to the ceiling.

"Oh. In the room above?" asked Chipper.

The hippie opened bloodshot eyes and stared in silence. If there was even a trace of expression, it was lost beneath the black beard that seemed to creep up and choke the eyes.

"We'll take that to mean a 'yes,' Maharishi," Peachy said as he shut the door.

Chipper shook off the remembrance of his personal excursion to Otherworld as he was constantly haunted by the notion that the journey had not been a complete roundtrip.

"Thank goodness that wasn't Brewster," said Peachy as the two continued upstairs.

Peachy knocked this time on Room #14, and Chipper was relieved when a short, slightly-built kid answered, trying desperately to force a smile. The laws of genetics seemed loose, though, by this runt who had clearly mutated to Chihuahua from his bulldog father.

"Hello. I'm Brewster. Brew for short. Please do come in, fellas."

"I'm Chipper DeHart, and this is Peachy Waterman."

Relief was short-lived. It wasn't the boy's lisp that forced Chipper's blood to his feet, but the dainty steps as Brewster, or Brew, floated to the sofa where he sat after a silly wiggle into the cushion, legs crossed at the ankles with knees together, slender hands resting in his lap with fingers spread as if to allow his nails to dry.

Chipper wrestled to find a word or two that might crack the silence. "I—uh— we're from—uh—" He looked to his erstwhile motor-mouthed friend to bail him out.

Peachy had transformed into Bazark the Robot. Frozen round eyes, rigid rectangular mouth, cubed head locked onto larger cubed torso that moved as a single unit. Speechless.

Sabotaged, Chipper was forced into propping the conversational bridge to Brewster. After stuttering his way through the ideals of Sigma Zeta Chi, the lifelong commitment, the bonds of brotherhood, Chipper was startled by the interruption—

"I know why you're here," said the boy, eyelids fluttering, "and I want you to know that I have no intention of pledging Sig Zeta, or any other fraternity for that matter."

Chipper felt his blood starting to circulate again as Brew continued:

"*However,* I'm willing to take the pressure off you—and I *know* how my father can apply the pressure—*only* if you agree to one promise."

"Anything!" bubbled Chipper. "I promise."

* * *

"You're up shit creek without a paddle *or* a canoe," said Peachy on the way back to the fraternity house. "If you tell the old man that the kid's not getting a bid, he'll tear you a new asshole. But if you tell the old man the truth, that his son doesn't even wanna pledge, the kid claims he'll pledge out of spite, then he'll be levitating in his loafers on initiation day. Chipper, you peckerwood. That kid's got you hostage. You've promised to lie for him."

"Dang it, Peachy, you heard him. He said his dad would beat him to a pulp if he refused a bid to pledge. We just gotta say we never offered him a bid. No big deal."

"Don't you get it? The old man's desperate. His son's a homo, and he's countin' on the fraternity to make a man out of him. If you tell Senior that Junior doesn't get a bid, your ass is grass."

"But if I tell him that Junior doesn't give squat about pledging, he'll kill the kid."

"Better him than you, my friend," Peachy said. "You've just been hoodwinked. What a friggin' sucker you are. The kid blackmailed you. Do you really think he'll show up at our front door to pledge if you don't keep your promise?"

"I don't know."

"Hell, no. It's an idle threat. He knows there aren't any homos in fraternities."

* * *

After a Monday night meal, with Actives scattered on the front lawn to fly their Frisbees, Chipper stood inside and stared out the panoramic picture window in the living room. A bizarre parade of radicals ebbed and flowed through the gates of the Alamo apartments across the street. The front yard at the Sig Zeta house was the size of a football field, so it was difficult to be sure of identities at such a distance, but Audora was unmistakable with her fanny-length black hair crowned by a wreath of flowers. Standing near the front gate, she kissed Smokey Ray, then skipped toward the central court of the apartments.

Chipper had pressured Audora to the point of confession last week after Art Linkletter's daughter leaped to her death while spaced out on LSD. His all-consuming research into the wacky chemical cousin in Heavenly Blues—LSA—indicated that it caused altered perceptions of reality rather than the full-blown hallucinations he had experienced. After hounding Audora, after preaching to her about Dianne Linkletter ("Propaganda," Audora replied), after finally scolding her for her blasé attitude regarding his young, fertile mind, she finally admitted she had added mescaline to his morning glory seeds, unbeknownst to Smokey Ray. "You have the gift, Chipper. You *must* turn on. Use the gift." And ever since, he had been steaming at the realization that his bouquet had included not only morning glories, but also peyote cactus extract. But perhaps the steaming was really just to cover the sadness. Somehow, his dalliance with organic chemistry had left a languor without shape, form, or identity.

As he stared at the white stucco walls of the Alamo, a peculiar golden cast filled the sky near sunset. The metallic browns of oak and maple leaves glittered from a cyclonic swirl in a corner near the front door. Late fall at college was a beautiful time, and he had the foresight to log the moment for future reference, even if the scene was giving artificial color to a world gone mad.

Although lasagna-stuffed Actives were roaming everywhere, dodging and catching flying Frisbees, Chipper felt alone as he stepped outside and looked at the large gold cross on the front of the house, gilded in bronze.

"Hey, there's Al Marlowe," he heard someone yell.

Spinning from his reverie, Chipper saw his Big Brother, the former President, for the first time in over a year. But something was wrong—terribly wrong. Al Marlowe was smiling. No, he was *laughing* as he strolled down the long, skinny sidewalk to the Sig Zeta front door, glad-handing and backslapping the brothers as he walked.

And he wasn't alone. He was walking with an older-looking guy, huge, almost the size of Kong. And the big guy was smiling, too.

Chipper's feet were melded to the sidewalk as the two men approached the front door.

"Chipper, my little brother, good to see you again," said Al, one arm thrown around Chipper's shoulders. "Let me introduce brother Ross Loveland. Ross was an All-American tackle at Florida in '63 and a Sig Zeta there as well. Now he's on full-time staff of Varsity Voyagers here on campus."

"Varsity Voyagers?"

"Yeah, let's go inside and talk."

* * *

In the air-conditioned President's room, with RFK watching from the poster on the wall, where Chipper had been hot-boxed as a rushee, a place now called home, Chipper listened to Al Marlowe talk about his conversion experience.

Al talked about a "God-shaped vacuum" where his heart should have been, how Christ had filled that vacuum, how the simple act of accepting Christ bridges the gap between God and man and allows you to live life as God would have you do it, rather than the self-destructive path of our own desires.

Ross Loveland joined the conversation like a giant panda (close-set eyes with dark circles) so gentle and soft-spoken Chipper couldn't even conceive of the man as a bone-crushing tackle. Ross talked about "joy" as distinct from "happiness" and how much he en-*joy*-ed working full-time for Varsity Voyagers where the fruits of labor were eternal.

And when the serve switched back to Marlowe, Chipper focused not so much on Al's words as the bursting enthusiasm written all over his face. The bright, glowing eyes that appeared to be seeing something not there. The smile that stretched on and on, gleefully anticipating something that hadn't even happened yet. The shifting crinkles in his skin caused by facial muscles that previously sagged like molten wax, now fueled like Mexican jumping beans. To Chipper, it looked like a new human being sitting before him. Once morose, Marlowe was spirited, savoring life, and downright silly to the point of childlike.

Loveland mumbled something about wanting to start a Bible study at the Sig Zeta house, which seemed appropriate in a Christian fraternity, then the two men left the room.

Chipper shut the door behind them, then collapsed in the same overstuffed chair that had swallowed him as a rushee—a chair that seemed to be providing increasing mystical comfort every time he sat down. He bowed his head and said, "Lord, if you're up there, I think I'd like to have whatever you gave to Al."

* * *

"Smokey Ray, here's a question for you—now don't think it's stupid—but do you believe in God?" asked Chipper, curious as to how the architect of enlightenment might respond.

"Not the same as you, probably. Why?"

"Just curious. I figured you've given it lots of thought."

"Well, I'm fascinated that man is the only animal that contemplates itself. But rather than dig this privilege, isn't it amazing that diggin' isn't enough, and we dream of something greater still? Perhaps the heaven of our own awareness is really hell in disguise, stoking the fire that makes men search for God."

Chipper remembered that with Smokey Ray there were no yes-or-no answers, and he was sorry he'd asked.

Smokey Ray continued, "I bet I know what's going on with you. You're in comparative anatomy this semester, aren't you? And you're studying the brain. I took that course last year. It's too baffling to believe the brain is an accident of nature, isn't it? Makes you wonder about a God?"

"Actually," said Chipper, "That's not what prompted my question, but the brain is so overwhelming that it just jams my circuits. I can't even start to appreciate it. No, to tell you the truth, the organ that blows my mind is the eyeball. The design is more understandable, so it makes it more unbelievable. The eyeball is no accident. I gotta think we were made by a Creator."

"Fine enough for you, cowboy, but if you're planning to start some pilgrimage, don't ever forget the denizens of the deep dark ocean—they've got eyeballs, too, you know. But why? In the darkness, the miracle is nothing more than a useless ball of jelly."

* * *

With the new academic year and thus improved seniority, Wickiup Enterprises relocated its international headquarters across the hall from Chipper on Officer's Row. While Chipper enjoyed the cool air and wall-to-wall carpeting of the President's palatial suite, Social Chairman-for-Life Peachy and sidekick Drywall were his neighbors, though Drywall was pretty scarce these days.

Peachy's latest brainstorm flowered from *The Magazine of Sigma Zeta Chi*, which all initiates and generous alums received quarterly. In the back was a listing of the officers of all the Active Chapters in the country. From this list, Peachy recruited a network of distributors for his products, most of which still came from Mexico. With the addition of chapters at Case Western, Ball State, and USC (Brother Chisum's old chapter), Peachy now had 37 distributors to complement his fleet of seven trucks already serving the Big Eight and Southwest Conference schools.

Sig truck drivers wore Wickiup-issued World War I leather flying caps and goggles, along with jackets bearing the Wickiup logo. The trucks formed a caravan en route to Mexico, then split on the return trip to cover the central and southern U.S. And after the enormous success in sales of 3,741 alarm clock-radios, Wickiup even bore a slogan: "Wake up to Wickiup."

* * *

Peachy was juggling his Wickiup books when he heard a knock at the door. Before he could answer, Chipper came into his room.

"Hey, peckerwood, invite yourself in, why don't you? Ready for your execution tomorrow by the House Corporation?" asked Peachy.

"I hear Brewster Stone has a bounty on your head, only it's not dead or alive—just dead."

"Hi. What's going on, Peachy?"

"Just going over profits for the month. And thinking what I might do for an encore our senior year. You know I have to end on a bang."

"Peachy, do you do *anything* else? I mean, how are your grades this semester?"

"C'mon man, who appointed you my parole officer? You know I ain't been to class since September. I figure I'll start studying next year. I should still have time to bring my grades up to a two-point for graduation." Peachy resented Chipper when he started pulling his holier-than-thou shit.

Chipper sat on the edge of Peachy's bed as he reached over to turn down the radio.

"Leave the dial there and listen. It's another groovy tune from Three Dog Night. That's three hits in a row. This one's called 'Eli's Coming.' I'm tellin' ya' these guys are gonna be big." Peachy sang along, "I walk to Apollo by the bay, everywhere I . . ."

"Yeah, I agree. It just seemed a little loud."

"That's the advantage of living in this hall. You can rattle the pictures of the dead-and-dying Presidents on the wall out there, and no one cares." Peachy turned around to his accounting ledgers, wondering what had prompted Chipper's visit. "Hey, by the way, guess what I'm hot on the trail of."

"What?" Chipper asked.

"World War Two Harley-Davidsons, hundreds of 'em, never used, still in their crates, still pickled in Cosmoline petrolatum and stored in a desert in southern Arizona. You can get 'em for 25 smackeroos apiece. You just gotta dissolve the Cosmoline with kerosene to bring 'em outta hibernation. I'm gonna make a killing."

"How'd you hear about that?"

"A Beta friend told me. Says they've been trying to locate the bikes for years, but I think I've found 'em, so I'm sending Kong in a truck to Arizona to—"

The familiar sound of someone crashing through the drywall overpowered Three Dog Night and sent Peachy and Chipper scrambling out in the hallway.

Ernie Dumas was standing over Mitch Addison, who was curled in the hallway at the head of the stairs. "Now get out of this fraternity, you faggot," yelled Ernie.

Peachy turned to Chipper, both of them assuming the word "faggot" was just an expression, as the two had tangled before. But Peachy was stunned when Ernie spun around, his white-striped eyebrows furrowed at the base of his mushrooming red hair as he pointed at Chipper. "Okay, Mister President, it's official now. I want it brought up next Monday night at chapter meeting. Our pledge brother here is a real live faggot, and I want him voted out of the house."

* * *

Chipper could barely concentrate on the proceedings of his first House Corporation encounter. Looming over the roundtable was the thought of tomorrow night's chapter meeting with a single agenda item—Mitch Addison. Plus, the no-nonsense, nose-to-nose meeting with Brewster Stone Sr. to follow today, just as soon as the men pushed their chairs away from the poker table.

In the midst of his preoccupation, Chipper offered only one ear to listen to the names of the Actives delinquent in their house payments. But worse, more and more Actives were living out of the house and not even paying basic dues. And one name stood out from all the rest, a member who had demonstrated supreme insolence during a Grand President visit last year—in essence, a blight on the name of Sig Zeta, and for whom immediate measures should be taken to jerk his pin.

"President DeHart, by the time of our next meeting, all the appropriate paperwork will be in the hands of headquarters to relieve this C.C. Chastain of his pin. Understood?"

Chipper nodded yes.

Within seconds of the closing gavel, Brewster Stone Sr. had Chipper backed against the ropes in a corner near the chapter room, pounding him left and right with a tongue-lashing over Chipper's failure to deliver a bid to his son. Beaten, bruised, and bleeding (at least in his mind), Chipper finally sung like a canary: "He didn't want a bid, Mr. Stone. He didn't even want to pledge at all. He could care less about fraternities."

The bout was over with a come-from-the-ropes, first round knockout. Brewster went down for the count.

* * *

"Peachy, d'you remember the night at Pringle's Pool back when we were pledges, when I gave my speech and all?"

"Does the Pope shit in the woods? Is a bear Catholic?"

"Well, I thought I had more courage that moment than ever before in my life."

"If you say so . . . rat fink." Peachy chuckled. "I bet young Brew is floatin' down the river as we speak."

"And I sorta thought that maybe that much courage would stick. You know, that I was suddenly this really brave person and all."

"Your point being . . . ?"

"When I let Brewster scare me, when I broke my promise to the kid, I felt like a punk—a real coward. I still do."

"Hey, chum, there's no shame in lookin' like a yellowbelly. The shame is when you're too stupid to know the difference between running fast and running slow."

* * *

The seating choice in the chapter room was jumbled, as no one knew where they stood on the shocking allegations, and like minds tried to sit together. The smoking possibility that Mitch Addison was a genuine fairy had diffused to every corner of the house.

Mitch was barred from the meeting. A point in Mitch's favor was the fact that the allegations were being brought by the fraternity's two most unpopular members—Ernie Dumas and Uno Guilford, partners in deceit. Their credibility was *always* in question, at least heretofore.

"I figured it out first during the pledge class walk-out," Ernie testified. "You remember how Uno here set a new record for barfin' on the bus trip down to Dallas? He beat the old record by pukin' just before Pauls Valley, and he was passed out by Gainesville. Anyway, we stuck him in the back seat of the bus. Remember? So old Mitch up and volunteers to go back there and sit with him to make sure he's okay the rest of the trip. Well, I sat across the way and I saw old Mitch slip his hand onto Uno's goods. So then, I played like I was passed out, but still peeking, you know? And what I saw was no accident—Mitch was playing Uno's skin flute, my friends. He stopped real quick-like when I opened my eyes, and I let him know just by looking at him that I seen what I saw."

"You're a damn liar, Ernie," said Kong. "There's no one on this campus that screws more ballshakers than Mitch."

And a verbal maelstrom was launched as some members vouched for Mitch's manliness, while others recounted "little stories," once private, now public, by virtue of the effervescing effect of accusation.

Most damaging was an allegation that Mitch had been seen in a car with Monty Day, a frat guy living off campus who, to anyone's knowledge, was the only bona fide homo in any fraternity on campus.

After an hour of charged debate, Chipper felt more pummeled than by the hands of Brewster Stone the day before. He called upon the wisdom of Solomon, hoping for a baby to divide, but settled on this: "I'll talk to Mitch. I'll explain what the accusations are. And if he wants, he should have his day in court. It's pretty crummy for us to sit here throwing things out about him when he's not here to defend himself. If he decides to address all this stuff, we'll have a special chapter meeting."

Later that night, Mitch told Chipper that *all* the allegations were ridiculous, and he demanded an opportunity to address the chapter.

* * *

John Tatum's dark star rose farther and faster than imaginable. From his curdling experience of rejection by Sig Zeta, the "Tom" turned toxic after he pledged the all-black fraternity. Shortly after initiation, he was elected president, and rumors held that the fraternity was actually a front for the Black Panthers.

Then, in an implausible reversal of campus karma to a mood already entrenched "back East" and "out West," Tatum was elected Student Body President of the whole university, replacing the perennial three-piece suits that had held the position for eons. Tatum's hair had Brillo-ed into a spongy Afro, and his black-rimmed sunglasses became a trademark for all the members of Alpha Phi Alpha.

C.C. Chastain remained wounded that his best friend Tatum had cut off all ties, leaving the search for the ultimate lead guitar ongoing, not to mention the dream of racial harmony. But wounded as C.C. was, he understood, and the institutional prejudice that caused the rift played second fiddle to C.C.'s anger when he received his letter from President—and Outstanding Pledge—Chipper DeHart: "You are hereby given 30 days' notice that failure to pay back dues for one year in the amount of $600.42 will result in proceedings for the revocation of your membership in Sigma Zeta Chi Fraternity."

* * *

Amy was pleased when Dot Turco selected her to participate in a small "consciousness raising group" held at Turco's home on Sunday nights. And she was elated when Dot asked her to serve as one of two student hosts to shuttle the new wunderkind of feminism—Gloria Steinem—around campus during her celebrated visit. But Amy was horrified to learn that Dot had selected "dear Monty" Guilford to serve as the other student-host.

After Steinem's presentation at the Student Union Ballroom—attended by several hundred women, a handful of bleeding-heart men, and one scoundrel (Uno)—the two student hosts and Steinem grabbed a few beers at the Peninsula, a local bar on an oblong strip of vacant land abutting the campus where, every midnight, a choral sing-along to "Hey Jude" was the tradition. Uno sat between the two women, dominating the conversation.

"So, *Ms.* Steinem, would you dismiss Freud in his entirety as patriarchal?" asked Uno with a smarmy emphasis on the 'Ms.'—Ms. Steinem's invention.

What a worm, Amy thought. *That very issue was one of Dot Turco's essay questions on last year's final exam.*

"No, Monty, it's better not to reject Freud, but use his writings to understand the inner workings of patriarchy, and how it has painted women as negative and passive."

Uno Guilford hung on every word, halting his chugalugs each time Gloria began to speak. Amy was appalled. *He's flirting with her! And that stony expression of hers doesn't fool me. I think she likes it!*

Then, beneath the table, Amy felt Uno's large hand grab her thigh, massaging her, while he continued to talk to Gloria without missing a beat. Horrified, Amy dropped one hand beneath the table and slapped it onto his while he tried to slide upward, along the inside seam of her slacks. "I especially enjoy reading Wollstonecraft," Monty said calmly to Steinem, "and how she describes oppression starting at home, where a woman is taught to be the toy of a man." Amy curled her fingers and dug her nails into the back of Uno's hand, hard enough, she thought, to draw blood. He didn't even wince as he slithered his paw from between her legs. "More guys like me need to read the early feminists. I especially like Woolf and Brittain."

Gloria said, "Monty, you are the exceptional man, I can tell you."

Amy knew she would never, *ever*, be able to tell Chipper what had just happened, all in a span of 10 seconds.

* * *

Amy was royally peeved that Audora was missing Cassie's candlelight. And with no good reason. "Bourgeois middle-class traditions," Audora had said. "Silly rituals that play no role in my life anymore."

As the candle went round and round the Beta Chi merry-go-round, only Amy knew for sure that tonight's girl was Cassie who would blow out the candle to announce she'd just been pinned by Larry "Drywall" Twohatchets.

Amy smiled as she looked at Cassie's squinty and excited expression, her eyes reduced to slits, while her freckles seemed to glow like stars in the dancing light of the candle each time it passed.

Amy caressed Chipper's pin over her left breast.

When Cassie blew out the candle in a moment of lustrous joy, Amy thought to herself—just as she had done at her own candlelight—how odd it is that the announcement of a new burning love is celebrated by blowing out a flame.

And when one of the Beta Chis flicked the lights back on, Amy looked at Cassie's beaming face, but felt uneasy for her friend who was so hopelessly lost in love.

* * *

The Trial of Mitch Addison was arguably the worst event in Chipper's fleeting political career. He lost control of the crowd somewhere shy of three minutes.

The most damning accusations came from the most damnable witnesses. Ernie and Uno poured out their boiling oil while Mitch sat in a chair, stony-faced, next to the President, where the spirit of the accused should have been evaporating.

Others joined in the slaughter with puny swatches of evidence ("I remember once when I offered Mitch my old copy of *Playboy*, and he said 'no,' like he didn't even care about naked girls or nothin'") that so flabbergasted Chipper he had no idea where to bang his gavel.

Mitch volleyed each of the charges lobbed his way, unflappable, always with a plausible explanation. Chipper was astonished that Mitch could sit there and defend himself so calmly against accusations considered by the mob as worse than murder itself, accusations so vile that someone should invent an 11th commandment, then highlight it with Magic Marker.

And as the southern flow of steam was met with the northern tempest of Mitch's defense, aimless eddies of emotion ripped at the hearts of everyone in the room.

A terrible monster seemed to have crawled back from the grave—the resurrected spirit of Black Jack DeLaughter. Some of Jack's lackeys were still seniors, many living off campus, but they were here tonight to maintain the purity of the chapter, and to make sure a friggin' junior President didn't do something stupid like protect a faggot pledge brother.

And pledge brother C.C. Chastain didn't help his own cause to save his own neck when he had the gumption to show up for the first time this year—dues still unpaid—to denounce his fraternity brothers for their prejudice and bigotry. Most felt C.C. would have been better off defending Mitch's manhood rather than offering tacit approval of queerdom with worn-out epitaphs best suited for racial issues.

Kong stood directly behind Mitch, an unofficial sergeant-at-arms, glaring at all those members spewing poison, as if he planned to break bones at a later date. But the spoken word was not Kong's forte, and Mitch had few articulators who were capable of neutralizing the acidic atmosphere that was growing so thick that Chipper thought he could feel his skin starting to sting.

Just at the moment when it seemed that those with pointy fingers were about to go outside to gather wood for the base of the burning stake, tongues slobbering in anticipation of the fiery conclusion to a vexing problem, former Pledge Trainer Ted Boone entered the chapter room.

Chipper hadn't seen the Mentor of the New Breed for at least a year, though his fame was chronicled in the student newspaper—"first student-written play ever produced by the School of Drama." And, more recently, the big city newspapers—"Ted Boone, who recently received his Masters from the College of Fine Arts, is holding city audiences spellbound with his new play. Certainly, one of Oklahoma's rising stars . . ."

As Ted strolled into the room, hipbones still leading by a smidgen, he looked neither left nor right. As he approached the President, Chipper could almost feel the epaulets being ripped from his shoulders for his failure to lead, his gross inadequacy in perpetuating truth and fairness as they had promised themselves in pledge meetings, in a time that seemed so much longer than a mere two years ago.

Chipper was sure that Boone was about to launch into one of the most grandiloquent soliloquies of all time, that his incisive words would dart about the room and puncture all forms of prejudice and deceit and backbiting, rendering the chapter whole again. It would be a speech talked about again and again for years to come. Not a Moses-come-down speech of anger, but a compilation of words so powerful that even a gentle voice could not contain them.

And then, with an arched black eyebrow that hooded a dark, scary eye, scanning the room like a kryptonite laser, Mother Emeritus uttered his entire speech: "Why? *Why? Why-y?*"

Boone's voice had the same musical tone, and the exact same word—each "why" a few notes lower than the last—that he had used to shame them as pledges after the panty raid.

Chipper agonized through each second of silence that passed, each second adding an hour it seemed, as he wrestled to understand the moment. Heads started to hang, eyes searched the salmon terrazzo floor, big-talkers became little-men. Then Ted Boone walked out of the chapter room after a mere one word, used thrice.

Mitch Addison was exonerated by a vote of 62 to 13, thus ruled "not queer" by a clear majority.

* * *

Al Marlowe encouraged Chipper to attend a hootenanny called "Campus Life" that rotated through the Greek houses where there would be singing and joking and revelry—delicious fun without a drop of alcohol, without so much as a wisp of weed, and certainly no Heavenly Blues.

Expecting to participate as a back-pew sleeper, Chipper was startled when a cute brunette greeted him at the door of the Chi O house with, "We've been worried about you. I thought maybe you wouldn't make it at all. Let me show you where you'll be performing." Rattled, Chipper felt her grab his hand and drag him into the spacious living room where the army of chairs had been regimented to stations at the periphery, and a lonely microphone stood at one end of the room.

Chipper began fighting a wooziness that threatened to end up as a kerplunking faint before he managed, "What are you talking about? I'm not performing."

"Oh, you're not the leader of the New Bloods? You're not Chase Callaway?"

"No." Chipper was rejuvenated at the prospect of mistaken identity.

"Oh," she giggled. "I'm sorry. I was told that the leader, the main guy, the guy who writes their hit songs, that he's—well, you know—heavenly. And, of course, they never show their faces on the album covers."

Chipper was both flattered and relieved, but still nervous to be so alone among these God-fearing strangers since there wasn't one Sig Zeta in his right mind who'd—but then again, Al Marlowe was a Sig. And so was All-American Ross "Let's start a Sig Bible study" Loveland.

"Don't you just love the New Bloods?" continued the girl. "I have all their albums. I can't believe they're coming here tonight, all the way from California."

Chipper had never heard of the New Bloods.

Finally, the familiar face of Marlowe arrived, along with Loveland who emceed the meeting of 60 or so kids, told fair-to-middling jokes, then introduced the real Chase Callaway, leader of the New Bloods. Music with a message.

Afterward, Al, Ross, and the real Chase Callaway took Chipper to the nearby coffee shop of the Wallaby Drive-In, where the three laid out their strategy to save the world one person at a time, in this case, starting with the Sig Zeta house.

Songwriter Chase told Chipper how he'd scored highest ever on the MCAT from his school at Far West Texas University, but he decided against going to med school at the last minute so that he could "lay my treasures in heaven." As the little Chi O had projected, Chase was heavenly, all right. Chipper worried he was a little "too heavenly" if he had chucked med school for religious songwriting. Then he realized his own hypocrisy as he was walking a similar razor's edge. Of course, journalism was a higher calling than—well, there was something more grounded about his dilemma.

The final group-chug of coffee secured their resolve to start the Sig Zeta Bible study next week, led by Ross. They would start with the *Book of John*. And they would meet in the President's room. Chipper would recruit the core attendees, and they would branch out from there, as the spirit moved.

And as spirits go, he felt least among these four. But when he shook hands, saying good-bye to Chase Callaway, he felt an uncanny kinship to this stranger.

* * *

And the Word spread. It spread down Senior Row, it spread through the pledge class, and it spread through the factions so sharply demarcated by these strange times. And the Word brought young men to a doddering knee as they prayed a simple prayer to relinquish control of their lives to God. The converts were the young men who formerly banged bottles of beer or smoked a little weed; the men who charged a dollar-a-head for Saturday night porn movies—8mm black-and-whites—where the men wore black socks and the women wore no shame; and, the men who proffered their barf to that sacred vomitorium—the Puke Pit. And the Word changed them.

Added to the Antiwar Movement, the Civil Rights Movement, the Women's Movement, and the Environmental Movement, came the Jesus Movement and the new moniker for its members—Jesus Freaks. Indeed, Jesus made the cover of *Time*. And if a loaf of bread were cut in the usual fashion according to these many movements, then the world had become fresh slices—save the Jesus Movement, where yet another cut was longitudinal, turning protester against protester, activist against activist, women's-libber against libber, tree-hugger against hugger.

And from the nonbelievers in the fraternity, a delegation arose and approached their President who was uncomfortably involved in the movement. And they told him that he was harming the House, and that if he continued, he would go down in history as the most divisive President in the history of the chapter.

And the President shuddered as he remembered a verse from Ross Loveland's Bible study—"And brother will deliver up brother to death"—a bizarre reward for all those who preach the gospel. And as the great champion of unity and synergy in Sigma Zeta Chi, the President was torn in two.

* * *

> *When dreams fade away*
> *As they sometimes do,*
> *And you've lost the light in your heart . . .*

Drywall Twohatchets fractured the chilly night air as his warbling tenor made every Beta Chi on the vast porch swoon. In his arms, a dozen roses. In his heart, a love for Cassie St. Clair, the likes of which few of the sorority girls had ever seen. To further seal Cassie's pinning, the entire fraternity was wooing the Beta Chis with "The Sweetheart Serenade," joining Drywall after the intro:

> *. . . And the starlight streams*
> *On the girl of my dreams . . .*

Chipper felt no stronger fraternal bonds than when music put every man on the same note. Factions melted. Lines were undrawn. Bygones were gone. And in those few lyrical minutes, all that was ever said about Sigma Zeta Chi was true.

After the serenade, Chipper held Amy in his arms by one of the white Corinthian columns near the front door. "All the guys are sayin' they want you for Sweetheart next year, you know."

"That's nice of them, but it's not a big deal to me."

"I wish it were."

"Besides, the way your popularity is crashing," she said, "I doubt I'll have the same chance this time next year."

"Not funny."

She kissed him with a smidgen more heat than usual. "You know I respect your opinions, Hon, whether it's God or anything else. We don't always have to agree. Just remember, you can take *anything* too far."

* * *

December 1, 1969—At least 60 Sigma Zs crowded into the TV room, overflowing the banks of sofas and chairs, extending to the entryway of the fraternity. How many frat rats could squeeze into a Volkswagen bug? Not nearly as many as could cram into Holy Hell to watch their own lives unravel on television.

Like everyone else, Chipper hoped to be in the final third. While the first third would definitely be drafted, the middle third was a maybe, but the final third was home free.

An estimated 850,000 young men were likely in fervent prayer with foxhole faith at this very moment. The honor in serving in Vietnam had just about evaporated.

On the TV screen, a water-cooler bowl contained 366 blue plastic balls, each marked with a birthday. A congressman in a suit, too old for war, gripped the side of the clear glass bowl with one hand, while he reached for the marbles with the other.

"September fourteenth," he announced.

The Sigma Zs in the TV room craned their necks in silence, searching for an unlucky bastard born on September 14 who, after his II-S college deferment expired into I-A status, would be off to BCT (basic combat training), then AIT (advanced individual training), then to the central highlands of Vietnam in the blink of an eye.

The TV room was quiet.

"April 24th—December 30th—February 14th—October 18th—"

Twobits let out a bloodcurdling scream and tore out of the room, proclaiming in the wind of his jet stream that he was headed for Grady's Pub where he intended to drink himself to death.

With a collective gulp, the entire fraternity realized, perhaps for the first time, that the Vietnam War had just waltzed into their home and snatched Twobits away, others to follow.

As the evening wore on, Sigs evacuated the TV room one by one, always alone. Friends couldn't leave to console the walking dead on their way to Grady's until their own numbers were called. Peatmoss finally joined his best friend Twobits when January 19th was announced, the 58th plastic ball. Now, together, they could be two tunnel rats in Vietnam, where bamboo booby traps shish kabobbed U.S. military intelligence.

The population shift from the TV room to Grady's Pub took hours, and even those whose lives were spared in the final third joined their fallen comrades. Chipper thanked God for #257, while Peachy thanked Lady Luck for being born on June 8th, a splendid #366.

Those who bunkered at Grady's first, of course, became the drunkest. And as Chipper toasted with the others, singing Sigma Z songs, laughing at graveyard humor, he was overcome by the horror of it all—each man had just traded his initiation number for a lottery number. Drywall was no longer #1408, he was #154; Twobits was no longer #1411, he was #5; Smokey Ray switched from #1407 to #291; and Chipper gladly dropped his #1401 for #257.

And he thought back to ninth grade in El Viento where they had studied a short story in English class called "The Lottery." How absurd the story had seemed at the time. And in the fraternal inebriation, he wondered if the symbols that writers use don't necessarily have to be symbols at all. Maybe writers just lay it out as it is.

* * *

Greek Review, directed again by C.C. Chastain, boasted another successful tour of the military bases, with frat boys and sorority girls singing and dancing and telling jokes to the young men on their way to be annihilated in Vietnam.

Incensed at the letter from that arrogant asshole President Chipper DeHart, who had threatened C.C.'s membership in Sig Zeta, Chastain told said President to "get screwed" when this same President had the reckless audacity to try out for percussionist.

"And don't bug me to play the drums for the annual Varsity Sing, either. Some buddyfucker you turned out to be."

Rumor held that C.C. Chastain was also in the process of providing the tunes to playwright Ted Boone's lyrics, and that the duo was closing in on a deal for an off-Broadway musical based on an old comic strip, "The Sorcerer of Siam."

* * *

Peachy Waterman Junior enjoyed the view of his world from the summit. Elected Campus King at this year's Campus Chest festivities, he was, for all practical purposes, the most popular guy on campus. The big-name bands, the flashy dancing, the once-only dates, made him simply irresistible.

Sure, his old friend, foolish Chipper DeHart might be Top Ten Everything, but none of that stuff mattered one iota.

Reigning over an empire that stretched from Canada to Mexico, embracing 71 Sig chapters, the Big Eight, the Southwest Conference, smaller colleges in Oklahoma, and approximately one-third of the Kickapoo Nation, Peachy named himself Generalissimo of the Wickiup World, and gave all his employees military rank.

"Peachy, I was wonderin' something," asked one of his semiloyal subjects who also happened to be the semiimpeached President. "With all the guys moving out of the house so that they can smoke dope and screw and stuff, well, we're not making ends meet here at the house. Treasurer Graham tells me we have six rooms empty, and we're losing hundreds of bucks every month. It's crazy 'cause we're pledging and initiating more than any house, thanks to you and your bands, but no one wants to live in the house. And no one wants to pay dues *out* of the house. I was thinkin' maybe if Wickiup could pay the dues of the out-a-house guys, we'd probably be all right."

"Well, well, well. Finally. After all these years. *Finally,* the great Chipper DeHart has to come crawling on his knees to his old buddy, begging for dough. I don't remember you needin' me before. I don't remember you helping me since Day One when we walked on this campus, when you started pretending to be Mister BMOC."

"Let me tell you something, before you start spoutin' off, Peachy. Number one, we're in financial trouble. The whole Greek system is in the red. Some say it's near the end for fraternities. And before you go struttin' your stuff, let me just inform you right here and now that I got you your Sig Zeta bid in the first place. I—"

"What?! What did I hear you say? *You* got *me* my bid? Well, aren't you just about the most arrogant sumbitch on the planet. Listen, peckerwood, you didn't get me nothin'. I conned my bid fair and square. It was my own doin'. I got me a bid, and I got Drywall a bid. Me, myself, and I, you dipshit. You want Wickiup money? Well, take a hike. You want to juggle the books so's the House Corporation will think your shit doesn't stink? Well, screw you. Must be some heap big awards coming up next year for Mr. I-Love-the-Golden-Cross-of-Sigma-Zeta-Chi. And now, you're toppin' it all off with that Varsity Voyagers crap. A Bible study, for chrissakes, right across the hall from me. I don't friggin' believe it."

* * *

And the Word spread not only through the Sig Zeta House, but also through Chipper's arteries, coursing to his fingertips, then back to his heart. The loneliness that had been gifted to him by Otherworld disappeared, and he began to remember Chase Callaway's claim of "storing treasures in heaven."

Chipper dropped out of all campus activities, save Sig Zeta, and became a regular at the outreach hootenanny Campus Life, a regular at a campus-wide Bible study, leader of the Sig Zeta Bible study, and then—as if his identity-switch with Chase Callaway had been prophetic—Chipper ended up as the weekly emcee at Campus Life, which was soon peopled by members of all fraternities, sororities, and independents.

"You're dropping out of everything?" came the collective cry.

"Yes."

"But you're the Comptroller-General of the Model United Nations. Next year you'll be Secretary-General. Do you realize how *huge* that is?"

"Yes."

* * *

"When I was a little girl, Chipper, when I looked at numbers on a page, I saw colors around them. Colors that no one else saw. I don't really remember as I got older when I couldn't see them anymore." Audora spoke so softly that Chipper could barely hear. They sat together in the TV room, waiting for Smokey Ray to arrive and escort his lover across the street to the SDS apartments.

"Yeah, Amy told me that story."

"When I was in high school I started having to wear glasses, and I remember we had this terrible ice storm in Dallas. Once every hundred years, they said. The trees were coated in a thick glaze, and the day afterward, the sun came out. It was so-o groovy. We had this honey locust tree out back, and when I feasted my eyes on it after I first got out of bed, it was decorated with thousands and thousands of prisms, tiny rainbows all over that tree that were more spectacular than any Christmas tree you could ever imagine."

"And your point?" Chipper's suppressed anger was masked as patience. *I'm trying to forgive you, Audora. I really am. Why can't you just apologize? I know I could forgive if you'd just say those two measly words:"I'm sorry." I take my half of the blame. So why can't you take yours? I'd forgive in a flash if I knew you were sorry. But I'm havin' a heckuvalot of trouble with this Christian bit about unilateral disarmament.*

Audora reached over and brushed Chipper's hair from his eyes, then stroked the side of his face, following his new sideburns with her forefinger down to his chin where she tapped him once like pushing an elevator button.

"The point is that when I got out of bed and put on my glasses, it happened again."

"What happened?"

"The color went away. When I wore my glasses, all the beautiful prisms disappeared. I knew then that clarity makes the world drab."

Chipper wasn't so sure that the secrets of the universe were revealed through freak ice storms, but he tried to act interested until an old conversation with Smokey Ray popped up from his memory. "Audora, you say that clarity makes the world drab, but Smokey Ray told me once that he considers himself a fog-lifter. That his whole purpose in life is to get people to see more clearly."

He had her, and he was proud of himself. *Yesiree, the old high school debate tricks can always come in handy.*

"My poor simple prince," she said. "You talk about being a writer, don't you?"

"Yes."

"Well, my dear, you're mixing your metaphors."

From the front door, Smokey Ray shouted, "Let's go," and Audora rose and left the TV room, a mixed twosome heading for the Alamo apartments where they could parallel their paradoxes.

* * *

On the day that Apollo 13 launched, a foreboding came when Paul McCartney announced he would no longer record with John Lennon, presumably because of Yoko. Drywall and Cassie might as well have been on another planet.

"Did you hear that the Beatles broke up?" said someone in the TV room while Drywall and Cassie necked.

"Really?" panted Cassie.

Days later, again in the TV room, Drywall and Cassie sat in the corner armchair, two pretzels interlocked, when astronaut James Lovell announced:

"This is the crew of Apollo 13 wishing everybody there a nice evening, and we're just about ready to close out our inspection of Aquarius and get back for a pleasant evening in Odyssey. Good night."

Nine minutes later, an oxygen tank blew, and the command module lost its normal supply of electricity, light, and water. The Apollo crew was a mere 200,000 miles from Earth.

Then, when Drywall and Cassie went to the second-run theater in Oklahoma City the next night to see "Marooned," the story of three astronauts stranded in space—playing again, no doubt, to capitalize on the fact that the U.S. currently had three astronauts stranded in space—they didn't really notice when the movie retro rockets failed, nor when ground supervisor Gregory Peck remained calm and cool, nor when it was finally suggested that one of the three astronauts volunteer to cut off his own oxygen supply to save the other two.

Later still, parked in a quiet nook near the river bottom, Cassie turned on the radio, twisting the dial through the channels:

"Like a bridge over troubled wat—"

"Today, the Milwaukee Bucks' center Lew Alcindor was unanimously named NBA Rookie of the—"

"SALT talks between the U.S. and Soviet Union resumed today in Vienna—"

"Well we all shine on, like the moon and the—"

"And now with our continuing coverage of the disaster in space, Apollo 13—"

"Leave it there, pumpkin," said Drywall.

"They never should have named a space mission using the number thirteen," said Cassie. "Numbers are powerful, good and bad."

They made love, never once hearing the radio as it continued:

"To recount, with only 15 minutes of power left in the Command Module Odyssey, the crew made their way to Aquarius, the Lunar Module. The Aquarius was only built for a 45-hour lifetime, so it was a miracle to last 90 hours. And now the whole world waits as the crew reenters the Earth's atmosphere at a speed of 24,680 miles per hour. The ill-fated Apollo mission is currently in a total radio communication blackout, dear listeners, that is lasting forever . . ."

* * *

Prepare yourself, you know it's a must;
Gotta have a friend named Jesus.
So you know that when you die,
He's gonna recommend you to the spirit in the sky . . .

Chipper, energized by Norman Greenbaum's new hit, turned off the radio and prepared himself for Mark 16:15 (And He said to them, "Go into all the world and preach the gospel to all creation."), with no less emphasis on Romans 1:16 (For I am not ashamed of the gospel, for it is the power of God for salvation to everyone who believes, to the Jew first and also to the Greek.).

Chipper had resisted the dictum to evangelize. In fact, part of the enormous appeal of All-American Ross Loveland's leadership in the Bible study was that Ross, too, seemed more content with "touch-other-lives-by-your-own-example" rather than the "grab-'em-by-the-collar" approach some Voyagers seemed to extol. But Chipper could never completely shake Otherworld, and he thought it his mission to tell Smokey Ray, then Audora, about Another Way.

As he made his way from the President's room to the downstairs one-man room of the guru, Chipper remembered that Smokey Ray was his only friend of whom he was half-afraid.

"Hey, what's doin'?" asked Chipper, soft-pedaling as he entered Smokey Ray's room.

"Reading. Always reading. So many thoughts, so little time."

"What're you reading?"

"*On the Road*, by Kerouac."

As usual, Chipper had never heard of the book or the author. Smokey Ray somehow knew how to tap the underbelly of the world.

Recognizing Chipper's ignorance, Smokey Ray continued, "Come on, daddy-o, you call yourself a writer? Kerouac's the architect of the Beat Generation, a hippie before his time, a beatnik before they even had a name."

"Is it any good?"

"Not all that it's cracked up to be, in my opinion. Stream of consciousness, free-associating prose, funny language like 'he's a real gone cat', and whatnot. At times, it sounds like it's being written by a kid in grade school, but then the grooviness starts to spin if your ears don't flap over."

"Oh."

"So, why'd you want to meet tonight, Chipper?"

"Well . . . I . . . you know how we have the Sig Zeta Bible study every week—"

"Say no more, my man. Count me out. I know why you're here, and you have no idea who you're talking to."

Chipper felt his career as an evangelist sliced, diced, and pureed, all in a matter of seconds.

"You know, cowboy, we've played golf and been friends for a long time, but you never really get to know a guy 'til you start talkin' religion. And odds are you'd lose 90% of your friends if you let it all hang out. That's why it's usually best to keep such things to yourself. Dig?"

Chipper recalled Mark 16:15 to be in direct conflict to "keeping things to yourself."

"Did I ever tell you, Chipper, that my old man was a minister of sorts?"

"Of sorts?"

"Yeah. Didn't go to school for it. Just announced it one day. Plumber turned preacher. I didn't grow up in Pottawatomie per se, but in a little craphole my old man renamed Grace after he became Brother Divine or Preacher Divine or Father Divine, whatever folks wanted to call him. About four hundred people there, two hundred living in wooden shacks, two hundred living in mobile homes, and just one brick building—the church my old man built with poor folks' spare change. My whole family lived there in a wing of the church. My mom, sister, me, and the old man.

"The old man was a faker deluxe. Handled snakes, cast out demons, spoke in jibberish that he practiced beforehand to make folks think it was tongues. And he humped a good portion of the women in the congregation while Mom turned her Christian cheek.

"But none of that holds a candle to what the old coot did to my sister."

Chipper rued the moment that he memorized Mark 16:15, and he hoped to wipe it from his memory soon.

"After my sister got her boobs, the old man would sit there at dinner praying to his phony god, begging forgiveness for the lust in his heart for my sister. Right there in front of her. In front of Mom. Never touched her to my knowledge, but in the evenings, he'd force my sister to take a cat-o'-nine-tails and flog him for his sins of lust. 'Consecration,' he called it. 'Sick,' I called it, and I moved out of the house and lived in one of the empty mobile homes my last two years of high school. Just me and my golf clubs and my yellow pickup in that old rat trap."

"What about your sister?" asked Chipper, remembering how Smokey Ray had refused to discuss the subject when they'd made out their biographical crib sheets for pledgeship.

"I don't know. She's probably dead. She ran away from home when she was 16, got into heroin in L.A., started making cheap porno movies, turning tricks, and who knows what else."

What else is there? thought Chipper.

"I tried to find her that summer two years ago, you remember, when we were on our way to California right after Audora worked so hard to turn you on? Well, we dropped down to L.A. after the Santa Clara rock festival, and I found out my sister was last seen when a john picked her up on Sunset, just east of the Strip. No one saw her after that. I figure she's probably dead. So see, there's the fruit of my old man's ministry. I think sometimes you do more harm to people with your words. You don't even have to touch."

"I'm sorry, Smokey Ray. I really don't know what to say."

"Don't get me wrong, Chipper. I'm not ruling out some kinda God out there. I'm just not sure how he works. Look at this—"

Smokey Ray pulled a three-ring binder from a bottom drawer, then handed it to Chipper. "Leaf through that, will ya'? I put it together myself. See what happens to the folks who believe the stuff my old man was handin' out."

It was a scrapbook. Newspaper headlines, photos, and stories, all taped neatly in place. Chipper flipped through the 50 pages or so, reading such items as: "Freak Mud Slide Covers Church Bus, Killing 22 Children en Route to Bible Camp," "Lightning Strike Kills Church Organist during Service," "Basketball-sized Meteor Crashes into Church Picnic, Killing Four, Injuring Eleven," and the last entry, "Drunken Minister Hails Congregation with Bullets, Three Dead, Six Wounded."

"That one you're looking at might well have been my old man, but it's not. You see, he just keeps on keepin' on. Just added a new brick wing to his mighty fine church, profiting well. I made that scrapbook after I moved out of the house to remind me to come to my senses if I *ever* was tempted to believe in my old man's god. You see, cowboy, it's far easier for me to believe there's a Devil."

"But the guys in the Bible study, uh, we're not talking about that god, we're talking about—"

"Don't kid yourself, Chipper. I can rattle off my old man's sermons, and it wouldn't sound a darn bit different. Leave out his snakes, leave out his bullshit rehearsals to speak in tongues, leave out his impregnation of choir members and the mysterious miniepidemic of gonorrhea that he cured with prayer and penicillin, and he was sayin' the same thing you Varsity Voyagers are saying in that Bible study.

"I know the Bible very, very well," continued Smokey Ray, "and I can quote hundreds of verses. Don't underestimate me here. What's more, I can quote from the Gospel of Thomas. You ever heard of that one? It's almost as old as the four gospels. But it ain't in the Bible, is it? Your Bible was put together in its present form a long, long time after Jesus walked. And I can hear you guys talkin' in the halls and at meals about the original Greek, the original Hebrew, the original this and that. Let me tell you something, cowboy, *none* of the *original* documents exist. That's why the Jews have a different Old Testament. Theirs is from the *Massoretic Text*, while the Christians use the *Septu-*

agint. And I won't even go into the *Vulgate*, the Latin version that the Catholics go by.

"But like I said, don't get me wrong. There's a damn good chance there's a God out there. I told you once I was searching for enlightenment. For all I know, Apollo is the real God of Light. Maybe the Greeks had it right. But one thing for sure, I ain't buyin' into a God that lets meteors kill his followers.

"By the way, I hear tell you've been selected to be on some debate team for those Voyagers, going to colleges all over arguing the Christian way. Well, just remember something for me, will you? If you could explain and argue and prove every little tidbit of Christianity, then it wouldn't require faith at all, would it? Be careful, cowboy; don't go shovin' things down folks' throats. Remember, your precious John Calvin once approved the burning of a Unitarian—a slow fire, with the heretic's published book strapped to his leg as he roasted. But don't fret. Calvin, being the nice guy he really was, actually wanted to use a more humane approach—decapitation."

Chipper was decimated. His rehearsed presentation seemed as empty as the decorative bottles of Weller's whiskey on Smokey's shelf. Now he understood why they called the art of Christian persuasion *apologetics*.

"I don't know how to explain all that stuff, Smokey Ray. There're dark forces at work in this world, and it makes no sense sometimes. But I kinda try to stick to one thing that Ross Loveland told us in the Bible study—Man says, 'Show me and I'll believe.' But God says, 'Believe and I'll show you.' I think there's a reason that the words 'faith' and 'leap' go together."

And Chipper left the room, apologetically, but not sorry.

* * *

Smokey Ray and Peachy left the local head shop where they had been checking the inventory for the addition of sundry products into Wickiup Enterprises. Smokey Ray would be a lieutenant, in charge of the new Counterculture Division. Peachy had resisted including drug paraphernalia in Wickiup for fear of drawing attention to those annoying fiscal details, but the prospect had grown too lucrative. Pot had infested every campus in the country. Whereas Greek pledges had been de-pledged three short years ago for smoking dope, now the officers were dealing. It was time for Wickiup to take its rightful place in this new economy.

As they started to climb into Peachy's red Vette, they heard a woman scream—

"Stop him! Somebody stop him! He's trying to kill my baby."

A young girl stood 50 yards away on an overpass, while a long-haired guy tried to pry away a bundle from her arms.

Before Peachy could wiggle out of his seat, Smokey Ray was in a dead run. And before Peachy could muster a run, Smokey Ray was on the scene. And by the time Peachy arrived at the scene, Smokey Ray had pushed the guy away from the bawling girl, then forced the monster away with the evil eye as only Smokey knew how to deliver.

And when Smokey reached to comfort the girl, she said, "Please take her. He'll just kill her later if you don't take her. Please, she's got to have a good home." And she thrust the Indian-blanket bundle into Smokey Ray's arms and ran away.

Peachy peeled back the blanket, and a soft pink tongue tickled his fingers. "Well, I'll be," he said. "She's a puppy."

"I wonder what kind she is. Looks like a mutt. Maybe part-cocker with those big eyes. But maybe golden retriever."

"Hey, let's keep her," said Peachy.

"Are you crazy?"

"She can live at the Sig Zeta house. Hell, with everyone movin' out of the house, we got empty rooms. Make one for her. Get the pledges to clean her shit and all."

"Hmmm."

"What should we call her?"

"How 'bout Toto, like in *The Wizard of Oz*?"

"No. The Sig Alphs already have a dog named Toto."

"I got it then," Smokey Ray said. "Rickelbell."

"Rickelbell? What kind of name is that?"

"Rickelbell. After our two founders — Clovis Rickel and Thatcher Bell. She'll be our mascot."

And the sweet mistress of serendipity was wed to 60-plus guys who treated her like a queen, who fought for her attention, who gitchy-gooed like babies as they played with her endlessly. And Rickelbell became more than a mascot. She became a force that insisted that her men keep at least one heartstring soft and supple just for her.

And the President was pleased that, once again, there was a unifying spirit in the house.

* * *

"My gosh, it's just like that old panty raid when we were freshman," said Amy as she and Chipper tried to make their way into the Microbiology building for class.

Swarms of students, in swirls and streams, were crisscrossing campus in aimless desperation.

"No. Back then they were more organized. This is complete chaos."

The clamor of the crowd almost drowned out their conversation.

"They really did it this time," said Amy. "Just when I thought things might be turning the corner. But killing college kids, girls even, Chipper, I'm scared."

"I'd never heard of Kent State."

"Me neither. Did you ever think we'd see a day when troops came onto a college campus? And that they'd open fire?"

"Where's it gonna stop? The whole world's on fire, seems like. The radio this morning said there's rioting on almost every campus in the country."

A hippie riding a bicycle spun to a stop in front of Chipper and Amy, then hopped off, letting his bike fall. He sprang like a mad dog toward Chipper, knocking him to the ground. The hairy radical grabbed one of Chipper's books, then began ripping out pages. It was his Micro text. "Biologic warfare!" screamed the hippie. "Don't you know what they're doing in that building? Germ warfare! Army research. Pull your head out, buddy, it's revolution—NOW!"

The hippie heaved the mangled book at Chipper, and their eyes met. It wasn't a hippie at all! Not in the normal sense, that is. It was Oliver Kirby, ex-President Perry Crane's other top choice, along with Chipper, to pledge Sig Zeta back on that hot box day in the fall of 1967.

Two days later, over four hundred colleges and universities were closed.

*　*　*

Al Marlowe got engaged to one of the most beautiful coeds on campus, Susie Walters, a Varsity Voyager girl with a smile so bright her entire face seemed to be the corona for the dazzling white of her teeth. And she laughed every bit as often as Al. And they visited the Sig house often. As did Ross Loveland, tackling the fraternity with joy.

While the power behind the Word was an ill-defined spirit, fiancee Susie gave striking visage to the power, effecting one of the greatest revivals in fraternity history. At least 20 more Sig Zetas, and countless others from other houses, dropped to their knees and prayed for someone like Susie.

And so it became standing room only for the Bible study in the President's suite, as a group of hard-cores dedicated their lives, surrounded by a crowd of pulp that fully intended dedication while maintaining a modicum of personal liberty, as well as a rind of curiosity-seekers. Multitudes pondered a bite into the fruit, especially if they could taste such plums as Susie Walters.

* * *

"Peachy, get line two," said roommate Drywall. (Peachy was the only guy on campus with two lines.) "It's your lieutenant at Ball State. Says he's got a hot tip on air-conditioners."

"Air-conditioners!" Peachy stumbled across the room to the phone.

Air-conditioners had been both Holy Grail and Nasty Nemesis for Peachy who knew the windfall would be boundless. Small window units with large profit margins had been surprisingly impossible to come by. Exhausting his Mexican pipelines, Peachy had all but given up hope. Yet he clung to the belief that out there, somewhere, was a unit so small, so efficient, so cheap, he could refrigerate the world of fraternities, sororities, and dorms nationwide, while setting fire to Wickiup's bank balance.

"Yeah . . . sure . . . you bet, Dave. Earthquake damage? Okay, I guess. If the coils are damaged in only five percent, we'll be able to offer free replacement with that kind of markup. Sure, we got double-hung windows, but some houses don't. Lots of dorms don't. That'll sorta limit our market, but. . . . yeah, sure. Ten per cent finder's fee? How 'bout five per cent with increasing yield depending on sales? Remember, I've got capital *and* distribution. That'll be copacetic. Deal."

* * *

Chipper beamed that his creative brilliance was so elusive. The circuit-riding rep from Headquarters was baffled by the trick photography in the Rush Film, so Chipper explained his special concoction of stop action coupled with sharp-eyed editing.

"And all those old movie clips you spliced in," said the touring Sig, "it's really good. Tell you what I'm going to do. We're still making out the schedule for Workshop this summer, and I'd like you to give a presentation on how you made that Rush Film. If they do films at all, most chapters are just shooting the parties, and poorly at that, but you've really captured the life of a Sig Zeta. Would you be willing to do that?"

"Sure." Chipper relished the thought of delivering a talk on film-making. After all, his work of art was nothing short of an 8mm backyard masterpiece.

"But what I'm really here to ask you is if you'd be willing to come one day early to Workshop. Headquarters is asking 10 Presidents from around the country to brainstorm a day before the General Session begins, on thoughts to save the Greek system. To be honest, we don't think we're going to survive the radical changes underway, certainly not in our present form. Who'd ever thought we'd be longing for the good old days when the only major problem was alcohol?"

"But it's not just drugs, and it's not just psychedelia," said Chipper. "It's a whole new way of thinking. And the Greeks who've stayed traditional, in just the three short years I've been on this campus, have gone from running the campus to being dinosaurs."

The slick young professional Sig Zeta, sitting on the edge of the President's desk, enjoying the refrigerated air, said, "That's the point. We can't seem to get a handle on what's happening. I'm hoping you'll come early for that session. I'll finish my report on your chapter tonight, then I'll be headed back in the morning. So I can count on you then? For both the Rush Film session and the other?"

"You bet."

"By the way, I think there's a real chance that next year's International Aegis Award Winner will come out of that group of 10 Presidents."

Chipper felt an electrical surge inside like he hadn't felt in years, just thinking about being named the outstanding Sigma Zeta Chi in North America. And he began to rehearse his resume in his head: *Phi Beta Kappa, Top Ten Greek Men, Pre-med through . . . Journalism? Jeez, what am I going to do with my life?* Then he remembered ex-pre-med Chase Callaway, storing treasures in heaven, not to mention Al Marlowe's recent pledge to leave law school for the ministry.

***

Chipper thought he was late to the Bible study taking place in his own room, but given the customary revelry and hallelujahs that came through the cheap wooden door, he checked his watch to make sure he had the right time, for there was odd silence at his doorway. And before he could open it, the door swung open and two escapees—Peatmoss and Twobits—said, "We're outta here" before Chipper could see the problem.

And the problem, so blatant upon entering this Bible study turned funeral parlor, was a new member of the group—Ernie Dumas.

Chipper's faith plunged precipitously. And during the meeting, Chipper was sickened by his own skepticism while Ernie droned on and on about his life-changing experience, and how the born-again Ernie had to sever his friendship with Uno Guilford over his commitment to God.

Afterward, Chipper went to the Student Union with leader Loveland, where they met Marlowe, and where Chipper confessed his incredulity and his poor attitude. He told the two men that Ernie had done "the most horrible things" since he'd known him, and it was one thing for a lackluster dude to shine with the power of God, but quite another for the rotten-to-the-core to suddenly proclaim being the apple-of-God's-own-eye. The placating response of Ross and Al wasn't enough for Chipper. Obviously, they didn't live in the same fraternity with Dumas. They didn't understand. God's "mysterious ways" didn't cut the mustard this time.

Quite simply, Chipper couldn't believe the conversion. And if he believed it, his own conviction was simply too weak to be excited about this allegedly saved soul who, as Chipper put it, would alienate people from Christianity faster than if Billy Graham said, "Don't come forward." It was horribly judgmental, he knew, but Chipper couldn't imagine how the same God who had set the fraternity ablaze through Al Marlowe (and Susie Walters) would turn right around and undo everything with Ernie Dumas.

Although the year was winding down, Chipper knew that *next* year, there would be plenty of available seating in the President's room for Bible Study. Then Chipper felt the demonic pull of a thought so vile he couldn't believe the voice inside him: *"Hey, don't worry. With summer coming, Ernie will probably smoke enough dope (or worse) to put himself into a major backslide, and we'll never have to deal with him."*

* * *

Amy was in a great mood. She had placed second in the first official Big Eight Women's Golf Tournament, and the team came in second as well. She had scored well on her first MCAT—in fact, well above Chipper—for medical school interviews next year. She had her fifth straight four-point GPA in the bag. And Peachy had paid her a small fortune for assuming the Wurlitzer jukebox distributorship on campus. But she couldn't understand why Chipper was such a grump.

She and Chipper were on their way to the popular second-run theater in Oklahoma City to celebrate the end of finals. The double feature would be showing last year's hits, *Easy Rider* and *Midnight Cowboy*. On the car radio, the Sandpipers were oozing their new version of the hit song from *Sterile Cuckoo* that she liked so well, and she started to sing along.

"What's the matter, Hon? Why aren't you singing?" she asked.

"I dunno."

"Are you still grousing about Ernie showing up at your Bible study?"

"I suppose so."

"That's silly. It's not that big of a deal." Then she began whistling with the song.

"You *do* remember that Ernie darn near raped Cassie once upon a time, don't you?" he asked with a sarcastic snarl. "It's only 'cause Cassie didn't want to tell anyone that he didn't end up in big, big trouble. And remember, too, it was Ernie who led the charge to destroy Mitch Addison?"

(She stopped whistling.)

Chipper continued, "So how do you think I feel associating with the guy, especially every time I look at Drywall or Mitch?"

Amy sighed. "I don't know, Hon. I don't know what the answer is. Time will probably tell you if he's serious or not."

Inside the theater, they settled into a back row where smooching couples were the norm, surfacing for air periodically to watch previews of future old movies. Over the past few years, Amy had noticed fewer and fewer couples kissing, whereas more and more were openly firing up joints, so much so that the smoke formed a visible haze in front of the screen. And when the previews for the old classic *Reefer Madness* showed, the audience howled at the antidope message in its archetypical form.

But when the previews for the religious epic *In the Beginning* started to play, the crowd quieted again in slippery reverence. A never-ending string of stars was introduced to the half-stoned audience, all huge names, playing major roles, minor roles, cameos, while a booming radio voice announced each with the same pomposity.

And with a celluloid flicker, hero Jake Chisum appeared on the screen, standing on a rock ledge, proud face to the thunder and wind, dressed in a pleated skirt made of metal plates. The announcer called out, "And Jake Chisum as the Roman Centurion," and the theater crowd roared in laughter with quadruple the force they'd expelled at *Reefer Madness*. And the hilarity wouldn't stop.

Amy could feel Chipper stiffening in his seat before he said, "How—*how* did it come to this? Not two years ago, guys were signing up left and right to volunteer for Vietnam after watching Brother Chisum in *Silver Wings*. And now, we're sitting here with a bunch of dope-smoking freaks who are pretending to be intellectuals, and Jake Chisum is nothing but a joke?"

And she knew Chipper well enough to know that he was angry, and maybe afraid, because, indeed, Jake Chisum did seem quite the joke.

Senior Year (1970–71)

38

The President—the *senior* President, unfettered from last year's intimidation wrought by premature investiture to the throne—was enjoying the fact that *this year*, the roundtable would be peopled by his pledge brothers. His knuckles could go unpopped; his fingernails could grow.

Actives had been streaming into the President's quarters since the beginning of the school year with vexing frequency—complaining without solution, pontificating without a point, haranguing just for the hell of it—but always depositing well-heeled information that added nothing toward omnipotence for the President, yet it did allow a taste of omniscience.

Now, in the overstuffed wingback that engulfed him more and more with blissful security, Chipper sank into its softness while a pageant of thoughts and calculations roved freely. In a way, the chair had become a talisman that dissolved time, allowing him to wallow in the past and revel in the future, all in the now.

* * *

Last summer's Sig Zeta Workshop left a lasting, resonating glory. From the gang of 10 Presidents in the Greek-preserving brainstorming session, Chipper had been chosen as "one of three" to report to the General Assembly of several thousand. *Could this mean I'm in the middle of the hunt for the International Aegis Award?*

Then, feeling the power of the podium, Chipper had taken his shining moment to admonish the vast congregation of Sig Zetas to reclaim their Christian roots, to dedicate their lives to the glory of God, as distinct from the praise of Men, and to lay their treasures in Heaven. *A tour de force, O, Great Lion of God.*

Never, in the quiet months that followed, did it occur to Chipper that his holy pride served as an intoxicant, numbing his mind to the notion that Phariseeal espousals could whisk away communion with God without leaving a footprint. While the message may have been an arrow of truth, the archer may have been drunk.

What perplexed and consumed the President, though, was the delight he felt through leading the miniworkshop on "The Making of a Rush Film." Every moment was bliss, every question a spark, every challenge a thrill. But there was no filmmaking beyond college. This path was a cul-de-sac. In fact, it didn't seem to be a path at all, and he stuffed away the joy.

During the summer that followed Workshop, Chipper concocted a master plan, a scheme to fuel a growing obsession and to inspire the Sig Zetas to win campus "Fraternity of the Year," no easy feat since the Betas were systematic, perennial winners. And if such accolades were to incidentally bolster his chance at the International Aegis Award— well, then so let it be written.

Most remedial in this quest would be the chapter's overall GPA, up from nineteenth to fifth last year by virtue of New Breed study habits, still considered heinous by Dying Breed remnants. Einstink— the sweating, body-building genius—always devastated if his guaranteed 4-point was sullied by any test score less than 100—agreed to serve as Scholarship Chairman. Twobits was ordered to remove his pet skunk from its home in the study hall, and—of course—the room would have to be furnished. There would be rules, fines, even public humiliation if necessary, to ignite a love of scholarship.

Intramurals carried as much weight as chapter GPA in the Fraternity of the Year point system (thank goodness), and the Sig Zeta house was jubilant at the very real prospect of capturing the title. New initiate Kevin Morrison would, amazingly, stoop to serve as Intramural Chairman. Kevin was a senior, having pledged Sig Zeta as a junior after serving as student body president while still an independent. In fact, Kevin was the last three-piece suit to hold the office before revolution placed Afro-sporting John Tatum in power. Kevin had also served as president of the Big Eight Student Government Association and was a national debate champion, following in the footsteps of former President, now Harvard Law, Perry Crane.

Kevin had chosen a fairly focused life-goal: to become President of the United States of America. But before pointing his compass in that direction, he had decided to pledge a fraternity and raise hell his final year in college. After that, law school and the primary elections. Six-foot-three Kevin—with unflinching grin and a seemingly outstretched hand even when sitting on his thumbs—was a former state tennis champ. While the chapter was almost embarrassed to ask him to serve in this "minor" office, Kevin secretly considered it the most exciting post in his career. It became his raison d'être.

Actives would be required to enter a minimum number of events to snag points wherever possible (the Betas had pulled this stunt for years). No sport was so small as to render it pointless. Even President Chipper set an example by playing B-team volleyball, C-team basketball, swimming, badminton, Ping-Pong, racquetball, and bowling (he refused golf).

Kevin secured his station as exemplar when he recruited two independents—5th-year seniors—to pledge Sig Zeta in order to shepherd A-team football. The quarterback-receiver twosome had been the Hanratty-to-Seymour ("Fling and Cling") equivalent at an anonymous small college national champion, transferring to Oklahoma after eligibility expired, in order to complete their engineering degrees.

In an excruciating moral dilemma lasting all of three seconds, Chipper okayed their "special pledgeship," later confirmed by a knee-jerk unanimous chapter vote. The duo would be treated like the varsity jock-pledges—no inquisitorial "meals," no Worksessions, no mental hazing—though they would still have to study the pledge manual and pass the test for nationals that, conveniently, took place after football season.

The offensive line was so pumped they couldn't wait for the start of the season. They drove to Ardmore High School two-a-days where the delirious coach mistook them—even balding Kong—for new kids in town, announcing them as starters and predicting a state championship season. When Rush Week began, the poor Ardmore coach lost his entire front line.

Then, Chipper and Amy plotted for the Sig Zetas and Beta Chis to join at year-end for Varsity Sing, the ensemble talent show that carried its own fair share of points for Best in Show. Dance King Peachy Waterman and Amy would codirect the act. Hopefully, C.C. Chastain would help, though his unpaid dues remained a dark cloud.

And there would be "community service" until it hurt.

No points were given for parties. And this was unfortunate, for Wickiup Enterprises International and its Generalissimo had gone beyond legend already. Last year the fraternity had enjoyed the Kingsmen, the Ventures, and the Spencer Davis Group, to name a few.

Granted, these bands were separated by a few years from their glory hits, but any one of them could have mopped the floor with the local bands that entertained the poverty-stricken frats with half-filled houses.

But a subtle current had started coursing through the veins of the Sigma Zs last year—band boredom. Big Names became the norm. Bigger Names became a bigger norm. The people wanted more. In spite of the fact that the Turtles had provided their repertoire for the first party of the year already, Actives had scattered to their rooms after the first set ended with "Happy Together." Tucked away in their private dens, the brothers smoked dope, watched the boiling permutations in their lava lamps, and enjoyed the soft comfort of coeds, under new and wonderfully lax university rules that finally allowed girls in their rooms.

And the texture of these parties blended flawlessly with Three Dog Night's latest Number One Hit, "Mama Told Me Not to Come."

While the new Wickiup product line—air-conditioners—was cooling campuses across the Southwest, simultaneously heating revenues, trouble was brewing.

Peachy, unaware that pinnacles are precarious, started down that well-worn path common to even the most benevolent autocrats— he flaunted his wealth. And it came in twos. No one cared when he installed his second phone, or his second refrigerator, or his second television. And his second car—a red 1961 "bug-eyed" Austin Healy Sprite—raised nary an eyebrow. But when he made his grand entrance at the Western Party with a blonde ballshaker on each arm while the Turtles played, "She'd Rather Be with Me," there was more pissing and moaning than a hundred soldiers in Saigon suffering from the clap.

Overnight, Wickiup truck drivers demanded more pay and fewer trips to Mexico. Some drivers even refused to wear their jackets with the Wickiup logo. Bribing their acquiescence was not enough, and Peachy finally agreed to a cutback on sorties to Mexico and thus, a cutback on cash flow.

Profits on the air-conditioning front were countered by losses in several of the subsidiaries. The Phi Delts managed to steal back the campus bookie concession, and the Women's Line collapsed completely. "Colonel" Mitch Addison did not return for his senior year, transferring to a small college somewhere near San Francisco. Peachy was livid that his peddler of women's wares left him holding the bag, having just received a truckload of platform shoes, matching sets of crocheted hats and scarves, bales of pantyhose, velvet chokers with cameos, and the latest rage—hot pants.

While turning points are sometimes difficult to define when rounding the bend, perhaps the Beet Rebellion should have been seen as such a signpost. When the Actives returned for fall semester, they were greeted by beets. Beets for lunch. Beets for dinner. Optional beets for beet-lovers at breakfast. Beets au gratin, beets au jus, but no beets au revoir. Just beets and more beets for every meal, day after day, until a posse nearly lynched the Kitchen Manager, brother Wallace Johns. Threatened with a frying pan, Wally finally squealed: "It's Peachy's fault. Peachy made me do it. We've still got three more months of beets to go!"

And the investigation did not stop there. Sig Alphs, Fijis, Delts, Betas, Sigma Nus, Phi Delts, Kappa Sigs—turns out, every probing phone call found a Fort Knox of Beets. Everyone was steeped in beets. Sororities, too. Even the dorms. And yes, the inquiry extended to the schools in Kansas, Colorado, Missouri, Iowa, Nebraska, Arkansas, and Texas. Beets were pandemic. It seemed that Peachy had cornered the world market.

Then, one evening after Mom Miller excused herself from the meal (beet-kabobs), the Actives, led by Wally the Kitchen Manager, staged their revolt. Several hundred gallon cans of beets were opened and readied as ammunition, and with Mom's exit, the entire Chapter single-filed into the kitchen where each Active took his stockpile and exited the swinging doors to hand-dump the contents onto the Generalissimo's head. But there was no '*Et tu, Brute?*' from Peachy, who was honored by the attention.

After four or five orderly dumpings, the moment escalated into full beetmania with slinging, heaving, and tossing beet bombs across the dining room, first at Peachy, then randomly.

Peachy, covered in the gooey blood-red of beet syrup, joined in the melee until all were likewise covered, and the salmon terrazzo floor became a skating rink for a throng of Hans Brinkers slipping and sliding through the crimson slime.

Always aspiring to become the ultimate gross-out artists, Twobits and Peatmoss assumed their ongoing competition by trying to eat the most beets off the floor, joining Rickelbell, without using their hands. When Peatmoss pulled ahead in the competition, Twobits upstaged him, winning the event by his grody-to-the-max coup d'etat, using a sweeping reach into the drooling mouth of Peatmoss, pulling out the red mulch, and swallowing the cud himself.

Peachy thought it all great fun, forgetting the financial loss, oblivious to the possibility of a turning point.

Although food fights were expected as a college norm, this beet bath was the only such event at the Sig Zeta house during these years.

Indeed, with the elegant Mom Miller at the roundtable, members were consistently adept at feigning gentlemanly ways.

The fact that Rickelbell was routinely allowed to eat at the table with the members was not considered out of the realm of decent manners; however, to be on the safe side, the house mascot was not invited to sneak through the sliding glass doors and jump into her chair until Mom had excused herself each evening.

Rickelbell was mostly golden retriever, it was assumed. And she ate her Alpo and leftovers du jour gracefully, barely dropping chunks on the tabletop. She blended well, for her chair of honor was at the senior gross-out table staffed by Peatmoss and Twobits, whose place mats were every bit as chunky by the end of mealtime.

The mascot's wardrobe had recently been switched from red bandannas to velvet chokers with cameos (unlimited supply), and a Sig Zeta pin was attached to this sweetheart's choker as well.

She had no single master, and she refused to sleep in her own room as was the original design, slinking instead to those rooms with an abundance of snacks and petting hands, mostly the former. A nightly ritual at the house became Rickelbell going door-to-door surveying the food supply. At least 12 rooms kept beds ready for her if her midnight snack led to slumber.

The lodging she chose most often was the Social Chairman's room across from the President where Peachy and Drywall competed for her devotion, Peachy favoring snacks, Drywall affection.

Peachy also taught the tricks, with everyone's favorite being, "Make Like a _____," where the blank was filled by the name of the sorority apropos for the moment. On command, Rickelbell would jump onto the nearest couch or bed, roll on her back, spread her legs and pant.

"Rickelbell, make like a Tri Delt," brought howls of laughter for Theta dates when the golden girl spread her legs, but then "Rickelbell, make like a Theta," created identical howling for the Tri Delts at a later time.

Rickelbell, in her finest velvet choker with cameo and fraternity pin, attended every football game, serenade, and party. On rare eventless days, she hung out mostly in the TV room, or wherever most of the Actives were planted. Other than a 20-dollar fine against Uno Guilford for the first offense, and a 50-dollar fine on the second offense, for getting Rickelbell drunk on Coors, life at the frat house was sweetened by her gentle spirit and wagging tail.

On the human side of life, Amy was a sweetheart for the chapter, the preseason favorite for an official crowning next spring at the Gala.

As president of the Little Sigma Z Auxiliary, she served as confidant for the lovelorn Actives, mother to overwhelmed and lonely pledges, and chief advisor to the President who generally chose to ignore her wisdom, adding fodder for the Actives' sport of quibbling with the President.

And she managed this all, even as she applied to 12 medical schools, far more than her male counterparts, having calculated her targets in consideration of male chauvinism ingrained in the selection process. Lukewarm Chipper applied to one—Oklahoma.

As mothers go, the new Pledge Trainer was Smokey Ray Divine. And for every sentence carved by Smokey Ray to instruct his pledges, he had two subjects in mind and maybe a verb, but only one of the subjects was ever mentioned. As always, his true message was concealed, or lost. Some pledges could hear the hidden subject, some couldn't.

Chipper could feel Smokey Ray's influence on the pledges as early as the first week, the day that NASA announced cancellation of two of the remaining six Apollo moon landings as a result of budget short-falls. In response, Pledge #1 said, "Good. The country's in chaos right now. They need to spend that money to solve all the problems at home." Then Pledge #2 answered, "But don't you see? They know money can't solve our problems. That's *why* we go to the moon." *Pure Smokey Ray*, thought Chipper at the time.

Smokey Ray had been promoted to Psychiatric Aide III at the local mental institution, Building #19 (the "experimental ward"), and it was reported by other college student-orderlies that the psychiatrists routinely turned to Smokey Ray to help them assess the wonder of their new drugs.

Inspired, Smokey Ray announced his plans to pursue a Ph.D. in a new division of psychology called "psychopharmacology." Connecting new synapses through neurochemistry was an area where Smokey Ray had done some field work and where comfort lay in his self-described role as a "fog-lifter." Sometimes, it seemed, the stodgy and sober transcendentalism of Emerson needed a kickstart.

While advised by Chipper to go for the M.D. so he would be able to write prescriptions, Smokey Ray rejected the advice, obsessed with the prefrontal cortex and limbic system. "Why waste my time on all the garbage from the neck down?"

Girlfriend Audora was spaced-out. Completely dissociated from Beta Chi sorority, she wasn't positively enrolled in school anymore. Apparently, she worked full-time on the Antiwar Movement. Shortly after the school year began, Chipper had seen her in the courtyard of the Alamo Apartments on his way to do his laundry. He had paused at the gateway long enough to watch her method of protesting the war in Vietnam—spinning to sitar music among a group of hippies, a flower wreath in her hair, a short diaphanous dress, while on her back she sported of set of fairy wings—about two feet across, made of translucent silk, with painted purple veins branching to wing tips. In her hand was a wand with a spangle on the end, which she dubbed onto the heads of her fellow hippies in time to the music. *Always transforming others*, he groused to himself.

On the other hand, Smokey Ray managed to straddle both worlds easily, always denying membership in the S.D.S., yet acting like a blonde Abbie Hoffman. Smokey Ray's motivation to be Pledge Trainer defied the average Joe College. Certainly, as a freshman he had been profoundly absorbed in intellectual jousting with Pledge Trainer Ted Boone. But after initiation, Smokey had never held office. When he announced his Pledge Trainer intentions the idea was such a novelty that he was swept into office by the "heavy" longhair majority in a landslide. The cowboy hat was long gone, and the headbanded hippie became known as Moguru (mother + guru) Divine. His pledge brothers, though, stuck with Smokey Ray.

Minority opposition to the Moguru's election was led by Ernie Dumas who drew upon the supernatural to explain and fortify his stance. While many of the brothers had reservations about a pot-smoking acid-head serving as Pledge Trainer (including Chipper), Ernie exerted a powerful anti-fluence on the chapter. If Ernie was agin' it, all others were for it. In the end, Ernie's claims that Smokey Ray's genius, his glib tongue, and his quixotic charm were entirely fueled by Beelzebub, brought the Unbelievers into staunch union *supporting* the new Moguru. So, very little effort was required to explain the mystery of how Smokey Ray became Pledge Trainer.

Ernie's limburger presence nearly decimated the Sig Bible study, reduced to a platform upon which Ernie ruled with long passages of memorized verses, while offering sanctimony so steep that Chipper couldn't recognize his own leanings, and he began to waffle in his commitment.

Al Marlowe and Susie married, then joined the full-time staff of Varsity Voyagers, where their first missionary assignment was to reach the restless natives of darkest Arkansas (University of). Thus the two ultimate role models for Christianity were gone, replaced by the ultimate dumb ass—Ernie. Chipper, who had devoured the works of C.S. Lewis to squeeze into his rightful spot in the Christian intelligentsia, was dumbfounded. *If God is trying to reach mankind through mere mortals, why the heck would he pick loud-mouthed Dumas to be an ambassador?*

Al's conversion had been such a sea-splitting event that the impact was felt by all, including the most hard-hearted. Even those who had not converted held a powerful respect for Marlowe's decision, and they had maintained a healthy, arms-length respect for Christian ideology. But this was not the situation anymore with Ernie in the fold.

All-American Voyager Ross Loveland spent hours with Chipper over coffee, trying futilely to explain the futility of trying to understand a God who did not recognize the word "futile." Ross admitted in so many words, it seemed to Chipper, that Ernie had single-handedly destroyed the Bible study, as there were now only five hard-core attendees. But it went beyond that, all the way to the Dumas-induced phenomenon of reverse-evangelism, with mass migration away from the Christian roots of the fraternity. Chipper was horrified at himself for praying for Ernie to *stop* spreading the Word. In apparent desperation, Voyager Loveland even groped for the verse that said something about, "Not everyone who says to Me, 'Lord, Lord,' will enter the kingdom of Heaven" in his efforts to explain the unexplainable.

And every time Moguru Divine kidded Chipper about Ernie being his Bible-thumping brother, Chipper's faith was taken down a notch (or perhaps changed). And these notches proved to be blurry units of measure, for Chipper came to realize that his proclamation of faith before a thousand Sig Zetas at Workshop hadn't demanded anywhere near the gumption as claiming his faith—in light of one foul doofus—to one measly Moguru.

But inside, Chipper's heart had a Dumas-ache for a particular reason. Last spring, one week before Ernie announced his conversion, Drywall Twohatchets had attended his first Bible study as a leery spectator. Afterward, Drywall stayed in Chipper's room for one hour as they discussed the life-changing power of conversion. Drywall had presented his gentle arguments and concerns to Chipper, who returned a well-matched C.S. Lewis-inspired apologia. The words "I accept" were about ready to roll off Drywall's tongue, but he said instead, "I want to think about it 'til next week." Next week, Ernie Dumas was there, all spit and no polish.

Chipper had never mustered the nerve to ask Drywall if he knew about the near-rape of Cassie their freshman year, but he assumed the truth was known. Once Drywall saw Ernie in the President's room for Bible study that next week, he joined the mass exodus and refused to discuss the Christian experience with Chipper ever again.

Drywall resumed his submersion with Cassie, introducing her left ring finger to a one-carat princess diamond (Wickiup does it again), prompting a newfound chorus of support from her sorority sisters.

After the carat, insensitive mutterings about the interracial love affair gave way to less insensitive comments like, "He's so handsome, just like Michael Ansara, you know, the Broken Arrow warrior on TV." Or, "Oh, your babies will always have such a nice tan all the time." Or, "My, he has such a beautiful voice for an Indian." Cassie accepted them all as wonderful compliments.

At the sorority candlelight announcing their engagement, the flame traveled around the circle three times before Cassie blew out the candle.

Yes, the times were an epochal hodgepodge. While the undulating buzz of the fraternity hive provided backdrop, the world had gone mad. President Nixon's Commission on Campus Unrest came to this conclusion: *A nation driven to use the weapons of war upon its youth is a nation on the edge of chaos.* Draft evasion cases rose tenfold. After taking top honors at the Cannes Film Festival, the movie "M*A*S*H" was banned from all U.S. Service bases. A black serviceman killed in Vietnam was buried in an all-white cemetery in Florida, prompting whites to remove the bodies of their relatives. Dr. Timothy Leary escaped from prison in California and resurfaced in Algiers. Nixon announced a three-point plan to deal with the new fad of terrorist hijackings. Jimi Hendrix, whom Chipper and Amy had seen perform on campus last spring, died a drug-related death. Three weeks later, ditto for Janis Joplin. No less than 25 people were indicted by a grand jury in the Kent State shootings, while the National Guardsmen were completely exonerated. And the beat of the Manson trial went on and on . . .

* * *

Yet, as Chipper sat in the President's room, his mind Rolodexing through news and places and events and people, he was gripped with a sober euphoria—a rush so powerful he knew this was a singular moment in his life. *What, or where, was the source of this ecstasy?*

He knew the euphoria was not the illusion of Presidential omnipotence. Was it this peculiar omniscience? Was it the "knowing of all" that was happening in this little Sig Zeta sliver of the world? Or, better yet, was it knowing the future? *Knowing* it would be a banner senior year. Knowing that Peachy would pull in the top name bands. Knowing that the Intramural Trophy was in the bag. Knowing Fraternity of the Year awaited his brothers—and the unthinkable Aegis Award, maybe, for him. Knowing of his own ultimate success, *regardless* how the coin landed as to the role he'd choose. Knowing that Vietnam was bound to wind down eventually. Knowing that his rock-solid

Amy would be beside him, and that they would never have to experience the tragedies born from the dissolution of love.

But the euphoria had an odd paradoxical side—it paralyzed him. And it was a magnificent paralysis. Certainly, the deep and cavernous origin of this strangling ecstasy, holding him bound in the wingback chair, was—*knowing*.

If he heard the knock at the door, he didn't respond.

"Hey, Chipper, you in there? Quit playin' possum, you fink. It's the Peach. Open up, dipshit, I know you're in there. Oh well, go screw yourself. Drywall and me are going to get in nine holes before dark. We'll be taking Rickelbell with us if anyone asks. Our friggin' Intramural Hitler says we all gotta play 18 holes every week 'til the tournament next spring."

As the sounds trailed down the dark hall of former Presidents, one voice said: "Jeez, I'm startin' to worry about that peckerwood. I think he's losin' it."

39

Peachy eyeballed his lie — a small basin of dirt shored by dead tallgrass and a decaying tree stump, in a forest nook of a par-5 dogleg. He removed his glasses and pinched the skin between his eyebrows as he considered his two options — chip out or cheat. By the time he secured his glasses back in place with a finger-nudge on the bridge, the answer was clear.

Drywall, with a nearly identical fate, was practice-swinging a few yards to the rear of the Peach, both of them having failed in their attempts to cut the dogleg. Rickelbell waited in the fairway with Smokey Ray and Uno Guilford, wagging her tail, anticipating the next opportunity to serve her multiple masters by retrieving their golf balls.

"I told you so. No way to reach the green in two," Drywall said. "Not even when the wind's from the east."

"I'll try to remember how friggin' right you were when we're each paying 50 bucks to our asshole friends on the 18th green," said Peachy, referring to their lowball wager. "It's not the money, it's the thought of losing to that banana-nosed jerk-off Guilford."

"Come now, Peachy. Remember — we're all the same team next spring. Same fraternity, same —"

Peachy closed his ears to his disturbingly upright friend. Then, from his pocket he pulled a wooden tee, checked the perimeter for scrupulous observers, went back to his bag for the driver, and teed his ball smack dab in the middle of the dirt spot — a spot heretofore foreign to wooden tees.

He could hear Drywall stuffing a laugh behind him. "Don't you think those guys can see you're using a wood out of the rough?"

"So what? They can't see I'm using a tee. Nothing illegal about a driver out of the rough. Hell, if I can launch it between those trees up there, I got a shot at the green. On in two, my friend, on in two."

Peachy addressed the ball with vestigial remnants of his hacker's swing of old. He had evolved over the years to a legitimate 12-handicapper. The Quasimodo stance was detectable only if one had a good eye for hunchbacks. Wiggle to the left. Wiggle to the right. Backswing, overswing, downswing. Crack. Master's pose.

But the echoing pop of the shot was followed in a millisecond by another crack, the sound of the golf ball in head-on collision with a tree, and Peachy ducked as he saw the ball ricochet his way. Then— another pop as the ball hit the tree stump near his feet.

Peachy turned to Drywall. "Well, my fine Polack friend, don't never forget—cheaters never wi—"

The stinging needle on his cheek set his face ablaze—"Goddam mutherfuggin' sonuvabitch"—and the simultaneous buzzing about his head let Peachy know that he had trespassed on the home of a hornet. He rubbernecked to look for the culprit, but the sky was clear. Within a second, though, the buzzing seemed to come from all directions so it was no surprise when he saw three, then four, then countless black shapes orbiting and buzz-bombing from everywhere.

Through useless reflex, he gripped his driver. Then, as if the first sting had simply been a teaser, the buzzing converged on his face, and he felt pinpoints of acid burning all over his head, neck, arms, then into his shirt where his chest and back were caught up in the fire.

"Oh—my—gahhhhd—," he yelled as he closed his eyes and gave the driver a roundhouse swing through the air as if the thin silver shaft with a knobby tip could slow the assault. "Oh—shit—mutherfugger—." And he swung again, a final-stand prelude to a dead run. But it was a hit-and-run, as he felt the crack of his driver against a . . . tree? A scream accompanied the smack—*What in the hell?*—overpowering his own howling as he let the driver drop from his fingers, eyes still shut.

Peachy was afraid to open his eyes for fear of a direct hit by a stinger, so he managed shutter-like peeps to guide his run to safety. "What's going on?" he heard Smokey Ray say in the distance, and he used the voice like sonar to guide him to the fairway. As he flailed his arms, sprinting, Peachy turned and saw Drywall lying on the ground, hands to face. And between his own curse words, he could hear Drywall moaning. By the time Peachy reached the fairway and Smokey

Ray, the wasp squadron had retreated, save one straggler that he smashed beneath his shirt.

When he looked again at his fallen friend curled into a question mark, red was oozing between Drywall's splayed fingers. Stunned, Peachy forgot that the upper half of his own body was burning still.

"What in the hell did you do, Peachy?" asked a shocked Smokey Ray as he began running toward Drywall.

"No shit, Sherlock. What did you do?" chimed Uno.

"I—I guess I hit Drywall accidentally with my driver. I thought it was a tree. Not that I was trying to hit a tree. I was—"

Peachy turned and followed Smokey Ray back to the woods and to Drywall's aid. Rickelbell got there first, and she tried to lick at Drywall's face. When he pushed her away, he dropped his hands long enough for Peachy to see one eye socket as a bloody mess with a gelatinous ooze.

"Jiminy fuggin' Christmas, I'm sorry Drywall. I was getting stung like a sonuvabitch. I couldn't see nothin'. I just—"

"C'mon, we gotta get him to the hospital, guys," said Smokey Ray who reached down and helped Drywall to his feet.

Drywall started to throw one arm around Smokey Ray's shoulders, but Peachy pushed the Moguru to the side so that he could offer his own shoulder. Rickelbell was making a sound Peachy had never heard before, a high-pitched squeaky-wheel noise, and she raised herself up to land her paws on Drywall's thighs.

"Good girl," said Drywall as he patted her down with his bloody hand.

"Can you walk? Do we need to carry you?" asked Smokey Ray.

"No, I can walk."

The fivesome stumbled out of the forest, leaving an anemic swarm of wasps circling in the air above the tree stump.

"Honest to God, Drywall, it was an accident. I was getting stung like a—"

"I know, Peachy."

"Does it hurt? Shit, of course it hurts. What am I saying? I mean, are you hurting much?"

"Like hell, as a matter of fact."

Peachy thought it odd that Drywall's face was so calm, as if there was no pain at all. But his friend seemed to be stutter-stepping, as if he were spooked every time he tried to put the next foot forward.

"Peachy, is there anything wrong with my left eye?"

Shit-o-dear. Your eye is a friggin' bloody nightmare, thought Peachy. *I mean it's hamburger. No . . . wait, he said "left eye." It's the right one that's smithereens.*

"Uh . . . your right eye looks pretty bad, Drywall. We'll get you to the doctor right away."

"No, my left eye. I can tell my right eye's gooned—it's like a grenade went off. But what about my left eye?"

"Your left eye looks fine." Peachy twisted his head around to be certain. Drywall's low slung eyelids kept Peachy from a real good look, but "Yes, it looks fine. Why?"

"'Cause I can't see anything. Not out of either eye."

Peachy felt his heart eject from his throat, dragging his stomach and entrails like the string of a kite.

Drywall held his left arm out like a curb-feeler until he felt Rick-elbell's tail. When he grabbed the golden tip, she seemed to know it was time to lead.

40

Every seat in the waiting room was occupied, and the spillover carried down the hallway where Actives filled the plastic seats in the emergency room as well. Chipper had never witnessed such perfect attendance, certainly not at a chapter meeting. Girlfriends, pinmates, friends from other fraternities, at least a hundred filled the hospital, waiting for the word on Drywall.

C.C. Chastain made his fraternity debut for the year, though aloof toward triggerman Chipper who still was "a slimeball after my pin." Ty Wheeler crawled out of his hole in full Orbison array, guitar included, strumming and singing off-key to Roy's hit, "In Dreams." Sig Ross Loveland was there, offering sanctified support. Countering the assuaging effect of the All-American Voyager, Ernie Dumas was working the crowd, trying unsuccessfully to form small clusters for prayer.

Amy sat by Chipper, their backs against the wall, while Cassie sat on the other side of Amy. Rickelbell was tied to metal pole outside and was pawing at the glass doors to get in. Chipper stole glances at Cassie whose tears were fauceting on and off until she spotted Ernie Dumas, prompting a look that could kill. Chipper didn't know for sure if Drywall knew about the panty raid three years ago, but Chipper knew that Cassie knew, and that was enough.

In order to break Cassie's deadly glare at Ernie, Chipper felt compelled to distract her. "You know, Cassie, I read about an operation they did last year in Houston. They transplanted an entire eyeball."

"You mean cornea, don't you?" added Amy, as if to cover a blunder.

"No. The whole thing." Chipper was certain he had read about it somewhere.

"Did it work?" asked Cassie.

"Well, no. But they're doing amazing things these days."

Amy scowled at him.

"I just keep thinking," said Cassie, "that Drywall always said his favorite thing in the whole wide world was watching me dance. He would get real misty-eyed about it. Said he could watch it all day and all night. It brought him peace. You know he's had a much harder life than ya'll know. It gets to him sometimes. But when he watched me dance—." And her tears began to flow again.

Peachy was slinking in the seat next to Chipper at the end of the row, and with Cassie's words, Chipper could sense him slouching even further trying to reach oblivion. Peachy was almost unrecognizable with welts and blotches covering his puffy red face. Though his mask offered little in the way of sympathetic support, perhaps it provided a measure of deluded anonymity.

Moguru Divine and Audora made a striking entrance, he in a black top hat with Indian-braid headband and shoulder-length blonde hair, she devoid of her fairy wings but with her spangled wand that she kept parked like a flower above her ear. Audora seemed to float toward Cassie as she pulled the wand from her hair and touched the spangles to Cassie's head. "Oh, my dear sweet baby Cassie," she gushed as they hugged, "how short the seconds 'tween dream and teardrop—how harsh the pounding rain." (And then some more gibberish that Chipper ignored.)

Usually, Smokey Ray looked fondly at Audora, but it seemed to Chipper that the Moguru, too, could see the dark halos about her sunken eyes and the floating emptiness of her head as it bobbed aimlessly.

A surgeon walked through swinging doors, then halted, apparently surprised at the multitude. "Any family for Mr. Larry Twohatchets?"

Everyone in the room stood. "All of us," called out random voices.

Cassie marched to the front of the crowd. As the surgeon removed his green cap, the overhead light bounced off his bald head, rimmed at the base by a gray strip of hair about the width of duct tape.

"His sister's on the way," Cassie said. "I'm his fiancee."

"Well, we had to take the right eye," said the surgeon.

"Take it?"

"Remove it."

"Oh."

"But there was a freak injury to the other eye. Bone fragments from the orbital fracture on the right crossed over to the left where they lodged in the region of the optic nerve on the good side. We've removed the fragments, but he's going to lose most of his vision in that eye as well."

The group gasp was accented by Cassie's sunny reply, "But not *all* the vision is gone on the left?"

"It's too early to tell, but it looks like some of the nerve might still be intact. He might have a small window of vision on the left."

Cassie kept a smile plastered in place as she received the news. Chipper couldn't imagine how she could stand there and look so hopeful.

The group had been inching forward in a huddle around the surgeon as he revealed the news, and Chipper was standing shoulder-to-shoulder with Amy on one side, Audora on the other. Audora muttered something along the lines of "How the naked sword doth clothe its foe in darkness." Annoyed every time Audora spoke, Chipper wondered if she was referring to the golf club as the naked sword. He turned to look for Peachy, but the Peach was gone.

* * *

Peachy sat alone in his darkened room, headquarters for Wickiup. He wasn't prone to depression. As a matter of fact, he wasn't sure depression even existed ("I think it's all in their heads.") Hell, he had a lifetime of reasons to be depressed, but he wasn't. Yeah . . . reasons a damn sight better than most folks had. His friggin' mother had walked out on the family on a Merry Christmas morning, thank you, when he was just a kid. His old man whacked him when he cried about it, and whacked him later on if he ever mentioned her name. Shit, oh dear, the list went on and on.

So he damn sure wasn't gonna be depressed now. Sad, sure. But not depressed. It wasn't his fault. It was just a bad roll of the dice. It was roulette with a green zero on a red-black bet. It was all in the game.

Using a wooden tee in the forest was, of course, on the slippery slope for those that followed the rules. And if he hadn't been cheat—

But he wasn't about to turn over a new leaf, and he damn sure wasn't going to offer up a prayer to an empty sky.

Drywall was the best friend he'd ever had. So it was natural to feel terrible . . . and sad—very much like he had years ago on that Merry Christmas morning.

41

Exiting the President's room, Chipper crossed the hallway to the headquarters of Social Chairman-for-Life, President of Wickiup Enterprises International—Generalissimo Peachy Waterman Jr.

After a few knocks on the door, Chipper heard a muffled "Come in."

"Hey, Peachy, whaddya up to?"

"Studyin'."

"You've got to be kidding."

"What's so funny about that? Didn't you hear I'm going to law school?"

"Law school?!" Chipper held his laughter in check.

"That's right, amigo. Law school. You didn't know I was that smart, did you?"

Chipper could sniff out a loaded question a mile away. "Smart has nothing to do with it, Peachy. You've gotta have grades. I mean, for gosh sakes, your GPA is sittin' on the wrong side of the decimal point."

Peachy turned from his open book and frowned at Chipper who was easing into a beanbag chair in the corner.

"Do you have any idea how many times I've cracked a book here at college?" asked Peachy.

"Not many."

"Take a guess."

Chipper thought for a moment, then said, "I dunno."

"Never. I've never opened a single friggin' book for a single friggin' course."

"You don't go to class either, Peachy, so let me correct myself—now that I think about it, your GPA is pretty darn good, considering your closed book policy. Maybe it's the cold copies."

"Hey, the Peach doesn't go that route any more. Besides, I didn't always have cold copies. I osmosed stuff from the brothers in the courses, plus friends in other fraternities. But most of the time, it's just common sense, my friend. I'm a good test taker. That's why I'm studying for this LSAT thing. I'm also going to classes now, I'm studying, and you know what? I'm making over a three-point, so put that in your pipe and smoke it."

"I'm impressed."

"I figure they'll reject me this year, but I'll go another year, then reapply when my grade point's higher."

"You gonna be the next Ty Wheeler? A super-duper senior? I hear he's finally movin' on next year."

"Very amusing, dipshit. Nope. I figure another year will do it for sure. And this LSAT deal is going to be a chip shot."

Chipper knew Peachy had been acting differently, but he didn't want to probe. Ever since the accident, the Peach had disappeared from public life. Instead, he helped his roommate Drywall with the day-to-day stuff, so that between Cassie and the Peach, the bases were covered for the nearly blind.

"I guess Drywall's with Cassie tonight?"

"Yep. She's using my cassette recorder to tape all Drywall's lectures, then she plays them back for him."

Chipper remembered back to high school when Peachy was one of the first anywhere to own a cassette recorder, and how the music they'd taped soothed the savage shank that plagued his golf game.

"You know he can take his tests pretty well," continued Peachy. "That one spot where he can still see okay lets him read the questions if he holds his head just right. And they're giving him extra time for exams, too. Yep, it's pretty amazing, but I think that one-eyed Indian is going to do okay. I'd like him to go to law school with me, maybe be partners someday, but I don't think he's very gung ho on that idea anymore."

"I gotta tell ya', Peachy, I'm kinda confused where this law school thing came from. I haven't really thought about you and the law in the same sentence."

"It's just I never paid much attention to problems in the world before, but I got to thinking after the accident, especially when Drywall was in the wheelchair that first week, when I was pushing him around campus, but we couldn't get anywhere. I couldn't believe it. There were only a couple of ramps, some buildings we couldn't get in to at all, and jeez, trying to get him into the crapper was damn near impossible. There oughta be a law. And that's where it started."

"At the crapper?"

"Damn straight. At the crapper. I'm the perfect asshole to be a good lawyer."

As Peachy droned on about social injustices, Chipper was spellbound. If anyone was ever a scholar-in-residence as to the art of nurturing injustice, it seemed that Peachy was the man. Now it seemed his friend's heart had done a flip-flop.

"Did Drywall tell you about our new deal for Wickiup?" asked Peachy.

"No."

"Well, when we took Black Jack down to Mexico that time, we saw some awful stuff going on with the Kickapoos in Eagle Pass. They were just wandering around town, drunk on paint. It was unbelievable. But there was this one chick, pregnant, who'd been sniffin' paint, and you could see the silver on her T-shirt, and some gold paint was all over her bloated belly. It kinda made me sick at the time. Well, Drywall and me we're gonna start a counseling center there in Eagle Pass, using Wickiup money."

"I don't believe—"

The pounding of a fist on Peachy's door interrupted. "Mister President, are you in there? President DeHart?"

Chipper buried his head in his hands. Ernie was the only guy in the house that called him President DeHart.

"Yes, Ernie, I'm in here, but I'm busy right now. Can I talk to you later?"

The door opened anyway. "This can't wait. I gotta talk to you *now.*" Ernie stood there, his white eyebrows angled into a chevron, while the hose of a gas mask dangled from his fist.

"What are you doing with that gas mask?" asked Chipper.

Peachy nodded to Chipper as if to say, "We'll talk later," then he turned back to his books, the student-at-work.

"The mask is what I've got to talk to you about. I've had a revelation."

Chipper squirmed his way out of the black beanbag, then escorted Ernie to the President's room, site of all-knowing nonpower. He asked Ernie to sit in the wingback, but Ernie was too agitated to sit anywhere. Chipper eased behind his desk, beneath the poster of RFK and Perry Crane, hoping for some protection from the dead and gone.

Ernie tossed the gas mask onto the President's desk, remaining silent, apparently believing that the mere sight of the Army green mask with its black corrugated hose, would serve as its own bombshell.

Chipper sighed. "What is it, Ernie?"

"You don't remember?"

"No. I don't."

"President DeHart, I'm here to tell you that our own Pledge Trainer, Moguru Divine, is demon-possessed."

The bonds of brotherhood had their limits, be they fraternal or biblical. Chipper couldn't take it anymore. "Ernie, where do you come up with this stuff?"

Ernie turned his back on the President, as if spinning to another source for more power. Then he twisted his head over his shoulder to speak, "I'm telling you—*the Moguru is possessed.*"

Clearly, the President wasn't on the same wavelength, so Ernie approached the desk, leaning forward, while he braced himself with palms on the desktop, elbows stiff.

"Don't you remember how we used this gas mask when we were freshmen, during the takeout on Black Jack?"

"No. Not really. Well, sorta."

Ernie let out a groan of exasperation. "Maybe I should back up a bit. Do you remember the dinner we had before the takeout? Or, as the Devil would have it, our *mockery* of the Last Supper?"

"Er-nie . . ."

"Think about it. Smokey Ray organized it, then he sits at the head of the table and says something like 'This is our last supper.' (Chipper faintly recalled something more about it being the last supper *without self-respect.*)

"Then, Satanic Ray—excuse, me—Smokey Ray stands up and fingers a traitor. A Judas."

"But there *was* a traitor," protested Chipper.

"So what? Judas was a real traitor, too. But it doesn't end there. What did we do after that? To make sure there was plenty of piss for the Puke Pit, Smokey Ray has them bring out the beer. And then *bread* to keep from getting too drunk. The wine and the bread! *Don't you get it?*"

"You're making too much of this stuff, Ernie. It was nothing but a freshman stunt. Come on now."

"You are so naive, my friend. *So naive.* Don't you know the Devil works by twisting and warping the truth? By perverting religion and its sacraments? That Last Supper was Smokey Ray's message from the underworld to the pledge class, to force our apostasy."

"Aposta-what?"

"And what was the grande finale for our Prince of Darkness in his ridicule of God? Well, my friend, he turned the Puke Pit into a satanic baptismal font. Thank heaven for my grandfather's World War I prize, this gas mask that saved gramps' life. My gramps was a God-fearin' man, and the answer to his prayer was this mask. Then, don't you remember? The pledge class took turns putting the mask on to escape the stench of Hell as we cursed Black Jack DeLaughter. All under the watchful, guiding eye of one of Lucifer's own demons."

Ernie stood up straight, so very pleased with his analytical coup.

Chipper was speechless. The way Chipper remembered it, the main reason for the mask was so the pledges could curse Black Jack in the comfort of anonymity. The stench was secondary. And if anyone was wildly enthusiastic that night, it was Ernie who had added to the stench with his own puke, and who knew what else.

"And here's the part that'll give you chills, my good brother, and this is the revelation that dawned on me tonight as I was looking at the mask—only *one man* who went into the Pit refused to wear the gas mask that night. Do you remember?"

"No."

"Drywall. Everyone else had the protection of my grandfather's mask, a mask I now realize was blessed at the time. But not Drywall, and look what happened to him. An eye for an eye."

"Jeepers, Ernie, you're giving me the creeps. Are you trying to tell me that Drywall lost his eye because he was living by the Old Testament 'eye for an eye'? We were *all* playing that game. Every one of us wanted revenge. Your revelation is—'an eye for an eye'? That's insane."

"Yes, we were all in the wrong. But we all had the blessing of gramps' gas mask. All except Drywall, who was so proud of his unrighteousness that he walked into the Puke Pit with his face exposed."

Chipper used every ounce of energy he could muster to keep from blurting out, *"You hypocritical, lying sonuvabitch. You damn near raped Drywall's girlfriend before she was his girl. The only reason you failed is because Audora came to the rescue and two girls humiliated you. And now, you've got the balls to attack Drywall? To attack Smokey Ray? To attack anyone who knows what a piece of shit you are?"*

Instead, Mister President said, "You're wrong, Ernie. I don't want to ever hear this garbage again. I don't know where your so-called revelation came from, but I wouldn't hang it on God. Now please. I need to be alone."

Clearly stunned, Ernie backed away, first with a look of hurt, second with a look of derision, but then those white eyebrows relaxed with smug insight, and he said, "Woe unto him who waivers in the ways of the Lord."

42

Its eight-foot diameter made it, perhaps, the world's largest ottoman. Like a big blue trampoline, it waited for jumpers to enter the front door of the Sig Zeta house. Since it had no back to it, the ottoman denied prolonged sitting. In fact, by design, it seemed worthless. Yet, like many inert and unavailing objects at fraternities, a utilitarian force overcomes it, consumes it, defines it. And so it happened with the big blue ottoman. Over the years, it had become Grand Central Station for the party pic proofs, tossed most every Monday into the center of the trampoline by the party pic man, whose company was now operating as a wholly-owned subsidiary of Wickiup Enterprises International.

Drywall sat on one edge of the ottoman, holding the large squares of tiny proofs up to his remaining eye, where he slid the rows by his little window through which he now viewed the world. And this window, it seemed, was like looking backward through a telescope, with Vaseline covering the lens. More than losing the one eye completely, he was most upset that this remaining window of his good eye forced him to lower his chin to see. In order to be sure of his footing when he walked, he had to drop his head to a cowardly pose that he detested. Much better, he thought, to hold his head high and let the world witness him using the crutch of Cassie's arm or the touch of Rickelbell's tail, than to let his jaw drag on the concrete.

Accompanying Drywall on the perimeter of Grand Central Ottoman were Cassie, Amy, Chipper, and Peachy, all groping for proofs and more proofs, scribbling their names on the backs, to add to their brimming collections.

"Hey Drywall, you look like a pretty cool dude in these pix," Peachy said. "Sorta like 'the man in the Hathaway shirt,' what with your black eyepatch and all."

Drywall had become terribly frustrated with his glass eye. It hurt. It didn't move right. Adjustments brought only more adjustments. Cassie said the color wasn't a good match. His eyelid was propped open too wide. So what the hell, a patch it was, a patch it would be.

"Doesn't he look good?" gushed Cassie. "Gives me goose pimples."

He felt his lover poke him in the ribs, and Drywall tried to laugh, but he knew things had changed.

"Look, here's a good one of Chipper and Amy," said Cassie. "You two should have this one blown up."

Amy was dead quiet.

It took some effort for Drywall to twist his head around like an owl. He wondered if Amy was smiling as widely as Chipper in the photo. After all, Chipper had been offered a position in next year's medical school class immediately after his interview. With far better credentials, Amy hadn't made the cut. Though Chipper claimed "everything's cool with Amy and me," Drywall knew Amy must be seething.

Peachy said, "Wow, here's a great one of me, if I do say so myself. I'm up front at the bandstand, surrounded by the Box Tops."

"Hey, Peachy, you dickhead," said a new voice. "They haven't had a hit in two years. You're slippin', man."

Drywall looked up to identify the new yakker. He had guessed Peatmoss, and he was right. He knew most all of the Actives by voice now.

Then Twobits added, "Yeah, when are we gonna have a real band? What did the Box Tops have? Two whole hits? Hell, my mother could do that."

"Yeah, Peachy. Time for a big name. Word on campus is that you're a has-been. Past your prime."

"Screw you both," said the Peach. "Our worst band is better than the best at other houses."

Their voices disappeared in the distance as Drywall contorted his neck in an attempt to see Peatmoss and Twobits head to their gross-out rooms on Senior Row.

"Assholes," said Peachy in a kidding way. But Drywall knew the ongoing "has-been" tease had been eating away at his friend.

"Look, here's a pic of C.C. Chastain."

"I didn't see him there," said Chipper.

"Takes a lotta gall to show up for the parties when you haven't paid your social dues in over two years," said Peachy. "Hey, Chipper, that reminds me. Isn't the House Corporation meeting coming up? They're gonna cook your goose if you haven't turned in the paperwork to jerk C.C.'s pin."

"Thanks for reminding me, Peachy."

"Look. Here's some pix from the football finals," said Amy.

Drywall could feel that everyone on the ottoman scooched in her direction. Since the ottoman was on rollers, this joint response set them in motion, with one roller slipping off the rug onto the floor, newly polished by the pledges.

"Could you believe it? What a romp!"

"Thirty-five to seven. Musta had four hundred yards passing."

"And the B-team won their championship, too."

"It's gonna be quite a year."

Drywall kept silent while the others oohed and aahed over the black-and-white pictures, the trophies, the memories. For him, the world was different now. Before the accident, he felt "the velvet touch of life" was stolen and enjoyed only by the whites, leaving burlap and bristles for red, black, and yellow. How trivial that seemed now in light of his darkness. Touch was not as important as sight. Now, too late, he understood that the world had been an album of colorful photographs. How precious was his remaining little window that permitted one frame at a time. But there was only one color for his future—dark.

Poor Cassie. Poor oblivious Cassie. Because cold shoulders are hidden by a shawl, the world's cool response to her white hand interlocked with his brown seemed to fly right by her. But there would be no getting around the delicate oddity of a husband who could barely see, a quarter-eyed Indian.

What cruelty had come his way. He didn't blame Peachy because the world was moved by unseen spirits. But how blessed he'd been to find Cassie, only to have a veil crash down between the two of them. Yes, there were many beautiful women in the world, but they were portraits, to be admired in a two-dimensional sense. Cassie was a sculpture that he could feel. A flower he could smell. And as he held her hand now, he could feel so much more—the smoothness of her skin, her heat, the moisture of her passion—all disconnected from the fate about to unfold.

How deadly for him to drag her into his dark pit. She deserved so much more than hanging onto the elbow of a husband to keep him from bumping into telephone poles on the street—more than a husband whose palsied head bobbed around in circles until the window of sight spotted its object—more than a husband who hung his head in shame as he walked, lest he trip over a curb onto his face and lose the remaining window.

Cassie made a strange sound when she tried not to cry. She had groomed her larynx to freeze into a spastic fit that wouldn't allow air or speech. Drywall had heard the odd noise only a few times before, and how he dreaded that awful suffocating sound that would seize her throat the moment he set her free.

43

"I thought we made it clear at the last meeting that this was to be settled by now," said Brewster Stone, never raising his eyes from the written agenda, eyes that ignored the roundtable hot seat occupied by the President.

"It's not as straightforward as it seems," said Chipper, hopelessly hoping that Mr. Stone could forget Chipper's role in not pledging the alum's son two years ago.

"Looks pretty straightforward to me. A man doesn't pay his house bill, then you kick his tail out. We're not running the Salvation Army, Mr. DeHart. This isn't a charity. I thought we, as the House Corporation, made our position perfectly clear on this issue already."

"Well, there's a bit of a technicality here," offered Chipper, "you see—"

"Does this C.C. Chastain—if I remember right, the kid that attacked the Grand President—does he owe the house money, or does he not?"

"He does, but—"

"Brother DeHart, we don't really need to hear excuses. We realize he was one of your pledge brothers, but there's such a thing as fiscal responsibility."

"—ends to meet—"

"—financial security is the backbone—"

"—no room for dead weight—"

Boxing ropes seemed to form around the ring, and the Actives, instead of walking by, stopped and formed a crowd at the perimeter.

Occasional taunts from members were tossed into the ring to let the
House Corporation know they were outnumbered, the Actives being
oblivious to the basis of power.

As the other members of the House Corporation provided chorus, Chipper was haunted by Drywall's words to him before the meeting: "Don't forget. No one loved and lived the ideals of Sig Zeta more
than C.C. Chastain, and we ran him out of the house. *We* ran him out.
Don't fall into the Black Jack trap. When you meet C.C. on the street
in 20 years, his unpaid dues won't matter one bit. The only thing that
will matter is how you treated him as a friend and a brother."

Chipper tried to sound confident: "There's a technicality. When a
brother lives out of the house, he only has to pay social dues. To cover
the parties and all. But what you all don't realize is that this chapter has
been operating with a—a para-economy that pretty well covers social
stuff. Our social parties, and therefore the dues, have already been
paid for with outside money. For the past three years, the chapter has
not spent one penny on . . ."

And with the words that followed, the role of Wickiup Enterprises
International as the fuel for the brilliant success of the chapter was
divulged to the House Corporation. And rather than revel in praise
due the chapter for such ingenuity, Chipper was shocked to bear the
brunt of criticism and condemnation. Apparently, it was better to jerk
the pin of a brother who owed a few bucks than to receive "donations"
of tens of thousands of dollars from Wickiup (especially when said
donations were used exclusively to book top-name bands).

As Chipper tried to argue his point, Brewster Stone's face turned
from pink to bright red. Chipper thought, *Here we are, on our way to
becoming Fraternity of the Year, and the leadership is bashing me?* He
pushed his chair away from the table to make his final point: "I'm
not going to sign the papers to jerk C.C.'s pin. I just can't do it over
a few bucks."

Brewster Stone silenced some ringside taunters with a single stare.
"Let's move forward on this agenda, because—believe me—I'm just
getting started. Next item. It's come to my attention that you've been
allowing girls in the rooms of this chapter house."

The words from Stone oozed through such a sneer that Chipper
could feel a torrent of adrenaline rush into his veins, then his heart.

"It's a new rule with the university," stated Chipper, proud to have
the full force of the university administration on his side.

Brewster answered, "They have a rule now that you're required to
bring girls into your rooms?" The members of the House Corporation
laughed on cue.

"No, you know what I mean. It's a new rule that it's *okay* to have girls in the rooms. Campuswide. All university housing. They did away with the old rule."

"Well, *they* might have done away with it, but *we* haven't," said Brewster to the boos from the crowd. "There will be no girls in the living quarters of this house."

"We can't compete in rush if we're the only house on campus where you can't take girls into your room," protested Chipper, aware how mindless the argument sounded the second the words left his lips, not to mention the fact that members had been sneaking girls to their rooms since the beginning of time. So, in fact, the only modification in this construct was the legitimization of "sneak." But that didn't stop the crowd from jeering, being led now by Peatmoss and Twobits, as hooting and hollering filled the dining room.

Brewster Stone stood up, scraping his chair across the floor and plowing his fists into his waist. "Let me tell you something, Mr. DeHart, you've got a fraternity here that's out of control. You've got girls in the rooms, skunks in the study hall, and for cryin' out loud, I hear you've got a dog living in the house! You're runnin' a goddam zoo. Get the girls and the animals outta this house!"

Chipper stood at the opposite corner of the ring, the swell of the crowd noise urging him on toward a knockout. "We had a great rush this year, we're in great financial shape, we're winning every intramural sport, our grades are up—and you stand there telling me we're out of control?"

The crowd screamed for blood.

But blood did not come. As if the entire House Corporation at once appreciated the ridiculous escalation, Brewster Stone chuckled (sadistically) and said, "Okay. Let's all stay calm now."

Stone sat down. Chipper sat down. The room quieted, and the agenda rolled on. The crowd lost interest and left. It was a tsunami that never seemed to hit the shore.

But when the meeting ended an hour later, Brewster Stone took Chipper aside and spoke softly through a smile, the same sardonic smile he had used earlier in the meeting when the wave of rebellion had crested. "That was quite a show you put on in there for your buddies. But I want you to remember something next spring when it comes time for the Aegis nominations. You have to be nominated at the province level by your Province Advisor. And the advisor for this province happens to be my old pledge brother from way back. Now, I heard you were some big hot shot last summer at Workshop, but let me tell you where smart aleck hot shots like you end up—nowhere, bud. You can kiss that sweet Aegis Award good-bye."

* * *

Later, nursing Chipper's wounds in the TV room, Amy listened to his account of the altercation with Brewster Stone. Although she pretended concern, she had little patience for the negotiating inadequacies of men. In her mind, history was merely an account of the failed diplomacy of mankind, where periods of delusional peace were punctuated by the raw virility of war. She refused to take sides, resisted Chipper's pressure for sympathy, and was more than ready for Chipper to stop whining about losing the Aegis Award before the process even started. Amy believed there was strong evidence for unanswered prayer, for if God answered every beck and call, men would annihilate themselves praying for the death of their enemies. Certainly, God listened first to the prayers of forthright women.

She was relieved when Chipper finally stopped rambling and when he apologized for sniveling. "I'm sorry," he said.

And as she tucked her feet beneath her legs, she cradled Chipper's head in her lap and stroked his hair. She had just finished reading a book that was sweeping the campus as a tear-filled epidemic— *Love Story*—and the ubiquitous message from that book was in her fingertips.

Peachy entered the TV room at the start of *Bonanza* and squeezed onto the couch beside Chipper and Amy with a burrowing wiggle too tight for comfort.

"Have a seat," said Amy. "There's plenty of room."

"Believe I will."

Amy felt Chipper struggle to sit up, then he twisted around, smiling, and they kissed.

"Hey, cut the lovey-dovey crap around the Peach, will ya'?"

"We were here first," said Amy.

Then, an inhuman sound whisked behind them, and all three turned their heads over the back of the couch toward the living room. Having sneaked legally into Drywall's room earlier, Cassie was now sprinting out the door. Her face was pale and wrenched into an ugliness that Amy had never seen before. She thought the noise Cassie was making had to be the same squawk that occurred when the hangman's noose cinched its victim. No air in. No air out.

"Uh-oh," said Peachy.

Rickelbell was on Cassie's trail, but the front door slammed shut and the golden mascot was stopped short. Rickelbell turned to the threesome staring over the back of the couch as if to plead for intervention.

44

Two weeks later, after wading with Cassie through streams of anguish, Amy took her friend and Beta Chi sister to the practice tee at the university's golf course. The tree leaves were dead and gone, Bermuda brown, winter winds in the making, the vestiges of life meager, and the golf course had been forsaken for the warmth of campus fire.

Still, golf was diversion. And Cassie needed diversion. Dance had been her life before Drywall, and it was her life with Drywall. So Amy decided to divert. Life after Drywall was today's dance.

"You bent your left arm again," said instructor Amy as Cassie hit dirt, not ball. "It's hard to remember at first. It's not really natural, but you have to make that left arm like a rod until it becomes natural."

"I know it must be so-o frustrating for you to watch me muff shot after shot," said Cassie. "After all, your being second or thirdish—which was it?—at the Big Eight tournament last year. I'm so-o embarrassed." Cassie began making that weird choking noise again, subverted tears it seemed.

Amy smiled and said, "Cassie, don't be silly. Everyone has trouble first time out. Golf is not the sort of game that comes natural. It's hard." Amy knew a weentsy liability was built into golf-as-therapy, for this was the very place where Drywall had his eyesight drawn and quartered.

Cassie skulled her next shot, but its airborne status, for two seconds, gave hope.

"I don't understand it. I did everything right. Everything," said Cassie.

"Actually, your left arm was still a little bent. You think it's straight, but—"

"No, I mean with Drywall. I did everything right. I gave him everything. There's nothing more I could have done."

Amy reconsidered her geographic choice for this session. Perhaps she should have taken Cassie to a course in Oklahoma City. "Cassie, men are impossible to figure out. They want to be our great protectors, then they turn right around and need us to say, 'You poor, poor thing. How you've suffered.' Don't try to figure it out. It's just them. I'm sure Drywall is going through a phase where he doesn't think he can be your protector, your hero. So it doesn't matter how much 'poor, poor thing' stuff you lay on him. He *has* to be your hero."

"But he *is* my hero."

"*You* know that, but it's not enough. *He* has to believe it," said Amy. "And—you need to play the ball a little more off your front foot."

Amy noticed that Cassie stopped to hit after every fifth practice swing, pulling one ball out of the neat lines she had arranged after dumping her basketful on the ground.

"How do I do that?"

"Your front foot is your left foot and—"

"No, how do I get him to believe he's still my hero?"

Amy was stumped, but she didn't want to let her friend down. There was no higher calling than the petition for feminine counsel. "Being the hero has to grow inside him. Something he believes about himself. You might be able to plant the seeds, but he's got to accept it. No easy feat, I'll admit. I'm sure with his eyesight almost gone he's thinking that he's nothing more than a lifetime burden for you."

"But how do you accomplish the hero deal with Chipper?"

Given Chipper's penchant for heroics, Amy often considered her situation quite the opposite, that is, keeping Chipper's feet nailed firmly to the floor. "Chipper and I are different," she said. "Chipper gets carried away by dreams, and I keep him focused." Amy felt herself shaking her head, as if to say, "Don't even *try* to find any similarities here."

"Is he still thinking about going into the ministry?" asked Cassie as she lifted her first clean shot into the air.

"Good one, Cassie. That's over a hundred yards. Uh, he's not ever considered the ministry per se. He's talked about joining the full-time staff of Varsity Voyagers, that college outreach, but not as a real minister. And not because that's really what he wants. You know how much he admired Al Marlowe, after the conversion that is, and then how much he liked the Bible study guy, Ross Loveland. But he was *really* captivated by the guy he met just once—Chase Callaway, the song-writer for that Voyager folk group, the New Bloods. Chipper's got to learn to follow his heart more, and role models less."

"What do you mean?" asked Cassie, practice-swinging with her 5-iron.

Pulling the hood of her red windbreaker over her head, Amy tried to block the chilly gale that was announcing resolute arctic air on the way. She pulled long and loose strands of wind-whipped, "mousy brown" hair from her mouth and tucked them into her jacket (her colored blonde and lacquered flip long gone with the times). "Chipper," she said, "trusts too much, I think. I don't suppose you've heard him talk about Chase Callaway, but Chase almost had Chipper sign the dotted line to join Voyagers after just one evening. Chase apparently has a genius IQ and all that, but he gave up med school for full-time Christian work. 'Storing treasures in Heaven,' as Chipper would quote. And Chipper thinks Chase walks on water, skipping on the surface with Marlowe and Loveland."

Cassie laid down her 5-iron and picked up a second sweater with avocado-colored flowers to cover her first, a cable knit of harvest gold. "So would it be so bad for Chipper to join them?"

Amy felt as though she were blushing now at the secret she'd been holding inside. "Well, I've got a bit of a zinger for Chipper. So much so that I haven't had the heart to tell him." Amy let her eyes slide down Cassie's abbreviated stature, from pigtails to freckled ankles, then her view crept along the driving range and slipped into the forest.

"Wha-at! Tell me." Cassie planted both hands onto her full, unballerina hips.

Maybe such an unveiling would be the diversion Cassie needed rather than golf, so Amy decided to confess. "You know I had to apply to lots of medical schools because they really don't want girls."

"Yes, I know."

"You also know Chipper applied to just one here in Oklahoma, and he was in like Flynn the day after his interview."

"Yes . . ."

"Well, at the last minute I applied to the new medical school at Far West Texas University. That's where I got in, and that's where I'm going."

"And Chipper? What's going to happen? Long distance romance? Chipper didn't even apply there, did he?"

"Oh, we'll work something out. He's not sure what he's going to do with his life. One minute it's journalism, one minute it's Varsity Voyagers, then it'll be medical school, so who knows?"

"Wow. That *is* a zinger." Cassie headed toward Amy and started to offer a hug.

"No, that's not the zinger," said Amy to Cassie's puzzled look. "Chipper already knows I was accepted there."

"I don't get it. So what's the zinger?"

"Just this—I found out about this new medical school in the first place because it's the one that Chipper told me Voyager Chase Callaway gave his brush-off to several years ago so he could be part of the New Bloods. But when I went for my interview, guess who was there? None other than Mr. Walkin'-on-the-Water Chase Callaway! Turns out he got engaged, and wifey-to-be isn't quite as excited about 'treasures in Heaven' when there're bills to pay on Earth. Or so it seemed to me. Too many IQ points to waste on songwriting."

"So you met the guy? You talked to him? Is he going to med school there?"

"Yes, yes, and yes."

"What's Chipper going to think?"

"I hope he starts to think about his heart, rather than role models. It'll surely rip the water from beneath his feet when it comes to Varsity Voyagers because he *really* identified with Chase Callaway the most. Chipper's heart is talking to him, but he's simply not listening, Cassie. Sometimes, I think that's our job as partners. We have to get our men to listen to their hearts."

Cassie backed away and reclaimed her 5-iron. "I just wish I *had* a man. One in particular. It's my only dream."

"I'm sorry. I didn't mean—. Don't be fooled by Drywall taking the ring back. You can make him believe he's a hero again. Just get him to listen to his heart."

Cassie's bladed shot flew past the hundred-yard marker. "I'll never get it, Amy. It's just not natural."

"Sure it is. You'll get him back."

"No, I meant this crazy game."

45

The party pic man tossed the proofs into the center of Grand Central Ottoman, beneath the recessed spotlight above. The piranhas swarmed.

"Lookit here, you were so-o-o drunk."

"Lemme see."

"Not as bad as Lawner. He was in the Puke Pit before the first set was over."

"Sure was groovy to see C.C. Chastain back with the Rickel Four. They sounded far-out, man."

"Hey, Chipper, here's one of you playing the skins with the band. First time C.C.'s ever let you jam, isn't it dude? I'm having trouble gettin' used to your new moustache."

Chipper checked out the photo, confirmed his triumph on the drums, then flipped the proof sheet over and ordered five copies. His mother had advised him not to return to hometown El Viento until the moustache was gone, but "the look" of hair—shining, gleaming, streaming, flaxen, waxen—had bled its way from Haight-Ashbury to Everytown, and mothers everywhere were simply going to have to adjust.

Playing with the Rickel Four at the house party last weekend hadn't come close, though, to the thrill of serving as drummer for the Greek Revue variety show that had toured the local military bases during Christmas break. After Chipper promised C.C. he'd protect his pledge brother's Sig Zeta pin unto death, a whole new world opened for Chipper. And that world was located smack dab in the middle of the orchestra pit, surrounded by bass, snare, toms, hi-hat, and cymbals.

At the Ft. Sill show on Christmas Eve in Lawton, the all-Greek entertainment troupe was told that one-third of their audience would be shipped to Vietnam the next week. When a drop-dead coed sang, "I'll Be Home for Christmas" as the finale, Chipper scanned the crowd from his perch of safety in the middle of the trap set and saw a theater full of soldiers sobbing like babies. And while his accompaniment to this lullaby was meant to include shimmering sounds made with wire brushes on cymbals, he added the disharmony of his own choking and snorting as he fought back tears for the doomed faces located just beyond the orchestra pit.

"Yeah, this was my first time to play with the Rickel Four," he finally answered. "But C.C. had me play for Greek Revue during Christmas. It was lots of fun. The soldiers came up after every show to the orchestra pit. Some guys wanted to play guitar or piano, but most of them wanted to sit at the trap set and bang away. It was neat to let 'em—" And with those simple words, Chipper's throat snagged. If one more word had escaped, tears would have followed, and he was stunned by his own emotion.

"Someone told me C.C. is going to direct our act in Varsity Sing at the end of the year," said one of the piranhas.

"Cool, dude. What a talent that guy is. Do you suppose our old Pledge Trainer will help? Aren't they still working on plays and stuff together?"

"Mother Boone won't help officially, but I bet he'll work behind the scenes."

Two piranhas after the same proofs ripped the paper in half.

"Say, Chipper, how many points do we get if we win Varsity Sing?"

"Twenty-five," said Chipper. "Believe it or not, it's the same as winning A-team football."

"Who we gonna do it with?"

"The Beta Chis," Chipper said. "Amy's going to be the girls' director, Peachy's going to be in charge of the guys, and C.C. is going to be the overall director and handle the music."

Conversation stopped when Drywall, wearing his pirate patch, edged his way from the living quarters into the living room using Rickelbell's tail as a guide, his fingers flirting with the tip, navigating by a hair. Drywall had skipped the party sans Cassie and was seen less and less these days. He cocked his head and lowered his chin so as to look through his window, then he nodded to the group at the ottoman and kept right on going. Rickelbell wiggled away from him for a moment to say "hi" and get strokes from the crowd before she scampered to join Drywall as he closed the oak doors behind them both.

"Jeez, I wish he'd get back with Cassie. He's starting to spook me out."

"Chipper, I hear C.C. got the old rejecto from medical school."

"Yeah, he spent too much time goofing around with his music. If he'd studied, then he'd be in. A three-one-five GPA isn't gonna cut it, no matter what your MCAT is. But C.C.'s been accepted to that new med school where Amy's probably gonna go, down at Far West Texas."

"So what are *you* going to do, hot shot?" asked one of the voices on the ottoman.

"I don't know yet," Chipper replied. "It's too late for me to apply to Far West this year, so I might go here, then transfer, or I might go to the J-school at Far West, or I might—who knows?"

Peatmoss and Twobits joined in poolside at the blue ottoman. Grabbing proofs from pledges and underclassmen, they scoped out the party scenes. Already fast friends before winning their losing numbers in the lottery, the duo had formed their own fraternity of two that they called, "The Body Baggers," based on the finery that clothed dead soldiers returning from Vietnam.

Twobits was short and stout, having served at the bottom of a cheerleading pyramid in a Houston high school. Since males as cheerleaders were foreign in these parts, excusable only for Texas A&M, his nickname had been nailed to his forehead the day he pledged almost four years ago ("Two bits, four bits, six bits, a dollar—"). But no one teased Twobits beyond the nickname, for all held healthy respect for his gold nugget noodle. Twobits was a lazy genius whose insatiable quest for facts was countered by the absolute triviality of the minutiae he memorized. He was a Master of the Inconsequential, and to anyone's knowledge, he had never studied a single day in his life.

Peatmoss was born below sea level near Lake Pontchartrain in Louisiana, and his slow, stumbling steps disappeared every time this towering beanpole became airborne to catch B-team footballs floating into the end zone. Hero status was confirmed this year with his game-winning touchdown in the finals (10 more points for Fraternity of the Year).

Chipper was saddened when Peatmoss and Twobits led the exodus out of the Presidential Bible Study the day that Ernie Dumas had joined the circle. And now, he was even more concerned that "The Body Baggers" had changed even further since the Lottery. They hung out at Grady's Pub. They crashed at the Alamo Apartments across the street. They reeked of marijuana, but that was not the larger concern. Like twins, they developed their own secret language. More than the usual hippie lingo—narcs and pigs, bongs and bread, keys and tokes, rap sessions and roach clips, making the scene, making a score, free love and freak out—they spoke of marmalade dreams and rosemary clouds. And they giggled as they spoke, exchanging knowing glances like schoolgirls choking back a juicy rumor.

Without making a sound, but all eyes drawn his direction anyway, Smokey Ray Divine appeared on the landing near the TV room, a few steps above the ottoman. The Moguru was followed by a handful of duckling pledges. "Now don't forget, guys, at pledge meeting tonight, we're going to start going over the alumni history. Just because you've passed the test from nationals doesn't mean you're in the club yet. In many ways, the alumni history is harder. And you've got to know it all. I'll see you tonight."

Smokey Ray leaned into the intercom to announce that the party pic proofs had arrived, then he joined the feeding frenzy already in progress and began sifting through photos. Peatmoss and Twobits had seemingly adopted Smokey Ray as their shaman, and Chipper considered Smokey Ray's safe lottery number 291 to be the shaman's source of clarity and inspiration.

Peatmoss said, "Hey, did you guys hear about our old pledge brother?"

"No. Who?"

"Mitch Addison."

"What?"

"Almost died in a car wreck. By himself. Drove his car off a bridge somewhere in California."

Chipper was sick inside as he remembered one of the theories behind the lyrics of "Ode to Billy Joe," as to why the kid jumped off the Tallahachee Bridge.

"Is he okay? Where'd you hear this?"

"I guess so. Heard it from Kong who heard it from C.C. who got it from our old Pledge Trainer."

"Well, Mitch always did drink too much," said one of the guys.

Chipper took note that their pledge brother Mitch would probably never be spoken of again—persona non grata—here yesterday, gone today. So much controversy had surrounded his name, grounded in unthinkable accusation, that his absence, sadly, was a relief to most all. Out of respect for the nearly dead, no one resurrected the horrible trial of Mitch Addison.

"Speakin' a-dyin'," said another, "I heard that another one of our chapter alums went kaput in Vietnam."

"Who?" came the communal cry.

"He was a super-senior when we were pledges," said Twobits. "Ricky Watson. I only met him once at Monday night meal. Nice guy. Only Active at the table that didn't chew my butt."

"How'd you hear about it, Twobits?"

Twobits offered his source, then repeated the version he'd been told: "Ricky was a 1st lieutenant and his position was being overrun by the gooks. He grabbed his radio to call for an air strike, but the radio drew lightning—*literally*. He was killed by a lightning strike while screaming for help into the radio."

A hush fell over the room. Peatmoss turned to Chipper and asked, "Is that what you'd call answered prayer?"

Chipper recoiled at being asked to defend his faith after a punch below the belt. "Maybe that was quicker and easier than what was going to happen to him."

"Now you're reaching," replied Peatmoss. "Why would God have him over there in living hell in the first place?"

Good questions. No answers. The Apologia was wearing thin.

Chipper drifted back to the unthinkable scene at Ft. Sill where he had considered every third face in the audience to be a corpse. The obsession was so strong that during one song in three-four time ("Wives and Lovers" with new lyrics as "Knives and D'ruthers," poking fun at the military while still assuring Our Support for the Vietnam Cause), Chipper had counted one-two-three, one-two-three, as he marked time with his percussion, each beat matching a face in the audience—row after row—so that every downbeat was a dead man.

Moments earlier, he had tried to describe the Ft. Sill experience for the group at the ottoman. The sudden spasm in his throat had halted his story, leaving him mystified as to the power and the source of the paralysis.

To prove his mastery over silly emotion, he tried again. "You know I was talking earlier about the soldiers down at Ft. Sill. It was kinda weird looking out in the audience while I was playing the drums, thinking about every third guy going to Vietnam. What really made it bad was the show being on December 24th and all, what with Nan Breedlove singing, 'I'll Be Home for Chris—' "

The Invisible Hand clutched Chipper's throat and squeezed, as if to say, *"One more word out of you, and you will embarrass yourself to death. You may fear me now, but you'll thank me later. For you, this story means tears. I'm here to help you, to keep you from looking like a sappy dope."*

The power of the Invisible Hand was frightening. Chipper realized that all eyes were turning his direction, waiting for him to continue. *"One more word—"* cautioned the Hand.

"Uh . . . I forgot what I was saying," said Chipper as the neutral words squeezed through frozen vocal cords. "Look at this picture of Peatmoss and Twobits. You two are on stage with the Rickel Four. Remember? You were leading us all in 'Who Do You Love?' "

"Who do you love?" sang Twobits.

"Sigma Z," shouted the group.

And as the refrain went on and on, Chipper congratulated himself on the diversion. But he knew now that the Invisible Hand was relentless. And he knew he could never, ever, speak the story of the soldiers on Christmas Eve. Not to anyone. Never again. Invisibility was not his enemy, but a friend, and its hand was guiding him now.

Over the brick planter separating living and dining areas, Chipper spotted Peachy running full steam toward the chapter house from the parking lot. The Peach *never* ran. Yet even before Peachy slid the glass doors to enter the dining room, Chipper could hear him howling.

"This is it, guys! This is the biggest friggin' thing ever. I told you sumbitches I'd go out in style." Crossing the floor, Peachy punctuated his exclamations with dance steps. The Hully Gully was followed by "This is history, man. We're making history." The Swim and the Mosquito were followed by "No one, and I mean *no one*, will *ever* be able to top this." As he strutted from dining room to living room while Walking the Dog, he shouted, "THREE – DOG – NIGHT."

The room froze.

"Three Dog Night." The Peach waited for a response.

"You mean—" said someone.

"Three friggin' Dog Night."

The piranhas left the ottoman pool and swarmed around Peachy, His Highness. The shouting and screaming almost kept Chipper from hearing the story as Peachy continued, "Three Dog Night happens to be performing on campus the same night as our Sweetheart Serenade. I finagled a deal with the old man, I coughed up some Wickiup dough, and they're coming to the house after they perform on campus. They've got to leave their sound equipment at the Field House to be packed for their next stop in Dallas, but they'll come afterward for one set. Their backups will use the Rickel Four's instruments. Since most everybody'll be going to the concert, we'll have a short dance before we crown the Sweetheart" (everyone looked at Chipper), "right there in front of Three Friggin' Dog Damn Night!"

Pandemonium struck, and Chipper could hear phrases out of the crowd, such as "do a story for 'The Magazine of Sigma Zeta Chi,'" "contact all of next summer's rushees," "get every sorority chick on campus over here," "sell tickets," and "ol' 558 is gonna make history."

And from the chaos, someone began singing, "Eli's Coming." Soon, a musical melding brought the entire group together in a sing-shout, surrounding Hero Peachy at the center. The noise brought Actives and pledges out of the TV room, adding to the chorus.

Chipper backed away from the group, stepping slowly onto the landing so that he had a bird's-eye view of this pivotal moment in time. And standing alone, he thought of Amy and how they would share the Three Dog Moment forever, after crowning her as the Sweetheart of Sigma Zeta Chi.

46

For Chipper, the strategy was simple. Given a college curriculum over-loaded with pre-med musts, the untraveled path toward journalism had to be paved with copies of *TIME* magazine. He had subscribed during his junior year when he made a solemn vow to read each issue cover-to-cover in a self-designed correspondence course.

But the hours needed for a piercing scrutiny of style and content in *TIME* began slipping further and further from his grasp. Initially, he fell a week behind, then two, and so forth, until now he was staring at a stack of 12 copies sitting on the corner of the President's desk, laughing at his folly.

He scooted the top copy of the red-rimmed journal from its perch and started reading the Letters to the Editor. After stumbling through railings against (and kudos for) the Harrisburg Six and their plot to kidnap Henry Kissinger and blow up the heating tunnels of federal buildings in D.C., he looked back at the stack, then to the copy in his hand, back at the stack. And then he did the unthinkable—he *skimmed*.

He skimmed through the cyclone in Bangladesh that killed 200,000. He skimmed through the Appalachian plane crash that killed the entire football team at Marshall University. And he skimmed from magazine to magazine, week to week, month to month.

He skimmed through the first vehicle with wheels on the lunar surface, placed by the U.S.S.R. (unmanned, of course). He skimmed through the Beach Boys' command performance for Princess Margaret, Jerry Lee Lewis' divorce from his cousin, the estimated number of communes at 15,000 and growing, the review of a TV debut that hailed *All in the Family* as a "revolutionary" show, the opening of Senator McGovern's single issue presidential campaign ("Stop the War"), the conviction of Charles Manson and three followers for the Sharon Tate murders, the growing concern over a My Lai Massacre (charges dropped on the enlisted men, but three officers still facing troubles), Apollo 14 astronauts Alan Shepard and Edgar Mitchell playing golf on the surface of the moon, and a review on brother Jake Chisum's new movie release this coming spring—*Rio Rojo*.

And as the skimming went faster and faster, it got easier and easier. But one page in each magazine slammed the brakes on Chipper's autobahn—the Essay. He read, he studied, he reread, he studied again. The Essay seemed to be a magnet, sucking him into every eye-opening word. He remembered Smokey Ray's life-goal of fog-lifting, and Chipper had to weigh this against his own upbringing that considered the red-rimmed border of *TIME* to be symbolic of its radical leftism, a red flag for Commie pink. (He never told his parents of his decision to subscribe to the radical rag.) But even when he didn't agree with the essayist, he at least *felt* something. And it seemed that the feeling, good or bad, came from a friendly crowbar that pried at his skull.

"Hey jerkoff, whaddya doin'?" asked Peachy as he barged into the room.

"Just reading my *TIME*s."

"What a waste. Well, here it is," said Peachy, holding his hand to the light. "Not quite as big as Drywall's, but hell, a diamond's a diamond."

Pinched between Peachy's thumb and forefinger, the stone almost disappeared, but when Peachy plopped it into Chipper's cupped hand, the diamond started to glimmer.

"Looks pretty good to me," said Chipper. "Same price?"

"Yep."

"I'll borrow the money from the folks, but my mother'll probably use my moustache for collateral, making me shave it so it's not in the wedding pictures."

"Does Amy know, d'ya' think?"

"Probably. You just know stuff when you've gone together as long as we have. But she *doesn't* know I'm gonna give it to her as she's crowned Sweetheart, with Three Dog Night playing in the background."

Peachy beamed. Since the accident with Drywall, the Peach had seemed unusually quiet. Chipper could tell Peachy was proud to be on top of his game again. His friend had secretly admired Amy for years.

And while his puppy crush was buried beneath many layers of leathery scales, the Peach seemed pleased to offer his humble service with both contraband gem and celebrity music to assist in the engagement of Chipper and Amy.

"Here's my down payment," said Chipper, handing Peachy a check for one hundred dollars. His friend's mop of bushy hair had grown longer like everyone else's, but it seemed to be thinning as well, with long strings festooned across the front that had forced a remarkable likeness to Roman Polanski. And, forsaking his old horned rims for granny wire-rims, Peachy had adopted the universal look of the pondering intellectual, a style that made both the gifted and demented appear to be kin.

"Hey, Peachy, is that a moustache you're growing? Or'd you forget to shave?"

"Screw you. Just 'cause I'm no Zhivago like you doesn't mean I ain't cool."

"Zhivago?"

"Yeah, that's what Peatmoss and Twobits are calling you. You know, the poems you've written for chapter meetings and stuff, then bein' a doctor almost, and now this moustache of yours. They're trying to get everyone to change their nicknames. Twobits calls himself Major Major, you know like in *Catch-22*."

"And what's Peatmoss calling himself?"

"Major Error." Chipper laughed as Peachy continued. "They're still calling me Generalissimo, but those days are over for me. I am, and always will be, the Peach. Just plain Peachy."

47

While Amy stared at the white worm of glue creeping along the backbone of the eyelashes she held in her fingertips, she remembered remarks by Germaine Greer: "I'm sick of peering at the world through false eyelashes, so everything I see is mixed with a shadow of bought hairs—"

On her stereo, Three Dog Night wailed, "This is the night to go to the celebrity ball . . ."

How naive of Chipper to think he could surprise her. Still, to receive your engagement ring in the same breath as being named Sweetheart, with Three Dog Night in full force—it would certainly be a night to remember. Not prone to silly sentimentality, Amy was buzzing inside, and she almost shivered with excitement.

Ignoring Germaine, she leaned forward into her vanity and pressed the lash into place, held for a moment, then released. But the glue had crawled onto her fingertips and the lash chose her finger rather than her lid. She was back where she had started, only now with a rubbery goop sealing spaces between the strands.

In times past, the Sweetheart was announced at the Gala as if it were a beauty contest. However, a recent tradition of personalized gifts, including her gown courtesy of Sig Zeta (or more accurately, Wickiup), mandated the winner be foretold.

The only variable in tonight's celebration would be the timing of Chipper's proposal. Would it be during the proclamation of Amy as Sweetheart? Would Three Dog Night play something special? Surely, the threesome didn't know the Sweetheart Serenade. Would Chipper make his move in private or public?

She peeled away the rubber goop and tried again. This time, the lash stuck, but it was caddywompas, making her look decidedly drunk. She pulled the furry caterpillar away from her lid and started over.

Amy knew the carat, the clarity, and brilliant cut. (Peachy had always been a pushover.) But she didn't know the timing.

Yet, one horrible thought clouded the evening. Cassie would be alone.

To make matters worse, in spite of Amy's vigorous protest, Cassie had insisted on ironing the Sweetheart's gown. And when she thought of Cassie in such morose servitude, on the biggest night ever, she felt herself starting to cry. She understood good tears or bad tears when the reason was pure. But comingling tears were confusing, forcing a strange solitude.

When she squeezed, the glue squirted out in a pool that bound the lashes together into a rubbery Frito. She should have listened to Ms. Greer, and she threw the mess into the trash and reached for her mascara, though she would wait until her teardrops cleared.

* * *

Never in the history of the chapter had there been more goldfish crammed into the mouth of the Sig Zeta house. Actives and their dates seemed the minority. Stag sorority girls. Ticket-bearing frat boys. High school rushees. Alums. Townies. At least three hundred filled the living room and the dining room dance floor, with another two dozen perched on the brick planter that divided the two rooms. Outside, several hundred were milling around in groups on the front lawn, hoping to catch a glimpse of Three Dog Night as they entered the Sigma Z house. Peachy had even hired a professional photographer, just in case the party pic man blew it.

Most had attended "the best concert ever" moments earlier, but the distinction between watching celebrity and touching celebrity was magnified now by the eager mob at the Sweetheart Gala.

Amy, in formal gown, stood near the bandstand with the tuxedoed President, squished by the crowd to the point that Chipper clutched one of the three microphone stands to secure their position—and, to secure the access to his pending announcement.

As he looked in Amy's eyes, he wondered if she knew. Her eyes were green in the sunlight, blue at night, but always clever. Even if she did know, she'd never guess that he'd sent a copy of "The Sweetheart

Serenade" to Three Dog Night (via Peachy's old man) and that *they* would be singing the tearjerker while Chipper waited for the exact lyrics—"and the starlight streams on the girl of my dreams"—before producing a star-shaped treasure box that held the diamond, freshly mounted. Chipper was absolutely smitten by his own ingenuity.

The crowd was oddly sober. The concert at the Field House had kept bottles from lips, though weed and its "sobering effect" was rampant. But now it was 11:40 p.m., and the tummy-to-brain transit time of alcohol only took minutes. Soon, sobering would be slobbering.

Peachy was pacing near the bandstand when Chipper grabbed him by the shoulder.

"Everything's all right, isn't it, Peachy?"

"Sure, man. They gotta get away from that crowd at the Field House and make sure their gear's in the truck. All sorts of stuff."

Chipper was reassured. Peachy showed no signs of doubt.

Near midnight, the catcalls began. Mostly from foreigners—the guys from other frats, showing off for their girls. Out the front window, after boring a hole through the haze of cigarette smoke—mixed with the fog of Panama red, Kona gold, and Maui wowie—Chipper could see some of the outsiders leaving.

"Hey, Peachy," someone yelled, "are you sure it was Three Dog Night? Maybe it was Three Pooch Screw."

"Yeah, or better yet, maybe Question Mark and the Mysterians—but only Question Mark showed up."

"I think they done did you in, Peachy. Doggie style."

Then some half-wit fell to the ground on all fours and began barking. Within seconds, the entire dance floor was covered with barking, howling, and yelping dogs, while three such dogs grabbed the microphones and began bowwowing "Eli's Coming" with lyrics replaced by permutations of "bark," "ruff," "howl," with a few "yelps" tossed in for harmony.

One hour of patience had been replaced by riot in a mere minute.

Chipper and Amy stared at each other, mouths gaping, she in her long formal gown, he in his formal tux. It was quite the Celebrity Ball.

Chipper reached inside his pants pocket and fiddled with the star-shaped treasure box. The moment was gone, so the gem in its shell would have to wait for another day.

After canine debauchery waned, the non-Sig crowd began to leave. And when Chipper heard the pay phone near the TV room ringing, he wondered how long the faint bell might have been clanging, lost in the cacophony.

Peering beyond the planter and through the living room, Chipper saw an Active pick up the phone and call for Peachy. The Peach made his way through the dissipating crowd until he finally reached the receiver and held it to his ear. Peachy's lips didn't move as he listened. His eyes shifted around the room through narrow squints as he seemed to be assessing the number of potential assailants. The crowd quieted as more and more revelers saw that Peachy was on the phone, looking thoughtful. The barking stopped, and all dogs returned to an upright position.

When he hung up, Peachy announced: "They've been delayed."

"Oh yeah, by how long?" shouted one of the few remaining non-Sigs.

"Well, so long that they're not gonna have time to make it over—"

"That ain't delayed, man, that's a rip-off. I want my money back."

"Don't worry, those that had to pay will get their money back."

"Hey, Peachy, nice job for our Sweetheart this year."

Mob rule began to stone Peachy with insults. Chipper spotted C.C. Chastain across the room, so he made his way to the rejuvenated leader of the Rickel Four. Crowd control would be simple. The Rickel Four could start playing "Who Do You Love?" Then, when the crowd answered back, "Sigma Z," tempers would calm, and all would be forgiven.

C.C. was game and started rounding up the band. Having left Amy at the bandstand, Chipper moved toward the landing near the front door where Peachy stood wiping imagined, but palpable, rotten vegetables from his face.

Holding up his hands, palms forward to the crowd, Chipper began pleading for quiet. But quiet did not come until every last townie, every foreign frat boy, every stag sorority girl left. And when the quiet was smooth and soft and nearly genuine, Chipper spoke: "Lest we forget that tonight is really our Sweetheart Gala—"

For some reason, not a single person was looking at Chipper. And when he turned to follow their eyes, he spotted Drywall standing near his side on the landing, a few steps above the crowd. Rickelbell was sitting at Drywall's side, tail wagging, tongue hanging, waiting for Drywall to speak.

But the Kickapoo did not speak. He sang. A cappella. And the tremolo of his tenor stroked soothing fingers over the mongrel's and brought the house into peace:

When dreams fade away
As they sometimes do
And you've lost the light in your heart . . .

One by one, the members began to join Drywall in "The Sweetheart Serenade," and the Actives near the bandstand escorted Amy to the landing beside Chipper.

> *Then close your eyes*
> *Bid sadness farewell*
> *Light the fire 'neath your shrine of dreams*
> *And dream the face of your Sweetheart there . . .*

Chipper hugged and kissed Amy just in time for the key lyrics, which sent his hand scrambling for the star-shaped box . . .

> *And the starlight streams on the girl of my dreams . . .*

But he froze. Amy was crying, so he froze. He let go of the star, and kissed her again for the crowd-pleaser. The moment didn't seem right. Amy was crying. Peachy was bathing in overwhelming disgrace. Drywall was spearheading a chorus of love while his own true love had spent the evening ironing Amy's dress. The moment didn't seem right.

* * *

Sitting in the wingback chair of the President's room at 2:00 a.m., waiting for Amy to return from the ladies' head, Chipper relived the evening. The Rickel Four had covered nicely. Everyone had a great time except for Peachy, who evaporated after the phone call. Memories had been made all right, but Chipper flubbed his moment. He raked himself over the bad timing. Even RFK, looking down from the poster on the wall, seemed to be groaning at Chipper's stupidity. *Oh well, Amy was kinda distant tonight anyway, probably the stress and demands of being Sweetheart and all.*

Amy appeared at the door, hands on her hips—hips that were covered in some sort of luscious, shiny white material that made Chipper want to slide his hands across her and down her and up her, then a second round of sliding *between* the white and her skin, across her and down her and up her—

"Chipper, why didn't you give it to me?"

"Give you what?"

"Don't play dumb. The ring. Why didn't you give me the ring?"

"Who told— How'd you— Peachy, that asshole. I . . . uh . . . it didn't seem right. I mean you were crying and everything."

"I was crying at the thought of Cassie. Drywall was singing that beautiful song—" She caught herself, as if she were about to cry again. "Chipper, doggone it. It was the perfect moment. There'll never be another— You missed— oh, damn!" Amy hiked her gown above her knees and sprinted directly at Chipper. About six feet from the wingback chair, she seemed airborne, arms wide, white chiffon flapping, landing against Chipper and the chair simultaneously, bracing herself against the wings of the chair with enough force that it tipped backward and toppled them both to the ground. "Marry me," she said.

Chipper struggled for the star box and opened it. "I will," he said, with pure joy. Amy took the diamond ring from the box and they laughed together, rolling into embrace, still in the fallen chair, mostly. It didn't matter that the door to his sanctuary was wide open. Such was love.

He kissed her with a force that ignored the probing eyes of RFK on the wall. Then he lifted her gown above her waist, while her kisses in return let him know that she was ready as well. As they squirmed, still engulfed in the fallen chair, he fought her pantyhose—the scourge of passion—and finally stripped her down to the last stop. Amy had properly doffed *his* formal wear as well, at least below the waist, leaving his tux pants in a crumple by the chair. He was in his party-ware— white boxers with a big red heart for his sweetheart—along with starched white shirt, bowtie, and satin lapels.

Flat on his back against the toppled chair, with Amy perched on top, he placed his cupped and clinching palms on her buttocks and pulled her onto him, the simulated act covered by a tent of white chiffon. Celibacy could be a struggle, but it was better than no sex at all.

Chipper barely opened his eyes to see a stranger in the room, standing over them both. Chipper yelled. Amy screamed.

"Dammit, Ernie, what the hell are you doing in here? It's two in the morning."

Chipper caught his words as he scrambled for decency, grabbing his tux pants for coverage.

"A better question would be, 'What are *you* doing here . . . *brother*?'" The words of Ernie Dumas were greased with oil. "Granted, I'm normally in this room just for *Bible* study."

The guilt stabbed at Chipper, only making him angrier. "Then what the hell are you doing here now?"

"As *President*, I thought you might oughta know that Audora Winchester is tripped out, standing on the roof, directly above your head right now. We think she might fall off, or even jump. She's really spaced-out."

"Where's Smokey Ray?" asked Chipper, forgetting for a moment that the boyfriend was at Harvard interviewing for graduate school. "Oh, never mind. Jiminy Christmas, what the heck is going on around this place?"

"I knew it," said Amy, standing now, composed yet blushed. "I knew something like this was bound to happen."

The President and the Sweetheart hurried to the roof in formal attire.

48

From a dormer window squatting on the old wing of the house, Chipper emerged onto the shingled roof where he could spot Audora, standing like a weathervane at the precipice.

She was facing away from him, feet spread slightly on either side of the roof's peak, toes near the edge. Her arms were frozen in an odd configuration, outstretched, but curved upward, as if she were holding a giant, invisible beach ball. Her fingers were spread, each nail pointing to the night sky. She was silhouetted by the streetlights near the Alamo apartments, and the night breeze slapped around her long black hair in tandem with her loose and long dress. A quarter moon shone above.

"Audora?"

She didn't seem to recognize his voice. She didn't move.

He yelled again, "Audora?"

She was lifeless.

Chipper helped Amy out the dormer window, then they worked their way across the pitched surface to the ridge of the roof where they could balance by waddling, each step on opposite sides of the crest. Chipper led, while Amy was a few steps behind, cautioning him as they eased closer to the edge that held Audora.

"Don't do anything sudden," said Amy. "Use psychology."

Chipper cringed at the advice. He had no idea how to approach Audora, but neither did Amy. Audora looked as though she were spreading her wings, about to fly from the roof of the fraternity house. About 10 feet from her perch, Chipper stopped.

"Audora, it's me. Chipper."

She was a statue.

"I've been thinking about something. You know, we've been a little cold to each other ever since our freshman year, you know, the Holiday Inn deal and all. I guess I've wanted to put that behind us. I always kinda blamed you, but I shouldn't have swallowed that stuff, no matter what was mixed with the Heavenly Blues. These things get crummy when both sides think the other oughta apologize, so I'm sayin' it first. I'll meet you halfway. I'm sorry I've held that grudge."

Audora's black hair continued to swirl about the back of her head, so Chipper couldn't detect any response at all.

"See. I'm taking steps to meet you halfway," said Chipper as he inched forward toward the statue. "I'm halfway now. So if you're willing, come meet me."

Her hair whipped about, and her dress flapped in the wind, but Audora was motionless.

"It's not working," whispered Amy. Chipper returned a scowl.

Audora was lost in Otherworld. As a prior tourist, Chipper knew the terrain, and he decided to drive to Audora. He looked back at the dormer window where a cluster of heads were poking through to witness the spectacle. He hoped they didn't hoot or holler in their fear. Especially Ernie Dumas, who was crawling out the window to join him and Amy.

"Tell me, dear sister, what voices speak to you now? Is the moon your muse? Are you listening to her cool breath?" Chipper turned to the dormer crowd, anticipating confusion at his odd words. He couldn't tell if they had heard him.

"Little Prince," replied Audora. Chipper turned an ear to capture her next words. "I am a flower born with the sun. Four thorns have I, and my soft petals glow in the moon. But aye, it is my two green leaves that offer solace and stability to the two ends of the ecliptic—that black rainbow crossing the heavens where both sun and moon ride their chariots."

"Audora, why do you call me 'Little Prince?'"

"Because you live on a planet that is no bigger than a house."

When Chipper turned back to Amy, she said softly, "The book. She's talking about the book called *The Little Prince*," reminding him of the fantasy novel that had spread across campus, with nearly the fire of *Love Story*.

"If I remember right," said Chipper, "if I'm the Little Prince, then my tiny planet is called Asteroid three . . . three . . ." He prompted Audora, thinking that the concrete foundation of mathematics might draw her back to reality.

"Your planet is Asteroid 558, Little Prince."

The night chill bore its way through Chipper's tuxedo, for he shivered at her words.

He was afraid for the first time. Audora had not moved a muscle. From his vantage behind her, he wasn't even sure she was moving her lips. The last thing he wanted to do was prompt her into a hallucinogen-fueled jump. For some reason, she was absolutely rigid. Her arms continued in their odd posture. Amy was a blank, no help. A voice deep inside told Chipper to leave Audora alone. It seemed preposterous, given the natural history of people on ledges, but the voice he heard was strong: *You cannot understand her Otherworld. Leave her alone.*

From behind, Chipper heard the scraping sound of shoes sliding along the pitched roof, someone struggling to the crest, toward Amy and him—and Audora.

* * *

What glory to have been the Chosen One for this supreme design. But ohhhh . . . the pressure. I musn't move a muscle. Not for 26,000 years. The precession will complete its circle in the celestial sphere, the vernal equinox will continue its path along the ecliptic, leaving Pisces, then entering Aquarius, where I will hold the universe in place with my two leaves and my petals of peace, until the circle is complete. If my leaves move any at all, just one tiny bit, the ecliptic will collapse, the order is destroyed, chaos will reign, and I will surely die of my own thorns as the universe disintegrates.

"Tell me, dear sister, what voices speak to you now? Is the moon your muse? Are you listening to her cool breath?"

"Little Prince," said Audora, wisely using her telepathy so that even the trembling of her lips would not have an opportunity to disturb the universe. *"I am a flower born with the sun. Four thorns have I, and my soft petals glow in the moon. But aye, it is my two green leaves that offer solace and stability to the two ends of the ecliptic, that black rainbow crossing the heavens where both the sun and the moon ride their chariots."*

"Audora, why do you call me 'Little Prince?'"

Oh, the fool. I call him the Little Prince because he IS the Little Prince. He stands on his tiny planet, staring at this simple flower, yet he is such a fool he cannot recognize himself. For him, the mirror has no image. I will try to instruct him as to the danger he presents to all creation, and I must do it without moving my lips . . .

"Because you live on a planet that is no bigger than a house."

"If I remember right, if I'm the Little Prince, then my tiny planet is called Asteroid three . . . three . . ."

The Little Prince is playing games. Standing on top of his tiny planet, no bigger than a house, yet he thinks himself wiser than the cosmos. The madness of it all! Does he not realize that he is disturbing the order, that he could destroy us all? He must turn away. I must show him how tiny and insignificant his little planet really is, and again I will transmit my words through the night air, lips sealed . . . "Your planet is Asteroid 558, Little Prince."

Oh, the vibrations in my toes! A trampling herd of celestial monsters is coming my way. They will destroy everything! I should turn my head to see, but I musn't. Clairvoyance will need to serve me now. Oh, no. Not a herd of monsters, I see just one. Red-haired and wild-eyed, he lunges at me. But the universe must reign. My two leaves must hold the eclectic. I have no choice, or all will be lost. Does this monster not understand? Oh, he is so close. I must take to the air now and let the zephyr carry me to a safer planet, one where my leaves will not be disturbed for 26,000 years.

But why do they scream? All of them. The red-haired monster, the Little Prince, and his Princess? Don't they realize that their tiny planet is no bigger than a house? The universe is supreme. If they were anything but fools, they'd understand why I have to fly in order to save—

49

"I was there. Ernie pushed her."

"Bullshit. I was there, too. He was trying to grab her before she jumped."

"How would you know? I had the better look. You barely had your head out the window."

Such were the words that followed Audora's leap. Hallway discussions were led by eyewitnesses, or secondhand witnesses claiming firsthand experience, or Actives not even present that night who cast themselves as witnesses. One thing for sure—different eyes saw different things.

"Ernie's always hated Smokey Ray. He was getting even for all the times Smokey's made a fool out of him."

"You're talking attempted murder there, brother. If that's the case, why'd the cops let Ernie go?"

"Hell, the pigs didn't see nothin'. How would they know?"

"The cops listened to Chipper and Amy, that's why. No one had a better look than Chipper and Amy, who said Ernie was trying to be a big hero."

"But I heard Ernie and Audora had a run-in when they were freshmen."

More thoughts and opinions floated through 558 while Audora had her first surgery to remove her spleen, her second surgery to give her a new hip joint, and her third surgery to drain the abscess from her first surgery. After three weeks in the hospital, most of her drug-induced psychosis was gone (she no longer shrieked inexplicably when her rigid, outstretched arms were restrained to her side with lockbelt and wristlets). But her Thorazine requirements were still so rich that upon discharge she was admitted directly to Building 17 at the state insane asylum, where she continued her reentry to Earth's atmosphere.

Her location in 17 was a mere two buildings away from the experimental ward in Building 19 where Psychiatric Aide III Ray Divine had won fame as an amateur therapist, and where his supervising psychiatrist had written such a superlative letter of recommendation to Harvard that the Moguru was slated for their newly established graduate program in psychopharmacology. Since it was so close to the end of the school year, Smokey Ray quit his job to spend more time in Building 17 with Audora. Rumor held that of the inmates on Audora's ward, 10 were college kids trying to reenter a world they had once known.

* * *

"I just can't seem to get over it," Chipper said. "I've been through it a thousand times in my head, and I can't shake it."

Amy replied, "I know what you mean. Thank goodness she's okay. That's all I can say."

"I don't ever see Smokey Ray any more," Chipper said.

"Who'd ever thought he'd be so devoted to one woman?" said Amy, apparently remembering Smokey Ray's reputation in high school.

"I hear she's almost back to normal."

"I'm not sure Audora was ever what you'd call 'normal.' But you wanna know what's really strange?"

"What?"

"I've been having this dream," Amy said. "In this dream—I've had it four or five times now—Smokey Ray and Audora, the hippies, appear in a cave, like they live there or something. And while I'm looking at them, they transform into the old Smokey Ray and the old Audora. Smokey's in his cowboy hat, and Audora's in her black suit and heels she wore the first time I met her. Then, Audora spreads the lapels of her jacket and shows me her fluorescent lime green bra, and she says to me, 'Color your dreams.'"

"That's too weird, Amy. Far-out. I wouldn't share that with anyone else."

* * *

Words about the incident hopped and skipped and jumped through the Sig Zeta house, and it seemed that when it came to truth, there were at least three versions.

"I heard Smokey Ray decked Ernie when he got back from Harvard."

"Baloney, I was there. Smokey Ray cut him to shreds all right, as only Smokey Ray can do, without even raising his voice. But Ernie's too dumb to even know what Smokey was doing to him."

"That's not what happened at all. I saw it with my own eyes. Smokey Ray was a perfect gentleman."

* * *

Chipper and Amy recited the details of the incident over and over for weeks, as if reliving each and every second could scourge their memories. Then, one evening while Chipper and Amy were sitting in his '60 Thunderbird, watching a rerun of Jake Chisum's *Guts and Grit* at the Boomer Drive-In, they agreed to quit talking about Audora and Smokey Ray. They knew it wouldn't last, but they agreed nonetheless.

"Hey, I got the flyer from the School of Journalism at Far West Texas," said Chipper. "I'm going down for an interview next weekend. I'm assuming you'll go with me?"

"Of course, Mister Wishy-Washy. I wouldn't want to miss one minute of your torment."

"It's pretty bad, isn't it? Even Ty Wheeler, for gosh sakes, knows what he's going to do with his life—after just eight or nine years of college."

"Oh, really? What?" asked Amy.

"He's going back to Leadville where he's going to teach guitar."

"Well, what's a good college education for anyway?"

"He'll do fine. As long as he doesn't sing."

The newly engaged duo fell into a rhythm that chimed with the scenes of *Guts and Grit*. They necked while a stilted actress delivered her monotone lines, then they surfaced for air when the eye-patched Chisum came on the screen. Down for the girl, up again for the Man.

"Do you remember the girls' golf team is headed to Kansas tomorrow for a three-way match, including K-State?"

"I forgot. You still going in the coach's station wagon?"

"Yesss," said Amy, with ice in her tone. "Not one penny from the university for the girls' golf team. The coach pays for it all, and we chip in."

"Can't you let it go? Your college career is about over."

"You know how hard I've worked in that action group trying to get legislation like they got passed in—"

"I know, I know. Like in Title Six of the Civil Rights Bill. Let's just enjoy the movie."

Chipper thought he heard a sigh.

"Speaking of golf," she said. "Your intramural tournament is pretty soon. Who's taking Drywall's place?"

"A freshman, from El Viento of all things. Do you remember Booger Yarkey? Caddied for me in the state tournament?"

"Sure. The little guy with the white spot of skin beneath one nostril?"

"Yeah, he's a new initiate. Nearly a scratch player. And what a deal for him that moustaches are so popular. He's got enough fuzz to cover that white spot. Of course, everyone calls him Booger anyway."

"So what's the standing on the Intramural Trophy? I forgot to ask how tennis came out today."

"Ugh. Kenny Townsend—mastermind of our brilliant year in intramurals—got puking drunk with the poker players at the round-table the night before tennis finals. Hung over, he lost his match. First time to lose, ever. What irony. We'd have won the overall trophy if Kenny had won. Now we have to clinch first place in golf to win the whole shebang. What's more, do you realize that if we win intramurals, then if the Sig Zeta-Beta Chi act pulls off Best in Show at Varsity Sing, we'll have the points for Fraternity of the Year?"

Chipper found it hard to believe his fantasy as a freshman had become a very realistic, palpable dream.

"Gosh, you ought to have golf in the bag. The Sigs have won every year since you were freshmen. If Smokey Ray can get up for it, what with Audora and all—and if Booger is as good as you say he is—"

"Yeah, and Peachy has come along amazingly well. I can't believe that old hacker consistently shoots in the low-80s. And I hate to say it as much as I can't stand the guy, but Uno Guilford is a scratch shooter now. The jerk of jerks could easily play varsity, if he had a lick of ambition."

"Hard to be ambitious when you're anticipating a lifetime of frolicking in Daddy's money," said Amy, her voice oddly strained.

On the screen, the actress said, "They say he has guts. They say he has grit. I wanted a man with guts and grit."

Chipper and Amy crawled into the backseat, where bodies could slide across the black leather, and where Chipper's lofty intent could be maintained through *celibus interruptus*. After all, New Blood songwriter Chase Callaway had finked out in favor of the fair sex (dealing a serious blow to Chipper's flirtation with the ministry).

50

Forlorn, dejected, alone, Peachy Waterman Jr. sat at his desk, forehead in palms, at the global headquarters of Wickiup Enterprises International. He could no longer traverse the plains of 558 without some wiseacre yapping, "Arf-arf" or "Bow-wow" or "Ruff-ruff" or simply howling out loud to the moon. Three Dog Night had screwed the Peach. They had decimated his reputation and labeled him forever as a failure. His life as King of the Hop was over. No redemption rested in the cards.

Simply being the bastard that had blinded Drywall was bad enough. He had been max'd out from the moment the eye surgeon revealed the bleak future for his friend. His vow to forge his way into law school had been only a temporary salve for that wound. Now, after all his hard work to establish Wickiup, he was the butt of dog jokes from everyone. Even his financial empire was being threatened, not only from blowing all the dough on top-name bands for four years, but also from the fiasco in progress with Project Daddy-Cool.

Peachy had cooled a good deal of the southern United States with air-conditioners before the power failures began. First, it was the Delts at Sam Houston State University, then the ATOs at Emory, then a sassy Kappa from SMU called to say the coeds planned to load all their air-conditioners into a dump truck and pile them on the 558 lawn if Peachy couldn't deliver on the generators. But it didn't end there. Seventy-six collegiate domiciles had now registered vile complaints.

In the early days of Project Daddy-Cool he hadn't been able to keep up with air-conditioner orders and deliveries, but then lights began to dim, fuses began to blow, circuits began to break, and the universal cry came from refrigerated colleges everywhere to provide auxiliary generators. Business came to a standstill, and now the empire was imploding. Peachy had originally closed down five divisions of Wickiup to focus and finance the inventory for Project Daddy-Cool, but orders were on hold and the warehouse full. Now he was closing another seven divisions to arrange the instillation of generators at every fraternity, sorority, or dorm that had eight or more window units in operation. The buildings of the early 1900s had simply not been designed to keep up with technology.

Things went from bad to worse when his own drivers struck again for higher wages still, and fewer trips to Mexico, and when that was straightened out, the generators were on back order, and when that was straightened out, the warehouse in Mexico caught fire and destroyed the goods, and on and on. Now, 12 states from Arizona to Georgia, from Texas to Iowa, were screaming for emergency electricity. And being the smooth, deliberating businessman, Peachy would say, "The generators are on the way," while in his head, he was dying to say, *You spoiled, sorry, sumbitches—you didn't even have air-conditioning until I came along and now you're squawking at me? Why the hell don't you get your own generator? Or how 'bout this, you dimwitted baboons—why the hell don't you ration air-co time? Make a schedule so's you've only got five or six units on at any one time. Is that so freakin' hard, you bird-brained bozos? How the hell did you get into college anyway?* Instead: "The generators are on the way."

Peachy could hear Drywall groping down the hallway, fingering the doorjamb, then fumbling with the knob. The door opened.

"Hey, what's up?" said Drywall.

"Nuthin'. How 'bout you?"

"Nuthin' much."

Such intimate words of friendship could flow endlessly.

"Say, why'd you move Rickelbell's bed out of our room?" asked Peachy, puzzled, since the mascot was Drywall's seeing eye.

"She's gonna have some pups. I found out for sure today. I went with Kong to the vet, and the vet says she'll be delivering soon. I figured I'd move her down to the study hall where Twobits' skunk used to live. She'll just make a mess up here when she delivers. And no one uses the study hall anymore."

"No, not after our stellar GPA first semester to satisfy Heil President. Damn good thing second semester GPA doesn't count for anything."

Drywall plopped down on his bed and began thumbing through mail. "You didn't have anything in your box, Peachy, I already checked."

"So what else is new? Good thing Wickiup gets its mail at the post office. There ain't a box big enough to handle all the crapola I'm getting these days from the whiny bastards around the country that can't figure out how to get by without their precious air-conditioners until I can get 'em their generators. Air-conditioners that, I might add, they never woulda had if it wasn't for me."

Drywall ignored him, which ticked Peachy off just a little. After all, Drywall had once been an equal partner in Wickiup, but now he was a token Polack who made sure the border Polacks in Mexico did their deeds on time. He hadn't contributed one-tenth, but had shared equally in the spoils. But how could Peachy complain now? Especially after whacking Drywall in the head with his driver, in essence wrecking the copresident's life. Still, it ticked him off.

"What the heck is this?" said Drywall, holding a letter close to the window of vision that he still had in the corner of one eye.

"What?"

"This letter. It's addressed to Cassie St. Clair, but the address is 558 University Boulevard. Here, Peachy, you better figure it out."

"The return address is RCA Records in Nashville, Tennessee," said Peachy.

"Are you kidding me? What's it say?"

Peachy opened the letter and read it aloud to Drywall: "'Thank you for submitting your tapes to RCA. Unfortunately, we don't believe your style fits with our company, but feel free to send us samples in the future. Styles will change—yours before ours.'"

"I don't get it. I didn't send them anything."

"But it looks like Cassie did," said Peachy. "What I read you was scribbled at the bottom of *her* letter to *them*. It's on her stationery."

"*Her* letter? I still don't get it."

"This is Cassie's letter to RCA Records. It's dated *after* you broke up with her." Peachy translated Cassie's typewritten words: "She says in here that a friend of hers has the most beautiful voice in the world, and that she's enclosing some tapes. At the bottom, she asks them to write you at 558 University Boulevard if they're *interested*, but to respond to her at the Beta Chi house address if they're *not*. Looks like they sent this to the wrong place. Any rejection letter was supposed to be mailed to her. So what's this about? Did you make some tapes?"

"Well, yeah, but they were just for her. I like hillbilly music, but no one listens to it. Heck, most people haven't even heard of Nashville.

Anyway, I talked about singing western music once, but only to Cassie."

"You've never talked about wanting to be a singer," said Peachy. Drywall was a million miles away. He wasn't listening to Peachy, so the Peach simply looked at him and tried to guess his thoughts before proceeding with his special insight: "Ah, I see it now. This is the moment of truth, Drywall, my man. The girl who you dumped loves you so much that she works her butt off to see you succeed, even if you were a flaming asshole to her. What's more, she gives the record company two addresses—hers and yours. Hers if they reject you. Yours if they accept you. She's willing to take the Big Fat No for you. It's just that the record company sent the No to the wrong place."

Peachy was getting a kick out of his caring insight. He knew Drywall was suffering over Cassie, and it felt good to twist the dagger a little, to get his stubborn Polack friend to think. It was for a noble cause, after all.

"I'm going to leave you with your thoughts now," said Sigmund Peach. "And Drywall, I want you to think about how much that girl loves you. I tell you what—I'd give my right nut for a girl like Cassie who worshiped the ground I walk on. I got chicks on both arms, mind you, but their hands are a-sliming their way into my pockets lookin' for bread. You got yourself a girl who loves you for what you are, even with just one-quarter of an eye. In some ways, you're the luckiest sumbitch who ever lived."

Peachy closed the door behind him and took off down the Hallway of Dead and Decaying Presidents, muttering to himself, "Hell, Chipper ain't the only pissant around here who can give a good speech. I bet I sounded damn near as good as Smokey Ray."

Intending to go to Grady's Pub to drink himself into a state of mind where there was ample electricity for everyone, Peachy stopped at the landing near the front door when he heard someone say, "Which pledge forgot to light the candles for Brother Chisum?"

It was rhetorical, of course, as the only two guys near the front door were Peachy and the speaker, Kong.

Major rituals were important to Kong, and he opened the bureau where the fine silver was kept, along with a stash of candles and matches. The man-mountain set new white candles on their sticks at the base of the portrait of Brother Jake Chisum, just as they should be, ready for lighting every Monday night before meal and before chapter meeting. And it was the pledges' responsibility to make sure that fresh candles were lit on time.

Peachy looked at the countenance of Brother Chisum, the only man who ever lived and feared nothing. Jake Chisum didn't fear some annoying little coed threatening dump trucks full of air-conditioners, Jake Chisum didn't fear mocking and taunts when the band didn't show. No, Jake Chisum just blew the bastards away. But Peachy wondered how Jake would have felt if he had nearly blinded his best friend—because Peachy knew how it felt, and *he* felt like the biggest freakin' leper in this here colony.

"Hey, Peachy," said Kong as he tried to strike a match, "didn't you tell me once that your old man played poker with Brother Chisum?"

"Yeah, sure. Once," said Peachy. "Maybe twice. Yeah, the first time in Las Vegas, then at Chisum's house in Newport Beach. Took my old man for a bundle. The old man said he emptied Chisum's pockets, which means the exact opposite, given the fact that my old man's a damn liar. After all, Chisum told my old man that if he ever needed *any-thing*—meaning, of course, that Brother Chisum won a shitload—"

Thunderstruck, Peachy almost fell to the ground. "I can't believe I didn't think of this earlier."

"What?" asked Kong.

"My old man. Jake Chisum. The old man knows Jake Chisum, sorta. I can't believe I didn't—. Man, oh, man. Just when I was thinking the Peach was gonna leave college as the biggest joke that ever wuz. Here, gimme those matches."

Peachy's hands were trembling as he tried to hold flame to wick. When both candles were lit, he stood back with Kong and admired the flickering hero—America's hero—the one man who feared nothing—the Emancipator who held the power of redemption for the Peach.

51

Milestones can happen in millimeters or milliseconds, as fate doles out the degrees. Just as Peachy's golf shot had cracked the hornet-infested stump through improbable measure, so Peachy's phone call to his old man came in the nick of time. Poker pal Jake Chisum was already touring the country to promote his new release, *Rio Rojo*, and his scheduled flight from Dallas to St. Louis was easily rearranged for a pit stop in Oklahoma. His host for the overnight stay? The Sigma Z chapter of Number One Son, Peachy Waterman Jr.

As Chipper removed the poster of former President Perry Crane and RFK from the wall, he grinned at the new poster of Chisum that would take its place, not only for the Visit tomorrow, but also for All Time. The wall of the President's room would no longer support the likes of mere mortals. Future visitors—Actives, pledges, hot-boxed rushees, and smuggled girls—would forever see the countenance of Jake Chisum, cowboy hat tipped low and his left eye patched for his role in *Guts and Grit*. And by the time Chisum left the chapter, he'd have his autograph on this poster, as well as the candlelit portrait near the entry of the house. Chipper would vacate his room for the special night, allowing words to echo for generations yet unborn: *"Jake Chisum slept here!"*

But that wasn't all. Chipper had designated Senior Hall as the new Gallery of Brother Chisum, where black-framed party pics from the Visit would show Jake with his Oklahoma brothers, several hundred photos lining the walls at which great-grandchildren would gawk. And there would be more pictures in the rush manual, enduring year after year, on through the next Ice Age. Local television stations were on alert, and reporters were stumbling over themselves to grasp some measure of exclusivity on the "Twenty-four Hours When Jake Chisum Visited the Sigma Zeta Chis in Oklahoma."

Of course, there would be a staged chapter meeting where Jake would be "one of the guys." The agenda would be phony from top to bottom, all topics rehearsed (this was no time to reveal the true essence of discombobulation). The one real agenda item would be to bask in the glory of America's hero. And to take pictures of it all.

After chapter meeting, so that pledges and rushees and girls could join, the crowd would gather in the living room around the grand piano where C.C. Chastain would play, Drywall would lead, and everyone would chime in with "The Sweetheart Serenade." Chipper again borrowed his father's new Super 8mm movie camera, but was disappointed that there would be no sound. Nonetheless, he was investigating the possibility of renting a rare 16mm sound camera from a shop in Oklahoma City. Pictures. Movies. Proof. Documentation that the impossible can happen—that dreams come true sometimes even if you haven't dreamed them in the first place.

Peachy was even more wired than Chipper. No expense was too great for Wickiup Enterprises to make the Visit a legendary success. The restoring of Peachy's proud stature provided such ecstasy that he was determined to make the 24 hours last forever. In fact, he decided to make it begin before it even started.

On the day before the big event, Wickiup rented the Sooner Theater—the entire place! While the owner had never done this before, Wickiup paid him well. Wickiup paid him to show *Rio Rojo*. Wickiup paid him to keep the theater locked during the showing. Wickiup paid him to run the movie for Peatmoss and Twobits ahead of time, so that the duo could practice comedic timing to enliven the showing. Wickiup paid him to allow beer in the theater. And Wickiup paid him three thousand dollars in advance for potential damages.

The Wickiup plan was simple. In order to drive the Sigs and their dates into a feverish pitch the night before Chisum's arrival, they would, in fraternal bond, without anyone but Sigs and their girls in the theater, experience their own personal screening of *Rio Rojo*.

And so it went—

The Sooner Theater had a stage for live performances in front of its screen, which was mostly hidden by green velvet curtains with a gold brocade stripe along the bottom. When the curtains were drawn, the bunched curtains looked like rigid pillars on each side of the silver screen. The concrete sidewalls were covered by art deco graffiti that included masks of comedy and tragedy just about every 10 feet in any direction. Fixed curtains (more green velvet) draped these walls, serving no purpose whatsoever.

Four years earlier, an American flag had hung lifelessly on its stand near the velvet pillars on stage, and a spotlight beamed on the flag while the crowd stood for the national anthem prior to the flickering lights of a Road Runner cartoon, a short subject, Movietone News, then the feature. But the hippies destroyed the flag, the theater changed ownership, and the velvet curtains became filters for the residue of hashish that permeated the air with every showing.

But not tonight. Not the night before Jake Chisum. Tonight, they'd hauled in an American flag and American beer.

Chipper and Amy sat at the back, top row, the President and his Empress at Circus Maximus. Peachy was Ringmaster, but the clowns were Peatmoss and Twobits who, in an 18-hour marathon the day before, had watched *Rio Rojo* nine times to learn the lines and crystallize their cues.

With wondrous timing, the duo—calling themselves the team of "Major Major and Major Error"—dove into the Civil War epilogue plot with wit, repartee, and props. With microphones in hand, loudspeakers in front of the green curtains, they stood on step stools and ladders of various heights to join the actors on the screen.

In the second ring of the circus, Peachy led the crowd in cheering, "All honor to his name" every time Jake Chisum shot a bad guy. And whenever Jake so much as pulled out his six-shooter, the crowd—under Peachy's direction—yelled, "With this sign, victory reigns," a Sigma Zeta Chi slogan meant to apply to their symbol, the Golden Cross.

In the third ring, Kong and Einstink carried empty kegs of beer out of the wings of the theater, then full kegs in, holding the metal barrels in bear hugs as they walked.

"I feel like I'm missing half of everything that's happening," said Chipper to Amy, both of them trying to watch all three rings of the circus.

"Maybe that's best," she said.

"Remember Jake Chisum being cheered by the audience in *Silver Wings upon Their Chest,* then being such a joke a few years later at *In the Beginning*? What do you call this?"

"I don't have the slightest," said Amy. "Chaos?"

Waddling across stage, hugging a keg, Kong tripped, sprawling face first while the freed keg rolled across the stage and struck Twobits' ladder like a bowling pin just as he was attempting to smooch with the actress on the screen. Twobits tumbled with the ladder to the ground, and the laughter was nonstop for several minutes.

Drywall sat on the front row, sans Rickelbell, who was back in the maternity ward at the fraternity house, awaiting delivery.

From his perch near the top, Chipper took an informal roll call, wondering if all the members were part of this—this—this debauchery. For in its depravity, Chipper realized two mystifying hours where the members weren't divided by cliques, weren't bickering over idiotic trivialities, and weren't demanding that Chipper do something about nothing. How could such a night of folly be so right and so wrong at the same time?

Although he couldn't remember each and every underclassman in his personal roll call, he knew his own pledge class backward and forward from their initiation numbers. Missing were #1407 and #1429 — Smokey Ray Divine and Ernie Dumas, respectively.

52

Drywall adjusted his eyepatch from the blurry image in the mirror, then donned the black cowboy hat provided by Peachy for the Chosen One. As first greeter at the door, Drywall would be dressed as Jake Chisum's character from *Guts and Grit* in order to utter the soon-to-be historic line, "Welcome to our chapter, Brother Chisum," hand outstretched, anticipating the secret grip.

With Peachy and Chipper en route to the airport in Oklahoma City at this very moment, Drywall practiced his line to the federal marshal in the mirror, time and time again: "Welcome to our chapter, Brother Chisum."

In order to keep his chin up, he would have to target Jake Chisum through his small portal early, a periscope view of the movie star, then proudly lift his head high where Brother Chisum would then disappear from sight.

"Welcome to our chapter, Brother Chisum."

Drywall punched the power button on Peachy's 8-track, ending Paul Revere and the Raiders' new hit, "Indian Nation." Peachy's old man, of course, had been an entrepreneur in the early days of cassette recording, and now that 8-tracks were taking over, Peachy claimed his old man had arranged a mysterious meeting of the Learjet inventor—who had actually developed 8-track technology for his own airplanes—and Ford Motor Company. The spoils to Peachy's old man in the 8-track revolution had included poker parties with the high rollers, which numbered in their midst none other than Jake Chisum.

So here he was—First Greeter—an Indian in a cowboy hat, tipped just right so that the shadow of the brim eclipsed the eyepatch as it crossed his brow at a dark angle.

With a full, gut-twisting hour left before the Arrival, Drywall started for the basement to visit Rickelbell and her new pups that had greeted him late last night when he checked on her after Circus Maximus. Six wet rats, blind and deaf, with Rickelbell licking them dry, were twitching in their sleep in the birthing bed when he'd found them last night. Strangely, his impulse upon discovery of the pups had been to call Cassie to share the moment, but the joy of new arrivals was ruined at the thought of poor Cassie who had no business being burdened by a quarter-eyed Indian.

As Drywall edged his way down the hall, down the stairs, touching the walls ever so lightly to maintain his course, he realized how much he depended on echoes to guide his way. The returning noise of his own footsteps sounded different on the landing at the base of the first set of stairs than it did just a few feet onward at the top of the basement stairway. In fact, he practiced this trek with his good eye shut, counting the number of times he had to touch the walls to maintain bearings. On each practice trip, he had touched fewer and fewer times until he could make it all the way down two flights and into the study hall with only five wall-taps. He wasn't sure what prompted this exercise, other than the all-consuming fear of total blindness some day.

As he listened to the sound of his clicking heels on the linoleum of the basement floor, he knew it would be five more steps until he had to zig to avoid the U-bench in the middle of the room. Zagging back toward the study hall door, another eight steps clicked on the floor before he entered the delivery room, where he opened his eye to see Rickelbell proudly wagging her tail and greeting him with her too-human eyes. Like a metronome, her head swung back and forth between her babies to Drywall as if to mark time on everything important in her life.

"Hey, girl, how's your little pups tonight?"

Drywall squatted until he was resting on his hams. The six little ones were squirming on top of each other, some hunting for the rows of drinking fountains. As he petted each of the six—three golden, two spotted brown and white, and one black—he reminded himself of the names he had declared the night before—Jinglebell, Clarabell, Nellibell, Tinkerbell, Tacobell, and Pachelbel.

After feeding Rickelbell, he watched the pups for a half-hour or so, until the drone of the crowd upstairs began to rise. Only the Actives would be there for the initial greeting, and Drywall could feel their sparks even though he was tucked away in the basement. *Welcome to our chapter, Brother Chisum.*

"Bye for now, girl. I'll see you later. Take care of your pups." He could see her smiling, as dogs do, as he walked out the door.

Navigating up the stairs, he kept his eye open and head held high, hoping that the brothers wouldn't laugh at the federal marshal outfit. What peculiar solace this getup held for him, the eyepatch no longer a sign of infirmity. Peachy was a friend indeed to come up with the idea.

"Where the hell is Drywall?" he heard just before reaching the landing. "He's supposed to be up front at the door." Similar cries of feigned panic followed in chorus.

As Drywall rounded the corner onto the landing by the TV room, overlooking the living area, he was greeted by a crowd of federal marshals, each and every member in eyepatch and black cowboy hat. As the applause began, Drywall gulped to swallow the emotion that threatened to drip a quarter-tear from his quarter-eye. He wasn't really sure why they were clapping, but it seemed to be for him.

The Actives had formed a gauntlet to the front door where Drywall would stand to greet Brother Jake. And as he walked through the crowd, his eyepatched brothers patted him on the back and continued their applause. And for the first time since he had pledged Sig Zeta years ago, he felt like he was one of the guys. No, it was more than that. A strange sensation was creeping through him that said, "for this one moment in time, you *are* Jake Chisum." And stranger still, he wanted Cassie—just out of the clear blue—he wanted her right now. He didn't understand why, other than he needed her.

As he took his place at the open door, he looked back at the crowd, touching the brim of his black cowboy hat in thanks for their applause, whatever in the hell it had meant. Marshals everywhere, each eyepatched, each cowboy-hatted, all ready for the biggest moment of their lives. *Welcome to our chapter, Brother Chisum.*

Drywall lowered his head for just a moment to get a better look at Ty Wheeler who had cheated slightly with his eyepatch by simply knocking out one of the tinted lenses of his Roy Orbison glasses. When Drywall began to chuckle, the reclusive Ty smiled for the first time that Drywall had ever seen.

Inching outside, Drywall looked at the dusk and worried that he was losing his remaining vision until he heard someone comment on the "sumbitchin' fog" that had rolled in. He was relieved that no one else could see across the street. But 20 minutes later, he couldn't see the cars in the Sig Zeta parking lot. And 20 minutes after that, he couldn't see much beyond the front door as the fog consumed the house at 558.

"Gosh, when Chipper and Peachy get here with Brother Jake, just imagine them comin' outta that fog right before our eyes, just like in a movie or something," someone said.

Drywall kept looking back at the flickering candles at the base of Jake Chisum's portrait to make sure his remnant of sight wasn't failing. No, he could see the face of Brother Chisum through his window just like before. But outside, a thick green soup turned darker and darker by the minute as sunset was now well past. Usually, a fog meant cooler weather, but tonight was unusually warm and muggy.

Then, out of the fog, just like in a movie, the bodies of Chipper DeHart and Peachy Waterman Jr. materialized before the one-eyed crowd. The Actives gasped in a collective breath-holding that lasted for time immemorial—because only two bodies appeared.

Chipper and Peachy both held their heads to the ground. Drywall was sick inside. *The proud man looks upward.* No one could muster a word.

Finally, after stepping just inside the doorway, Chipper managed in a shaky voice, "The fog came in. They closed the airport. Brother Chisum was diverted on to St. Louis."

"Welcome to our chapter, Brother Chisum," said Drywall in long melodic tones like a mournful dirge. "Welcome to our chapter."

No one moved, with the exception of the party pic man who scampered out the door. The Actives were spellbound by their own grief. They stood in the living room, on the landing, and spilled over to the dining room behind the planter. Kong was standing beside the portrait of Brother Chisum, and he stooped to blow out the candles. Even Peatmoss and Twobits stood quietly, robbed of their last full measure of joy before Vietnam.

Drywall wanted to rescue the moment as he had done with the Three Dog fiasco by singing "The Sweetheart Serenade," but his throat was jammed. Then, Drywall spotted Smokey Ray Divine emerge at the landing, three steps above the crowd, his top hat gone, cowboy hat in place again. Smokey Ray lifted his eyepatch and spoke to the crowd with his Moguru voice like only Smokey could do, startling Drywall with the first line of "The Sweetheart Serenade" as if there had been unwitting telepathy:

"'When dreams fade away, as they sometimes do—'. Why, oh why, would a love song—a song of tribute—begin with a bummer phrase like that? I ask you. Why?"

No one spoke. Smokey Ray had the floor.

"Because, my brothers, the world—goes—wrong—and—dreams—fade—away. So I say to you now, you are the product of your dreams, and your view of the world is shaped by whether you distinguish fantasy from dreams and dreams from vision and vision from hope and hope from faith. There's a difference in those words, and the difference will make you or break you."

Smokey Ray lifted one hand, gesturing toward the front door where Chipper and Peachy and Drywall stood in total paralysis. From Drywall's limited view, it seemed that Chipper was, as usual, hanging on every word uttered by the Mad Moguru. Turning back to the Moguru, it looked to Drywall as though Smokey Ray saw a ghost standing at the front door of the Sig house as he continued.

"Aye, let us greet Brother Chisum as he enters our home." Smokey Ray's hand followed his imaginary friend into the living room, and the unpatched eyes of the Actives jerked back and forth from Smokey's fingertips to the void. "And we supped with him and he with us. And photographs we took and took and took. We sang our songs, gathering around the grand piano. And how we laughed when so many brothers sat on the piano that the legs broke, all tumbling to the ground. But Brother Chisum, in his generosity and gratitude for handing him such a splendid memory, promised the chapter he'd buy a new piano. And what joy we all had when we received the piano with his inscription carved onto a brass plate above the keys: "For my Sigma Z brothers in Oklahoma. With This Sign—Victory Reigns. Jake Chisum.""

Peachy leaned over to Chipper to whisper while Drywall eavesdropped, "Smokey Ray is totally tripped out, man. He's hallucinating. You'd better do something."

"No, I don't think so," said Chipper, "I kinda think he quit trippin' after Audora's accident."

But Smokey Ray went on and on, describing the events of the night in past, present, and future tense, as if there were no restrictions on time. And as he seemed to draw to a close, he lifted both arms to crowd.

"So, my brothers, remember and foretell a Creator in the Time of our youth, while evil days are kept at bay, with years drawing nigh when we will say, 'I have no pleasure come my way.' Not the light that heralds the sun, not the glow that follows the moon, nor the clouds that vacuum the rain, will wait before we dash to our deathbeds as bridegrooms to the bed of our lover. Indeed, we look to the rear to gaze upon the horizon of tomorrow as we walk with noiseless feet of Time, traveling back in a twinkle, but forth at a steady, deadly speed—60 seconds per hour. Only our vision holds still. So cling to your timeless

vision, see a new heaven and a new earth. Make your holy city, O
brotherly chapter, ready as a bride adorned for her husband. He who
sits on the throne makes old things new, vanquishing Time's thievish
progress to eternity. Aye, it is Time that brings truth to light. Write it
down—write it up—for a Creator's words are faithful and true—words
that must be passed to all generations—'I am the Alpha and the
Omega, the beginning and the end.'"

Then Smokey Ray "Moguru" Divine tipped his hat and disappeared, easing back to his hole on Senior Row. The fog seemed to have
slipped inside the Sig house as he vanished.

The dumbstruck audience began to stir in quiet tones and hyp-
notic shuffles. Then, out of the ranks, broke Ernie Dumas—no cowboy hat, no eyepatch—heading toward Chipper.

Drywall sat down on Grand Central Ottoman as if he were looking at the imaginary party pics that Smokey Ray had described in his
soliloquy. He didn't want anything to do with Ernie. But Drywall sat
still, sensing that Chipper might need a witness, or help. The crowd
drifted away.

"So now what do you think, President DeHart?" Ernie said.

"About what?"

"About *what*? How can you say that? Didn't you hear that blas-
phemy? Don't you realize Smokey Ray was perverting the word of
God."

"What are you talking about, Ernie?"

"Smokey was twisting the word. Remember, even the demons
call out, 'Lord, Lord,' but the really satanic part is claiming to be God.
Didn't you hear it? He said, 'I'm the Alpha and the Omega.' What
more do you need, Chipper? Smokey Ray is possessed, and if you're
not going to do anything about it, I will."

"Oh crap, Ernie, are you casting out demons these days?"

"If that's what it takes. Fight fire with fire."

"Well, the way I took it, if Smokey Ray was making any sense at
all—and you gotta remember that Smokey Ray is part Shakespeare,
part Bible, and part Smokey—was something about writing down
words for the next generation, about Alpha and Omega, as if the Creator's words need to be written. Not Smokey Ray claiming to be God.
But who knows? For goshsakes, whoever knows what he means?
Maybe he was talking about the Greek system, for all I know."

"You're way, *way* off base here, brother."

Drywall sneaked a peek through his window of light, and it
seemed that Ernie's white-striped eyebrows lifted as his blazing eyes
widened in a sort of moronic revelation.

"Why . . . *you* must be in league with the—. DeHart, I'm beginning to doubt your salvation."

Chipper's face looked red, even through Drywall's foggy lens.

"Let me tell *you* something, Ernie," fired Chipper with finger pointed. "I'm beginning to doubt your *sanity*."

Drywall lowered his head back to Grand Central Ottoman, trying to act invisible, which wasn't really that hard. Until tonight's convention of one-eyed federal marshals, he'd always considered himself the most invisible man in the house.

* * *

Brother Alex Wade, House Manager, noticed that the hallway lights started flickering and dimming as he headed to bed around 1:00 in the morning. Even though the night was suffocating, he'd have to shut down the air-conditioners on Senior Row, the wing of the house that had been built in 1928.

Banging on each of the doors to rouse sleepers, or using credit cards to pick the locks, he turned off all the coolers one at a time.

"Hey, screw you, Wade, why don't you make the underclassmen turn theirs off?"

"Feel this plug, wiseass. Do you feel how freakin' hot that mutherfuggin' cord is? The cords are all cool in the new wing. But they're red hot over here on Senior Row. Now turn your machine off."

And the same conversation was repeated at each room, except at Smokey Ray's abode where Alex Wade had to jimmy the door open after no answer—there sat Smokey Ray with headphones on, listening to his goofball music, staring out the window, legs crossed, back arched, as if he were in some sort of lunatic trance. Alex slipped in the room, turned off the air-conditioner and left, without ever disturbing the Moguru.

But after Alex Wade made his rounds and went to bed in his room in the new wing, he could not see the lights dimming again, nor could he hear the whirring sound of the recalcitrant air-conditioners on Senior Row.

* * *

Peatmoss and Twobits had adopted an elitist position with regard to their hallucinogens. No longer given to crass alcohol, even mocking the sponge brains that relied on such mindless revelry, they now limited their forays to chemicals conceived for the thinking man—lyser-

gic acid diethlyamide, first and foremost. The switch, of course, had
followed on the heels of the lottery that told the twosome that they
had better see a lot of the world—real or not—in the very short time
they had left before Vietnam.

But after the nonvisit of Jake Chisum, the twosome backslid to
Grady's, where they sponged their own fair share of brew and discussed "just another night closer to death." Now, resisting sleep that
would take them just another day closer, they ran through the halls of
the chapter house firing pop-bottle rockets at each other.

"Major Major, incoming at 3 o'clock."

Schwoooooooooosh. The sparkles flew.

"Major Error, Major Error, gooks firing from the jungle."

Schwooooooooooosh.

"Major Major, I'm all outta napalm—just kidding."

Schwooooooooooosh.

* * *

Smokey Ray maintained his lotus position, knowing it was Alex
Wade breaking into his room. Even through his headphones, he had
heard Alex chewing butt, one room at a time down Senior Row for
having air-conditioners on full blast, so he knew it was his turn when
the door popped open. He didn't have to turn around.

With the air-conditioner off and Alex finally gone, he was able to
purify his thoughts once again—embered incense, smoke pluming,
flower petals at his feet, Ravi Shankar transporting him to the banks
of the River Ganges with sitar music in his headphones, his pulse captured by the rhythm that lulled him closer to harmony.

Within moments, though, he thought he could hear the air-conditioners in the rooms around him kick in again with the clanky sound
of their cheap motors. Harmony disrupted, he thought again of
Audora's progress, with physical therapy predicting her first steps in
another month, and mental therapy predicting her first sober
thoughts any day. Their union would last because he remained convinced that he could lead them to a higher plane of consciousness than
the phony world of chemical transport. Then he erased his mind for
the ride once again.

The closer he could bring his heart rate to match the sitar rhythm,
the more peace he enjoyed. But the music became complex, with
irregular nuances in rhythm that threw his pulse into a twitter. Back to
calming purification again. *Plunck, plunck, plunck.* Another subtle

change in metre—*plunck* . . . *plunck-plunck*—seemed to electrify him, causing his heart to skip a beat.

He thought he heard the noisy hinges of his door opening again, but he wasn't sure. He didn't care. Alex Wade might be at it again, so he kept his gaze on the blurry full moon out his window, smudged light in pain and confusion, barely visible in the lifting fog—the fog that had destroyed the hopes of all Sig Zetas but himself. The door shut softly again, after just two beats of his heart and two beats of the sitar. *That was quick,* he thought.

He closed his eyes for peace. The smell of his incense changed, taking on a pungent fragrance, so foul he thought he had purchased a rancid lot. The sitar quickened and his heart raced. He felt himself coughing for no reason at all. As he opened his eyes to catch his breath, the glass of the window before him was a flickering orange, and when he twisted in his lotus position to the rear, he saw tongues of fire licking his matchbox door all the way to the ceiling.

53

As flames from the 1928 wing spawned black mushrooms of smoke against the night sky, Chipper clustered the Actives into three bouquets on the front lawn—seniors, juniors, and sophomores. The former president of each pledge class took roll, and Chipper could hear the initiation numbers being shouted from all three groupings at once.

Moguru Divine was the hero, having broken through the glass of his jammed window and rousing all the sleepers in the house, including Mom Miller. But after Smokey Ray answered roll call with his initiation number, #1408 was missing—Drywall Twohatchets.

Peachy, in near panic, said, "But he was right behind me. In fact, he was hanging onto my shoulders as we got near the front door. I remember spotting Smokey Ray on the pay phone calling the fire department, and I stopped for just a second. When I turned around, Drywall was gone, so I thought he went on outside. It was hard to see with all the smoke."

The blaze was rolling into the new wing, and smoke was gushing out the double doors in front, each door carved with a cross having thick and fluted arms, soon to be cinders. Chipper twisted his head in a futile search for fire trucks.

"Sophomores are present and accounted for," someone yelled.

"I bet he went after Rickelbell and her pups," said Peachy. "She was in the basement, and the study hall door's always closed."

Before Chipper could wipe the soot away from his eyes, Smokey Ray charged for the twin doors to find Drywall. But the rescue was short-lived, for Drywall emerged coughing, choking, and dogless.

"Junior class is all here," came the voice of an ex-president.

In the commotion, Chipper realized he hadn't finished the head count yet for his own pledge class. Inching toward Drywall and Smokey Ray at the front door, he took note of #1409 through dead last Ernie Dumas who, at #1429, was fidgeting a few feet away. By the time he confirmed no casualties, Chipper could feel the oven-like heat of the inferno as he heard the words of Drywall and Smokey Ray:

"The fire's not to the living room yet, but it's the smoke that stopped me," said Drywall. "I don't need to see. I know the way. It's just that I couldn't breathe."

Smokey Ray tried to placate him. "The firemen will be here any minute. They can try to get the dogs."

"Every second counts," replied Drywall. "Every second."

Chipper joined in. "What about using Ernie's grandfather's gas mask? He's been keeping it in his car lately." In this grave moment, Chipper struggled to dismiss the lunatic symbolism that Ernie had glued to the mask. In fact, Chipper spoke the words loudly so that, perhaps, nearby Ernie would hear and volunteer—for once—to do something honorable.

For Chipper, the gas mask idea had certain merits. But for Drywall and Smokey Ray, the idea must have been brilliant, for they were 40 feet en route to the parking lot, Drywall hanging onto the Moguru's arm to run, before Chipper had placed the period at the end of his sentence.

Struggling to keep up, Chipper saw the tandem backs of Drywall and Smokey Ray as they weaved through the cars in the lot until they targeted Ernie's brown Buick. But a shadow flew by the corner of Chipper's eye in a slant pattern that was zeroing in as well—Ernie.

By the time Chipper joined the threesome, blood was boiling through clinched fists and jutting jaws, and Ernie's intent was clear. No one was going to touch the gas mask.

"Calm down, dammit!" yelled Chipper, a command that seemed to travel only two inches beyond his lips before it dropped dead on the pavement.

Drywall, with head cocked to see better, jumped Ernie from behind in a Full Nelson while Smokey Ray circled to the passenger side of Ernie's locked car. Bracing himself against Kong's old Cadillac, Smokey Ray raised his cowboy-booted feet and began kicking out the window.

The trouble unfolding made the nearby fire shrink, it seemed to Chipper. Smokey Ray was yelling, "Twice in one night—breaking glass—I don't friggin' believe it." Smokey reached inside the shattered window and grabbed the gas mask off the dash. Ernie broke loose from Drywall and vaulted over the hood with hopes to retrieve his sacrament, but Smokey Ray stepped to one side and let Ernie fall to the ground. Drywall took the handoff from Smokey Ray and scoped the mask with its corrugated hose and shoulder pouch. Then, before Ernie could get to his feet, Drywall headed toward the front door holding the mask, his head tilted slightly and chin down.

As Ernie stood up, Chipper fully expected a brawl. After all, it had been four years in the making. Ernie Dumas was taller and stronger than Smokey Ray, but Chipper couldn't conceive of Smokey Ray losing a battle, be it one of wit or might.

Ernie's face reflected the nearby flames, with hues of orange dancing over his hollow cheeks and brick red, bushy hair. Even his chalk-stripe eyebrows seemed orange. But it was his eyes that were on fire. He began huffing and puffing as he moved slowly toward a cool Smokey Ray. His fists made two iron balls, and he began a slow back-swing by cocking his elbow.

Smokey Ray didn't budge.

"Why are all your clothes in your car, Ernie?" said Smokey Ray, with all the jitters of a cat in the middle of a yawn.

The elbow uncocked. The fists unclenched.

Chipper looked to the backseat of the brown Buick where hangers of shirts and slacks filled the rod that stretched from hook to hook.

"All of us lost everything," continued Smokey Ray. "You didn't lose anything, it seems. Why did you move your clothes? Finals aren't for another three weeks yet. Are you going home to *study*?"

Ernie dropped his arms and stood straight and proud.

"Yeah," said Ernie. "That's right. I'm going home to study."

Smokey Ray's arms were crossed, and he lifted one hand to stroke his beard.

"Then I guess you better get in your car now and get to studying."

Ernie was still. Then, "It was Twobits and Peatmoss—shooting off pop-bottle rockets."

"How would you know that? Let me say it again—get in your car *now* and get the hell out of here. I want you to drive off, and don't look back—and don't ever come back. As far as I'm concerned, when they circumcised you, they threw away the wrong part. If I so much as see your dickhead again, you'll be carted off to jail in handcuffs."

Ernie Dumas backed away, slithering around the car to the driver's side where he unlocked the door and got in. The Buick crawled away in a slow drive to the street where Ernie disappeared just moments before two fire trucks arrived.

"Do you think—?"asked Chipper.

"Think? I always think."

Both of them realized at once that Drywall was probably some-where in the fire, so they ran to the front of the house, leaping over squirming hoses that the firemen were positioning. In such a short time, Chipper couldn't believe that the new wing was burning as well, flames on the second story, smoke on the first.

The Actives were scattered, some getting too close to the firemen, others sitting on car hoods watching, but most standing still, speechless.

Chipper approached one of the firemen who was holding a hose and motioning to his comrade to turn the spigot. "There's one guy in there," Chipper said. "And some dogs."

"Whaddya mean? I was told everyone was out."

"Well, at first, yes, but now there's one in there. Probably down in the basement."

Water blasted out of the hose, and the fireman held his stance. "Well, it's too hot now and too much smoke. We'll beat these front flames for a minute, then send in a team. Where is he? Do you know?"

"Probably in the basement."

Peachy joined Smokey Ray and Chipper as they watched the inferno engorge itself on the chapter house. Chipper offered a silent prayer. As for Peachy and Smokey Ray, who knew?

So much water rained against the roof and upper windows that a waterfall developed from the ledge over the front door. And through that veil of cascading water, Chipper watched in amazement as the Creature from the Black Lagoon emerged—Drywall in his fish-eyed gas mask was carrying a cardboard box labeled "IGA Beets" while Rickelbell tangled herself between his legs as he walked.

Many of the Actives on the front lawn, distracted by chaos, hadn't even realized Drywall had gone back inside. But as he ripped off the mask and set the box of Rickelbell's babies on the ground, clustered brothers began to gather around Rickelbell and her litter.

Drywall kept coughing and choking, claiming the gas mask was nearly worthless, as he squatted near the beet box and began stroking each of the puppies.

Chipper stood behind Drywall, staring over his shoulders. Rickel-bell, alternating barks and hacks, jumped into the box and began lick-ing the six pups, testing each with a nudge of her sooty nose. She kept returning, though, to one pup that was lifeless.

"Which one is that?" asked Chipper of Drywall.

"Pachelbel, I think," answered Drywall, twisting his neck to see bet-ter. "The gold ones all sorta look alike, but Pachelbel was the littlest."

"What the heck is a Pacobell?" asked one of the 20 Actives or so that had gathered around the box.

"It's Pachelbel. The name of a composer."

"Like I said—Pacobell."

The puppy was dead, yet it didn't seem official until Drywall declared it so. Rickelbell wouldn't let go as she ignored the other five and fought at Drywall's arms with her paws as he lifted the dead one from the box. Neither Drywall nor Rickelbell seemed to accept it, but the pup was just a hunk of soft clay.

Drywall took a deep breath as he backed away from the crowd huddling near the box, holding the pup in both hands and lowering his chin so he could stare into its face. Chipper broke from the crowd as well to join Drywall steps away.

"I called it Pachelbel," said Drywall to Chipper, "because I was going to give it to Cassie as a peace offering. Pachelbel is her favorite composer, and she always said she wanted a song of his—a Canon or something—to be played at her wedding. This must be a sign. A bad sign."

Chipper couldn't believe that Drywall would allow a dead pup to be the fulcrum for such teeter-tottering. "You know what, Drywall? Those dogs don't know their names. Change 'em. Isn't one of them named Nellibelle? That's a crappy name for a dog. Change it to Pachelbel."

Drywall gave him a blank stare.

"Which one is Nellibelle?" persisted Chipper.

"The black one," said Drywall.

"Okay. It's new name is Pachelbel. Good enough, huh?"

"I'm gonna go bury it back where the soil is soft beneath the cedars," Drywall said, an odd thing to do while the fraternity house was still burning to the ground. Rickelbell followed him.

Chipper felt he was a one-man island as he stood in the front yard to watch the horrid end of the conflagration. Even Peachy's loud protest—"They ain't gonna hang this sumbitch on me. It had nothin' to do with my air-conditioners or the electrical wiring. I don't care what Alex Wade says. Hell, he's just the House Manager, not a fire inspector"—yes, even Peachy's protest seemed to be a gentle wave lapping at Chipper's shore as the Peach rolled by, proclaiming his innocence to anyone who would listen.

The fire was winning, the firemen losing. Thank goodness no one had been hurt, but everything material would be lost. Chipper was gut-wrenching sick for the first time since the blaze began. Sick that the Sig Zetas were without a home. Sick that he had lost all his personal mementos. Sick that the brothers would be separated for the final three weeks of college. Sick that collective memories would never be able to latch onto touchstones.

Someday soon, there would be bulldozers, and those reckless, uncaring monsters would raze the cinders and push dirt to bury the study hall, the U-bench, the melted jukebox, and the Puke Pit. Then, the alums would most certainly try to relocate the house to south campus — after all, the burning house at 558 University on north campus was nothing but a solo planet out of orbit.

Grass would grow, then someone bright and cunning would realize there's easy money in parking lots, and concrete would pour. And the unwitting would fight for spaces on game days, would empty their drinks onto the pavement, would flick their cigarette butts — never realizing for a moment that they were standing on a million memories.

And two thousand years later, after pavement returns to sand, and the dunes emerge, archeologists — famous, perhaps, for cracking the case at Stonehenge — would uncover the dwelling and whisk away the dirt and ash to discover a strange U-shaped structure, a concrete pit (theorized to be some sort of sacrificial altar), and a charred box of chrome and colorful plastic, black discs inside, melted into a meaningless blob.

54

Chipper turned onto the winding gravel road leading to the university golf course. Amy sat in her bucket seat, twisting the dial on the radio until she hit her new favorite song. She rocked her shoulders to the tune, while Chipper stole glances at pink shorts, long thighs, sleeveless blouse, tan arms with elbows bent, fingers clicking.

Over a week had passed since the "faulty electrical wiring" verdict, though rumors continued to swirl about pop-bottle rocket sightings, not to mention the early summer exodus by Ernie Dumas. The Actives had been farmed out to empty dorm rooms or houses of local alums, while many who lived nearby simply went home for the rest of the year.

"Hard to believe the chapter house that's about to win Fraternity of the Year doesn't even exist," said Chipper, though Amy ignored him, probably because this was the umpteenth time he'd said the same thing.

Amy sang, "Here comes the sun, do-dah-do-do . . ."

Chipper could see the course straight ahead, with a small crowd gathered on the 18th green for the finale of intramural golf.

"You know we're going to win Varsity Sing, don't you?" said Amy with more declaration than inquisition. "Do-dah-do-do . . . we're calling our act, 'Color Your Dreams.'"

"I'm counting on it for the 25 points, but how do you know you're gonna win?"

"I didn't, until the fire, but now I know. Do-dah-do-do . . ."

"Why? Sympathy vote?"

"No. We keep changing the act, and every time it gets better and better. And even though the Sig Zetas are scattered all over, they all show up for every rehearsal. You *do* know your old pledge trainer is behind the scenes helping C.C.? I just follow orders. So does Peachy, believe it or not. Do-dah-do-do . . ."

"Old Mother Boone is really amazing," said Chipper. "He won some new-young-playwright award in New York. It's hard to figure why he'd stick around here and help with something as diddly as Varsity Sing."

"Because he and C.C. are still collaborating on musicals. But to stop everything for Varsity Sing? Amazing."

"I don't know how C.C. is going to make it in med school and still pull off a musical career," said Chipper, comfortably denying his own career pickle, just weeks from graduation.

Chipper parked his T-bird beneath a tall elm with freshly budded leaves and sweeping limbs that hovered just above the heads of the spectators on the 18th green. He could see ex-team member Drywall standing greenside with Rickelbell at his side. Then, Peachy emerged from the crowd with a jackpot grin on his face. Amy wasn't even out of the car before Peachy cornered them near the front bumper.

"We got it in the bag, Chipper. Helluvalot closer than I thought it'd be, but we still pulled it off. Hurry up. You're about to miss the big finish and the trophy."

"I knew it. Fantastic." *And with Varsity Sing, we'll clinch the Big One. First time ever for Sig Zeta to be Top Dog.*

Peachy said, "I shot a friggin' 86, but Smokey Ray had a 75, Booger shot 77, and now Uno is even par with his approach near the pin. All he has to do is two-putt from eight feet for the win. The Betas are gonna take second. Delts third."

Amy gave Chipper a hug at the waist as they worked their way to the green. Uno Guilford set his bag down on the fringe, and the nearly delirious Peachy walked over and whispered something to the "banana-nosed bastard," which Chipper guessed to be hypocritical words of support, meant to last only until the winning putt dropped. After the whisper, Uno slowly scanned the rim of the green until his lifeless eyes met Chipper's. Then he lined up his putt.

After the ball rolled a foot past the cup, he stepped up for the tap-in. But before he stroked the ball, he glared again at Chipper. Uno's reptilian eyes struck the former pledge class president, and Chipper felt an unseasonable winter draft. Then Uno lowered his head toward the ball and pushed his second putt by the edge of the hole. When Guilford turned and stared at Chipper again, a sadistic grin smeared across his mug beneath his banana nose, and it was clear that his look of smug and righteous revenge had been fermenting for years.

Stunned beyond words, Chipper felt like his feet became blocks of ice while his heart froze, then shattered into icy shards. *The sonuvabitch is sabotaging the tournament—the intramural trophy—and Fraternity of the Year, to boot! Unbelievable!*

Uno still had a 10-inch putt to tie. He massaged his chin, scratched his head, faked a modicum of anguish, then bent over the putt, was statue-still for a torturous moment, then stroked it ever-so-lightly, leaving the ball short of the hole by the width of a dagger blade. Four putts from eight feet.

Chipper's whole life flashed before his eyes.

Uno Guilford walked off the green, making a point to stroll by Chipper where he stopped and said, "Looks like we lost by . . . *UNO* stroke, Mister President."

Chipper felt Amy squeeze his hand as she muttered, "Oh—my—God." Dazed and dumbstruck, Chipper couldn't move. Then, a scream came from his left and Chipper saw Peachy charging full steam ahead at Guilford.

Peachy hit Uno with a flying tackle that tumbled them onto the moist green turf where body imprints marked their struggle as they rolled from the fringe onto the green, Peachy using his marshmallow fists to pound Uno's face repeatedly. Smokey Ray and Booger rushed onto the green to pull the two apart, while the spectators were spewed with obscenities reworked into crude syntax such that "mother" and "god" were but light seasoning in the stew.

Chipper turned his back on the scene, wrecked and ravaged. Amy helped him back to the T-bird where he gripped the steering wheel until the white bones of his knuckles looked as though they would pop through the skin.

She tried to console him, but he couldn't really hear her speaking. Time lost its grip, and he thought back to Smokey Ray's speech the night that the house burned, something about evil days being kept at bay. And it was then that Chipper appreciated the full measure of evil, and that it was *not* kept at bay. Evil stalked and stared and waited for an opportunity to strike below the belt.

In an odd sort of way, the calamity on the 18th green was far more terrifying than the fire that had consumed the Sig Zeta house. For what Chipper had just witnessed was a solitary man who could wreck a four-year march toward top honors. Uno could neutralize the points offered by the winning football team, the basketball team, the wrestling team, and the baseball team. He could stomp on all the

Actives who had studied so hard first semester to bring the house GPA
to its highest point ever. He could neuter the whopping 25 points they
hoped to win in Varsity Sing, even before the competition began.
Ninety-odd men of different gifts and convictions, sharing a common
standard, could all be squashed by one fucking asshole who had quietly
waited his turn. And it wasn't the trophy loss itself that made the world
look so bleak, it was the fact that one person, one measly subhuman,
so steeped in malice could lie in wait, quietly, for so many years, seizing one millisecond of opportunity to flex his muscles. How would it
have played out if that millisecond had never lent itself to Uno's ugliness? Would Uno have waited another four years, or 40 years, to deal
his perverted revenge? And how many other Unos were out there,
waiting to sting for the sheer hell of it?

Whereas before, Chipper had considered Uno's wealthy future
lucky, now he was incensed at Uno's unearned privilege. Uno would
inherit the family fortune and assume the Throne of Society. He would
win all the outstanding citizenship and leadership awards that money
could buy. His name and face, for the rest of his life, would be plastered
everywhere local nobility was honored. Yet, inside the man, his heart
was stone cold evil. A scary evil that can sit and wait, year after year,
waiting for its chance, waiting for its opportunity to blossom. Then
with one stroke of the putter, it could wreak destruction a hundred-
fold greater than anything cast its way.

Yes, more than hellfire itself destroying the Sig Zeta house, Uno's
stroke was the commanding blow. For it was then that Chipper realized that Smokey Ray was right when he pondered the words to "The
Sweetheart Serenade"—*When dreams fade away, as they sometimes do, and
you've lost the light in your heart*—only sometimes dreams don't fade
away . . . they explode. The world goes wrong all right, and what's even
more sickening—Noiseless Evil has the edge.

55

The President called the chapter meeting to order, under the stars, the moon, and an inscrutable night sky from which Chipper hoped to draw a message from Above.

The ashes of brotherhood, scattered across campus in dorms and homes, had convened tonight at Chipper's call—minus one banished Ernie Dumas and a shunned Uno Guilford—for their final meeting of the year and for Chipper's valedictory. The chosen venue was the banks of Pringle's Pool. Willow trees, oaks, and cedars, all had their roots dipping into the pool like straws, exposed where erosion left a grassy overhang.

Seniors, juniors, sophomores, and newly initiated freshmen were herded near the water, each Active wearing the gold cross crest of Sig Zeta, either on T-shirt or sweatshirt.

Chipper spoke of his phone call from Brewster Stone of the House Corporation who had arranged a ramshackle house as temporary home for the brothers next year (a death knell for the rush effort). The chapter house had been underinsured, so there was no possibility of rebuilding, and the alums had confirmed their intent to switch to Fraternity and Sorority Row on south campus. Asteroid 558 would not orbit this way again.

Chipper warned the freshmen that they might never live in the new house since the alums anticipated a fund-raising effort taking at least five years. But he had more to say:

"Almost four years ago, the senior class, my pledge brothers, in an act now considered legendary, right here on the very ground where we stand, turned the Black Jack takeout into a takeout of the entire chapter. Our goal was to raise a giant mirror for the Actives, to let them see how far they'd drifted from the original goals and traditions of our fraternity.

"At the time, we considered it a huge victory, unlikely to be matched ever again. But I say to you tonight, especially the freshmen, you new initiates have a much harder task. You are the ones who will have to keep a spirit alive when there is no house to speak of. It is you who will pass the stories of 558 down to the next generation. It is you who will need to create a vision of the future to attract rushees as you paint the way things will be again some day. It is you who will need a victory greater than the story of Black Jack. And as they say, history is written by the victors, not the losers."

As Chipper spoke, he kept glancing at the half-moon overhead where small, puffy clouds blocked the light at predictable intervals. Chipper needed a sign. He had prayed and prayed for a sign that would guide his decision as to life's calling. Placing no restrictions on the Almighty whatsoever, he had waited and waited, months on end, but still no sign. Therefore, it occurred to Chipper that the expectation of unilateral, heavenly intervention might be a bar too high, and perhaps he should set the stage for God, to make it a little easier on Providence, so to speak.

Earlier in the evening, Chipper had noticed the puffballs crossing the moon, and he laid out the following plan so that God would simply have to fill in the blanks: when Chipper closed the chapter meeting with the secret ritual soliloquy, the final words—"my life"—would serve as the gun at the finish line. If the moon was unobstructed by a puff cloud, the answer would be medical school. If the moon was covered, journalism was clearly the plan. And if he witnessed a miraculous lunar eclipse, he would join Varsity Voyagers full-time after all.

"—for us, the job was easy to identify evil, for it came in a transparent package. But in the dark years ahead for the Sig Zetas, and in all of our lives for that matter, the job won't be that easy. For evil comes with a smile, a handshake, and a long arm that wraps around your shoulder while the other arm reaches inside and plucks your heart out like a cherry."

Chipper wondered if anyone guessed he was talking about Uno. Hopefully, his generalities would come across as senior wisdom rather than the targeted attack it really was.

As he drew closer and closer to the final keynote—a closing speech from the secret ritual so beautiful that few could manage to hear the words without a throat-lump at least—Chipper kept one eyeball to the moon. The clouds were on again, off again.

Chipper had delivered the final speech for more chapter meetings and more initiations than any President ever, having served in the post for two years. The final address was the most expansive work that he had ever memorized in his life, more filibuster than simple charge. And each time he gave the speech at initiations, the alums in the audience would approach him afterward, all of them having heard it hundreds of times, and they would tell Chipper that they had never heard a delivery as fine as his, with each billowy phrase and each lofty word given new luster. Admittedly, if there were a choice of interpreting a compliment as a simple pat on the back or effusive praise, Chipper would likely choose the latter.

The puffballs floated by the moon as Chipper launched into his final rendition:

"My brothers—"

The Invisible Hand grabbed him by the throat, choking the rest of his words. No doubt, if he tried to speak, he would drown in tears, and humiliate himself to death. *I can't let this rule me. I have to try again.*

"My brothers—"

The Hand strangled him once more. He could feel his face flushing with embarrassment. The light of the moon bounced off quizzical faces on the front row before him. Smokey Ray, Peatmoss, Twobits, Kong, Einstink, C.C. Chastain, Drywall, even Ty Wheeler, all seemed to be in pain for his sake. Peachy put his hands on his hips and offered a scowl, as if to say, "C'mon, cut the sentimental crap." Chipper would simply have to force his way through it, tears or no tears. This was the same Hand that had throttled him when he tried to tell the story of the Army guys at Ft. Sill headed to Vietnam on Christmas Eve. He knew this speech backward and forward. He *owned* it. *No one* could deliver it like he could.

"My brothers—"

Choked by the Hand again, he was forced to abandon Plan A and salvage what he could. "My brothers, go in peace, and may the Gold Cross guide you in all your remaining days."

Fizzle, fizzle, pfffffft.

"Seniors will be meeting at Doyle's," yelled Peachy, as if to rescue Chipper from the humiliating moment. "Same room where we planned the Black Jack takeout."

* * *

No one spoke of Chipper's bomb after arriving at Doyle's, the windowless restaurant/club where the over-21 seniors entered legally this time. The conversation was light and airy, full of collegiate memories, both altered and pure. Each senior recalled his pivotal role in the Black Jack takeout, everyone basked in the glory days of Wickiup, and no one missed the opportunity to claim the greatest personal loss as a result of the fire.

As a perpetual senior, Ty Wheeler had been asked to join the group tonight, and Chipper considered Ty's loss of his photograph with Roy Orbison and the rainbow's end to be the winner in the top tragedy competition.

After a while, Chipper couldn't stand the skirting of his botched performance, so he sought out a conversation with Moguru Divine who was easing toward the door.

"Ya' leavin', Smokey Ray?"

"Just about. You can only rattle the bones of the past so long."

"Well, what did you think about the meeting at the Pringle's Pool? Did it go okay?"

"The chapter meeting was cool, cowboy, very heavy indeed. But you sorta choked at the end, didn't you?"

Confirmatory words made the disaster much more real, and Chipper shrunk about three hat sizes.

"Yeah, I don't know what happened. Seein' all you guys out there, knowing we're going separate ways. I just don't know what came over me."

"Don't worry about it. Your gift is the written word anyway."

"What do you mean by that?"

"I've seen some of your stuff, your poems, especially that poem you wrote during Silent Week. I'd stick to carving out words rather than speaking, if I were you."

"The poem I wrote for that funeral? L.K.'s brother? How'd you see that?"

"You let Mother Boone have a copy. Remember? He showed it to me. Like I said, you're better with the written word. But all in all, it was cool thing to do, Pringle's Pool, I mean."

Chipper was cautious about revealing too much to Smokey Ray, but he finally managed, "The worst part about choking at the end was, well, I kinda figured I'd use a sign to tell me what to do with my life. And if the clouds were covering the moon when I said the final words of the speech, then—"

"Whoa, cowboy, I don't want to hear anymore. Do you know what we mean in psychology when we say 'magical thinking?'"

"No."

"Well, there are some principles of cosmology and causality that are so pervasive—. No, let me say it this way. When we're kids we think we can make things happen just by thinking them. If we don't get rid of this, we end up being superstitious as adults. Now usually, we think of superstition as something bad happening. But magical thinking can also apply to good, where we interpret piddly little—"

"Hey, dickheads, what's up? Ya'll talking about how Chipper choked?" A half-lit C.C. Chastain burst into the conversation, spilling some of his drink onto Chipper's bare forearm. "Say, Chipper, before I leave—one thing. I want you to play drums for our act in Varsity Sing."

Chipper was ecstatic, forgetting his failure in a flash. "You bet. But why are you asking me so late?"

"Well, the School of Music is providing the orchestra, but I'm sitting in with them on keyboards for our act, and it just occurred to me you did okay last winter in Greek Revue, so what the heck? We'll just bump their drummer for our act. Director's prerogative."

"But Amy said your rehearsals were over. How will I know what to play?"

"You know all the songs. And I'll give you a tape of the music tomorrow. You can practice with the tape, then show up Saturday night. It's not like there's a drum solo or anything. Just play along."

"Yeah, sure. Great."

C.C. Chastain buzzed around the room a few more times before he flew out the door. Pushing five feet-five inches, he was like a pinball David in a crowd of Goliaths.

The seniors began drifting away to their stopgap homes, and Chipper offered to give Smokey Ray a lift to the dorms so he could pick the Moguru's brain a little more. He considered it an honor of sorts when Smokey Ray rode in the T-bird.

"I guess Varsity Sing will be the very last time we're all together," said Chipper after they left Doyle's. "Although we won't be totally together there, I suppose. Most Sigs will be in the audience, some on stage, then C.C. and me in the orchestra."

After a short hesitation, Smokey Ray said, "You just named the three kinds of people."

"I thought the old saying was 'two kinds.'"

"I don't know about the old saying, but I say there's three. There's the performers on stage, there's the audience, and there's the orchestra. The orchestra's in between—part audience, part performer. Performers, audience, orchestra."

"Like that sign in Brewster Stone's office that says, 'Lead—Follow—or Get out of the Way?'"

"No. Not at all," said Smokey Ray. "That sign is just for goons who are really trying to say 'I'm the king in this little corner of the world so

shut the fuck up.' No, I'm saying that the performers on stage are the
doers, one type. Then, the second type is the audience where they get
their kicks out of sitting back, playing it cool and enjoying the
moment. But the guys and gals in the orchestra—your job is to enrich.
Enrich is the key word, Chipper."

"Hmm."

"The performers and the audience barely even notice that the
Enrichers are there. You're sort of invisible, but the experience is better for both stage and crowd because of the orchestra."

"Hmmm."

"Invisible. Like the atmosphere at the horizon. Everyone says it's
the horizon that makes the sun and the moon larger, but it's not—it's
the invisible atmosphere, like a hand with its palm cupping the Earth."

Chipper felt prickles on his neck when Smokey Ray joined the
words "invisible" and "hand" in the same sentence, making heavenly
bodies larger, because Chipper had identified and named the mysterious force that held back his spoken words—twice now—as "The Invisible Hand." But all he could say was, "Hmmmm."

As the T-bird eased into the parking lot at the dorm, Smokey Ray
continued, "Oh, one other thing, Chipper."

"What?"

"Whereas I agree with what you said tonight about the kind of evil
that wears a smile, it was pretty freakin' obvious that you were talking
about our buddyfucking friend Uno Guilford."

"So what if I was?" Chipper asked.

"Well don't let Uno take up any rental space in your head, okay?
Do you think for one minute Uno's going to take our memories away
from us? Memories that will be some of the best of our lives?"

"Well—"

"Remember that line from *Patton* last year—'All glory is fleeting'?
Well, trophies are fleeting, momentary bromides to take away the
pain. Uno can't take anything away from us, if your head's on straight,
that is. Remember, it's not whether you win or lose—" (Chipper
waited for the inevitable conciliatory ending to that phrase) "—'cause
both victory and defeat are masqueraders."

Masqueraders? Both defeat AND victory? Chipper halfway resented
Smokey Ray's defense of the buddyfucker. "What are you talkin'
about? Bromides and pain?"

"The pain of life, cowboy. The key is being able to deal with the
bummers, without having to depend on trophies and such. The Unos
of the world are everywhere. And most folks can't see them. Remember my deal about being a fog-lifter? Well, it ain't possible to lift the fog

for the majority. They'll see the Unos as good solid men, and they'll be passing out trophies to 'em right and left. If you let the Unos crawl into your brain, those simple strokes of the putter will turn into big swings of a pickax, and it'll destroy you. And what's more, the Unos never give it another thought while they're hacking away by remote control. You see, Uno has what we call in psychology—a narcissistic disorder."

"What? With that banana nose? That's the least of his problems. I don't see him as particularly vain."

"That's the lay use of the word, Chipper. People remember the Greek myth of Narcissus admiring himself in the pool of water. In psychology, we've got a different slant to the term. Look it up in a psychology text—while you're looking up *magical thinking*, by the way—it's not really about *vain*. It's about a shell of lies so to speak, but there's no pearl inside. Just the shell. And the shell fools the majority of folks. We all have our public persona, but the difference is that the narcissist will do *anything* to build his shell, and that includes harming others. Without remorse. And no ability to self-reflect, a pretty odd deal when you think about it since the name of the disorder is based on a reflection in a pool.

"Without self-reflection, he can't change, so he just gets craftier with time. If you were to talk to Uno right now, he'd tell you how important it was that he miss that putt in order to teach you a lesson that *you* so desperately needed to learn. In his mind, he's a hero. The key for you, cowboy, is not seeking revenge—even if it's in the form of calling a chapter meeting where Uno is obviously excluded—the key is developing mental muscles that are greater than the evil that comes your way."

Even if you disagreed with him, even if he spoke jibberish, Smokey Ray had a way of making you listen. Chipper thought it appropriate that the Moguru was going to be a doctor of psychology—Dr. Ray Divine—and, at the same time, wondered how an acid-head could be walking on a path so clear, whereas his own path was cluttered by doubt and second thoughts.

As the Moguru stepped out of the car, he lowered his head back through the doorway for final words. "Chipper, do you remember how I told you once about my wacko father?"

"Yeah."

"Well, there's more. When I was about 14, and not gonna take my old man's craziness anymore, I thought I had an ace in the hole with someone who'd vouch for me, someone who'd help—a deacon in my dad's church named D. Sol McCovey. He always came on like a big brother to me, like he understood there was trouble at my house. Encouraged me to trust him completely. As a result, I often laid my heart on the table for Deacon D. Too much so, it turns out. When I finally decided that the horror had to stop, and the full story had to be told, I went to Deacon D. He was my only hope in the world at that scary point right before desperation. I thought my sister might kill herself. I had to have *someone* believe me. My mother was struck dumb, it seemed. At the time, I was hanging by a thread, and I thought Deacon D would turn that thread into a rope I could use to climb out.

"Boy, was I wrong. The sumbitch cut the thread instead. Turns out he was in cahoots with my old man using church money for graft, so the two-faced asshole turned on me and tried to paint me into such a monster that I nearly got my ass shipped off to reform school, or worse. After that, I kept my mouth shut and just listened to the shit going on my sister's room through paper-thin walls. I lived with a pickax workin' in my brain. I even managed to get a hold of a .38 caliber Smith and Wesson, and every night before I went to sleep, I pulled the hammer back and cocked that sumbitch, fantasizing about a shot through the forehead.

"I could picture the blood spurting out. Every night, the same thing. Cock the gun, lay it by my side, just one tiny pull of the finger, one *tiny* pull, and the gun would fire. BLAM! I heard that click every night for two years 'til I moved out. Click, click, click. I held back. Somehow. But I can still hear the clicks, faint as they are."

"Man, that's heavy stuff, Smokey Ray. I mean, shooting your father? Gee . . ."

"No. Not my father. That's my point. It was Deacon D I wanted to kill. He was my only hope, my sister's only hope, and there's no worse feeling in the world than to lose all hope. It's hell on earth, cowboy. Hell on earth. You Voyagers go around talking about a life-changing experience, but let me tell you this—you haven't had your life changed until you lose all hope. You may think you're over it, but you'll *never* be the same.

"D'you remember the story of Pandora's box? Well, most folks remember the bad stuff let out into the world, but they don't remember the punchline. The Greeks understood the importance of hope. After Pandora let out all the evils in the world, the only thing left in her box was—the punchline—hope.

"Deacon D had the power to stop the madness. But he didn't. And it damn near destroyed me by destroying my hope. Let me tell you something now—it was my long-standing nightmare seeking revenge against Deacon D that served as my blueprint for the takeout on Black Jack, what with the whole chapter having to jump into Pringle's Pool, making the entire chapter reflect at the pool. We were focusing on the fog-covered guardians of evil, rather than the evil itself. Do you see where I've been comin' from now?"

"Well, the Black Jack takeout makes more sense, but I'm still confused," Chipper said. "You're saying the key is 'don't pull the trigger'?"

"It's enough just to *not* pull the trigger. The memories are still there, waiting to attack. Just the thoughts can kill you. Sure, I learned to keep the click, click, click muffled under my pillow, so that the rhythm matched my steady pulse. But the hard part is realizing that whatever evil has been spit on you, it's your challenge to gobble it up like an amoeba.

"We all have a war roaring inside. Be it yin and yang, or intuition and intellect, or whatever, there's a struggle. And as much as people want rid of what they think is dark, we'd be lunatics without all the parts. I've seen it. The thing that makes me click—the thing that separates me from the loons in the asylum—is that I've learned to make the dark the sculptor of the light. And that's it in a nutshell."

When Smokey Ray pushed himself away from the T-bird, Chipper remembered that this was the same place where they had loaded the bus bound for 558 on pledge day back in '67. It was this very spot where Peachy had threatened to de-pledge at the mere sight of Monte "Uno" Guilford. As Chipper watched the Moguru walk away, he felt his own pulse to see if it was steady at the thought of four putts to the cup from eight feet away. He couldn't tell.

Smokey Ray vanished into the dorm, clickety-split.

And for all the Moguru's emphasis on the importance of insight, Chipper had a different sense—he could *never* forgive Uno. And when he thought of Smokey Ray's prediction of Unos of the future lined up, waiting to strike, Chipper feared for his very happiness, his joy, as he knew he did not have the ability to forgive a unilateral strike. He only possessed one flawed weapon—anger.

How easy, he thought, to forgive Audora in comparison, where *he* had contributed to the fiasco. Or, easier still to forgive someone who says, "I'm sorry." But for the guy who's proud of his evil, there was no forgiveness in his heart, nor would there ever be. And Smokey Ray's phrase—simple strokes of a putter turning into swings of a pickax—began to haunt him.

For it was a new and strange emotion he felt now. Unlike other acute feelings where time tempers, this one grew stronger. In the days following Uno's four-putt, Chipper's attitude hadn't improved—it was getting worse. This wasn't "simmering" or "boiling," for such words described a static situation. It was a burning—a burning rage—where the fire progresses, consumes the fuel, and finally destroys everything in its path.

And there, in the parking lot where he had first boarded the bus bound for 558, Chipper asked for help from Above. He had been wrong to think that commitment to God came only in the form of joining Varsity Voyagers full-time. He had been wrong to think that God was lucky to have cool fraternity guys serving as lions roaring his name. He had been wrong to think that God would work through puffball clouds and the moon. Chipper realized, quite simply, that if he didn't enlist help, the four-putt pickax would destroy him. It was a matter of emancipation—his own.

56

A PLEA TO HUMBOLDT

O hallowed halls of Humboldt sing
With phantom notes forever ring

A maestro's wand, a cellist's bow
Decades lost six feet below

Weep not with eyes of spotlight glare
But flaunt your marquee if you dare

Silence the mikes and their silver tongues
With curtains shut, the crepe is hung

No aria now, the soprano's stilled
Old music hall, your glory's chilled

Instead, tonight, you must forbear
Your stage, a hand, holds talent rare

Sharp or flat you must adore
And forgive these off-key troubadours

A comic opera not to say
A slice of life, a time to play.

—a poem by Kyle B. "Chipper" DeHart
May 8, 1971

After introducing himself to the School of Music percussionist, drummer-in-waiting Chipper DeHart took his shotgun seat as part of the growing audience, near the Ludwig trap set, front row, stage far right, by an exit. The Beta Chi-Sig Zeta spectators would be cheering for their brothers and sisters from this designated section of Humboldt Hall, so it was a handy spot where Chipper could be close to the drums. He was a bit nervous, having never seen the act, so being able to watch the early performers in Varsity Sing, close to his clan, would help calm the butterflies.

The orchestra groaned its warm-up as the crowd assembled, and Chipper recalled that both his parents had played this music hall as college students, his mother as first violin, his father on cornet. Someone told him once that sound never disappears, that it gets softer and softer with time, while imperceptible reverberations last forever. He had dismissed it as rubbish, but now he wondered.

A new initiate, Jess Thomas, sat down beside Chipper while more Sig Zetas and Beta Chis streamed into the section from all portals of Humboldt. The side doors near Chipper's shotgun seat were odd for a music hall; they swung like a saloon entrance of the Old West. The opera house balcony added to the feel of antiquity, as did a musty odor that suggested ancient sweat of prima donnas and virtuosos performing under hot lights.

Chipper turned his head every few minutes to view the expanding crowd, chatting with Jess Thomas and, along with the others, predicting a Best in Show for the Beta Chi-Sig Zeta act, even though rehearsals had been closed and no one had a clue what the act was about.

When the auditorium was so full it seemed the oxygen had been sucked out, Chipper heard a loud *bang* to his side as the swinging doors flew open and a wheelchair burst through, pushed by Smokey Ray Divine. Sitting in the wheelchair, letting her toes slide down to the ramrodding footrests, was Audora Winchester, her large, bottomless eyes darker than ever. Her straight black hair fanned over the shoulders of her granny dress like silky paws of a wild beast locking her arms to her side. Chipper was one "I-I-" stutter away from speechless as Smokey Ray parallel-parked Audora's wheelchair next to him on the front row.

"Hello, Chipper. I want to apologize." Audora said. "I'm sorry for everything. I'm especially sorry about that stunt when we were freshmen. I truly believed I was helping you. That you were ripe for expanding your mind."

Chipper checked out a blank-faced Smokey Ray before responding. "You don't need to apologize," he said. "No one made me drink the stuff. I did it on my own." This brief and simple exchange served as a salve that, out of the blue, made a three-year stockpile of planned digs and clever put-downs disappear.

Smokey Ray looked different. He had started college in his cowboy hat, then top hat, back to cowboy hat, and now tonight, no hat at all. His long hair was cut to the nape, and his beard was trimmed from derelict to artist.

Audora continued, "Life, I've learned, is a series of forks in the road. But for me, it was a series of knives."

"I'm glad you're back," said Chipper. "I know Amy's gonna be excited to see you after the show. How are you doing and all? I mean, are you walking some?"

The orchestra conductor, in tails no less, walked to the front of the pit from the opposite set of swinging doors, his path charted by a spotlight. The audience applauded (with lowbrow hoots and howls from the guys).

"Yes," she managed above the crowd, "I can walk fairly well with crutches, and I should be pretty much normal by the end of the summer. The doctors tell me I'll probably have a permanent limp, though. One leg's longer than the other now."

Chipper replied with a nod as the sound of the overture preempted conversation.

Traditionally, Varsity Sing was a series of sophomoric spoofs about college life, but everyone knew it would be different this year. The world was exploding, or imploding, and jocular barbs at the administration for inadequate parking and skyrocketing tuition wasn't going to cut it anymore. Each act was limited to 20 minutes and five songs, with the music precariously linked to dialogue intended to form a chain of thought, although the linkage was often rickety. The Beta Chi-Sig Zeta act had drawn the final slot in the program, a distinct advantage for making an impact on the five judges from the College of Fine Arts.

The Lambda Chi-Pi Phi act started the show, with three of their five songs relying on the strength of their star soloist, Emily Jordan, while the Lambda Chis loitered onstage like part of the set decoration. Skewed reliance on true talent could actually hurt in the point system used to judge Varsity Sing, as it seemed to magnify the noncontributors, in this case the wooden boys delivering stilted lines. Even the gymnastic feats of Susannah Ryan and the comedic delivery of Jaye Bea Foster couldn't overcome the fact that of the 30 or so kids on stage, only three girls shone.

The Beta-Theta act blew the audience away, featuring the boys' barbershop quartet, but the opening and closing numbers were so sluggish that Chipper found himself looking at his watch to make sure the hands were moving.

The ATO-Chi Os had great production numbers, borrowing from the the Beatles, with "Hey Jude" prompting audience participation, but its message was garbled. Then, the Delt-Kappa act seemed to have it all, with foot-stomping music, blended voices, creative dancing, and clever dialogue. Overall, Chipper marveled at how much talent was unsung on campus, hampered from view by the oppressive monotony of the classroom. Periodically, he turned to look at the five judges who sat on the front row of the balcony. Their faces—three dour middle-aged women and two pudgy men, one of whom sported a pitch black beard—were inscrutable, or perhaps simply bored.

The independents entered just one act, testimony to the populous and "involved" Greeks on campus. Their dialogue covered the war, the women's movement, civil rights, and the environment, all with insight and polish, and certainly with the best writing so far. But their music sucked and there was no getting around it.

After each act, the performers joined their cheering section in the crowd, so seats filled quickly and the mushrooming audience jammed the five aisles.

The black fraternity-sorority experiment on campus had failed. From its ashes rose the Afro-American Student Union of which John Tatum served as its first president before his star lifted him to student body president for the whole university. The Afro-American Student Union act was next-to-last.

The otherwise lily-white audience was a little squeamish at first, but when the black girls sang "White Boys" from *Hair*, everyone relaxed. The comfort was short-lived, though, when John Tatum walked onstage, full Afro surrounding big-lensed sunglasses, where he soapboxed a call-to-arms in the war for racial equality. With guitar in hand, Tatum mimicked Jimi Hendrix in "Are You Experienced?" with orchestral accompaniment. The finale was a haunting song, part chant part threat, listed in the program as "If You Were Black, Would You Be a Panther?" that ended with 40 black, clenched fists high in the air.

The audience was afraid to clap. Audora leaned over to Chipper and said, "Smokey Ray told me Tatum wrote that last one."

A few brave souls gently patted their hands together with caution, then the slow crescendo grew to a sustained applause that was the longest of the night. Chipper figured that everyone was afraid to *quit* clapping. In fact, Chipper was hesitant to leave his seat for the trap set. The room was silent. No one moved. *Jiminy, if I get up now, the whole place is going to look at me.* The 40 black fists held their clenched ideals as the curtain closed and the applause waned.

Director C.C. Chastain appeared at the swinging doors for the final act and walked proudly under spotlight to the keyboards at the center of the pit. Chipper, stooped at the waist, with Audora's "good luck" following him, sneaked to the trap set where the music school percussionist turned over the drumsticks. Chipper set them on the large tom, knowing he planned to start with wire brushes rather than sticks. Maestro C.C. nodded to Chipper to make sure he was ready. In the stillness, Chipper heard a faint humming, even though no instruments were being played. He finally realized the sound was coming from his cadillac cymbals — top-of-the-line Avedis Zildjian — two golden discs hovering above the skins, still resonating from the earlier applause. Reaching out, thumbs and index fingers trying to touch in a gesture reminiscent of a papal blessing, Chipper pinched the crash cymbal and the ride cymbal. The humming stopped. Humboldt was quiet.

As the Beta Chi-Sig Zeta act was announced, Chipper turned to Smokey Ray, who seemed almost in a trance, and to Audora in her wheelchair, then to his section of the crowd where most of the applause originated. But when the curtains opened, the polite clapping escalated into wild cheering as a spotlight beamed on one man — Kong — dressed in Roman Centurion garb wearing a skirt of metal plates, holding a giant stick with a white ball for a tip, as if to strike a gong with a giant Q-tip, all while perched on an eight-foot pedestal. Next to him, instantly winning a full 10 points for set design, was a realistic 15-foot jukebox, complete with five buttons across the front, a black disc spinning inside, and a rainbow arch across the top — an arc-en-ciel — with blinking lights, all to signify the title of their act — "Color Your Dreams."

When the crowd quieted (especially the Sig Zetas in the audience who were chanting: "Kong—Kong—"), Kong slowly swung his mighty hammer until the white ball kissed the first button on the jukebox. When the huge button lit up and blinked, the Sig Zetas and Beta Chis in the audience cheered again, as if each snippet of the act was a masterpiece. Kong returned to his frozen pose, and a translucent curtain of black gauze dropped in front of the Centurion and his jukebox. The stage went black.

A single spot then beamed onto Jerri Lane, a pretty Beta Chi with rump-length brown hair, who wore a peasant dress and toted a 12-string guitar. With a Joan Baez voice, she began singing the haunting introduction to "Safe in My Garden" by the Mamas and Papas.

The orchestra joined her on C.C.'s command, and Chipper began with brushes sliding across the surface of the snare drum. According to custom, the acts began with a "big production number," so Chipper was skeptical about the opening song, "Safe in My Garden," an obscure, commercial flop. A ballad was a shaky choice for a start, especially an unfamiliar ballad.

From the wings of the stage, the Beta Chis and Sig Zetas strolled in, adding their voices to the swelling tune. The costumes were rather bland—black and white—with the girls looking like Peter Pan in black overblouses and white tights, the guys in simple black slacks and white shirts, early Lawrence Welk.

The boys began answering the girls as the ballad had an echoing verse that accompanied the main song. The surging tune filled the auditorium as the full cast stood behind Jerri Lane, and their combined voices moved Chipper to lay the brushes aside and switch to sticks, while pounding the bass, and adding cymbal crashes to a hard rock rhythm. Then the guys and gals hit the pinnacle as their voices joined, "Man, can't they see the world's on fire?"

Just as it had peaked, the music softened and slowed, until it ended with a mere whisper from the honey-voiced Jerri Lane, "Take me away . . ."

Chipper grabbed the wire brushes for a final swish on the ride cymbal that was lost in the applause. Amy was on stage as one of the troupe, and Chipper caught the moment when she spotted Audora on the front row in her wheelchair. With one of those telepathic things that girls do with just their eyes, Amy said to Audora, "Welcome back."

At this moment, when the stiff actors and the trite plot and the sophomoric taunts should have begun, C.C. Chastain, it turned out, had dreamed and directed another path that Chipper thought perhaps too daring. In the quiet darkness that followed, the spotlight leaped from one Sig Zeta or Beta Chi to another as each spoke mystic lines of monologue that sounded more like Mother Boone than C.C. or any other mere mortal. And it seemed as though Humboldt Hall turned into a giant coffeehouse, with beatnicks onstage, under smoky spotlight, delivering those weird and awkward poems that don't rhyme and, for that matter, don't make sense.

At first, Chipper thought the strategy much too daring, but then he got caught up in the flowery language that was reminiscent of the first time he had heard Ted Boone during Rush Week. And the words themselves became the music, even though their meaning wasn't completely clear. These peculiar words—delivered by an emoting Peatmoss and an overly sincere Twobits, along with other thespians—

talked of gardens with black and white flowers tucked securely into their little private world, safe from the horrors outside. Phrases such as, "Our garden where life is so full that it renders hope a mere frill," and "Hold tightly to the reins of your dreams, lest those dreams reign over you," were spoken in lyrical singsong by a girl, then a guy, then another girl, and so forth, each under a shifting spotlight that somehow landed on the speakers with perfect timing.

Then, the backlit jukebox reappeared and Kong swung his mighty stick to touch Button Number Two. The large, spinning disc in the jukebox lowered into playing position that prompted the second production number, "Up, Up, and Away," the song that launched the Fifth Dimension.

More verse followed. No acting, no plot, just attempts to paint with the color of words. After the second number, cast members began to emerge in different costumes with the same cut and style, only with a touch of pale blue and pink and pineapple yellow.

Once again, Kong launched the next production number— Chicago's "Does Anybody Really Know What Time It Is?" The poetic verse that followed this third song—Amy and Peachy alternated many of the lines—dealt with the effect of time, serving to ripen fantasy in a fashion analogous to fine wine. And when the heady words claimed that fantasy ages to dreams that bloom into visions that cry out for goals—and that the goals will be thwarted, forcing us all to walk "the wooden plank of hope and the invisible plank of faith"—it occurred to Chipper that the script sounded every bit like Smokey Ray as it did Mother Boone. And when he looked from his trap set to Smokey Ray standing behind Audora in her wheelchair, Chipper saw that Smokey Ray was mouthing the words.

Again, the stage went dark, then the backlighting behind the curtain of dark gauze revealed Kong swinging his giant hammer. The fourth button lit up on cue, the jukebox and Kong faded from sight, and the auditorium grew deadly quiet and black and cold.

A candy-colored clown they call the Sandman . . .

The unmistakable voice of Roy Orbison pierced the silence as a tiny spot illuminated a single hand strumming a guitar at center stage. And as Chipper thumped the bass drum with the downbeat that started the orchestra, the spotlight expanded to include the top half of Ty Wheeler in early-Roy garb, pompadoured to perfection, the spitting image.

The crowd went crazy. Everyone on campus knew of the oddball Sig Zeta, the skeleton they kept in the closet; yet the power of the stage could not be denied—Ty Wheeler was an instant hero. A guy with enough guts to go out under the lights and just flat *do it*. The Sig Zetas continued in their screams, drowning out much of the pantomime. . . . *Pantomime?!*

The realization struck Chipper cold. Perhaps he was the only one. But the crystal clear tenor of Roy Orbison was not coming from ever-off-key Ty Wheeler, and pantomiming records was not allowed in Varsity Sing. They would be disqualified. The voice was clearly that of Roy Orbison, being piped in. How had C.C. or whoever managed to get a copy of the vocal? After all, the orchestra was really playing.

And with the next phrase, a second Roy Orbison who had been standing back-to-back with Ty Wheeler stepped out into a second spotlight and turned to face the audience. Whereas the first Roy was in all black, the second Roy was all white, including peroxided hair combed back, white-rimmed sunglasses, and white suit. It was the second Roy that was singing, "In dreams I walk with you."

From the wings of the stage, Cassie St. Clair appeared, dressed in a white sparkling leotard, trailing breezy ribbons of iridescent satin. When she engaged the second Roy in dance, Chipper realized that Roy Number Two was Drywall Twohatchets. Of course, the Voice was unmistakable, but it had never occurred to Chipper how much Drywall sounded like Orbison.

While Roy One continued to strum and pantomime at center stage, Drywall and Cassie moved in tandem to the song.

Just as most everyone in the crowd knew the story of spook Ty Wheeler, so they knew the story of Drywall Twohatchets and his Peach-induced blindness—and why Drywall had to tilt his head downward to see. While waves of cheering and applause tried to drown the song, audience gasps were blended in each time that Drywall took his choreographed steps to the edge of the stage, only to turn back again for a twirl with Cassie. For Cassie's part, she timed her jumps and leaps around Drywall perfectly with the violin responses in the song as the twosome continued their pas de deux.

Then Cassie pulled one of those backward scoots that ballerinas do, floating off stage with rapid piston-steps where only the feet move. She was bent at the waist with her 10 fingers wiggling good-bye beneath her chin. Drywall acted as though he could see her as he continued to sing, "I awake and find you're gone."

And with these words, the Sig Zeta and Beta Chi performers appeared at the perimeter of the stage, crouched so as to be nearly invisible, whereupon they released streamers of orange and red and yellow, held fluttering aloft by wind machines in the wings. All streamers were pointed toward Drywall at center stage, suggesting that Roy Two was being enveloped in a house of flames. Smoke of dry ice poured onto the stage. The Sig Zeta fire was burning again, symbolic for something else, Chipper was sure.

As Drywall moved to the song's conclusion, he stepped to the front edge of the stage, so close that even Chipper feared he might miscalculate. Ty Wheeler was at his side, still pantomiming perfectly. Drywall's chin jutted out as he hit the remarkable falsetto notes perfectly on key.

The final note was as if the seats in the auditorium had been electrified. Everyone shot up at once, and the noise seemed to last forever while both Ty Wheeler and Drywall took their bows.

And then, Chipper felt the Invisible Hand around his throat once again, only this time he wasn't even trying to speak. He was simply looking around the room, watching a mesmerized audience applaud, many with their hands above their heads. For a moment, in the back of the auditorium, he thought he saw the skinny phantom of Ted Boone standing against the far wall beneath the balcony. But when he looked again, the dark figure wasn't there.

The audience wouldn't quiet down, or even sit down. They continued applauding even while Kong was striking his fifth and final blow to the jukebox.

C.C. Chastain sat at the piano with his mouth pressing the microphone where, with a frenzied scream, he pounded his fists onto the keyboard and began wailing the song, "Do You Like Good Music?" adding a soulful rasp to his voice.

The cast members popped up in multicolored costumes, letting their streamers go, the smoke still straggling as a low-lying fog. The white spotlights doused, and black lights at the foot of the stage flipped on, making the dancers' bodies disappear while only their costumes— fluorescent blue and gold and green and scarlet—gyrated in the night.

Peachy and Amy ran front and center to lead the dancing as C.C. and his orchestra played on. Gradually, Amy stepped back as Peachy, with every ounce of talent he had ever mustered, began dancing like no one had never seen before. And while the performers took cleverly choreographed steps, Peachy was spinning, falling to floor where he gatored face down, face up, even twirling somehow on his back.

The black girls couldn't stand it. The men were struggling to look proud and sullen and angry. But when the girls saw a pirouetting Peachy, they moved to the aisles to rock and dance. Chipper watched the black guys check each other out, waiting for a first move, before their leader John Tatum began to clap with the music. With the go-ahead, all of them, still in sunglasses, began to bob their Afros in unison as they clapped with the music.

Peachy, as a fluorescent blue gyro, spun, jumped, twirled, hit the floor in splits, bounced back like Flubber into the air where he twirled again, splits again, bounced again. The Peach made the audience laugh, it seemed, louder than their continued applause. Even Kong started laughing, dancing on his pedestal like a bull on its hind legs.

Smokey Ray and Audora were smiling and clapping, and Chipper couldn't recall seeing either of them smile in years. And for Chipper's part, he just kept time with the music. The rhythm carried itself.

Then, Chipper saw movement in the Afro-American section. It was John Tatum, sliding out of his row into the aisle, walking toward the orchestra.

Chipper felt the jitters for a moment as John Tatum was no longer smiling. C.C. wailed away at the mike while old friend Tatum leaned into C.C.'s ear and shouted something. Then Tatum stepped over to the orchestra's guitarist where an exchange was made and the university's black student body president took over lead guitar mid-song.

Chipper wasn't sure, but it looked as though C.C. Chastain, being the sensitive asshole that he was, might actually be a little teary-eyed. Chipper then recalled C.C.'s dream years ago that it would be music, and music alone, that would bring all together as one, if only as long as the music lasts. As Tatum hit his guitar licks, the blacks joined the rest of the kids in the aisles and in front with the orchestra, dancing to that sweet soul music.

And when Chipper looked back to the stage, Roy One was still front and center with Peachy buzzing about, but Roy Two had backed away and was moving offstage into a lane between side curtains where only Chipper had a good view from the far end of the orchestra pit. Peering over his crash cymbal that was rocking and hovering like an alien spacecraft in a B-movie, he watched Cassie and Drywall kiss to the music in the wings. Obviously, "Pachelbel" had found a home.

C.C.'s sandpapered voice seemed to be failing, but the wailing continued: "I gots to get the feelin'—" John Tatum, holding his guitar to his side, was screeching into the mike with C.C.

Chipper knew there was no need to tally the votes for Best in Show when he looked to the balcony and saw the stony-faced judges all smiling, while the bearded sourpuss on the end clapped with Peanut Gallery enthusiasm. C.C. continued the reprise much longer than the original record. Cassie and Drywall came back to center stage to greet another crescendoing swell in the applause. Peachy finally wound down and joined the troupe as they inched their way to the front as a single, multicolored line where sudden house lights made the fluorescence disappear. Amy eased over to the side of the stage nearest Chipper as he continued freestyle drumming, rocking hard. She gave him an "I told you so" look and smiled.

And just when he thought he was the luckiest guy on the planet, he heard a subrhythm on his drum set—a click, click, click—that forced him to switch his style and move from crash cymbal to high-hat, from snare drum to toms, and from forte to pianissimo. He whispered to himself the word "rhythm," the word "enrich," and the word "invisible," all in beat with the I-gots-to-get-the-feelin' music—as if he'd never heard those three words before—and the Hand seemed to release its hold, allowing him to breathe again. *Click, click, click. Rhythm, enrich, invisible.*

Chipper decided there would be no more waffling in the offing—that his future was in writing to enrich. And, to borrow a phrase from Smokey Ray, he would rest his palm on the horizon to see if he could—just maybe—turn the setting sun to fire and the rising moon to gold.

57

Fidgeting with his necktie as he hurried to catch up with Amy, having parked their new 1986 Thunderbird Turbocoupe, Kyle "Chipper" DeHart was struck by the realization that two distinct streams were filing into the church. One tributary was composed of ornate walking sticks, berets, ascots, capes and multicolored panchos on somber men with Vandyke beards, along with weathered women, bobbed and crewed, while some rosy-cheeked matrons sported tightly coiled braids. The second stream came in waves of dark suits and striped ties redolent of Danner's clothiers, accessorized by lovely wives or girl-friends. The two streams reminded Kyle of the article he wrote for *National Geographic* where he described the surrealistic, inky waters of the Rio Negro that joined the mocha Amazon, flowing side by side for miles before intermingling in the "Wedding of the Waters."

"Chipper, you old sonuvabitch," called Brother Kong while Kyle was still steps away from Amy. "Haven't seen you in years. Oh, I guess it's *K.B. DeHart* now, isn't it?"

"Kong. Great to see you, but I guess Kong doesn't work too well either, what with your being mayor of Bartlesville and all. I didn't know you had it in you."

Peachy Waterman Jr., Esq. joined Kong and Kyle at the edge of the stream. Stricken with a bald pate crowning above a rim of mostly gray hair, the Peach was fighting time with a row of transplanted plugs in front that looked as though he were a quarter-way to victory. But the smirk was unchanged. "Gentlemen. How goes it?"

"And speaking of overachievers," Kyle said to Kong, "have you ever seen a finer specimen? Peachy was just named Outstanding Young Lawyer in Oklahoma, not to mention Bachelor of the Year last winter."

"Screw you, Chipper, you know you'll always be an A-1 loser in my book," said Peachy with a smile meant to be opposite his words. "Speaking of books, it took you long enough to get your first novel published. What's it been? Fifteen friggin' years since you started working on it? I'll admit the book wasn't half-ass bad, but you exaggerated a bit much. Hell, we never did half that stuff."

Kyle chuckled at the mention of his debut novel, *Two Shots per Man per Round,* a treatment of high school golfing days intended as metaphysical allegory, where it failed miserably. Yet the book ended up finding a comfortable home as plain ol' coming-of-age fiction (a.k.a. Bildungsroman). He said to Peachy, "You *do* know what *fiction* means, don't you, Peachy?"

"Of course, but—oh, hell, let's get inside the church before the good seats are all taken," said the Peach. "We've got all day and night to catch up on everyone. Leave it to our old Pledge Trainer to exit stage right on the very day we're dedicating the new chapter house."

Kyle felt himself looking to the ground, as did Kong, while Peachy fiddled with his silk necktie and the gold collar bar beneath, a lever that forced the knot to bob up and down as he talked. The Peach spun around and jumped into the Danner's stream trickling into the church. Kong, still with downcast eyes, having served as a champion for Mother Boone, turned to Chipper. "We didn't know, did we? We just didn't know. We thought there were maybe two or three at most in the whole state. It makes so much sense now, what with the Mitch Addison deal and all. But at the time—"

"His plays were going like wildfire, I hear. The one he was working on when he died was supposed to be his best. C.C. Chastain told me the title was, 'Paging Mr. Howard, Mr. Fine, and Curly Joe,' based on a conversation with his last three remaining T-cells. Terrible disease, just terrible."

"Where's C.C. these days?" asked Kong.

"Still in Hollywood. Same old doctor-songwriter he intended to be. He and Ted had a rift years ago. 'Lifestyle choices' C.C. would say, so the guy's still trying to find the perfect collaborator."

Amy joined Kong and Kyle at the edge of the stream. She was starting to show at five months, but the empire waist on her black jersey dress kept the trimester news for later today. "How have you been, Kong? I haven't seen you in, gosh, I don't know."

Kong enveloped her in a hug. "Our sweetheart," he said. "Always will be, too. Or, should I say 'Dr. Sweetheart?'"

The threesome entered the church, though Kong drifted away to join pledge brothers in a pew near the front. Chipper (as only Amy and Peachy called him anymore) sat shotgun in a back pew, with Amy to his right, joining Peachy who had already taken dibs on a spot. The Wedding of the Waters maintained separatist seating inside, as if the capes and berets were seated on the bride's side, while the suits and ties — aging Sig Zetas — sat on the groom's.

The "all-year fraternity reunion" with dedication of the new Sig Zeta chapter house was scheduled for later this afternoon, so the crowd at Ted Boone's funeral was replete with brothers, many wearing their gold cross pins, who remembered Ted as the Yearbook Man of Distinction, the man Kong had called "The Biggest Stud in the House."

And for Chipper and Amy and Peachy, the reunion had an encore phase the following week. A golf team reunion was planned in their hometown of El Viento, timed for one purpose — to discuss a recent estate settlement creating the Buster Nelson Foundation to honor their teammate killed in Vietnam.

Chipper held Amy's hand in the black hammock of her dress while he wiggled in his seat trying to identify old fraternity brothers from the backs of their heads. He finally spotted Smokey Ray and Audora — the celebrated Drs. Ray and Audora Divine — on the front row where Smokey Ray would have easy access to deliver a eulogy.

Smokey Ray was also to be Master of Ceremonies at the christening of the new chapter house at tonight's banquet where Chipper, significantly less prominent as a minor novelist, would introduce Dr. Divine. But after all, Drs. Ray and Audora Divine (or their "work") had graced the covers of *Psychology Today, Scientific American,* and *Nature*, not to mention a spot on *60 Minutes* and a spread in *People Magazine.* Audora's Ph.D. had been something about neurotransmitters as related to conflictive thought, while Smokey Ray had carried out his dreams of bathing the human brain in psychopharmacology. But together, fused in purpose, they had established themselves as the Harvard pioneers in mapping the cognitive and emotional centers of the mind, using fancy new imaging techniques, with the idea of altering behavior with drugs and/or stereotactic surgery, essentially shortcircuiting faulty circuitry.

Peachy, whose hero worship of Smokey Ray had diminished over the years in light of his own personal success as an attorney, once said, after watching the Divine couple on *60 Minutes*: "Best I can tell, 'mapping the centers of the brain' sounds an awful lot like phrenology, and the stereotactic surgery racket seems like it should be spelled l-o-b-o-t-o-m-y." Nevertheless, the great Doctors Divine had fallen face first into a pool of media saturation and had emerged drenched in idolatry by scientists everywhere. Chipper hadn't seen them since college, except on television, and he wondered if Audora walked with a limp.

"Do you see Smokey Ray?" he whispered to Amy. "And Audora?"

"Yes. Can't wait to talk to them afterward. I've spotted most everyone, but I still haven't seen Peatmoss or—"

"You aren't gonna see Peatmoss," interrupted Peachy, leaning across Amy to target his conversation at Chipper, as if she weren't there. "You know he's still running that liquor store in New Orleans. Calls it 'Peg-Leg Peat's,' given his blown-off leg and all."

"I heard it was one leg and one arm," said Chipper, barely above a whisper.

"Nope, just one leg. I was down there about five years ago at a seminar. I dropped by the liquor store and told the clerk who I was. The clerk fakes it like he doesn't know if Peatmoss is there or not, goes to the back, but comes out and says Peatmoss ain't there—that some days he's there, and some days he ain't. I got the distinct impression that the clerk was talking about *mentally* there or not, if you know what I mean. Several of the brothers have told me that Peatmoss was pretty much destroyed after Twobits was blown up guarding that Michelin rubber plantation near Saigon."

The Episcopalian priest began the service and Chipper was surprised that the opening hymn was "Faith of Our Fathers." When the second line rang, "In spite of dungeon, fire and sword," Chipper turned to his left and witnessed the late arrival of Drywall Twohatchets, led by a black lab mix whose twitching tail served as an antennae for Drywall's fingertips. Drywall had enjoyed a brief flirtation with celebrity himself in the year that followed the movie *Urban Cowboy*. In the wake of "country mania," Larry Hatchet (stage name) had three back-to-back hits as the "Kickapoo Cowboy" (nickname), earning enough bread to settle down with Cassie and their five little boys on the outskirts of Nashville.

Chipper leaned across Amy's stomach again to talk to Peachy, the only person who had kept in touch with Drywall, serving as his attorney-partner in several spectacular business deals. "Is that Pachelbel?" asked Chipper. "Yes," came Peachy's reply. "Rickelbell died seven or eight years ago. Hell, Pachelbel's 15 now." The thought of a 15-year passage had a chilling effect on Chipper.

Cassie lagged a step behind Drywall, holding his arm until she spotted Amy, then she left him standing in the aisle holding onto Pachelbel's tail as she tiptoed over and gave Amy a mouth-kiss, Chipper a mouth-kiss, and Peachy a cheek-kiss. "I can't wait to talk to y'all tonight. I miss you so much."

Drywall, his right eye socket covered with a standard issue black patch, lowered his chin and cocked his head, trying to aim his window to see whom Cassie was talking to, then he smiled and nodded when he finally zeroed in on the back row threesome. Drywall and Cassie settled in the back pew on the opposite side of the aisle. Pachelbel sat in the carpeted walkway, tail stilled as though in reverence.

"Drywall's gonna show us some tricks on the golf course this afternoon," said Peachy, referring to the fraternity tournament scheduled as a prelude to the reunion banquet. "You know he's president of the National Blind Golf Association, don't you?"

"I hadn't heard," said Chipper. "But I gotta ask . . . how do they—?" Chipper felt Amy's forefinger silence his lips as the priest launched into a lamenting prayer.

As the priest marched through Ted Boone's life and accolades, Chipper found himself lost in reverie. He wandered from Larry Twohatchets to Drywall to Larry again—from Smokey Ray and Audora to the Doctors Divine—from Kong to Hizzoner the Mayor—from Peatmoss and Twobits to just Peatmoss and his liquor store—from Rickelbell to Pachelbel—from Peachy to—well, some things never change.

When Dr. Ray Divine was introduced, Chipper focused again on the casket covered in white roses and the funereal words that filled the air. Smokey Ray was mostly bald, though he combed a forelock straight back, and he sported a short, blonde ponytail that was flattened into a ribbon and curled on itself. He spoke with all the elegance of years past, where words were quarter notes and eighth notes, syncopated, independent of meaning. But when Dr. Divine began talking about dreams and vision and hope and faith, Chipper perked his ears, for it was a sermon he had heard before:

"Ted and I used to debate for hours the subtle nuances that distinguished these words, these ideas, these concepts that give our lives sustenance. And we argued the nebulous shades between hope and faith, which we considered natural endpoints of seasoned dreams, the preferred course over abandonment. As I recall, we agreed that hope was rooted in the tangible, whereas faith was one step beyond, a sister concept. So, when I visited Ted last week, shortly before he died, I was not completely surprised that he remembered our old debates, for he revealed to me in somewhat mystic tones that the key was faith more than hope. And yet he remained perplexed by the elusive concept of love as being *the greatest of these*. He wondered if Providence would give him extra credit for arriving at faith, in light of the fact that he felt the Almighty had never intervened clearly on his behalf—offering, as he put it, 'a lifetime of unanswered prayer.' Surely, he said, the faith of a skeptic must mean more than the faith of a fool.

"But even if Ted found the concept of love elusive, I would have to add that of all the things Ted taught us so many years ago, we are indebted to him the most—not for his creative genius—but for teaching us perhaps the most important lesson in life. Quite simply, being kind to all. Not simply 'tolerant,' a word so used and abused today, but kindness to the point of *encouraging* each other. Ted was a gentle soul who felt we'd all been tossed into a salad of trouble, and that we needed each other's help. All of us could learn from that. I choose to believe that he loved, maybe even without knowing it.

"In his final hours, Ted spoke of the story of Constantine, and he made a point of the fact that Constantine acted on the command to put the sign of the cross on his soldiers' shields, even though he still worshiped the Greek gods, primarily Mars and Apollo. Faith came *before* reward, not after. Ted was wearing his trademark mischievous grin as he spoke, as if he were the audience in one of his own plays. I can't say that I know exactly what he meant, for Ted was fading in and out while we talked. But he also said, 'I wonder—I just have to wonder—what life would have been like if faith had come at the beginning, instead of now at the end.

"It was then he asked me to speak today at his funeral, and he made another request as well. He asked me to read this poem." Dr. Divine pulled a folded paper from the inside pocket of his dark suit, allowing a peek at his broad suspenders with Indian blanket color. "Apparently, he kept this verse as a link to the life he chose to leave years ago, but my thoughts are that the rhyme might also have been his link to faith."

Then Dr. Divine began to read:

> *No rhyme or reason can explain a life*
> *That from dawn to dusk is yoked with strife.*
>
> *Did Heaven's touch leave fingerprints to maim?*
> *Or did Vapor from Below cause you to be lame?*

Chipper's ears grabbed something familiar. *That's my poem!* Why wasn't Smokey Ray giving credit to the author? Had he forgotten this was Chipper's very own Reflection Week poem, written for a different funeral entirely?

> *You viewed the world between bars of pain*
> *Yet somehow smiled through drops of rain.*

> *The cause of suffering remains unseen*
> *Above, Below, or In-Between.*

"I wrote this poem," he whispered to Amy, desperate for someone to know, as amateurish as the poem might seem. After all, there was no greater torture for an artist than to be denied credit. Maybe the Great Dr. Divine had forgotten, but Chipper distinctly remembered Ted Boone having shown the poem to Smokey Ray years ago.

"What are you talking about?" she said, scrunching her nose as if her husband were half-crazed.

"During Reflection Week," Chipper said as he stiffened his back and scooted to the front edge of the pew. "Remember when they wouldn't let me go to Benny Taylor's funeral? I wrote this poem and they read it as a eulogy for Benny."

> *We know it's love that wins the gold*
> *That faith is second, we're also told.*

> *As you hoped to walk on legs of faith*
> *No rhyme or reason explains your fate.*

But then again, did it really matter? Weren't such trophies nothing more than masqueraders, as Smokey Ray had said once?

"Maybe you're confused," said Amy. "Are you sure it's the same poem?"

> *A trophied image now seems like mist*
> *Your father's knee replaced the fist . . .*

> *And in that twinkle of primal joy*
> *Love said man should become the boy*

Then Chipper eased back into the pew as he remembered the three words that, while playing the drums years ago, had led him to make his decision to become a writer—*rhythm, enrich, invisible*—and now the poem, "No Rhyme," was doing all three as he sat quietly next to Amy, content with his poetic anonymity.

> *My sorrow now is full and rife*
> *For no rhyme or reason can explain a life.*

* * *

Neither Chipper nor Amy played in the golf tournament that sunny afternoon, held at the old university course. As an OB-Gyn, Amy knew it was safe for her to play golf while pregnant, but what she told her patients and what she did for herself were two different things. It had been too hard, too long, too difficult getting pregnant. Instead, she and Chipper drove a cart around the course, taking pictures mostly, of Drywall, Cassie, and Peachy, while Pachelbel chased all shots in all directions.

The DeHarts were mesmerized by the art of blind golf. Drywall, with just a quarter of an eye, was going to break 80, with Cassie serving as coach. Tragedy had granted Drywall one small favor—the golf swing was perfected with the chin down, and this was the very position where Drywall's small window let him see the ball. If he moved his head during the swing, even a titch, the ball would disappear from sight. Given no options, Drywall's rigid head allowed a flawless swing. Of course, he needed Cassie to help with the aim.

After Peachy and Drywall made their approach shots to the 18th green, they loaded onto their cart with Cassie steering. Chipper began turning his cart to go back onto the course for more pictures of reunited brothers when Amy pointed out a lost soul in the woods off the 15th fairway, sporting a Sig Zeta T-shirt. The kid was wandering in circles looking for his ball. "Look where his ball is," she said. "He doesn't see it behind that surface root."

"Helluva lie," said Chipper. "Maybe he'd be better off not knowing."

"Reminds me of the lie you had in high school state tourney before your *legendary* final shot," she replied. "Only *your* ball was *under* the root. Circle over there real quick, and I'll show him where his ball is."

Chipper eased off the path and drove into the woods where he called out to the young Sig Zeta and pointed to the ball. The kid nodded, chipped the ball away from the root, then used another chip to get back to the fairway. Apparently in appreciation for sparing the cost of a lost ball, or perhaps because Chipper, too, wore a Sig Zeta T-shirt, the kid approached their cart.

"Brother Stephen E. Clay," said the smooth-chinned boy who seemed too young and scrawny to be in college. The kid extended his hand for the secret grip, and Chipper obliged by stepping out of the cart to shake.

"I'm brother Kyle DeHart. You're an Active, I suppose, since you've got the crest on your shirt."

"New initiate," Stephen said. "Number 2,012. We're really pumped about moving into the new chapter house next week."

"Sounds strange to have numbers that high. I was 1,401."

"Wow. That must have been a long time ago."

"Initiated in 1968. I was President for two terms—'69 through '71," he bragged, pleased that he didn't have to reveal how flustered and bumbling he'd been the junior year.

"1971?" Stephen's eyes widened and he backed away a few steps. His lips parted in shock and veneration, so strangely that Chipper looked to Amy in the golf cart to check her reaction. She saw it, too, for she shrugged her shoulders.

The young Sig Zeta then tried to speak, but it looked as though the kid was getting ready to drop to one knee to kiss Chipper's ring. "You're—you're—"

"What? What's wrong?" asked Chipper.

"DeHart. That's right. You said you're name's Kyle DeHart. I didn't recognize it like that. I mean, when you said it, it didn't click at first. Now it clicks. Brother, does it ever click. We all learned it as *Chipper* DeHart. *You're Chipper DeHart!*"

Chipper turned to Amy again, both of them beyond bewilderment. "What are you talking about, brother?" Remembering that all pledges had to learn the names of the 10 most recent Presidents, Chipper knew his name should have been dead and buried years ago.

"You were the President—. You were there! You were the President for the biggest event in our history—when Jake Chisum came to visit our chapter!"

Chipper thought he heard his own voice scream, *"WHAT?"* But, in fact, the word came out like a stretch limo: "Wwwhhhaaaaaaaat?" He turned to Amy for help, but she looked as though she was about to keel over in shock.

"You were President when Jake Chisum visited," he repeated. "You were the one in '71."

"Where did you—? Who told you—?" stammered Chipper.

"We learned all about it after we took the pledge test for nationals. It was in the local chapter history stuff we had to memorize as pledges. All of us learned it by rote. Every detail of the visit by Brother Chisum."

"What details?" Chipper backed away, stung by disbelief, needing to touch Amy's soft shoulder to make sure he wasn't in the middle of some sort of flashback hallucination.

"All the details. We learned how Brother Chisum showed up dressed like he was in *Guts and Grit,* what with the eyepatch and all, and the Actives were dressed up the same way. Everybody was wearing an eyepatch. Then, for dinner, you had big, fat T-bone steaks, and Brother Chisum ate three of them. Then, afterward, everyone gathered around the grand piano to sing fraternity songs, and during 'The Sweetheart Serenade' there were so many guys sitting on the piano that the legs broke, but Brother Chisum promised he'd buy another piano. The new one had a brass plate above the keys that said—. Wait a minute, why am I telling you? But still, I'm sure it's neat for you to know that pledges have had to memorize the details of Jake Chisum's visit for years, ever since it happened."

Chipper felt so weak he had to sit back down in the golf cart. He turned to Amy for a clue, but they were both so perplexed that they couldn't even send signals to each other.

"One question, brother Clay," managed Chipper. "Have you ever seen any pictures, or anything, to look at? I mean, a lot of the guys had cameras back then. Or newspaper clips?"

"Of course not. You should know that. Everything was lost in the fire. Everything."

"But—"

"I can't wait to tell my pledge brothers that I met the real Chipper DeHart, the guy who first shook hands with Jake Chisum."

"Brother Clay, I've got something to tell you," began Chipper, starting to recover from his shock. "You're right. I was President back when Jake Chisum was sup—"

"You've got it all wrong, partner," came a voice from over Chipper's shoulder. It was Drywall, standing behind Chipper, Pachelbel at his side, with Peachy and Cassie parked back on the cart path. "That's not the way it happened."

Chipper looked at the eyepatched Drywall, then back at the kid, and back to Drywall. With his head cocked, chin down, for a better look at the kid, Drywall continued. "*I* was the guy, not Chipper, who first shook hands with Jake Chisum."

Chipper shuddered as the situation shifted from quirky to bizarre in a matter of seconds. And when he remembered how close they were to the spot where Drywall had lost his eye, Chipper wondered if his trembling was visible.

"And the words that I used," Drywall continued, "when I stuck out my hand, surrounded by all my brothers, all of 'em wearing eyepatches like me, went like this—'Welcome to our chapter, Brother Chisum.' Now, you'll want to remember those words exactly, to pass 'em on and keep the legend alive."

Then Drywall turned to Chipper, gave him a quarter-eyed wink, and walked back to join Peachy and Cassie in the cart. As he walked away, Drywall's right hand hovered over the tip of Pachelbel's tail as a guide.

Amy whispered to Chipper, "Now *that's* what I call coloring your dreams." Chipper felt like he was wilting at the wheel of the golf cart as he said good-bye to the new initiate who walked away proclaiming, "I can't believe it," over and over and over. The other golf cart started coasting down the path toward Chipper and Amy.

"Am I shaking?" Chipper asked. "I feel like I'm shaking. Maybe I overdid it in a speech I gave once to the new guys at Pringle's Pool. You know, that speech I blew so badly when I—"

"You didn't overdo anything, Mister President," said Drywall as the other cart coasted to a stop. Peachy, Cassie, and Pachelbel were squeezed in tight. "To quote one of our lines from that old Varsity Sing act," he continued, "sometimes you just gotta 'walk the wooden plank of hope and the invisible plank of faith.'"

"I think you're probably right, Drywall," he said.

Chipper put his right hand on Amy's tummy to remind himself of their success after an exhausting, frustrating decade of wishing and struggling and praying to conceive their own dreams. He patted Amy where triplets swam in the amnion. He hoped for two boys and a girl, but she had faith it would be three girls.

Amy had already figured she was carrying one girl shy of a complete golf team.